BLEACHER
Report

KENNA KING

Anya
An Imprint of Meredith Wild LLC

This is a work of fiction. Names, characters, places, and incidents either are the product of the author's imagination or are used fictitiously, and any resemblance to actual persons, living or dead, business establishments, events, or locales is entirely coincidental. The publisher does not assume any responsibility for third-party websites or their content.

The author acknowledges the trademarked status and trademark owners of various products referenced in this work, which have been used without permission. The publication/use of these trademarks is not authorized, associated with, or sponsored by the trademark owners.

Copyright © 2025 Kenna King
Cover Design by Anna Silka
Chapter Header Illustration by @art_of_azeem

All Rights Reserved.
No part of this book may be reproduced, scanned, or distributed in any printed or electronic format without permission. Please do not participate in or encourage piracy of copyrighted materials in violation of the author's rights. Purchase only authorized editions.

Paperback ISBN: 978-1-966300-90-8

BLEACHER Report

DEDICATION

To my amazing Development Editor for always saying YES to my crazy ideas.

One of our real life conversations:

> **Kenna:** That was a lot of foreshadowing for a custom-designed dildo... maybe that should be my Dedication on this book, ha! 😊

> **Michelle:** Haha. Oh my god! I can't wait to read it. 😊

PLAYER POSITION & NUMBER

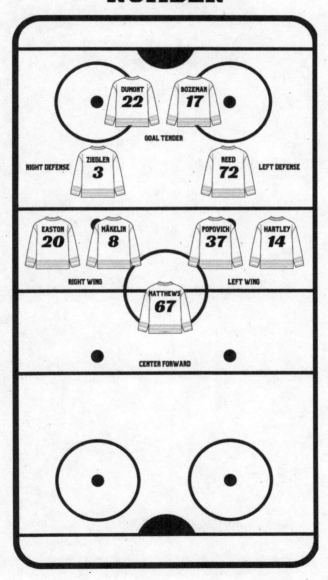

CHAPTER ONE

Peyton

The buzzer screams. The crowd groans. And just like that, the Hawkeyes lose. At home.

The Hawkeyes gave it everything—but effort doesn't always equal points.

Final Score: 3 - 2

"Well, that was shit," I hear a fan behind me mutter to the person sitting next to him.

His friend responds with the same annoyed tone. "Can you believe number seventy-two missed that goal in the second period? Maybe New Jersey was right to ship him off to their farm team for the last four years."

"How the hell did Coach Haynes think Reed was a good enough replacement for Kaenan Altman? What a downgrade."

Another voice cuts through the press box chatter.

"Fifty bucks says Kauffman trades him before midseason. They need a stronger defender."

Number seventy-two.

Hunter Reed.

BLEACHER REPORT

The Hawkeyes' newest left defenseman—and the player every network executive is foaming at the mouth over.

Not because of his stats, though those speak for themselves.

Because of the scandal.

Everyone wants to know what really happened between Reed, his old team in New Jersey, and Kevin Richards—the billionaire franchise owner who benched him just months after drafting him out of college at twenty-two years old in the first round five years ago. It was supposed to be a career-making move. But instead of headlines about hat tricks and rookie awards, the only thing the media got was silence.

Then the whispers started.

About Richards's wife. Young. Beautiful. Always in the owner's box for every home game.

And, allegedly, very interested in the team's new star defenseman.

Since then, Reed's been a walking headline—fast on the ice, faster off it. The league might've buried the gossip, but fans haven't. Especially the female ones sitting down by the plexiglass in REED jerseys and glossy lipstick, snapping selfies and begging for his attention.

They don't care if he broke the rules or just broke hearts. All anyone wants to know is what kind of off-ice skills Hunter Reed has between the sheets—because apparently, they were enough to lure a billionaire's wife straight out of her country club life. Even if it was just for a few stolen minutes in a dirty locker room.

Or so the rumor goes.

His demotion to the farm team didn't hurt his *game* with his female fans—not even a little. The charm, the wit, the hockey uniform...even without an NHL crest on the front of it for the past five years, it still worked just fine for him. Now, at the ripe old age of twenty-seven, Reed is a rookie again, and it hasn't changed his serial dating ways.

For half a decade, Hunter Reed's been snapped with puck bunnies, models, and a rotating roster of weekend companions who he rarely keeps around longer than a brunch reservation.

For a guy who parades his flings through upscale restaurants and velvet-rope nightclubs, you'd think he'd be more open about his personal life. But when the topic comes up in interviews? He smirks, shrugs, and claims he just likes meeting new people.

Cue the chuckles from the boys' club press pool. The occasional follow-up gets the usual brush-off—"No comment," "Nothing to tell," or my personal favorite, "None of your damn business."

It's cocky. Infuriating. And—if we're being honest—a little bit effective.

But now? Now he's in Seattle. Back in the NHL, wearing Hawkeyes colors and carrying more than just a bad-boy reputation.

Because if he wants to keep Everett Kauffman happy—the new team owner who signed the purchase deal, with one of the conditions being that Hunter got a spot on the roster—then he needs to start heating up the ice, not just the sheets.

And me? I need to convince him to spill every last scandal-soaked secret if I want to lock down this syndication deal.

Hunter Reed has never talked about New Jersey. Not to the press. Not on any podcast. Not once.

Which means if—and that's a massive if—I can land the interview, it could finally be enough to clinch the syndication deal I've been chasing.

Rebecca Jones, the only woman on the board of network execs making the decision, is rooting for me—quietly. She let it slip that one of the other execs is a massive New Jersey fan and would kill to hear Reed's side of the story on *their* network.

It's the biggest lead I've ever had.

My *in*. My opportunity. And the stakes couldn't be higher.

Two months. That's how long I have to prove I can do this—to land Reed, boost my subscriber list from seventy-three thousand to one hundred thousand, and convince the board that *The Bleacher Report* podcast deserves to go syndicated.

But none of it matters if I can't get him to say yes.

And that's the part that's been gnawing at me all game.

Because this guy only does post-game press.

No appearances. No interviews.

Just his stick, his smirk, his dating record, and the rumor mill nipping at his heels.

He also just so happens to be the holy grail of podcast guests that the execs are looking for—and the most ungettable.

And honestly? I don't know if I'm enough to land him.

Not when I'm competing against sports podcasters with million-follower platforms and full-time teams. Not when half the board still thinks women in sports media are a cute PR move instead of a serious voice. Not when my twenty-six years of life have most broadcasters mistake me for some press exec's personal assistant when I walk in the door instead of their equal with a press badge of my very own.

Not when the only real edge I have is hustle. And one exec quietly whispering, "I believe in you. Don't take no for an answer."

I pack up my notebook, fingers twitching with nerves as I glance down toward the ice. Reed's mad after that missed puck. It's evident in his rigid body movement when he's usually smooth on the ice.

He skates toward the tunnel, helmet off, jaw tight, hair sweaty and perfect in a way that shouldn't be allowed.

If I want this deal, I need Hunter Reed.

And if I want *Hunter Reed*?

I'll need to be strategic. Persistent. And maybe a little lucky.

Because there are only two months left. And if I blow this shot…

I don't get another.

I watch as the rest of the players follow suit, skating off the ice with shoulders sagging. Coach Haynes trails them in a sharp navy suit, his jaw clenched like he's chewing on the taste of defeat. Coach Wrenley is the last to leave the bench, and the scowl on his face could melt the damn rink.

With most of the old roster retired in the last two years,

the Hawkeyes are still trying to find their rhythm—though with December breathing down their necks, they're running out of time to figure it out. If they don't lock in soon, playoffs will just be another pipe dream.

All around me, fans rise from their seats, the air thick with stale beer, frustration, and hope circling the drain. Turquoise and white jerseys shuffle toward the exits, crumpled popcorn bags and half-empty drinks littering the floor like battlefield debris.

My phone buzzes in my pocket.

"Hi, Mom," I say, plastering my phone up to my ear, unsure if I'll be able to make out a word she says over the crowd around me. "Can you hear me? I'm still in the stadium."

"Yeah, I can hear you. What a tough loss. How's the crowd?" she asks, a little loud to make sure I can hear her.

"Pissed off as you can imagine."

"I'm sure they are. Have you gotten a chance to talk to Hunter Reed yet? That's who Rebecca wants you to score an interview with, right?"

I let out a sigh, remembering the sight of Hunter skating off the ice only a few minutes ago, chucking his helmet into the player box as he stepped off the ice and then stormed down the player tunnel and out of sight.

He's not happy with his performance tonight—that I can be sure of. I have a feeling tonight might not be the best night for asking for a favor, but I have to try. If Rebecca is right, and I can deliver on a podcast interview that one of the other network executives wants, it will be worth putting myself out there.

A little self-doubt creeps in as I consider the other players I could ask tonight, who looked a little less pissed off at the loss than Hunter, and might agree to my podcast guest request. But I know who I need.

"Yeah. That's the one. But maybe I shouldn't press my luck. He hasn't interviewed for a podcast in years, and I'm running out of time to get these interviews in before the network makes a decision. Maybe I should just ask someone else who's more of a sure thing."

I hear the faint sound of the TV on in the background, and I imagine her sitting on her couch, probably with my nephew Jesse somewhere close by.

"Don't back down. You can do this. You just have to play by their rules once, and then you're home free. Besides, your numbers aren't just going to magically appear because you want them to, and getting this interview with Hunter Reed is going to do wonders for your female listeners."

She's right, of course. She usually is—even when I don't want to hear it.

"My female listeners?" I ask, though I know exactly where she's going with this.

"Of course. Hunter Reed is a sex pot. And have you heard that deep voice during post-game interviews? Girls will be tuning in just to hear him read the warning label on a bottle of paint thinner—just you wait."

I laugh, though I know she's right. "Sex pot? You're aging yourself, mother. And even if I did convince him to come on my show, I doubt he'll give me the story everyone wants."

"Then find another angle that gets him more comfortable. You're Peyton freakin' Collins. You didn't let a blown-out knee stop you from staying in the game, and you're not going to let one stubborn hockey player tank your shot at syndication."

Her voice is sharp, encouraging, and exactly what I need.

"Maybe you're right?" I say.

I could use the vote of confidence right about now.

"I am right. About everything, too. Have you seen him stretch out on the ice before the game? That man can do the splits. On ice. In slow motion. I'm widowed, not dead, Peyton."

Despite everything, I laugh.

Dad passed away three years ago. A heart attack out of nowhere. One day he was cheering for my podcast launch, and the next...he was gone. He and Mom had been married over thirty years. Since then, she's taken care of everything and everyone.

"I'm just not sure it's going to be as easy as you think. He's impossible to pin down. Unless you're a puck bunny." I say the last part under my breath, pulling the phone's mic away from my mouth as I weave past a couple arguing about missed penalties. "Reed treats basic questions like they're classified military intel. I doubt he'd even tell me his favorite cereal."

The guy in front of me wears a REED, seventy-two jersey.

Of course he does.

It's like the universe is taunting me.

"That's motivation, sweetheart. Nothing worth doing in life is easy. That's just a fact. And while I have you, I'm just checking to make sure that you're going to Jesse's career day. He's been telling all his classmates that his aunt is famous."

I laugh at how my twelve-year-old nephew, Jesse, might be my biggest fan.

"Yeah, I'll be there."

Jesse was born with spina bifida. He's brilliant—wicked smart—but the world isn't always built for kids in wheelchairs. This is his third school in four years, each move just to find a building that could accommodate his needs without treating him like a burden.

I get it—I do. Everyone is trying to do the best for Jesse.

But it's hard enough as a kid to make new friends in a new school, and Jesse's had to do it more than I feel he should have.

My brother Noah re-enlisted in the Army for medical insurance, and to pay to put him through special physical therapy and surgeries that insurance won't cover. He's currently stationed overseas for another three months. Abby, his wife, works full-time as a nurse and saves all her PTO for Jesse's surgeries and appointments.

Mom's the one who picks up the slack. Retired, full-time grandma, chauffeur, and emotional backbone of the family. My dad left her a good enough life insurance policy to make sure that she could pay off the house and focus her energy on us instead. His way of still taking care of us even after he left this earth. That's the kind of man he was.

I'm on for career day—again. And I'm happy to do it. I just wish he had someone besides me—the same aunt he used for career day at his last school.

We chat quickly about my brother Will's call home from Japan, and we agree on a time for Thanksgiving dinner next week.

"Gotta go. Kiss the kid for me," I tell her.

"Will do. And Peyton?"

"Yeah?"

"You've got this. He's just a man. A very limber, very attractive man—but still just a man."

Sometimes I swear her belief in me is so strong, she could convince me I can walk through brick walls.

And at this very moment, I'd probably rather do that than try to convince Hunter Reed to do an interview with me.

Soon enough, I make my way down to the belly of the Hawkeyes Stadium, flashing the press badge Cammy Wrenley forwarded me earlier.

After two months of trying to wedge myself into Penelope Matthews's calendar for last week's interview, Cammy and I have exchanged enough emails to qualify as casual friends.

Or co-conspirators.

She gets it—what it's like trying to be heard in a room full of men who think their opinions come with a whistle and a clipboard.

The network's words from two weeks ago still echo in my head: "We love your content, Peyton, but we need to see at least one hundred thousand subscribers and some high-profile interviews before we can talk syndication. You've got eight weeks to show us what you can do."

That was two weeks ago. This means I only have six weeks left and no winning interview guest in my sights—until today.

Twenty-seven thousand short. And one elusive, too-charming-for-his-own-good hockey player who could change everything—if he'd just spill a few details about past or current relationships.

I hang up, shaking my head. This isn't going to be easy, but I don't need *easy*...I just need it to be *possible*.

Inside, the press room is chaotic. Cameras. Elbows. Six-foot-something reporters with zero spatial awareness.

A pissed-off Coach Wrenley steps up to the podium. I have a feeling that's how these interviews are going to go. No player enjoys the press when they have to talk about a loss.

I get it—I've been there. And as a tennis player, you don't have a team's shoulders to help carry a loss. The loss is all your own.

Just like this network loss will be only mine to bear alone if I don't make something happen.

I rise onto my tiptoes and catch a glimpse of Hunter Reed walking in now.

Jaw clenched. Eyes dark. No signature smirk in sight.

He looks like he'd rather be anywhere else.

I open up my phone recording app and hit play, doing my best to ignore the twist of anxiety tightening beneath my ribs.

I'm not usually in person for press conferences post-game. I can get the intel I need from watching playbacks online when I'm researching a guest who will be on my show, but since I'm here... why not get the full experience?

However, the experience is turning out to be less than optimal.

I'm squeezed in, wedged behind a wall of tall reporters and a cloud of sweat, post-loss frustration, and whatever cologne the guy from *The Seattle Sunrise* is practically bathing in.

Perfect.

But it still beats sitting at home before I created *The Bleacher Report*, pretending I don't miss the world that used to be mine.

Career-ending injury at fourteen.

Professional tennis dreams—gone.

Wimbledon finals—just a fantasy now.

I tried walking away from sports. Tried pretending I could be someone else.

But it didn't stick.

I kept looking back in from the outside like a ghost haunting my own past. Until I found podcasting.

Well, podcasting and a push from my dad before he passed for me to find my place in the sports world where I truly wanted to be. He knew me better than anyone, and after his passing, *Bleacher Report* has been sort of like my therapy to deal with his loss.

His exact words? "If you can't play—talk. Your voice is just as powerful."

What would he think now, seeing me vying to get an interview with a player just because he's clickbaity. Would he tell me that I'm wasting my voice with airtime garbage? Or would he champion me to do whatever is necessary to get a syndication deal to put *Bleacher Report* on the map?

All I want to do is make him proud.

And now here I am. Back in the game. Just...in a different way.

Hunter's voice slices through my thoughts—and the crowd. Sharp. Cold.

"No comment on personal matters."

His eyes sweep the room, daring anyone to try him again.

But I'm buried in the back.

Tucked behind cameras and cargo jackets—too far for his gaze to find mine.

I rise on my tiptoes, catching sight of his profile. His jaw is set, those forest-green eyes hard as he fields questions about tonight's loss. A muscle ticks in his jaw.

Tension, not nerves. He looks like he'd rather be anywhere else than here, answering questions from reporters he clearly has no patience for.

"Hunter, that missed goal in the third—" someone starts.

"I saw it happen. You saw it happen. Next question."

His voice could freeze hell over.

The room falls silent for a beat. Then, the questions resume.

I stay quiet, scribbling notes and pretending I'm not the tiniest bit curious about the man behind the headlines.

I've only seen him in person twice before—once in preseason warm-ups and once outside the locker room. Both times, he barely looked in my direction.

But tonight, up close? The tension rolling off him hums like static—sharp, charged, barely contained. Controlled fury pressed into short answers and that ticking jaw.

My phone buzzes again.

> **Cammy: Oakley's. After media. No excuses.**

I start to type back, but she follows up immediately.

> **Cammy: Don't even try to bail. I can hear you overthinking from here. Everyone wants to meet you.**

No pressure. Just the well-known WAGs group of the Hawkeyes players all wanting to meet me.

After the press conference, I grab my bag and head for my car.

Oakley's is only a couple blocks from the stadium, but I've got a longer drive ahead of me after—back to the shiny new townhouse I bought six months ago.

It was a splurge.

Between the down payment and the remodel I did on the second bedroom—now fully converted into a soundproof, pro-level podcast studio—I'm officially the most broke I've been since college.

But every time I step into that room, hit record, and hear my voice come through crisp and clean, it feels worth it.

My savings account disagrees, but my soul votes yes.

The drive to Oakley's gives me just enough time to lie to myself.

It's just a bar. Hunter is just a player. And the WAGs are just a group of girls. No pressure.

Oakley's is packed. Post-game buzz is in full swing.

The usual mix of beer, wings, and chatter of people dissecting plays hangs in the air, along with the sports network commentary blaring from every flat screen.

Cammy spots me first. She waves me over from a table near the bar, already deep in conversation with a mix of ladies and team staff.

I'm halfway there when I spot Hunter sitting at the bar, shoulders slumping, elbows leaning over onto the bar top, a whiskey glass in his hand.

Oh...it's going to be that kind of night, huh?

She turns to see what I'm staring at and then turns back to me.

"Hunter?" she asks.

"I need an interview for the podcast syndication that I was telling you about. An exclusive with him would make the network lose their minds. He's exactly what I need, but he's—"

"He's great," Cammy says. "Really. I know that he was having an off night in media, but he really is a good guy. I bet he'll say yes."

Her smile says she believes what she's saying, but her eyes tell me that she's seeing what I'm seeing. A drunk Hunter Reed who had an off night.

The thing is...I don't have the luxury of waiting for Hunter to have a good night. My opening is closing with every day that passes. It's been two weeks, and I haven't been able to come up with any better options. And the man is just sitting there in the flesh.

"Let me introduce you to the girls," Cammy says and then points to Penelope Matthews first, the gorgeous blonde General Manager for the Hawkeyes who is as down to earth and a sweetheart. Interviewing her for my podcast was a dream. "You already know Penelope, but this is Dr. Kendall Hensen, our team doctor..."

Kendall is beautiful, too, and I've seen her interviewed plenty of times during post-game media. She's smart, quick with an answer, and takes on the "boys club" with a finesse that I admire. I've seen her take down a reporter who asked her if she has a hard time focusing in the locker room with half-naked men all around. She said, and I quote, "If you've seen one set of hairy, ungroomed balls, you've seen them all. Now, if you have a more intelligent question to ask, I'd be more than happy to answer."

Which earned her a room full of chuckles, though she wasn't laughing.

After I get through the chaos of making the network happy and delivering on the guest they're hoping for, I have to convince Kendall to come on my show. She'd be hilarious to interview, I just know it.

Kendall lifts her glass to me. "Nice to meet you." She smiles.

"You too," I say quickly.

"Then we have Isla Altman."

I smile back, knowing Isla as the wife of a retired Hawkeyes player, Kaenan Altman. Kaenan and Isla made Seattle home after he retired, and they're still very involved with the Hawkeyes. Kaenan is one of the head coaches for the Hawkeyes kids league, and I believe I heard that his seven-year-old daughter plays the same position he did in the league.

Cammy starts darting around, looking for someone else. "I'd introduce you to Brynn and Aria, but they disappeared somewhere."

"No problem. I'm actually here for work as well, but it was lovely to meet you all."

Cammy turns back to me as if to give us a little privacy.

"You're going to go over there and ask him?"

"The worst he can say is no, right?" I ask.

He's just a player. I remind myself. *A player who could make all my dreams come true if he'd just loosen those lips a little for the mic like he does on the ice, chirping at the opposing team to get them riled up.*

She shrugs with an optimistic nod that I wish I could buy into. "Exactly," she says.

"Okay, I'm going. Wish me luck."

I head straight for him, ignoring the fact that Trey Hartley—tatted-up ex-special forces turned walk-on left winger—is sitting next to him, nursing a beer and looking every bit as intimidating as his reputation. My pulse kicks up, but I keep walking. I didn't come here to be intimidated—I came for Hunter. And this might be my only shot.

If Hunter turns me down, it'll be in front of half the Hawkeyes. But if I don't ask now, I'll run out of time to get my interviews up and win the syndication deal.

My heart is pounding so hard I can feel it in my toes.

Stress sweat is already creeping through my shirt.

Here goes nothing.

I walk up behind him and clear my throat. Trey glances over his shoulder first but then clocks that I'm trying to get Hunter's attention and turns back to his beer.

I can already smell the whiskey on Reed. I'd bet my career he's half-drunk, but I'm not turning back now.

Who knows...maybe he's a happy drunk.

Or maybe he'll be so belligerent he forgets he doesn't give interviews and agrees to mine out of pure spite.

"Hunter Reed? Hi, I'm—"

He barely turns his head.

Just enough to even pass as a glance. Then dismisses me.

"Not interested," he mutters, voice flat. "Find another jersey's lap to sit on."

I yank my head back as if his words physically struck me. "Excuse me?" I manage, heat flooding my cheeks.

"Don't take it personally. You're beautiful," he adds, like that's supposed to soften the blow. Then he takes a slow sip of his drink—dark amber, definitely whiskey. "I'm just not in the mood to fuck anyone tonight. Including you. I'm sure you'll find a player who's willing to take you home."

I see the moment Trey shoots a confused glance at Hunter but then realizes it's none of his business and turns back again.

The humiliation punches me square in the chest. Not only is he calling me a puck bunny and turning me down before I can even ask the question...but I have a witness to it all.

I straightened back up. Pinning my shoulders back.

Six years of tennis training and a career in male-dominated sports journalism. I've taken worse hits and turned them into wins.

"Wow. And here I thought your game was the biggest miss of the night. I didn't realize that you're a sore loser too."

That gets his attention, and I see Trey's shoulder shake with a muffled laugh.

He shoots a glare over his shoulder, brows lowering, eyes narrowing. It's the first time he really looks at me—because the first glance didn't count. He'd already made up his mind.

"I'm sorry, what did you say?"

He's not actually sorry. He just can't believe I hit back.

"Don't strain yourself to listen. I wouldn't want you falling off that tall pedestal you have yourself perched upon. You're drunk enough that a fall might do some damage, and based on the game you played tonight, you can't afford any more setbacks."

I hear Trey squeak out another chuckle he tries to hide while Hunter's eyes blink in a drunken stupor, and his eyebrows knit together in shock at what I just said. He attempts to mutter some reply, but I beat him to it.

"Besides, I'm not interested in anything you have to offer. You're probably too drunk to get it hard anyway, so I understand why you're not interested in taking anyone home tonight. That's the kind of rumor you wouldn't want getting around..."

"Whoa, whoa, whoa...hold on just a second," he says, trying to get his wits about him.

This conversation has gotten too far out of his control.

"Is that the excuse you planned to give her when you couldn't get it up?" I ask, knowing that I've now gone too far. Goodbye syndication deal...nice knowing you. "This was an obvious mistake. I see that now," I say, turning around to leave before I say anything else to make this whole situation worse. "Have a nice life."

I make it to Cammy's table in record time, my hands shaking a little and my heart pounding like it's trying to break out of my chest.

She takes one look at me and slides a glass of wine across the table, but I shake my head. "No, I can't drink because I'm not staying. I need to get out of here, and I live across town."

"That bad, huh?"

I thought the worst he could do was say no.

I didn't expect him to treat me like some puck bunny he couldn't be bothered to screw—and somehow make me feel smaller than I have in a long time. And I didn't expect that I would snap back that hard. Maybe all this pressure is finally getting to me, and I just released my pent-up frustrations on Hunter—though he deserved it...mostly.

I can see the moment all the girls at the table notice me in distress and then shoot daggers at Hunter. Good to know whose side they turn to first.

"He thought I was trying to get him to take me home and..." I can't even finish the sentence. His voice is still in my head. That tone. That dismissal.

"I'm sorry," Cammy sighs, patting my hand. "I should've figured he'd be like this tonight after a loss like that. But don't worry—I'll get you set up at the charity auction in three days."

She starts ticking off names like she's building me a fantasy lineup.

"Olsen clams up in interviews, so I wouldn't waste your time there. Trey's got the whole ex-special-forces mystery vibe—he's taking those secrets to the grave. Luka, though? Loves talking about himself. Aleksi's a total chatterbox. Scottie's chasing a sponsorship deal and could use the visibility, and Wolf...okay, people think he's a jerk, but he's actually a sweetheart off the ice. He could really use some good PR."

She leans back with a smirk. "We'll find you someone."

She doesn't mention JP Dumont as an option to interview, which has me wondering what's going on with Cammy and JP. Seems like there might be some tension there.

But it's not my business. We're still newly minted friends, and with me being a podcaster looking for a story, I would never want her to think I was fishing for something.

Even if the tension between her and the Hawkeyes' new goalie is practically its own subplot.

I take a long, cleansing breath, trying to forget the burn of Hunter Reed's words.

And the fact that I pinned my best shot at a viral interview—my last chance at network syndication—on a guy who just treated me like a groupie looking for a hookup.

I appreciate Cammy for trying to get me another player to interview, but Hunter is the one I needed to have a shot at the syndication deal. And that just went up in flames.

Happy Thursday to me.

CHAPTER TWO

Hunter

The pounding in my head matches the rhythm of my phone buzzing against the nightstand. I crack one eye open and immediately regret it as sunlight knives through the blinds and into my skull. Every inch of me aches.

Last night was a blur after that third whiskey, though I vaguely remember Aleksi and Trey dragging me out of Oakley's and something about me trying to recreate the *Mighty Ducks* speech.

I groan and blindly swipe for my phone. Seven texts from my agent, three from my mom, and—perfect—a push notification from a sports blog calling out my post-game attitude.

I squint at the screen.

REED'S RETURN TO THE NHL: IS THE ATTITUDE WORTH THE TALENT?

Because apparently, four years in the farm system wasn't punishment enough for dating the wrong girl my rookie year. The same girl who my mother still calls "the daughter she never had."

"Shit," I mumble at the headline.

I sit up slowly, swinging my legs over the side of the bed. My head spins, and I'm not even sure I slept so much as blacked out. I wipe the dried residue of drool from my chin. The taste of whiskey and regret still coats my tongue, a bitter reminder from last night.

Still clutching my phone, I shuffle out of my bedroom and out toward the kitchen, the light from the hallway an assault on my retinas. I yank open the freezer and grab the ice pack I keep there for bruises and hangovers alike, pressing it to my forehead as I lean against the counter, trying to gather my thoughts amidst the swirling chaos.

Another buzz.

> **Mom: Honey, you played well. Don't let them get to you.**

I type back with one thumb while keeping the ice pack balanced against my temple.

> **Me: Did you hear back from the doctor about the tests they ran? Do they think it's coming back?**

It's been almost two months since she let it slip that her doctor wanted to run more labs. She brushed it off, but I've had a bad feeling about it ever since—one that gnaws at the edges of my mind like a persistent itch.

Her reply pings in.

> **Mom:** Don't worry about that. I'll let you know when I hear back. No news is good news. Anyway, don't think about me. I want you to focus on your comeback. That's more important.

> **Me:** My offer still stands to move you out here to Seattle. There are a lot of great doctors, and I'd be closer if you need anything.

> **Mom:** Who would run the salon? Who would keep the a cappella group going? No, I'm good here.

Of course, she'd say that. My mom's never been the type to burden anyone, especially not me. She's still in Jersey, won't leave the salon, her friends, her doctors—even when I've practically begged her to move west. Says she's "content." But I know what that means. She doesn't want me to worry—which only makes me worry more.

I move to the couch and drop down with a grunt, still clutching my phone, the ice pack now resting on the back of my neck.

Only child. Single mom. We've always looked out for each other. She gave up everything to raise me. I owe her a lot.

The door swings open.

"Reed! You alive in here?"

Trey Hartley's voice pulls me from my spiraling thoughts.

Thank God. If anyone gets the push-pull of family guilt, it's the guy who gave up special forces to raise his niece after his brother and sister-in-law passed away in a car accident. He's seen the worst life can throw at someone, and still, he managed to walk on to the Hawkeyes team as a starting left winger after being off the ice since high school.

"It's open," I call out, wincing at the sound of my own voice.

Trey steps in, dressed in sweats for practice this morning, while Aleksi Mäkelin, the Hawkeyes' right winger, trails behind him, way too chipper for this hour.

"You look like shit," Trey announces, crossing his arms over his broad chest and a teasing grin spreading across his face.

"Feeling the love, Hart," I mutter, slouching deeper into the couch, wishing it could swallow me whole.

"Maybe next time don't try to drink your weight in whiskey," Aleksi suggests, his Finnish accent always thicker in the mornings. "Though watching you try to convince the bartender you could recite the entire *Mighty Ducks* movie was entertaining."

I groan. "Please tell me I didn't."

"No, we stopped you," Trey says. "Though you did try to challenge Wolf to a dance-off. Something about showing him your 'sick moves' from your middle school roller rink days?"

"Jesus Christ," I mutter, running my hand over my face, genuinely embarrassed.

"Don't worry, he said no," Aleksi drops onto my couch next to me and grabs the remote out of my hand, changing the channel to some cooking show. "But you might want to apologize to Cammy's friend from last night. Word is you were kind of a dick."

Trey chuckles. "Kind of a dick?" he asks, shooting Aleksi a glance and then back to me. "I'd say that's an understatement. I was sitting next to you, and you were in rare form last night. More dick-ish than I've ever seen you towards anything with two X chromosomes. I watched a ninety-year-old woman blush and give you her number once on a napkin at 5th Avenue Cafe... So I don't know what crawled up your ass and died, but Cammy's friend sure as hell didn't do anything to deserve what you said to her."

I try to pull the memory from last night, but everything seems blurry post-media and walking down to Oakley's from the stadium. "Cammy's friend?"

Aleksi glances over at me, his brow furrowing in thought. "The hot blonde from *Bleacher Report*. Her name is Peyton, I think. I don't know why she didn't just ask me to be on the show. I'd do it."

Peyton? The name doesn't sound familiar, but now a vague memory of exchanging heated words with a woman at the bar is starting to come into focus...though hazy at best.

"She didn't ask you because she's heard your post-game rambles," Trey says, casually tossing a protein bar from my cupboard into his gym bag. "Nobody's tuning into *The Bleacher Report* to listen to you talk about your nighttime facial routine and your moisturizing sock tips."

Aleksi stuffs a throw pillow in at his side, trying to get comfortable, unbothered by Trey's dig. "Don't knock it, man. The ladies love a guy in bed who doesn't scratch them up with callused hockey feet."

Trey huffs a dry laugh. "Mäk, no woman sleeping with you is getting anywhere near your feet. I guarantee it."

"Is that right, Hart?" Aleksi grins. "Then why don't you go ask your mom?"

Trey scowls and then grabs a pillow and chucks it at Aleksi's head.

Aleksi dodges it easily, still grinning like he just lit the lamp in overtime.

Trey's not offended. He never is. Not about stuff like that. Probably because he hasn't spoken to either of his parents since he was seventeen, back when he forged their signatures to enlist and left home for good. Whatever scars he's carrying, he keeps them buried under layers of military-trained resilience and loyalty to those who return it.

"She walked up and talked to me?" I ask, my memory still failing to remember a blonde that I rejected harshly enough that the team is gossiping about it.

Trey walks over to the fridge and starts filling his water bottle with ice. We've got morning skate in thirty minutes.

"She tried, but you said that you weren't in the mood to fuck her...I'm paraphrasing, but the word fuck definitely came out of your mouth," he says, topping off his water bottle and then screwing on the lid.

The memory crashes back—her face. That flash of surprise, of hurt. The way she blinked once, covered it, then fired back like she'd been waiting for a fight all night.

If I'd been sober, I probably would've found it refreshing. She wasn't simpering. She didn't cling. She didn't ask for a selfie or an autograph or the name of my hotel.

She was sharp. And I was an asshole.

Whether she was there as a fan or a podcaster—hell, even if she had been looking to flirt—I shouldn't have treated her like that.

I was pissed about the loss, worried about Mom, and feeling the pressure of proving to Everett Kauffman that he made the right choice to sign me. The last place I wanted to be was in that bar, surrounded by noise, pretending to be fine. And when she approached me, I went straight into defense mode. Sharp words. Crude assumptions.

Though, in fairness, most women who approach me at a bar after a game are looking to hook up with me or one of my teammates.

Cammy won't let this slide. Not when it's one of her people.

I sit up, hanging my head for a second.

Aleksi slaps my back. "Don't worry about it. You'll get another chance to make an ass out of yourself in front of her at the auction in a couple of days."

The auction—I almost forgot.

Kids With Cancer is a foundation started by Briggs Conley and his now-wife, Autumn, years ago when he used to play for the team. The Hawkeyes co-host two events each year to raise money for the families whose children are going through treatment, and this year, Cammy and JP convinced me to auction off a date with me to earn money.

I would have been happy to have just written a check, but where's the fun in that?

Luka and I have a bet to see who gets the highest bid. He hates to lose, so I wouldn't put it past him to cheat and show up in a breakaway suit with a man thong under it to get higher bids. That crazy Russian.

Though technically, this is a family event, so the new owner of the team, Everett Kauffman, would probably toss him out for indecent exposure.

Everett Kauffman is still a question mark in everyone's mind since the first owner, Phil Carlton, sold the team to him this year. But he wanted me signed while he was in negotiations to buy the team when Phil almost passed on me for another player. I need to prove to Everett that he didn't make a mistake.

"Great. Looking forward to it," I say sarcastically—though inside, I feel a flicker of excitement.

Until I choked out on the ice last night, I was looking forward to the charity event.

"Get up," Trey says, tossing my gym bag at me, and then hands me a glass of water and two Advil. "Best cure for a hangover is sweating it out. Plus, Coach will have your ass doing drills until you drop if you miss morning skate."

"I hate you both," I mutter, but I drag myself up off the couch anyway. The room spins slightly before settling, like a bad power play rotation.

"Bullshit you do," Aleksi says. "If it weren't for us, you'd be lying face down in a pile of your own vomit in the alley behind Oakley's. We dragged your drunk ass home."

He's right.

I had a shit night, and they did me a solid.

Any other night, it might have been one of them drinking away negative thoughts and I would have made sure they got home too. That's what you do for your teammates.

The locker room is lively by the time we arrive. Everyone is suiting up for practice. The familiar scene of Scottie wolfing down another protein shake and of Slade and Olsen taping up knees and shoulders from past injuries—a locker room full of teammates ready to get back on the ice after last night to prove we're better than that.

"Heard you almost challenged me to a dance battle last night," Wolf Ziegler, our right defender, calls out, pulling his practice jersey over his head. "Something about roller skates?"

"Never happened," I say, taking a seat on the bench to lace up my skates. "No witnesses."

"I have video," Slade offers, pulling his practice jersey up over his head.

"Delete it or I'll tell Coach who the mastermind behind filling his car with ping pong balls last month was."

That shuts him up. Some pranks are better left in the past.

Especially since the city had to get involved, bringing out the street sweepers to clean up all twenty-seven thousand ping pong balls to fill his four-door truck. The minute he opened his door, they spilled out into the parking lot and flooded the city streets.

The Hawkeyes got a fat bill for the cleanup, which Penelope made every player on the team split.

It was worth it.

I start my warm-up, trying to outskate both the hangover and my colossal fuck-ups with missing that goal last night and with Peyton. Tack on the fact that I have a sinking feeling that my mom's cancer has come back, and this week is shaping up to be complete shit.

"So," Trey says, following behind me as we make our way out onto the rink. "You want to talk about what's really going on?"

"Not particularly."

"Your mom's tests?"

I wish I had an answer for him—an answer for me, even, but I have neither. "She says she hasn't gotten any news back from the doctor yet."

"It's been over a month, hasn't it?"

I nod, the guilt creeping back in because if I were there, I could go to these appointments with her. I could talk to the doctors myself. I make enough money with my new contract that I can pay for any new treatments or any specialists they could recommend, but she turns me down every time I suggest that she move out here so I can take care of her.

"You know you can't control everything, right?" he says, matching my pace. "Your mom's health, last night's game—"

Some things you can't outrun, no matter how fast you skate out on the ice, no matter how hard the hit, no matter how many goals you score.

As we step onto the ice, the chill hits me, and I try to shake off the remnants of last night. My teammates are already skating, their laughter echoing off the walls—a reminder of the camaraderie we share—and for a second, I remember that last night is over and gone, and today is a new day with an upcoming game that needs our full attention.

Living in the past, focusing on last night's loss—and humiliating myself in front of Peyton—won't do anyone any good. We have to focus on what's ahead.

I take a deep breath, the cool air filling my lungs, and push everything else aside.

But as I start to glide across the ice, the weight of my mom's health is unwelcome company. It's hard to concentrate on the puck when my mind is a swirling mess of guilt and anxiety.

"Hey, Reed!" Slade shouts from across the ice, breaking me from my thoughts. "Let's see if you can actually hit the net today!"

Laughter erupts from the other players, and I can't help but roll my eyes.

"Yeah, yeah, don't worry about me. I'll hit the net when it counts," I call back, trying to shake off the tension.

The practice begins, and as we run drills, I focus on the rhythm of my movements, the sound of blades slicing across the ice, and the satisfying thud of the puck hitting the back of the net. For a moment, it feels like everything else fades away, and it's just me, the ice, and the game I love.

But every time I glance at the empty seats in the stands, I'm reminded of the auction tomorrow. The pressure is back, and the anxiety swells again. What if I make a fool of myself again? What if I can't shake this hangover? What if I run into Peyton, and she decides to call me out for last night?

Just as I'm about to zone out again, Trey skates up beside me, his expression serious.

"Reed, you need to talk to her," he says, his voice low. "You owe her that much."

"I know," I admit, the weight of his words sinking in. "But what do I even say? 'Sorry for being an asshole?'"

"Start with an apology," he replies, shrugging. "But you can't just let her think you're some prick who doesn't know how to treat a woman."

"Yeah, yeah," I mutter, shaking my head. "I'll figure it out. Just...let me get through today."

As practice wraps up, I can't shake the feeling that tomorrow is going to change everything. The pressure is building, but I can't ignore it anymore. I need to face it head-on, just like I do on the ice.

And surely I'll be able to find the right words to make things right with Peyton.

I push off the ice, adrenaline coursing through me, knowing that while I can't control everything, I can at least control my effort. And maybe, just maybe, that will be enough to get me through the chaos of this week.

CHAPTER THREE

Peyton

I tug up on the neckline of my borrowed gown for the hundredth time, trying to convince myself that the backless dress Abby, my sister-in-law, let me borrow isn't as revealing as it feels.

Abby has a closet full of them. A dress for every year she and my brother Noah have attended the Air Force Ball since he enlisted.

The light blue beading catches the chandelier light, scattering tiny stars across the Hawkeyes stadium, which has been gorgeously transformed into a ballroom for tonight's charity auction. It's beautiful. Elegant. And absolutely unrecognizable from the same space I stood in just days ago, surrounded by shouting fans and spilled beer.

I'd much rather be at home, curled up on the couch with hot tea and a book. But when your podcast dreams chew through your savings like Halloween candy, you wear whatever your sister-in-law lends you and fake confidence like it's your job.

> **Abby:** Stop fidgeting. You look amazing. Trust me—perfect for catching a hockey player's attention.

If only she knew that's exactly what I'm trying to avoid.

I'm not here to land a professional athlete. I'm here to interview one.

Just an hour of their time. A voice in a mic. That's it.

And even though I know Hunter Reed is the player I need to impress the network execs, after last night...I'm not even sure I could sit across from him in a recording studio for five minutes, let alone a full hour.

Selfishly, I hope he skips tonight entirely.

But Cammy already warned me—Hawkeyes players are strongly encouraged to show up for this event, and according to the program I was handed at the door, Hunter's not only here...he's listed as one of the players auctioning himself off to raise money.

Of course he is.

Judging by the crowd of women from every walk of life loitering near the stage, it's hard to say whether this whole idea of letting fans bid on players is noble or just a fresh excuse to stroke a few overblown egos.

Either way, it should be entertaining.

Though, I grow annoyed that I'll have to watch Hunter lap up the attention of women fighting over him.

Am I tempted to bid on a player just to score an interview? Sure, it crossed my mind. But not only would that be frowned upon in my industry—it's also a hard pass from my bank account.

The charity auction is already buzzing, the ballroom filled with Seattle's elite, media reps, and team fans. Glittering gowns and tuxedos swirl between tables topped with champagne and seafood hors d'oeuvres.

A stage is set at the front with bright lights, cameras, and a lineup of Hawkeyes players waiting to be auctioned off for charity dates.

"And here I thought I was early," Cammy says, sliding in beside me like a vision in an emerald dress and high heels that should be illegal. If I didn't know better, I'd say she was dressing for revenge. It has me itching to ask her about JP and if the rumors are true about them dating. It just still feels too early to barge in on her love life, and a work event is the worst time to do it.

She hands me a champagne flute without missing a beat. "Liquid courage. You look like you need it."

She has no idea. Though she did see me crash and burn a couple of nights ago at Oakley's.

I take the glass with a grateful nod and a half-laugh. "Is it that obvious?"

"Only to someone who's survived enough of these events to read the signs." She tips her glass toward the crowd. "Welcome to the social Super Bowl. Half the room's here to land a player. The other half is here to land a headline."

My stomach dips. Great. Just what I need—Seattle's entire sports media scene watching me fail in real time. It was bad enough when it was just the players and fans in a packed bar.

Cammy takes a sip of her drink and casually scans the crowd. "You've got that deer-in-headlights look. Don't worry. You'll adjust."

"I'm not used to...all this." I gesture vaguely to the dress, the champagne, the high ticket entry to get into this place. "It's not really my scene. I feel a lot more comfortable on a tennis court or behind a mic."

"It wasn't mine either at first," Cammy says with a shrug. "But you're here on a mission, and you deserve syndication, so put all of that behind you and find your target. Stay confident, and don't let anyone shake you. You're not here to blend in—you're here to make something happen. And honestly, the Hawkeyes boys are all great, though their talent agents can be overly protective."

I nod, gripping my champagne glass tighter.

No pressure.

A beautiful woman about our age with dark auburn hair and a sleek black trumpet dress waves Cammy down and heads our way.

"Cammy, there you are. I need help with the silent auction table. Do you have a moment?" she asks, giving Cammy a quick look before offering me a warm smile.

"Aria, this is Peyton Collins with *Bleacher Report*," Cammy says, gesturing between us.

"Hi, Peyton. It's great to meet you. I heard your interview with Penelope Matthews—it was amazing. I've worked in an office next door to Penelope for two years and didn't know half the things you brought up in that episode," she says with genuine enthusiasm. "Really great work."

Her praise catches me off guard. I didn't realize how much I needed to hear something like that until it hits me like a small, unexpected hug.

"Thank you so much for listening. That means a lot to me," I say. "So, you work for the Hawkeyes then?" I ask.

Aria's face turns a little green, her smile fading quickly. "Actually, I don't anymore. I was Phil Carlton's assistant when Everett Kauffman bought the team. It turns out that I was redundant, and Everett let me go."

Cammy reaches out and rubs Aria's arm quickly. "You're not redundant. He has no idea how incredible you are. I couldn't have gotten the silent auction table finished without you."

"Thanks," Aria whispers with a small smile and then turns back to me. "But forget I just told you my sob story. You should be here enjoying yourself."

Cammy beams back at me. "Speaking of which, Peyton's trying to line up a player interview tonight. She's getting a syndication deal."

Aria's jaw drops like Cammy just announced I won an Emmy.

"Oh—no, it's not a sure thing," I say quickly, shaking out a hand to brush away Cammy's attempt at propping me up.

Our friendship is still so new, and she's already the best hype man I've ever had. Maybe I should have had her in my interview with the network about my syndication deal.

"Well, if the interviews I've listened to lately are any indication, I think you've got it in the bag," Aria says with a confident nod.

"I really appreciate you saying that," I reply, cheeks flushing.

Aria gestures toward Cammy. "Do you mind if I steal her for a second? I promise I'll bring her right back."

"Oh...of course. No problem. I should mingle anyway."

I'm halfway through my second glass of champagne, making my way around the silent auction table when I catch sight of him.

Hunter Reed.

Standing near the bar in a black tux that fits like it was designed for his body alone. The jacket stretches just enough across his shoulders to be distracting, and the sleeves cut off right at his strong wrists. His hair is styled but not overly done—still that messy perfection that makes you want to tug on it just to see if it moves.

God help me, the man looks like a Bond villain and a GQ cover model had a love child. Tack on the scar across his eyebrow and a slightly crooked nose from too many hits to the face, and the man has a sexy hardness to him that sends flutters low in my belly.

I'm just about to pivot and walk the other way when I realize who he's talking to.

Cammy.

I slow down. Not enough to look obvious, just enough to let my ears catch the conversation.

"I'm just saying, she came to a bar trying to pitch a gossip podcast. It's not even real news," Hunter says, voice low but still sharp. "You know I don't do interviews like that. She should ask Aleksi. He'd be more interesting anyway."

A flush creeps up my neck. *Seriously?*

Cammy makes a face I can't quite see from this angle, but her voice is tight. "You were vulgar and rude, making wild assumptions about her when you didn't even let her speak. Besides, she's not like that, Hunter. She has this great way of letting you speak your mind and have a safe space to air out things that the media already wants you to speak about. You can do it on your own terms with her and get your side of the story out."

"I don't want my side of the story out. I think I've made that clear for the last four years. And if I were going to air out my dirty laundry, I wouldn't do it on a podcast."

Before I can react—or storm off—Cammy glances up and spots me.

Her eyes light up like she's been waiting for this.

"And look at that," she says with a little too much enthusiasm. "Peyton from *Bleacher Report*."

Hunter turns.

Our eyes meet.

He's as calm here as he is on the ice—so sure of himself—and I catch the flicker of recognition in his eyes. Then his expression smooths into something unreadable, and I hate how unfairly attractive he looks when he's doing absolutely nothing.

Out of all the Hawkeyes players on this team, why the hell does he have to be the one that the network wants to see me interview?

"Peyton, is it?" he asks, stepping forward and offering his hand like we're strangers meeting at a cocktail mixer instead of two people who've already exchanged public humiliation.

I don't take his hand.

Instead, I smile tightly and lift my glass in a mock toast. "Look who discovered manners. I'm shocked to see you without a whiskey in your hand."

Cammy lets out a soft cough that might be a laugh, quickly disguised as a sip of champagne.

Hunter's expression doesn't change, but I see the flicker of something behind his eyes. Embarrassment? Annoyance? It's hard to tell with him. He's a master of the blank face—years of press conferences and on-camera charm have made sure of that.

"About the other night—" he starts.

"Save it," I say, cutting him off with a wave of my hand. "You've made your opinion of my work crystal clear. No need to play nice now that you're wearing a tux and pretending to care. It's a good thing you didn't take me home that night, or this could have been really awkward." I say with a sarcastic tone.

His expression hardens slightly at my snark, but something flickers in his eyes. "I had a bad game. I wasn't in the mood for conversation."

"Well then, I'll remember that you're a sore loser and avoid you when you suck a big L on game days. Wouldn't want to be mistaken for a puck bunny again."

I want to kick myself for not just accepting his half-ass apology and using it as my shot to beg for the interview that could land me the network deal—but I can't bring myself to fake being nice to a man who clearly thinks he's above it all.

Hunter's jaw tightens, but before he can respond, Cammy slides a step closer to me, gently linking our arms. "Okay, on that note," she says, bright and breezy, like this is just another Thursday night at a gala. "Let's get you a refill and introduce you to literally anyone else. I can name at least four players who would kill for a podcast feature with your reach."

She starts to guide me away, and I let her—even though I can feel Hunter's eyes burning into my bare back in this dress as we walk away, making me wish I'd worn something with more coverage. Or better yet, something with armor.

I hate the way he leaves me feeling completely exposed.

Cammy and I are almost to the bar when the energy in the room shifts.

It's not loud. Not obvious. Just a subtle pause, like half the crowd collectively took a breath.

I follow the current and spot the source—tall, blonde, commanding the room in a way that's almost cinematic. A champagne silk slip dress skims her curves like it was poured on. Delicate diamond studs catch the light at her ears. Strappy heels. A designer clutch dangling from perfectly manicured fingers. She looks like she stepped out of a luxury ad campaign for trophy wives.

Somehow, I feel like I've seen her before, but I can't place her. From the way heads turn, everyone else can.

I follow her gaze to find her staring straight back at Hunter.

His whole body has gone still. His jaw is tight. Eyes locked. Hands clenched at his sides like he's resisting the urge to throw something—or run.

It's almost unnatural to see him like this. In fight or flight mode.

"Who's that?" I ask Cammy, since I know she helped with the guest list of the event.

Cammy's shoulders stiffen when she sees who I'm talking about.

"That would be Bethany Richards. The soon-to-be ex-wife of the owner of the New Jersey team."

Oh...that's right. I've seen her on TV once or twice, arm in arm with the owner of the team.

I remember when they first got married. There was a lot of buzz around their age gap.

There was gossip that the reason the owner sent Hunter to the farm team, after only completing half a season with the pros, was because his new bride was flirting with Reed, but when the noise died out, I figured that was all it was. Just noise.

But the look on Hunter's face right now, like someone let a jaguar loose in the building, tells a different story.

Why would the soon-to-be ex-wife of a team across the country be coming to this charity auction?

If I didn't know better, I'd say she didn't fly across the country for the crab cakes.

BLEACHER REPORT

CHAPTER FOUR

Hunter

Bethany Richards.

My ex-girlfriend and the reason I spent the last four seasons on a farm team instead of playing for the New Jersey NHL franchise.

Of course, she'd show up here when life keeps kicking me in the ass.

I watch her glide into the room like she owns it. Same confident stride. Same smug smile. Same overpriced perfume that somehow still triggers something bitter in the back of my throat.

She's wearing a silk dress that probably cost more than my first car—clinging to every curve like it was stitched on. Hair swept up, lips lacquered in that same power-hungry red. Bethany always did know how to make an entrance—elegant on the surface, but just polished enough to hide the claws beneath.

And just like that, it's like I'm twenty-three again. Standing on New Jersey's ice, unaware that the woman I was planning a future with was already planning her engagement party with someone else. Someone with more power. More pull. More money.

Someone who could erase me from a roster with a single call…and did.

Because in his mind, I was his biggest threat. He was blind to the idea that Bethany was setting him up to take half his wealth.

Oh, the irony.

I grind my teeth, forcing myself to breathe through the memories that I've tried hard to leave in that New Jersey stadium where they belong.

It's been four years of clawing my way back to the NHL—through injuries and rehab, brutal mornings and sleepless nights, while reporters questioned whether I was still worth the ink on my new contract. And now she's here. Waltzing into the world I rebuilt without her, like it's something she left behind and has every right to reclaim.

I've gotten her calls and texts—all thirty-two of them—saying she wants to talk. I haven't returned a single one.

Her eyes scan the room, slow and deliberate, until they land on me.

She smiles.

God, I forgot how manipulative that smile is. Sweet enough to fool a billionaire. Sharp enough to end a pro hockey player's career.

The fact that my mother still claims to see the good in Bethany has me demanding she see an obstetrician—or quit microdosing hallucinogens. Honestly, either one tracks.

"Hunter." Bethany's voice slides over me like ice water down my spine as she heads for me, weaving through tables, chairs, and other guests. "I've missed you."

I force myself to turn, to face the woman who derailed my NHL career with a smile and a wedding ring from a man twice her age and three times as delusional. She looks exactly the same—bleach blonde hair falling in calculated waves, red lips, and perfect teeth curved in that predatory smile. The only difference is now, she's not wearing the five-carat diamond ring Richards bought her.

The sight of her here, in my new life, makes my stomach turn. I've worked too hard to rebuild everything she destroyed to let her maneuver her way back in now.

"What are you doing here, Beth?"

"Can't a girl support a good cause?" She steps closer. "Besides, I heard you were up for auction. Couldn't pass up the chance to remind you how good we were together."

The memory of finding out about her engagement to Richards still burns. One minute, we were celebrating my newly minted NHL contract and planning a life together, the next I was being sent to the farm team to "develop my skills"—code for get me out of the way. Richards didn't like the idea of his new bride having access to her ex-boyfriend on the team. And from what I've heard from old teammates who still play for New Jersey, she made do with the other twenty-three players on the roster.

"We were never good together. You made that clear when you married Richards."

Beth rolls her eyes. "God, Hunter. I did it all for us, and now I'm going to have more money than either of us know what to do with. When are you going to get over it?"

"When your shrink finally diagnoses you as a raging sociopath. That's when."

She tilts her head condescendingly, not hearing a word I said. My point exactly—sociopath.

"Marrying Kevin Richards was a mistake I'm rectifying." Her perfectly manicured fingers trail up my arm, leaving goosebumps in their wake—not from desire, but from pure revulsion.

"The divorce will be final soon. The prenup gives me half the team, including player roster decisions."

Her smile is calculating. Cold. How the hell didn't I see this in college? She's always been this person—but all I saw were the big tits, the perfect smile, the pretty girl with a backstory that sounded like mine. I thought we were climbing together.

I didn't realize I was just her stepping stone to a bigger life. One that never included me.

My own personal Helen of Troy, burning my city to the ground.

"Once I pitch Everett Kauffman a trade deal too good to refuse, you'll be headed home. Back to New Jersey. Where you belong. We can pick up right where we left off."

Pick up where we left off?

She thinks she can just walk in here and destroy everything I've established here—and I'll thank her for it?

"Right where we left off?" I snap. "You mean right before your husband tried to ruin my career by sending me to the farm team?"

She rolls her eyes. "Water under the bridge."

Then she leans in, lips brushing my ear, her voice turning to poison-laced sugar.

"No one's ever been as good as you, you know. In or out of bed. The sex was incredible—you can't deny that. I got a place at The Commons. Two months to remind you what you've been missing."

She got an apartment in my building? *What the fuck?*

Typical Bethany move. Hit you where it hurts, then act like it's a gift. Though, this one catches me off guard. Before I can respond, she turns on her heels...but not without sliding her hand down to slap my ass.

"I've always loved you in a tux," she purrs. "See you on stage, baby."

I watch her sashay toward the VIP table, panic rising in my chest. This isn't happening. This can't be happening. Four years of rebuilding my life, my career, my reputation—all at risk because Bethany Richards is bored with her billionaire husband.

My eyes scan the crowded ballroom desperately for a way out of this when I spot Peyton at the bar.

The blue beading on her dress catches the light, making her glow like a beacon to my salvation. And damn if she doesn't wear that dress like it was made for her—elegant, understated, but cut low and sexy, making every guy around her take notice.

Including me.

A really bad idea jumps to mind, and I don't think.

I just move.

Bethany's scent still clings to my jacket, and I need it gone. Need her out of my line of sight, out of my brain. And I need someone to outbid her. And lucky for me, Peyton despises me enough that she's the perfect person to not twist this into something more than a simple deal—no strings.

She's at the bar, standing behind two men in suits. She's half-turned away, studying the crowd, completely unaware that she just might be my only shot at salvaging tonight.

The line moves. She steps forward, delicate fingers wrapping around the edge of the marble bar.

"Peyton," I say, my voice low. Controlled. A warning and a plea.

She doesn't even turn her head.

The bartender nods at her. "What can I get for you, ma'am?"

"Surprise me. Just no whiskey... It's triggering," she says, her voice smooth and cool.

I wince.

She said that loud enough for me to hear, yet she has no idea what kind of surprise I'm about to drop in her lap.

"Peyton," I try again. "I know you don't like me right now. We got off on the wrong foot, but I need to talk to you."

Nothing. Not even a blink in my direction.

Screw it.

I reach into my jacket, pull out my wallet, and slap two crisp hundreds on the bar—despite the fact that this is an open bar and nobody's paying for a damn thing.

"Keep her drinks coming," I tell the bartender.

He freezes, eyes bouncing between Peyton and me like he's trying to assess if I'm a stalker or just tragically stupid. Right now...I might be considered both.

Peyton finally turns her head toward him and lifts one brow. "Well, if he's just going to burn through money for no reason, you might as well take it."

The bartender takes the tip with a nod and then heads off to mix whatever chaos she just ordered.

She shifts just enough to glance at me out of the corner of her eye. Her mouth is a perfect, unimpressed line.

"What do you want, Reed?"

There's no warmth in her voice. None of the body language I'm used to from the opposite sex. No leaning in to touch my arm, no breathy laugh, no playing with her hair like she's waiting for me to make the next move.

She's becoming colder toward me the longer I stand here, her stiff posture making it evident that she's only interested in this conversation ending as soon as possible.

And yet somehow, there's this soft, unexpected scent—vanilla and honeysuckle—that doesn't match her closed-off stance. It's inviting in a way she isn't. And that messes with me more than it should.

The most important thing?

She hasn't walked away.

And right now, that's all I've got.

I lean in closer, quickly glancing around us to make sure no one is close enough to eavesdrop on our conversation. "I need you to bid on me tonight."

Peyton blinks slowly, like I've just asked her to help me bury a body. "I'm sorry, I think I must have blacked out just now, because I could have sworn you just asked me to bid on a date with you."

"Yeah, that's right."

She makes a scoffing sound and looks around like everyone nearby should be cracking up right along with her at the absurdity of my request.

I get it. I wasn't expecting to ask her either, but here I am, and I just so happen to know that she wants something from me too.

An interview.

"You're kidding, right? I can't think of anything I'd like less than to go on a date with you."

Her insult should sting, but it doesn't. I'm too focused on my goal.

"I'm not asking you to go on a date with me, and no, I'm not kidding. I'm serious." I drop my voice. "My ex-girlfriend, Bethany—she's here. She's planning to bid on me tonight. And I can't—" I stop, exhale. "I just can't let her win."

The bartender sets Peyton's drink on a napkin, muttering something about a blueberry lemon drop with a marinated vodka blueberry garnish, then glances at me.

"Nothing for me," I say, stepping aside so the next guest can order. Peyton follows.

"Hold on a second," she says, pulling the metal skewer from her drink. She slides one blueberry off with her perfectly straight white teeth and painted pink lips, chewing as her expression shifts—processing everything.

"Bethany Richards is your ex? As in, the soon-to-be ex-wife of Kevin Richards, the owner of the team you used to play for?"

"I dated her first," I say, sharper than I mean to. And stupidly, without thinking about the fact that Peyton is the last person I should be spilling this to since she has a podcast that she could use to air this information.

Her eyebrows lift in question. I know exactly what she's about to ask, and I cut her off fast.

"But that was a lifetime ago. And that's not what this is about."

Not exactly, anyway.

I've spent years killing the rumors—shutting down every whisper, every question about why I was demoted mid-season. I know what people assumed. What they still wonder. And the last thing I need is a podcaster sniffing around for a viral story to save her syndication deal.

That chapter of my life is closed.

Or at least, it was until thirty minutes ago.

"Okay, so why me?" she asks, arms folding across her chest. "There are at least fifty women in this room alone who'd sell their souls for a date with you. Ask one of them to outbid her."

"I can't ask any of them because you're the only person here who doesn't want something from me, except for an interview." I pause, watching her slide another blueberry off the skewer with her lips. "This is transactional. We both want something. We make the trade, and when it's done, you never have to see me again."

She doesn't respond right away. Her eyes narrow, she's considering it. She's sharp—too sharp for my own good.

"And you've already seen me at my worst," I add. "You've got more to gain than lose."

"I have plenty to lose," she fires back. "Like the last shred of professional dignity I have, after you basically accused me of being a puck bunny, then told me to find another teammate to screw in front of a packed bar of players and fans."

I flinch. No comeback. No defense.

"I deserved that."

"You did," she agrees easily, uncrossing her arms and shifting her weight from one hip to the other, clearly enjoying this.

I take a breath. "Let me make it up to you. If you bid on me—and win—I'll do the interview."

"You want me to bid against a billionaire's wife for an interview with you? Are you crazy? I don't have that kind of money. I just bought a new townhouse outside of town and renovated it for my podcast studio. I blew through my savings."

The news of her townhouse and a place to crash, away from The Commons, sparks a thought, but I need her to agree to one thing at a time. If I show all my cards, she'll bail out immediately.

"I'll pay for it. Whatever you bid, I'll cover the bill. You just have to win."

Peyton glances over in Bethany's direction, and I follow her line of sight, cringing when I see Bethany chatting up Everett, who's making his rounds with guests.

I was hoping I wasn't going to have to ask for this next thing, but by the looks of it, Bethany is making good on her threats to attempt to get me traded.

"Actually, I need one more thing."

Peyton's eyes snap back to mine. "Oh God...what now?" she

says, rolling her eyes.

"I need to live with you for two months," I say, "and I need you to pretend to be my girlfriend."

Peyton freezes, dropping the skewer with the last blueberry into her drink. It lands with a quiet plop, sending a few droplets splashing onto the napkin.

She blinks at me in disbelief.

"Okay," she says slowly. "Now I know you've lost your mind, and I'm going to do us both a favor and walk away."

She turns, clearly ready to bolt—but I gently reach out and catch her arm, just above the elbow. Not hard. Just enough to stop her without pushing my luck.

"Peyton, I wouldn't ask if I had another choice."

"You do have another choice. Pick someone else. I'm the wrong girl for this."

"Name your price," I say. "How many interviews is it going to take?"

That gets her attention. The word "interviews" is like a switch—her eyes narrow on me—and she's considering the offer in a whole new light.

"Five," she says, lifting her glass. "And I want the full story on you and Bethany."

"Two," I counter, "and nothing about my mom or my past relationship with Bethany."

"Well, well, turns out you're not as desperate as you said you were. Goodbye, and good luck," she says, turning like the conversation's over.

But I grip her elbow gently again, stopping her in her tracks.

"Hold on. Three interviews," I say quickly. "Nothing about my mom. And I'll cover all your townhouse expenses for the two months I live there."

She pauses, chewing on the inside of her cheek. I can tell she's close. She wants the interviews, and she already told me she's flat-broke after soundproofing her studio. I'm almost there—I can feel it.

"Fine," she says, her tone sharp and deliberate. "Three interviews. Two months of expenses."

"Deal," I say.

"...And you wash my car every Sunday," she adds quickly like she's scrambling to tack on more demands while she can.

Whatever. I don't care. I'll wash her car plus the neighbor's if it gets her to agree.

"Okay...sure."

"...In a Speedo. And Crocs."

I blink. "You're kidding."

She arches a brow, deadpan. "Am I? I'm giving up two interviews. You've got to give me something back."

"It's the middle of winter, and you want me to wash your car in a Speedo?"

"You're a professional hockey player. Cold is practically your natural habitat."

"I play hockey, Collins. I'm not a damn polar bear."

"Could've fooled me."

The way she says it—cool, casual, not quite daring me but absolutely daring me—almost makes me laugh. Almost.

It's not about the Speedo. It's a power move. She wants to see if I'll jump through hoops for her. If she's the one in control.

"Fine," I say, mostly because, at this point, I'll agree to anything. "I look damn good in a Speedo anyway."

"And," she adds, voice softening, "you come to my nephew's career day."

That one lands differently.

"Your nephew's career day?"

She nods. "My brother's stationed overseas. My sister-in-law's an ER nurse, and she's slammed. Jesse's a huge Hawkeyes fan, and he just switched schools again. This would mean the world to him."

It's a small task that she's asking for. And if a hockey player from my favorite team had come to my school for my career day when I was a kid, it would have been the highlight of my life.

"Done. Are we in agreement now?" I ask, catching Everett headed our way from across the room.

"I guess so. How much can I spend on the bid?" she asks.

"Whatever it takes. Bleed my bank account dry if you have to, but don't let her win a date with me," I say, my eyes shifting to Everett as he walks up.

"Bleed your bank account dry?" Peyton asks with a twinkle in her eye. "With pleasure number seventy-two."

Everett's voice cuts through the crowd. "Mr. Reed. We need you backstage."

I take one last look at her, unsure if she's going to follow through or if she agreed to all of this just to screw with me and leave me with no other options. At this point, I have no other choice than to trust she's going to make good on our verbal agreement as I follow Everett back through the crowd to the stage.

"Bethany Richards is a motivated negotiator," he says over his shoulder. "Do you two have history I should know about?"

Shit...she's serious about trying to make a trade for me.

"There's no history between us that's of any relevance," I tell him.

He nods, though I can tell that he's thinking through something she said to him earlier. "If there's anything I need to know, you'll be sure to tell me?"

"Yes, sir," I say.

Then he turns and heads for the podium as I head backstage.

Backstage is organized chaos. Luka's practicing his runway walk, completely in his element, while Aleksi critiques it. Wolf's adjusting his tie for the hundredth time. But all I can think about is Bethany out there, stalking the front row like she already owns the outcome. My stomach tightens.

I can hear the auctioneer warming up on the mic, already cracking jokes with the crowd. The curtain might as well be paper-thin—every cheer and laugh from the audience punches right through it.

Wolf adjusts his tie again. He's been doing it every thirty

seconds.

"Why does it feel like I'm about to walk into a shootout, not a charity auction?" I ask.

Trey claps me on the back. "Because you're about to be objectified for a good cause. Just smile and pretend to be charming."

I try. But the smile doesn't quite land. My hands curl into fists at my sides.

Bethany's sitting in the front row with a bid paddle in hand and a smile sharpened into something dangerous on her face.

"Hard to smile when your ex-girlfriend is out there with her soon-to-be ex-husband's money to burn," I mutter.

Trey's head snaps toward me. "Your ex is here?"

I nod toward the curtain. "Blonde. Red lipstick. Sitting between Penelope and Everett's empty seat."

Trey moves to the edge of the curtain and peeks out. "Isn't that Kevin Richards's wife?"

"Not for long, apparently."

"Jesus, Reed." He shoots a glance back at me. "If she's got Richards on the hook, then what the hell does she want with your ugly mug?"

"Shut up," I snicker.

But I know exactly why. It's not about me. It's about control. About seeing if she can still pull the strings and make me dance. Tonight, it's me. Tomorrow, it'll be someone else. That's who she is. Always has been.

And Richards? He deserves whatever mess he's in. He's the one who shipped me off like damaged goods to keep his wife in check. How's that working out for him now?

I glance back toward the crowd, my gaze locking on Peyton.

She's standing off to the side, her blue dress catching the light like a damn spotlight. Calm. Cool. Uninterested in the chaos swirling around her.

She's the only thing between me and a complete PR disaster.

I still don't know why she said yes. Maybe it's the interviews. Maybe it's for her nephew. Or maybe she just wants to watch me sweat after I embarrassed her at Oakley's a few nights back.

But I meant what I said. She can spend whatever it takes. I'll take the hit, so long as Bethany walks away empty-handed.

I hear my name announced after Luka's bid finishes.

Luka goes to a socialite who looks like she just stepped out of a country club catalog. He seems thrilled, already chatting about his Olympic medals.

Then it's my turn. The stage lights are hot, but Bethany's stare is hotter.

The bidding starts like a firecracker—fast, loud, and out of control. Ten different women, their paddles rising like birds taking flight. But I only watch two: Bethany, smugly confident in the front row, and Peyton, who hasn't moved her paddle once.

Come on, come on...

The numbers climb higher. Women drop out one by one as Bethany counters every bid. Still nothing from Peyton. Sweat trickles down my back under my suit jacket.

Then—finally—Peyton lifts her paddle, and the air in the room changes. Bethany locks in on her like a predator who just spotted a challenger.

The bids fly back and forth. Each time Bethany goes higher, Peyton doubles it. The crowd gasps and cheers, caught up in the drama. Even the other players have stopped their conversations to watch.

"Sold!" I shout, jumping off the stage before I can second-guess myself.

Gasps ripple through the crowd, but I don't stop. In three long strides, I'm in front of Peyton. She stares up at me, wide-eyed, stunned.

My heart is pounding like I just took a puck to the chest.

"Warning," I murmur, lowering my voice so only she can hear. "I'm about to kiss you."

Then I do.

I sweep her into my arms and crush my mouth to hers.

For a moment, she's frozen—surprised. But then she melts

into me, her arms wrapping around my neck, her lips parting against mine.

She tastes like vodka, blueberries...and possibility. Like everything I didn't know I needed until now.

And just like that, something dangerous—and completely unstoppable—releases in my chest.

Turning to the crowd, I announce, "Sorry everyone, but I couldn't let anyone but my gorgeous girlfriend win a date with me."

"You didn't say anything about kissing," she mutters, breathless but not exactly pulling away.

I just grin wider. The crowd awws appreciatively, eating up the romance of it all. Trey gives me a knowing look from the side of the stage while Aleksi whistles suggestively.

Only Bethany's cold stare reminds me that this is just the beginning. But with Peyton in my arms, soft and warm and already arguing about something under her breath, I can't bring myself to care.

Besides, how hard can fake dating be?

CHAPTER FIVE

Peyton

My voice echoes back through the headphones as I record the closing credits to a podcast interview I did a couple of days ago, trying to sound confident, casual—like someone who definitely hasn't just fake-bid on an NHL defenseman.

"...and don't forget to hit subscribe if you liked this episode and want to stay up to date on our new series starting next week: a deep dive into the rise of undrafted players making waves in professional sports..."

I stop the recording, click pause on my editing software, and let out a breath. My townhouse is blissfully quiet except for the hum of my recording equipment and the occasional creak of my chair—a reminder that I need to oil it or buy a new one that doesn't make noise during interviews. Although sometimes I think those little sounds bring character and authenticity to a podcast...as if there's a real person on the other side. In this room—the room I dumped my savings into soundproofing—I can almost pretend last night didn't happen.

Almost.

BLEACHER REPORT

I lean back in my chair, tapping my pen against the armrest, already starting to consider my interview with a University of Washington gymnastics superstar who competed in the Olympics and brought back a team medal for Team USA two years ago. And then my mind shifts to where I've been avoiding—my three interviews with Hunter Reed.

If I can just keep my head down and focus on the work, maybe the whole ridiculous auction scene will fade into the background, and everyone will forget that Seattle's entire social media feed is currently obsessed with me kissing the Hawkeyes' new left defenseman.

Maybe.

My phone buzzes on the desk, but I ignore it. Probably another group chat meme or a spam text from the podcast hosting platform.

Another buzz. Then another.

I glance over, heart sinking when I see the name flashing on the screen: Abby.

As in Abby Collins—my noisy, overbearing, and incredibly supportive sister-in-law.

In fact, she's more like a real sister than just my brother's wife. It's almost as if she's been around for my entire twenty-six years of existence.

Then, a text message when I just barely miss her call.

> **Abby:** Answer your damn phone. Why is my group chat blowing up with you and Hunter Reed?!

Before I can even process that, the phone starts ringing again. I swipe to answer. "Hey—"

"Peyton Elise Collins." Abby's voice slices through the line, all older-sister authority and no chill. "Why am I waking up to my entire group chat losing their minds over photos of you kissing

Hunter freaking Reed at a charity auction?"

I blink at my computer screen like she's speaking a different language. "Good morning to you too."

"I don't care about morning. I care about why my coworkers, my friends, and even Jesse's Little League parent group chat are blowing up with GIFs of my sister-in-law locking lips with Seattle's most infamous playboy."

I try to play it off. "No one even uses social media anymore. It'll die out over the weekend."

"Fat chance. You didn't think to maybe, I don't know, warn me before it hit the internet last night? The minute I walked into the ER, I had three nurses and a doctor grilling me about how long you've been dating an NHL player and why they were the last to know. Jesse came home asking about it."

My stomach sinks. "Wait—Jesse heard about it?"

"Of course he did. He's got it saved as his tablet background."

I groan and drop my head onto my desk. "This is not how this was supposed to go. We're faking it... It's not real."

Abby softens, but only a little. "Okay, spill. What's going on? Because that kiss did not look fake."

I let out a breath, knowing I can't keep this from her. "It's fake, Abs. The whole thing. We made everyone believe we're dating to keep his ex away from him, and in return, he's helping me with my podcast syndication deal."

"You're lying. That kiss was toe-curling good. There's no way that was fake."

A laugh slips out before I can stop it. Once I got past the shock, I'll admit—Hunter Reed is a damn good kisser, even when it's staged.

"Sorry to ruin the fantasy, but yeah. Totally fake."

"And the auction?"

"He paid for it. I was the bidder, but it was his money. He just didn't want her to win."

There's a pause on her end, followed by a dramatic sigh. "This is incredibly disappointing, by the way. Here I was, living vicariously through you while Will's still overseas, and you just kicked my hockey romance dreams to the curb. You should've lied to me."

I know she's teasing. She would have killed me if she knew that I waited two months to tell her that it was all fake. She'll thank me later.

"I have good news, though," I tell her.

"You know how I love good news, and you owe me after that big letdown."

"Well, this one, you're going to really love, because as part of our arrangement, Hunter is going to do Jesse's career day."

Abby squeals through my cell phone speaker. "Are you serious? Is he really going to do it? Because if this is fake too, I'll kill you. I've worked as an ER nurse long enough to know how to make it look like an accident—trust me."

"God...that was dark. But no, this one isn't fake. He asked me what my terms were for fake dating and him moving in for two months and—"

"Whoa, whoa, hold on just a damn minute. Did you just say he's moving in...with you? Like sleeping under the same roof in your one-bedroom apartment?"

"It's two bedrooms actually," I remind her.

"Yes, but the second bedroom you converted into a recording studio, which means you have to share a bedroom."

Oh wait... I hadn't thought about that. About sharing a bed. I just thought about not having to pay my mortgage for the next two months to help recoup my savings and I didn't consider much else.

Not that he gave me a whole lot of time to think through the logistics before the auction started.

Everything happened so fast.

"I didn't think about that. I'm sure he'll be fine on the couch," I say, shifting the phone to my other ear as I pace the kitchen.

There's a beat of silence, and then Abby's voice comes through, dry and skeptical. "Right. Because every hot guy wants to sleep on a couch while his fake girlfriend is tucked away in the next room."

I roll my eyes even though she can't see me. "It's not like that. We can barely tolerate each other. He's only staying here because his ex moved into his building and—"

"Oh my God," she cuts in, practically squealing. "Hate sex. This has all the makings of top-tier hate sex. I knew it. You're going to fuck this man silly. Finally. Now we're getting somewhere good."

"I'm hanging up now," I mutter, but my face is already on fire.

"You love me."

"Unfortunately. But I'm serious Abs...no one's fucking anyone silly."

"Oh, how cute. You're in denial. Your brother always told me he thought that you were a little naïve and I always stood up for you, but now I'm seeing the light."

I hear the sound of her repacking her lunch pail in the breakroom. "Shut up, I'm not in denial. It's just that keeping things clean and straightforward is going to be the best for everyone."

She snorts. "Clean and straightforward? With him? That man looks like the definition of a complication."

Before I can fire back, the hospital intercom blares through the line—paging Nurse Collins.

"Ugh, looks like my reign of terror on your fantasy world of disassociation has to end early. I'm needed back on the floor," Abby sighs. "Sorry to cut this short. I do want to unpack all these wild little delusions you're clinging to about not falling for the smoke show about to move in under your roof."

I hear the faint clatter of her locker and the thump of her shoes hitting the floor.

"But duty calls. My boss probably wants me to pick up a shift this weekend with the half-marathon madness. Time and a half, though, so—silver lining. Just remember, this conversation isn't over. Not even close. If I take the Saturday shift, can you take Jesse to his Little League game?"

"Of course. I'd love to. It'll be a good time to tell him about

Hunter coming to career day," I add.

Though Jesse can't play any of the field positions, he's the designated hitter for the pitcher, and he's good. He hit a home run last year and his entire team rushed the field, his coach lifting him up onto his shoulders as they all ran the bases as a team.

There wasn't a dry eye in the stands from the home and away teams. That was a great day.

Abby lets out a breath of relief. "Thanks. He's going to be so excited. Best Aunt of the Year award."

"It's just an honor to be nominated," I tease.

"Now go save lives," I mumble.

"Go get laid," she fires back, then disconnects before I can tell her she's completely insane.

I smile and say to the dead line, "Good, I didn't want to talk to you about this anymore anyway."

I should go back to editing.

I really should.

Instead, I reach for my phone, opening Instagram like I'm flipping over a rock I know has something slimy underneath it.

Sure enough, there it is—right at the top of my feed. The charity auction. Me. Hunter. That kiss.

The first video is on SportsNation's official page with the caption:

"Hawkeyes' Hunter Reed Auctioned Off for Charity... But Is That His Girlfriend?! #ReedAndBleacherBabe"

I click play, even though I know I shouldn't. My stomach tightens as I watch the scene unfold from an outsider's perspective—the crowd, the cheers, Hunter's name being called. And then me, paddle in hand, face flushed, caught in a bidding war I never expected to win.

But it's the kiss that makes my throat go dry.

It looks...different on screen.

Softer—sweeter—less like a PR stunt and more like the moment before something big and dangerous happens.

Now I get Abby's reaction and why she couldn't imagine that

we were faking it at first.

My thumb scrolls, and it only gets worse.

Another video.

This one zoomed in on Bethany's icy glare in the background as Hunter's lips crashed onto mine. The comments are a disaster:

@HockeyChick85: I'm living for this drama.

@PuckPrincess: OMG Hunter has a girlfriend?!

@BleacherFanGirl: Who is she and how do I become her?!

@GoalieWife77: Is that Bethany Richards in the background?! Someone grab the popcorn.

@SeattleSportsBuzz: Look at the way he looks at her after the kiss. That man is in love.

My pulse hammers in my throat. It's everywhere—there's even a trending hashtag:

#ReedAndBleacherBabe

There's a small, shameful thrill seeing myself on the screen, looking like someone who belongs in his world—the world of hockey and WAGs.

But it's tangled with something sharp and dangerous too.

Because none of this is real.

And no amount of headlines, GIFs, or internet theories can change that.

With Hunter moving in tonight, I need to make sure we set ground rules.

Boundaries. Clear lines in the sand.

Because no matter what Abby thinks, I am absolutely, one hundred percent not sleeping with Hunter Reed.

Hunter

There's a knock at my door.

I freeze, halfway through cramming a hoodie into the duffel bag at my feet. Sweat clings to my back from the morning run I cut short, my running shoes untied and damp against the hardwood.

The knock comes again—louder this time.

For one irrational second, my heart spikes in panic. Bethany. She already slid her spare apartment key under my door last night. I found it when I got home from the charity event, a shiny little threat lying on my welcome mat. I'd gone to Oakley's afterward with the team, staying out as late as possible just in case she was waiting in the shadows.

But when I crack the door open, it's not her.

It's Trey—already dressed for the gym, arms crossed, full-sleeve tattoos making him look more menacing than he is and giving me that you're a dumbass look he's perfected over the years in special forces for the Army.

I blow out a breath, the tension leaking out of my shoulders. "Jesus."

"You coming or what?" Trey asks, stepping inside without waiting.

"Just give me a minute. I had to cut the run short this morning." I nod toward the key and the folded note sitting on the kitchen counter. "Got a little...distracted."

Trey crosses the room, picks up the note, and skims it.

Hunter—

Here's a key to my place. Come by anytime, day or night.

Don't bother with the condoms... you know how I like to get messy.

He shakes his head. "Holy shit. You weren't kidding. She's out for you."

"Yeah," I mutter, dragging a hand over my face. "Welcome to the nightmare. She's trying to convince Everett to make a trade for me."

Trey's head snaps up. "You're fucking kidding me."

"Nope."

His gaze sweeps over the half-packed duffel, the shirts tossed over the back of the couch, my jacket slung across a chair. "You're really doing this?"

"Yep." I zip the bag shut and toss it onto the pile. "Moving in with Peyton."

Trey whistles low under his breath. "You know, I've seen you do a lot of dumb shit in the last ten months, but this might crack the top five."

"Yeah, well..." I scrub a hand over my jaw. "Last night was chaos. Bethany showing up, Peyton bidding on me, that kiss..."

Trey's brows lift, but he doesn't say anything.

I ignore him. "And now I'm packing a bag like a runaway teenager to move in with a woman I barely know—all so I can avoid another woman who's half my size."

Trey lets out a dry laugh. "You're a real inspiration, man."

I shake my head, slinging the duffel over my shoulder. This is really happening. I'm moving into a stranger's house to avoid the disaster that's been my love life and career.

For the first time since last night, I feel it hit me—how completely insane this is.

୶

An hour later, I show up at Peyton's place. I knock and she opens the door, stepping aside to let me in.

"You're early," she says.

"No better time than the present," I say, though I leave out that my ex is already leaving me apartment keys and all-access invitations to sleep with her day or night.

I couldn't stay there for another minute. I needed out.

"You're sure about this?" I ask, voice lower than I mean it to be. "You don't have to do this."

Peyton crosses her arms and leans against the wall. "I already signed up for this circus; I might as well ride the elephant."

My brows lift, and before I can stop myself, I toss her a

crooked smirk. "Didn't realize it was going to be that kind of living arrangement, but you're welcome to ride me anytime you want."

Her eyes go wide, cheeks flushing instantly. "No! I—God, that's not what I meant."

I can't help it—I laugh. The first real one I've had all day. "Relax, Collins. I was kidding."

She mutters something under her breath about regretting her life choices, but there's the smallest twitch of a smile at the corner of her mouth.

And damn it, my smirk turns into a full-blown smile. God help me, fake dating Peyton might actually turn out to be fun.

As I step further inside, I can't help but notice her décor. It's not just neat; it's curated. Framed photos line the walls, and my gaze catches on a framed tennis racket hanging just above the couch. A Wimbledon poster hangs nearby, and I can't help but feel a pang of curiosity mixed with admiration.

"Is that...?" I point toward the racket, trying to ask without sounding too interested.

Peyton follows my gaze, and her expression shifts slightly, almost wistful. "Yeah. That was my dad's. He played a bit when he was younger. I never got to enter the Wimbledon tournament, but it was always my dream."

"Wimbledon, huh?" I say, genuinely intrigued. "What happened?"

She shrugs, a flicker of something passing over her face, maybe regret or loss. "Injury. I had a really bad fall during a qualifier. It was one of those moments where everything just...changed."

I can see it—the way her eyes dim slightly, like she's recalling something painful but still precious. It makes me want to know more. "I'm sorry to hear that. I didn't know you were a competitive athlete."

"Yeah, well, not many do. I'm just a podcaster who knows a lot about hockey now." She chuckles lightly, but I can hear the undercurrent of sadness in her voice.

"That's impressive, though. I had no idea. You must've had

some serious skills to even qualify." I try to keep my tone light, but there's a weight to her story that pulls at me.

"Thanks. It was a different life, I guess." She shrugs again, but I can tell it's more than that. "But this is my life now, and I'm making it work."

"Moving in with a hockey player is definitely a shift," I remark, trying to lighten the mood. "You're in for a wild ride."

"Yeah, well, I'm not going to go all fangirl on you. Just remember, this is business."

I nod, but deep down, I can't help but feel a spark of something more—an interest in her that goes beyond the surface. This is a woman who's fought hard for her dreams, just like me, and there's something admirable about that.

I'm not just moving in with a podcaster; I'm moving in with someone who's had her own battles. Someone who might just understand what it means to fight for what she wants.

As I take a step further into her space, the tension from earlier begins to dissipate. Maybe this arrangement won't be so bad after all.

CHAPTER SIX

Peyton

The heat in my face still hasn't cooled from his offer to let me ride him whenever I want.

Not even close.

I push off the wall, trying to pretend I'm not wildly affected, and motion toward the hallway. "Come on," I say, my voice steadier than I feel. "Let me show you around the rest of the house."

Hunter falls into step behind me, a quiet chuckle under his breath that I pretend I don't hear.

My townhouse isn't big, but it's mine. And for the next two months, it's ours, apparently.

"This is the living room," I say unnecessarily since we're standing in it. "Kitchen's through there. You can help yourself to anything."

He grunts in acknowledgment, but I can feel his eyes following every detail—the shelves of books and tennis memorabilia of a life I don't have anymore, the barely-there scent of vanilla honeysuckle candles I forgot to blow out before he got here.

I lead him down the short hallway, his duffel bag still in his hands and a backpack over his shoulder.

"That's the hallway bathroom and the door across from it leads to the garage." A garage too small to actually park a real life-size vehicle in it. Instead, a treadmill I bought last January sits unused there. "The spare bedroom's my podcast studio."

He peeks inside, raising a brow at the foam-padded walls, the mic setup, and my desk cluttered with notes and cables. "Professional setup. Looks like your contractor did a good job."

"Thanks." I don't bother telling him how many late nights, maxed-out credit cards, and YouTube tutorials it took to turn that tiny room into something network-worthy. Or how much I'm counting on this room—and him—to help me land this syndication deal and recoup my expenses from this build.

We stop at the master bedroom, and I hesitate at the doorway. "And this is the main bedroom."

Hunter steps inside, giving it the same slow, assessing glance he gave the rest of the place. "And the guest bedroom? Where's that?"

"Guest bedroom?" I echo.

"For me to sleep," he says, like it's obvious.

Oh no.

I thought I'd been clear. Two bedrooms. One converted into a podcast studio. No spare bed.

"My guest room is my recording studio," I say carefully. "There isn't another room."

He frowns, brows pulling together. "There's not another bed in this house?"

"I have the couch..." I offer quickly, pointing back toward the living room.

Hunter's mouth presses into a thin line. "That's not going to work."

Panic flickers in my chest. "Why not?"

"I can't sleep on a couch and play at the level I need to. It'll wreck my back. Throws off recovery after a long game and hard practices. Bad sleep screws everything up."

He says it so simply, like this is a done deal. Like he's about to walk out that door and leave this fake dating circus behind.

And I can't blame him. I'd played at a professional level before my knee injury, though it feels like ages ago. Sleep and recovery are really important.

But I can't let him leave. I need those two months of living expenses covered to give my bank account a break until I land this syndication deal. I can't even think of my finances if the network doesn't pick me.

"We tried, maybe Coach Wrenley will let me crash in his basement," he says, and then laughs to himself as if there's no shot in hell that the grumpy goalie coach is going to let that happen.

Hunter turns to walk back out past me, but I take a step in front of him to stop him.

My brain is screaming that what I'm about to offer is a monumentally bad idea, and yet I can already hear Abby giggling with glee when she hears about this.

"We can make it work," I say before I can second-guess myself. "We'll share the bed. I wouldn't want you to have to worry about Bethany showing up at The Commons."

Right, sure, that's the reason.

Hunter glances at the bed again, then back at me—but something in his eyes has shifted. Lighter. Relieved, even. Like he didn't actually want to go back to his apartment and deal with the mess waiting for him there.

"Really?" His right eyebrow lifts. "You're sure about this? It's only a queen, and I'm not exactly a small guy. It's going to be tight."

I follow his gaze toward the bed and realize what he means. It's been a long time since I've shared a bed with anyone—years, actually. A string of bad dates, dead-end relationships, and one too many lonely nights made me realize I'm better off focusing on my career than wasting time on something that'll only fall apart.

And guys like Hunter Reed? They're exactly why I stopped trying. Too smooth. Too charming. Too temporary.

Which is why he's the perfect man to share a bed with.

Because this isn't real.

And in two months, I'll barely remember he was here, and he'll be back to chasing one-night stands.

"Yeah," I say, keeping my voice light. "It'll be fine."

What could possibly go wrong living with a man who just offered to let me "ride the elephant," after all?

I hope Abby and my brother aren't right about me being naïve.

I turn on my heel before he can see how hard I'm working to keep my expression neutral.

Behind me, I hear him drop his bags inside the door, footsteps falling in line as he follows me down the hall.

My phone buzzes in my pocket as we make it back toward the living room again. I glance at the screen—another text from Mom:

> **Mom: You know fake can get real, sweetheart. Careful with that hockey player.**

I quickly flip my phone over before Hunter can see it.

"Boyfriend?" he asks, one brow lifted.

"Nope. It's my mom." I clear my throat. "No boyfriend."

He huffs a quiet laugh. "I guess I should've asked that before I made the offer."

I ignore the way my stomach flips at the thought of him caring one way or another.

"I wouldn't have said yes if I had a boyfriend. I'm not like that—"

He cuts me off quickly. "No, of course you're not. I'm sorry." His jaw flexes. "When it comes to you, I tend to put my foot in my mouth."

I nod, letting his quick backtrack settle for a second. It's... surprisingly nice to hear him own it.

"Speaking of boyfriends, maybe we should set some ground rules," I say, leading him toward the kitchen island.

He leans a hip against the counter, folding his arms like he's settling in for a show. "Hit me."

"Rule number one—no sex."

His mouth curves like he's fighting a grin. "Wow, we're just diving right into the deep end, huh? No easing into the hard rules?" He tips his head. "Are you sure? I'd give you one hell of an elephant ride."

I level him with a flat look. "I'm serious. This is fake. We're selling the relationship to everyone else, but in here? Strictly roommates."

He lifts his hands in surrender. "Got it. Roommates. No funny business."

I nod.

"Rule two," he interjects before I can continue down my list. "You have to sit in my seats and attend all home games and Hawkeyes events for the next two months. Starting with the open stadium event this week. Everyone will expect you to be there now that you're my girlfriend."

"Every single Hawkeyes home event? That seems a little overkill, doesn't it?" I ask, my eyebrows stitched together. That's going to be quite a few.

"Bethany needs to see you as a doting supportive girlfriend. Let's put it this way, you only have to come if other Hawkeyes wives and girlfriends are going to be there. How about that?"

"Fine," I say, knowing this is going to throw off my calendar but this is part of the deal. "Then rule number three—no puck bunnies. I'm not running a brothel in my townhouse for your one-night stands."

"Got it. No problem. The only puck bunny I'm bringing home is you." He grins like he knows exactly what he's doing.

I stare him down. "Too soon."

"Okay, yeah. Too soon." His grin fades, just slightly. "And I am sorry about that night. The bar. What I said. If I hadn't been drunk, I would have done—" He stops himself.

"You would have done what?" I press, arching a brow.

He shakes his head. "Never mind—it doesn't matter now. It's in the past and this is a new slate."

He clears his throat and straightens. "Rule four, we're exclusive."

I blink. "Exclusive?"

"That's right. If we're going to sell this, we need to make it believable. No dating anyone else, no one-night stands, and no hookups." His eyes lock onto mine. "For the next two months, we're crazy about each other."

I fold my arms across my chest. "Correction—you're crazy about me."

That damn dimple appears when he grins. "That's fair."

"So...exclusively not getting any," I clarify. Which doesn't actually change anything for me. Not that I would ever tell him that the only thing making conjugal visits is my vibrator. "Even when you're on the road."

"Exactly. No one for the next two months. Same goes for you."

I nod, grab the spare key from the counter, and hand it over to him. "Welcome to the circus, Reed. I'll be your ringmaster for the duration of your stay."

After our conversation, I cleared some space in my walk-in closet for him, and then I excused myself, taking pajamas with me to the spare bathroom to change while he said he was going to unpack and then take a shower. A pair of loose-fitting shorts and an old Seattle football T-shirt. Nothing that screams "please let me ride your elephant."

Our earlier conversation about the ground rules still has my brain reeling.

I should feel relieved. We've got the terms clear. No sex. No puck bunnies. Strictly fake, strictly business. But instead, my brain won't stop spinning because apparently, I've invited six feet plus of NHL trouble to move into my townhouse and crawl into my bed every night—for the next two months, and he wants me playing the WAGs role like I'm actually a part of it all.

No big deal. I'm totally fine.

My phone dings on the nightstand, lighting up with another text.

> **Mom: Tell your "boyfriend" I expect him at Thanksgiving dinner.**

Shit. Thanksgiving is in three days, and with everything going on, I sort of forgot.

I groan, flipping the phone over to block the screen. The longer I stare at it, the more the weight of this entire fake arrangement sinks into my chest. This was supposed to be strategic—a way to get my interviews, my subscriber numbers, my future. Not... whatever the hell this is turning into.

And now, the most complicated man I've ever met is hanging his clothes in my closet.

I make it halfway through editing a new podcast teaser when my body gives up. One minute I'm scrolling through social media mentions, trying to keep my anxiety at bay about tonight, sleeping in the same bed as Hunter, and then the next I'm drifting off to sleep.

I don't know how long I've been out when I feel it—strong arms sliding under me, lifting me off the couch like I weigh nothing.

My eyes flutter open, groggy and disoriented. "What... What are you doing?"

"Carrying you to bed," Hunter murmurs, voice quiet but

steady. "You fell asleep."

I'm too tired to argue. My head lolls against his shoulder, and I catch a faint trace of his smell that I caught at the charity event.

When he nudges the bedroom door open with his foot, I realize he's made the bed. And not just made it—he's created a literal pillow wall down the middle, like some kind of amateur Great Wall of China. There's even an extra blanket folded neatly on his side.

"Seriously?" I mumble as he sets me down gently.

"Boundaries, Collins. You set the rules, I'm just following them."

He steps back, pulling the covers over me before grabbing his own pillow and settling down on his side—on top of the duvet, with a spare blanket thrown over him like he's camping out.

It should feel awkward. It should feel ridiculous.

But somehow, it doesn't.

Instead, there's this strange little bubble of safety settling in my chest. Like if someone broke in tonight, the hockey enforcer lying next to me would handle it without blinking.

And that's the problem.

Because the last thing I need is to get comfortable with Hunter Reed sleeping beside me.

But it almost can't be helped, because as I drift off again, the last thing I'm aware of is the sound of his breathing, steady and solid in the dark, and one soft, sneaky thought threading through my brain:

Hunter Reed might actually be a better man than I thought.

And that's dangerous.

CHAPTER SEVEN

Peyton

Waking up this morning to an empty bed almost had me wondering if Hunter moving in last night was all a dream.

Then I saw the pillow wall, a small block of his clothes hanging in my walk-in closet, and the image of his toothbrush in the hallway bathroom.

Yep, his signature is all over my place now.

I take a deep breath, sitting in my podcast studio down the hall from my bedroom, trying to calm the jittery nerves swirling in my stomach. Today is the day—the first interview with Hunter Reed—and somehow, it feels like the most important moment of my entire life.

I've interviewed arguably bigger names before—hall-of-famers, gold medalists, coaches with decades of legacy behind them—but none of them came with this much baggage. None of them came with the sharp edge of unresolved rumors or the kind of fandom that's ready to eat me alive if I mess this up.

Because Hunter Reed doesn't just come with a strong slapshot and a devastating dimple. He comes with a rabid fan base, a trail of half-true headlines, and a stubborn refusal to talk about any of it. He's never done a podcast interview before—never opened up on record. And now with our deal to help each other firmly in place, evident from the smell of his body wash from his morning shower still wafting through the hallway, I'd say it's my turn to cash in on our deal.

No pressure.

I glance down at the mic, already set up, double-checked for sound quality and levels. My notes are neatly typed and stacked beside me, along with a backup list of questions in case he clams up on the hard stuff. And he will. I can already feel it.

But I have a job to do.

And it's more than just scoring a good soundbite.

Because if this goes well? I'll be one step closer to locking in that syndication deal the network's been dangling in front of me like a carrot. And if it goes great? I could finally cement *The Bleacher Report* as a must-listen podcast in the sports world—no longer the underdog in a saturated market.

But if it flops? If I screw this up and Hunter Reed walks out of here with nothing but regret for the deal he made?

Then everything I've worked for over the past three years— every late night, every equipment upgrade I couldn't afford, every guest I begged to take a chance on me—goes down the drain.

And worse than all of that?

It'll feel like I failed him—my dad.

I roll my chair back from the desk and grab my favorite mug from the shelf—a white ceramic one with "Microphones & Mayhem" printed in bold across the front, a gift from Abby when I hit my first twenty-five thousand subscribers. I never do an interview without it.

Does that make me superstitious? Probably, but I don't care. Everyone has their thing and this one is mine. The hot tea and honey help to keep my throat from getting scratchy with all the takes I do in the editing process.

I hold it like it's a lucky charm as I glance at the framed

photo on my desk—me at twelve, drenched in sweat after a match, holding a plastic trophy in one hand and my dad's in the other. He's smiling like I'd just won Wimbledon. I hadn't even made it past regionals. But to him? Every win mattered.

He used to say, "Every match tells a story, kiddo. You just have to be brave enough to tell it."

When I blew out my knee at fourteen and my tennis dreams ended, I lost more than just a sport. I lost the one place where I felt like I knew who I was. And when I lost him, three years ago to a heart attack, I lost my compass completely.

But this podcast? It became my way back. My way to tell the stories he would've wanted to hear. To amplify the athletes who've fallen and clawed their way back. To find the people who've lived through the hard stuff and are still standing.

Just like me.

This isn't just about audience numbers or ad sponsors or nailing the perfect opener.

This is about making it count. For the girl I used to be. For the man who never stopped believing in her.

And most of all, for the story we're about to tell.

Because whether he likes it or not, Hunter Reed is part of it now.

My phone buzzes.

> **Rebecca:** Just checking in! Can't wait to hear what you and Hunter come up with. We'll be listening closely. The producer making the call on this just so happens to be a big fan of Hunter's.

A not-so-subtle reminder of the pressure riding on today's interview. Great.

I glance over at the extra mic I set up last night. Hunter still hasn't seen the inside of the studio. Not really. When he moved in, he peeked in the door, made a joke about how official it looked, and left it alone. Today, there's no avoiding it.

The door creaks open.

"Whoa," Hunter says, stepping inside. He's in a dark Henley and jeans, the kind of casual that shouldn't be allowed to look that good. His eyes sweep over the soundproofed walls, the acoustic tiles, and the shelf of guest mementos I've collected over the years—signed hockey pucks, tennis balls, a coffee sleeve from a certain world-ranked surfer who refused to drink from anything else.

He nods slowly. "This is...intense."

"It's just a studio, Reed. Not the Pentagon."

"Yeah, but it's your studio," he says, stepping closer to the mic. "This is where the magic happens, huh?"

"Only if you behave," I mutter, motioning to the seat across from mine.

He grins and drops into the chair. "I'll do my best."

The way he flops into the chair gives the dismissive, unserious vibe I'm used to seeing with him. Calm, assured...so cool he couldn't melt butter. But there's just a slight tension in his shoulders that I suspect he doesn't want me to see.

I check the levels on the soundboard and do a quick test record of our intro. He listens without talking, his gaze tracking me, curious.

"Are you always this focused when you're working?" he asks.

"Only when the interview might decide the future of my entire career."

That earns me a half-smile.

He reached for a bright pink Post-it notepad sitting between us in the shape of a French Bulldog.

"What are these for?" he asks, his thumb rubbing over the neon pink paper.

"Inspiration I guess? I don't have time for a dog, so this is the closest thing I have to a pet. But I'm hoping once I get this syndication deal and things calm down, I can get one."

He nods. "Too busy for real animals...I can relate," he says, and then sets the Post-it notepad back where it was.

I pull my "interview" mug up to my lips and take a sip of my hot tea.

"What are you drinking?" he asks.

"Peppermint tea with a little bit of honey. It helps soothe my throat during interviews...and it's calming."

He nods again and glances around the rest of my desk, trying to find new things he didn't notice when I showed him the studio yesterday.

"You ready to get started?" I ask, adjusting my headphones.

"Ready as I'll ever be."

I hit record.

"Welcome back to *Bleacher Report*, where the stories run deeper than the headlines. I'm Peyton Collins, and today, I'm sitting down with Seattle Hawkeyes defenseman Hunter Reed. Hunter, thanks for joining me."

"Thanks for having me."

The first few minutes are unexpectedly smooth. Hunter's good on mic—like, really good. He's got that natural charisma, the kind that doesn't need rehearsed lines or heavy edits. He's funny, confident, just the right amount of cocky. It throws me a little...in a good way. For the first time since hitting record, I start to relax.

And my mom was right. Hunter's voice is so sexy on radio that even I would tune in to hear him read the warning label on a can of paint thinner.

"So," I say, leaning into the mic with a smile in my voice, "you're known in the locker room as being the prankster of the group. Is that a Hawkeyes thing, or have you always been this much of a menace?" I ask, earning me a quiet chuckle from across the room. "And what's the best prank you've ever pulled off?"

He grins, eyes lighting with mischief. "Let's just say I was born with a calling," he says. "My poor kindergarten teacher still probably flinches every time she sees a whoopee cushion."

I laugh, already regretting asking. "Oh no, you were that kid."

"The worst," he confirms proudly. "But I only prank people I like. I don't do it with malice. The best one? Probably the time I hacked the mic during post-game interviews and turned the voice to helium before Coach Wrenley sat down. He had no clue until he started talking and everyone in the press room laughed so hard, tears were streaming down reporters' faces."

I choke back a laugh. "It was you who did that?"

I remember that post-game interview. It made its rounds for weeks. Coach Wrenley on the other hand, didn't seem very happy about it.

"Listen, it was either that or the life-size cutout of his wife in a ref's jersey. I'm saving that one for the playoffs."

"Oh my God," I mutter, shaking my head. "You *are* a menace."

He winks. "You invited the chaos, sweetheart. I'm just living up to expectations."

And somehow...I'm not even mad about it.

"Did he retaliate?" I ask.

"Yep, loosened one of the blades on my skates before he made me do laps the next day at practice. I didn't know until I was halfway around the rink and I lost my blade. He made me do ten laps with only one skate. He made sure we had leg day in the gym the next morning. I could barely walk for a week."

I cover my mouth to keep from busting up laughing. I can't even imagine picking on Coach Wrenley.

I glance down at my notes, and I wish that we could keep up this energy. It's going so well. But the network and the fans have questions, and it's my job to get answers...or at least try to.

"So," I say with a teasing tilt to my voice. "Hunter, the media has pegged you as a bit of a playboy. Love them and leave them type. How do you feel about that? And are they correct?"

His mouth curves into a smirk, like I just walked right into something he was hoping for. "I think if anyone could set that record straight, it would be you, wouldn't it, sweetheart? Do you think I'm the love 'em and leave 'em kind? And be careful what you say, honey. Remember, you have to sleep next to me tonight."

I blink.

Right. I forgot we're fake dating—though, his smug grin across from me says he hasn't. He just sidestepped my question like a pro, and there's nothing I can do about it without blowing our cover.

Fine. Two can play at this game.

"Of course," I say, recovering quickly. "I suppose our relationship dispels that rumor, doesn't it?"

It's not a question. We both know that as far as the public is concerned, our "relationship" makes him look like a reformed playboy. A guy who's finally settled down.

I glance at my notes and decide to push forward. Carefully.

"That's actually a great segue into the rumors about you that I'm sure your audience would love for you to address. You've been publicly connected to the New Jersey owner's wife, Bethany Richards. Some say that's the real reason you spent four years in the farm league. Would you like to set the record straight?"

There's a beat of silence—so still it makes my pulse roar in my ears.

Hunter's posture changes instantly. Gone is the relaxed slouch, the teasing smile. His eyes narrow. His jaw locks. The air shifts. He leans forward and—without breaking eye contact—reaches up and covers the mic with one broad hand.

We're not live but he's being cautious.

His voice is quiet but as sharp as a blade.

"I told you that she wasn't part of the interview deal."

"If you'll recall, excluding Bethany was only part of your initial offer. Your counteroffer included the townhouse, and your mother was the only exclusion you presented."

His eyes narrow and turn dark, maybe he didn't realize that he forgot to add Bethany back into his exclusion list but that's not my problem. His body stiffens from its previously relaxed position.

I've crossed a line he's not comfortable with, and I could have gone in softer than I did, but he's better at sidestepping questions than I thought he'd be which means I need to be more aggressive if I want to get what the network execs are looking for.

I glance at the mic under his hand, then back at him. "This isn't live," I say softly, trying to keep things from spiraling. "You'll have full control over the edit."

His nostrils flare. "And you think that matters to me? You knew that I didn't want to talk about my past—you knew I wanted to keep it off the record. Are ratings all you care about?"

"I care about finding the truth," I say, keeping my voice as steady as I can, "the truth that everyone else is already digging for. You've let them believe New Jersey's story for four years. This is a chance to set the record straight—your words. Your way."

He removes his hand from the mic.

"I'm not interested in entertaining trash rumors that no one should be reading into," he says tightly.

I can practically see the steam rising off his body now.

"So, New Jersey just made a bad call by signing you to a multi-million-dollar contract, only to bench you from the NHL? That's your story?" I press, my voice steady, but inside, I'm bracing for the fallout.

"I think that people should stick to the facts they know and not rumors circulated by every pop-up podcast with a microphone and sports media sleuths online that have no idea what the hell they're talking about. Maybe if they were real journalists, they'd have factual information to discuss instead of clickbait trash with no basis."

Was that a dig at me? Does he consider me a pop-up podcast or a sports media sleuth?

I remind myself to keep my cool. He's not the only guest I've ever hit a rough patch with, and I can usually iron out the issues, but the tension in the room thickens. I can feel the air crackle between us. I open my mouth to respond.

"So, you're saying that the rumors have no truth whatsoever?"

He leans forward, eyes intense, his voice dropping to a low, dangerous whisper. "I'm saying that you're walking on hot coals,

Collins, and you're a few more steps away from getting burned."

My heart kicks harder. His eyes burn like a warning that if I'm not careful, I'm going to lose this interview.

Whether I'm in the right that his relationship with Bethany and New Jersey should be on the table, there's obviously far more to this story that has him reacting like this.

I glance at the soundboard, wondering if I should pivot. Defuse. Walk it back. But I can't—not completely. This was always going to come up. We both knew that. It's part of the deal. His fame is tangled in this mess. And if I avoid the hard questions now, what does that say about me? What does that say to my listeners or to the network who are watching how I handle hard questions with guests?

Not to mention that part of our deal was that we agreed to discuss Bethany, whether he remembers it or not.

"I'm not trying to blindside you," I say quietly. "But this is the story people are already telling. I thought you'd want the chance to reclaim it."

His jaw ticks. A muscle pulses in his cheek. And then, for the briefest second, something flickers in his eyes—hurt, maybe. Or fury barely held in check.

"You think I don't know what people say?" he mutters, eyes flashing. "You think I haven't spent four damn years waking up before the sun, working through injuries, rebuilding every scrap of what I lost—just to have it all reduced to locker room gossip and rumors about a woman I never touched?"

I swallow hard. "Then say that. Say it into the mic. Tell people the truth."

He stands. Abrupt. The chair screeches against the floor.

"Hunter—wait," I say quickly, my voice catching. "Please don't walk out."

He doesn't move toward the door. Not yet.

"I don't owe anyone the truth," he snaps. "Especially not just so you can land your beloved syndication deal."

That hurts more than I expect it to. Maybe because he just

made an assumption that I have no heart or soul. That I'm willing to sell him out for a network spot. I just want to be taken seriously as a journalist who can give guests a safe place to tell their stories.

But he's not done.

"I didn't crawl my way back to the NHL just to be dragged back into the mud," he says, quieter now—but deadly serious. "I won't go willingly."

His gaze cuts into me, sharp and clear. "So next time you come looking for soundbites, maybe pick someone who wants to be part of your story."

Then he turns.

And this time, when he walks out, he doesn't look back.

The studio door slams behind him, the walls shaking from his force, and the silence that follows is louder than anything he said.

I sit there, blinking at the empty chair across from me. The mic still recording. The flashing red light like a heartbeat.

And then I hear it—the engine of his truck roaring to life outside, loud and angry. It fades into the distance like a match lit and blown out too fast.

I sit there, frozen, the silence in the room deafening.

Just me. The mic. The blinking red light that shows it's still recording, and the terrible ache of something I can't name.

A text from my mom lights up the phone screen.

> **Mom: How'd the interview go? Can't wait to hear it. I'm so proud of you, honey.**

I don't respond.

I just turn the phone face down on the desk and stare at the photo of my dad again. The edges are worn. His smile still steady. Still proud.

Even now.

BLEACHER REPORT

I wish I could believe he'd still be proud of me after this.
Because I don't know if I am.

CHAPTER EIGHT

Hunter

Leaving the house in a rush, I realize that the last place I want to head to is my apartment with Bethany roaming loose somewhere inside.

After driving around for forty-five minutes with nowhere to go, I get a text from my mom.

> **Mom: Sorry that I didn't return your text yesterday. The salon was slammed. Doctor's appointment went fine. Nothing to worry about. And don't think I'm just going to ignore the fact that you haven't told me that you have a beautiful new girlfriend. You better be bringing her home soon.**

Something keeps nagging at me that she's not being honest

about her health. That she's using my new relationship with Peyton to deflect the real conversation that she and I should be having, but what can I do? Call my own mother a liar? As if the issue with Peyton wasn't enough, now I have too much on my mind to just sit here in my truck. I need to work off this energy. Luckily, I tossed my gym bag with running gear in my truck before I stormed out the door.

A beat passes before I swipe the message away and pull up my texts, firing one off to Slade.

> **Me: You up for a run?**

> **Slade: We had morning skate and weights today. And my wife's still going to expect me to put out tonight. Have you forgotten that I'm not as young as you?**

> **Me: I need to run off some steam. Just left Peyton's place.**

> **Slade: Trouble with your fake girlfriend, shocking. Okay, I'm waiting at the stadium for Penelope to finish a meeting with Everett. I've got an hour to kill. Meet you at the park?**

> **Hunter: See you in twenty.**

I wonder for a second what the meeting with Penelope and Everett could be about. Are they discussing a trade for me to New Jersey? Has Bethany even made an offer for a trade yet? I have no damn idea.

Twenty minutes later, I'm pulling into the parking garage, kill the engine and quickly change into sweats, a hoodie, and running shoes before I head toward the park.

The evening air's already dropping degrees as the sun dips behind the jagged edge of the Seattle skyline. I pull the drawstrings of my hoodie tighter as I lace up my running shoes at the curb.

Slade's easy to spot—tall, lean, stretching near the trailhead like he owns the place. His breath mists in short puffs, sleeves pushed up to reveal tattooed forearms that still look solid for a guy who's always claiming he's past his prime. The man talks like he's retired but moves like he's got a few more seasons in him.

Gray clouds are rolling low above us, smudging out the last of the light.

Typical November in Seattle. Cold. Wet. Gritty. Perfect weather to run off regret.

It matches the knot in my gut.

Slade spots me approaching and nods. "Look who's still alive."

"Barely," I mutter.

"Looks like you escaped unscathed?" He pulls one knee to his chest, balance perfect, as I roll my shoulders.

I start jogging without answering and he follows, falling in line with me, the thud of our shoes against the frosty trail breaking the silence first. We settle into a steady pace. Trees huddle together on either side—a few orange leaves cling stubbornly to low-hanging limbs. The sound of traffic nearby, as Friday night kicks off in the city.

"Are you going to tell me what happened," Slade asks, "or do I have to guess?"

I let the silence stretch a beat longer than necessary. "She asked about Bethany in our first interview."

Slade's grunt is quiet but full of judgment. "The interview... right. I was wondering when that would come up. You can't be shocked she brought up Bethany."

"I told her I didn't want to talk about that."

"I thought you agreed to the terms at the charity auction. This didn't come up?" he asks.

I decide against admitting that it sort of did. But she knew I wasn't comfortable with it. At the very least, I figured she'd give me a heads-up about the kind of question she was going to ask before she jumped into it.

"She knew it was off-limits."

He shoots me a look. "Hunter, she's a journalist. It's her job to poke at things, and you told me you agreed to three interviews. You didn't think she'd ask about Bethany? Especially when the woman rented an apartment in your building and has been stalking the Hawkeyes' stadium, hoping to run into you every morning at early skate?"

"Bethany being in Seattle is temporary. She'll find someone else to manipulate and control. She bores easily...her best trait in my current situation. What I care about right now is being ambushed by Peyton."

"You weren't ambushed," Slade counters. "You were triggered. There's a difference."

My jaw clenches. "Same result."

"Nope. One makes her the villain. The other means you need to figure out your shit and apologize. And hell," he huffs, his voice strained from running and talking, "even if it were her fault, you'd still have to apologize. Might as well just get it over with."

We jog a few more strides before I respond. "She caught me off guard."

"She gave you a chance to respond. You got defensive. Then you stormed out like a pissed-off frat boy who just got benched."

"I was pissed," I snap. "You didn't hear her tone. It was like she was baiting me."

"I don't have to hear it to know how you would have reacted to it. I've seen you in post-games, remember? Bethany is under your skin, and you and Peyton barely know each other. She has no idea what Bethany did—what she cost you," he says calmly. "I've seen you pissed before. I bet you scared the hell out of her storming out like that."

That stops my thoughts. Just for a second.

Did I scare her?

That wasn't my intention.

I'd never hurt her, no matter what she said to me. But I keep running. "She'll be fine."

Slade's voice softens. "She might be. But will you?"

I don't answer.

"She's not Bethany," he continues. "She's not trying to screw you. She's trying to do her job while holding together a deal that means something to both of you. You blew that interview wide open. And based on the deal you made with her? She didn't deserve that."

"You don't know what it's like," I say, breathing hard. "Having people dig through your past like it's public property."

"Of course I do," he says, flashing me a glare. "Did you forget that I was slated for a first-round pick out of college, and Penelope's dad banished me to the farm team for five years to punish me for ruining Penelope's figure skating career? The media was all over me, asking why the hell I didn't enter the draft. The speculations were wild for years. Some of the headlines they came up with were nuts."

I glance at him.

"Shit...I guess I forgot about that."

We slow down at a crosswalk as Slade reaches for the *walk* button and presses it, then faces me, his hand on his hips, both of us catching our breath. "You're afraid to trust her. I get it. You've been burned before. But if you keep treating her like she's the enemy, this whole thing's going to go up in flames."

"She told me she wouldn't blindside me."

"Reed," he stops running, blocking my path. "You asked her to outbid your ex-girlfriend, and then let you move in with her. You owe it to her to help her get this syndication deal. She can't do that by painting you as some sanitized version of yourself. People want the truth. Even the ugly parts. Especially the ugly parts. If you're smart, and you work together, maybe you can both get something you want out of this."

"Maybe," I say, my voice low.

"It's worth a shot. Otherwise, you're the one not holding up your end of the deal, and that's not like you. I've never seen you back out of an agreement," the *walk* sign illuminates, and we start running again. "By the way, Luka says you cheated on your bet at the charity auction for the highest bid. He wants a rematch next year."

I laugh, not sure if I'm willing to put myself in that spot again if Bethany is still on the loose.

"You're going to fix it with her, right?" he asks after a beat.

"I don't know how."

"Start with showing up. A little effort. You don't have to spill your guts. Just...meet her halfway."

We slow as we near the parking lot. "Do something that says I'm sorry in your language. I don't know—pick up dinner. Show her that you care, even if you're too dumb to say it."

I snort. "You calling me dumb?"

"Emotionally? Frequently."

I laugh despite myself.

We reach our cars, breath still fogging in the cold air.

"Just fix it," he says, tugging off his beanie. "Before you burn the bridge with the only girl you've gone steady with in four years. Even if this is all for show." He pauses, giving me a look. "And maybe ask yourself if this is really about Peyton—or if Bethany, your mom, and everything else going on are messing with your head."

He's probably right. Not knowing what's happening with my mom, being this far away from her while she's going through it... it's weighing on me more than I want to admit.

"You might have a point," I mutter.

"I definitely do."

I huff out a laugh.

"Tell your wife I'm sorry if you can't perform tonight, old

man," I jab.

He smirks. "Don't worry about me. I'm getting some. And my wife's a fan of reverse cowgirl—I'll be relaxing with a nice view."

He claps me on the back, and I shake my head, grinning despite myself.

He's not wrong. Peyton and I agreed to two months of exclusive celibacy, which is already the longest dry spell I've had in years.

And he's right about her, too. I don't want to admit it—but I need to make this right.

I sit for a second in the driver's seat, fingers gripping the steering wheel. I let the engine idle as my heart rate starts to level out. Then I grab my phone and shoot her a message.

> **Me: What's your favorite kind of dessert?**

The screen stays quiet long enough that I think maybe she's ignoring me.

Then:

> **Peyton: That's...random. Why?**

> **Me: Because I was an asshole. And I'm trying to fix that. Starting with sweets.**

Pause.

> **Peyton: Anything chocolate.**

> **Me: Helpful. Thanks.**

I'm not sure if she can feel the sarcasm. I was hoping for more specifics. Candy bar, ice cream, brownies...something like that.

Then another message:

> **Peyton:** If you're really going to the store... I hate to ask but I'm totally out of tampons.

I blink. Then chuckle to myself.

It's not the first time I've bought tampons, and it won't be the last...I assume. Growing up with a single mom, and past girlfriends...I've done it before. What I don't want to do though, is be responsible for knowing what I'm getting.

Unlike the chocolate comment, I need exact information: Brand, size, color of box would be great too.

> **Me:** I'll need specifics for this. I'm not guessing.

She sends a photo. Blue box. Neat branding. Multi-size flow. Got it.

> **Peyton:** These. I swear I wouldn't ask if I wasn't dying.

I remember Slade's advice. Get her food. And now that I know she's on her period and probably not feeling well, I have an idea on how to smooth things over with her.

> **Me:** Have you eaten?

> **Peyton:** No. Thinking about ordering Thai.

Me: I got it.

I toss my phone on the seat, throw the truck in gear, and drive.

The grocery store is weirdly calm for a Friday afternoon. No frantic soccer moms, no screaming toddlers, no underage kids trying to use fake ID's at the cash register—just low hums of music and the occasional beep from checkout lanes. I push my cart down the candy aisle, scanning shelves for anything with cocoa, sugar, and a promise to buy me five minutes of forgiveness.

I toss in a double-fudge cake slice from the bakery section. Two pints of chocolate swirl ice cream—one for her, one for me. Chocolate-dipped pretzels. Milk chocolate M&M's—two kinds, peanut and plain, just in case. And chocolate milk...to cover my bases.

Next stop: the dreaded feminine hygiene aisle.

I pull up the picture Peyton sent and stand like a statue in front of the wall of pastel-colored boxes, blinking like I've never seen English before. I hold the phone in one hand and scan shelf by shelf, but it's like a damn eye exam—every box is a variation of the same color scheme.

A woman in her fifties pushes her cart past, glances over, and does a full double-take. "Need help?"

I offer a sheepish grin, holding up my phone. "Looking for this exact one. She said it was urgent."

She steps beside me, studies the screen, and then scans the shelf. In under ten seconds, she plucks the right box and drops it in my cart.

"There you go, darlin'."

"You've saved me from a total disaster."

She smiles. "Good boyfriend."

I open my mouth to tell her I don't have a girlfriend...then stop short. Technically, I do.

A fake one.

However, considering we've had our first fight, I'm buying her tampons, we're not having sex, and we're living together...it's starting to feel suspiciously similar to most real relationships I've heard guys complain about.

"Thanks," I say instead.

"It took my husband twenty years to buy the right ones. You're ahead of the curve." She gives me a wink and continues down the aisle. "She's a lucky girl."

"I'm tempted to record you saying that to replay for her when I get home," I tease.

She smiles warmly. "I think she already knows."

Fat chance. But maybe a little bribing with sugar will help my cause.

I glance down at the box in the cart, then shake my head, smirking. If someone had told me last year that I'd be in a grocery store picking up tampons and snacks for a girl I wasn't really dating, I would've laughed them out of the building.

And yet here I am.

I toss a few more comfort items into the cart—stuff I remember my mom asking for when she wasn't feeling great during her cycle. Heating pads. Chamomile honey tea. Midol. Whatever might make Peyton's day even a little easier.

As I move toward the checkout, something catches my eye—a French Bulldog Chia Pet planter, in its box, sitting near the divider bar. I think of her French bulldog sticky notepad that she keeps between the mics. Without overthinking it, I grab one and toss it on the conveyor belt.

If I'm going all in on this apology, I might as well stack the deck in my favor.

She mentioned during the interview that she wants a dog but doesn't have the time right now. That hit. It reminded me of all the years I begged for a black lab as a kid—something loyal, something constant. But with my insane practice schedule and my mom teaching full time, taking odd jobs to help pay for my practice gear and summer camps, the answer was always no. That conversation with Peyton felt like the first time we had something in common that had nothing to do with our careers or this fake dating thing.

I load everything into the back of the truck and climb into the driver's seat, firing up the GPS. A quick search pulls up a Thai place nearby with more than a thousand five-star reviews. That's good enough for me. I call and place an order for a handful of dishes that sound halfway decent—pad see ew, yellow curry, chicken satay. She's bound to like at least one of them.

The smell hits me before I'm even out of the truck—ginger, basil, and something spicy and rich.

I step inside the restaurant, grab the paper bag, and tip the girl behind the counter more than I need to. I'm not taking any chances tonight.

Good karma, all the way around.

Back in the driver's seat, I rest the food on the passenger side and glance at the rearview mirror. My hair's a mess. Hoodie wrinkled. And my nerves are doing a weird kind of twisty thing I haven't felt since my first NHL game.

This isn't a date.

It's damage control.

So why the hell do I care this much if she smiles when I walk in?

I pull up in front of her townhouse just as the streetlights flicker on. It's past dusk but not completely dark yet. My headlights sweep across the front of her garage as I roll into the driveway and cut the engine.

For a second, I just sit there.

Hands still on the wheel.

The smell of Thai food wafting through the cabin.

I think about the look on her face when I walked out of her studio. About the way her voice cracked just before I slammed the door. About the silence since.

This has to go right.

Because like Slade said—I never back out of a deal. She's been holding up her end and I need to do my part too.

I grab the food and the bags of snacks, tuck the box of tampons under one arm, and head to the door.

Time to fix what I broke.

CHAPTER NINE

Peyton

I'm sitting cross-legged on the couch with a half-eaten bag of popcorn beside me and my laptop open to a timeline I've been staring at for over an hour. I tried editing the interview with Hunter, hoping to salvage something usable. But every time I hear him snap back at me or watch the moment his body language shifts from casual to cold, my stomach tightens. The whole thing feels tainted.

After pausing for what must be the twentieth time, I gave up and clicked out of the project, opting for a brain break. That break turned into a social media rabbit hole, and now I'm watching a tiny, crocheted jellyfish bounce across a desk, wearing a mini bowtie. I don't know how I got here.

I texted Hunter back forty-five minutes ago but my stomach grumbles in betrayal just as I hear the front door open.

Hunter walks in carrying grocery bags in one hand, and a large takeout bag in the other. His sleeves are pushed up, revealing muscled forearms with the faint edge of a tattoo peeking out, and his hair is wet from the misty Seattle weather.

The savory scent of Thai food wafts up as he cracks open the takeout bag. I moan loudly and without shame at the smell. "Oh my God. That smells like heaven."

He gestures toward the grocery bag. "Did the best I could."

I walk around to help unpack. First, I pull out a bag of peanut M&M's. Then I see two pints of ice cream and a slice of cake. A pack of Midol and the exact box of tampons I asked for.

"You really did it," I say, setting the box between us on the granite island. "You actually bought tampons."

He shrugs as he continues to pull out the take-out containers, busting at the seams. "You said you were out. It's not a big deal."

Not a big deal? It's a big deal to me. After the last few years of bad first dates and even worse short-term relationships, a man picking up tampons for me without complaining is a big deal.

I turn back to the rest of the items in the bags. Next, I pull out a heating blanket still in its box.

"A heating blanket?" I ask, holding it up.

He shrugs again, less nonchalant this time. "Wasn't sure if you had one. My mom used them a lot when I was growing up for this kind of thing. I can take it back if you already have one."

I don't actually, but only because mine stopped working a few months ago and I forgot to buy a new one. The fact that he thought about it and went across the store to the home goods section to find it means a lot. It means he was thinking of me.

The snacks keep coming without end.

"You did all of this for me?"

"I didn't handle the interview well today. This is my attempt at bribing you with food to forgive me."

"I'll admit, it's working…"

Then I pull out the most unexpected item of the bunch—a box with a grinning French Bulldog on it.

"What's this?" I ask.

"That's Sproutacus. Our new plant pet."

I blink. "I'm sorry what? You bought a Chia Pet?"

"I got us a Chia Pet," he corrects. "Congratulations. We're

plant parents now. I was going to wait so we could name him together, but I had to kill some time waiting on the food and did some Googling. Sproutacus felt right. Strong. Resilient. He'll need to be, in this family of overachievers."

I stare at him, caught somewhere between disbelief and reluctant amusement.

"Oh my God...who are you?" I chuckle.

"I know what you're thinking," he continues. "Once this is over, how will we amicably co-plant-parent and split weekends and holidays? But I'm not worried. We're two mature adults. We'll work it out for the good of Sproutacus."

I snort. "Co-plant-parent? With you?"

"Why not?" he says, completely straight-faced. "I think we're doing great already. Look at us—functioning, healthy, thriving. Working through our first fight. Our relationship is ready for this level of responsibility now."

I shake my head, still stunned. Just hours ago, this man slammed the front door like he was never coming back. Now he's buying me tampons and adopting botanical dependents.

"Can we trade off claiming him on our tax returns?"

"That's the spirit." He grins.

Then, without breaking his weirdly charming stride, he pushes the box of tampons closer to me.

"I'll set up dinner. You handle...that. I'll meet you in the living room when you're ready."

And for the first time in the last couple of hours, I actually believe we might survive this.

By the time I come back out, the living room has transformed. There's a comforter spread across the couch, two big pillows, and a heating pad plugged in at the end. The coffee table is covered in takeout containers, chocolate goodies, and two forks resting on a paper plate.

Hunter is fluffing the blanket and queuing up a new chick flick on the TV. I recognize it instantly—it's one I've been meaning to watch for months.

"This is some kind of spread," I say, crossing my arms and watching him.

He glances over. "When I was a kid and I got sick, my mom would do this. Blanket on the couch, ice cream, dinner on the coffee table, cheesy movies. When she went through treatment years ago, we did this a lot. I thought since I screwed up today and you probably aren't feeling the best, it's a good night for it."

I sit down, the heating pad low and warm against my back and my muscles begin to ease right away. "Thank you."

He hands me a takeout box and a fork, then pulls the blanket over both our laps. "You're welcome."

We eat in silence for a while. Then he glances over. "I meant it. I was wrong. I shut down, and that wasn't fair."

"I pushed too hard," I admit. "I know you don't want to talk about your past. But that's part of what the podcast is about. It's my job. We agreed to that."

He nods. "Then maybe we should talk through boundaries next time. So we're not stepping on landmines."

"Deal."

After we finish eating, Hunter gets up and returns the ice cream to the freezer. When he comes back, he dims the lights and drops onto the couch again, tossing his side of the blanket back over his legs.

Somehow, I end up nestled into his side, his arm stretched out over the back of the couch. It's comfortable. Too comfortable. And how we got here from where we started is a wonder.

"Is this your move?" I tease, glancing up at him.

He snorts. "There's no move happening here. I just want you to feel better."

"I do," I murmur. "Thank you."

The movie plays in the background, but we're barely watching. We're talking and the conversation comes so easily. He's a great listener, but he's a great storyteller too. I bet he'd make a great podcaster someday.

"So, *Bleacher Report*—where did that name come from?" he asks, leaning into the corner of the couch, me up against him.

"It was my dad's idea," I say, smiling to myself and picking a tiny piece of lint from my sweats. "That's what he called himself—'The Bleacher Report.' His commentary was the best. Sometimes he'd even create commentary for when mom and I were making cookies in the kitchen, or while I was working on homework. He made trivial things seem so funny in his mock reporter voice."

Hunter looks over, more serious now. "He sounds amazing."

"He was. He passed away three years ago from a heart attack. It was completely unexpected."

Hunter goes quiet for a second and then runs a hand over his face. "Jesus, that's really rough. I'm sorry that you went through that."

I nod. "Thank you," I tell him, looking up into his green eyes. "When I got injured, I thought I'd lost everything. He never let me believe that. He kept pushing me to find a new dream. The podcast became that dream."

He nods. "I get that. When my mom was sick, I thought I had to carry everything alone. Sometimes you just need someone to sit beside you, hand you a blanket, and queue up a bad movie."

"You're good at that," I say softly.

"Years of practice I guess."

"Was it always just you and your mom?"

I ask the question carefully. I don't want him to think that he has to answer. This is the closest I've gotten to him opening up to me. I'd never use this for the podcast, but knowing more about him will help me navigate things more easily for our next interview.

"I never met him," he says, seeming almost distant from it. Void of any emotion. "My mom said that he was the bass player in some band she went to see. I'm the product of a one-night stand in the back of a tour bus."

"Stop it," I say.

He grins down at me. "I swear to God, that's what she told me."

I turn further to face him more clearly. I have so many questions, I don't know where to start.

"Did she tell you who it was? What band did he play in? Oh my God... Is he still touring?"

"I don't know any of that. She told me that she's taking that to her grave. She didn't want me to grow up with that lifestyle. My mom had just graduated from beauty school and inherited a salon from her aunt. She came into a lot of responsibility all at once, and she felt like it was her last summer to let loose. She didn't expect to be pregnant with me."

I reach out, gripping both of his shoulders. "Hunter...oh my God. You could be the son of a rock legend. Are you kidding me? This is amazing."

"She told me that they never made it big. One hit wonders on the radio, but that was about it. We haven't talked about it since I was in middle school."

"Wow. And here I thought you were going to tell me that your dad is an accountant or manages hedge funds. You just rocked my world."

"If you think that was rocking your world, then you haven't seen anything yet."

The smirk across his lips tells me that he's joking, but I'd be lying if I weren't curious how good Hunter is in bed with his reputation and all.

Luckily, we have rules in place, and I don't plan on breaking any of them for the next two months.

Later, I change into pajamas and head into the bedroom.

The pillow wall is fluffed and ready.

Hunter's already in bed, stretched out on top of the duvet, earbuds in, watching something on his phone. He pulls one out when I walk in, turning toward me.

"Just a reminder—we've got the open skate event tomorrow."

"Oh, right...okay."

I climb under the covers and face the wall.

"Sweet dreams, Collins," he murmurs.

"Sweet dreams, Reed."

൭

The first thing I register when I wake up is drool. A line of it, wet and warm, trailing down my chin.

The second thing I register is that I'm halfway sprawled across the pillow wall that Hunter made two nights ago because he doesn't believe in shared bed boundaries without a literal barrier.

I groan, wiping at my face as the fog of sleep slowly clears.

The room is empty.

Except for me and the pillows that, judging by my current position, I bulldozed in my sleep.

"Fantastic," I mutter, flopping onto my back and staring at the ceiling.

Did I climb over the pillow wall before or after he left for practice? Did he see me drooling like a feral animal? Was I starfishing across the entire bed like a menace?

Last night, sitting on the couch together, after everything he did to make it up to me from the interview, it felt like we got a little closer. But straddling the pillow wall was probably closer than he anticipated.

I grab my phone off the nightstand and hesitate for exactly three seconds before typing.

> **Me: Sorry if I woke you up. Pretty sure I staged a full-blown invasion over the pillow wall.**

It only takes thirty seconds before my phone buzzes in response.

> **Hunter: You didn't wake me up. You were too busy drooling on enemy territory.**

Another ping follows immediately—a photo attachment.
I swipe it open and groan out loud.
It's a photo of me completely unconscious with half my face mashed into the pillow barrier, mouth slack, and yes, an unmistakable drool stain front and center.

> **Hunter: Made it my home screen.**

I slap my hand to my forehead. "Oh my God."
Another ping.

> **Hunter: You're so angelic when you're fast asleep.**

He's flicking me crap. There is nothing about that picture that's angel-like in any capacity, and we both know it.
I type back quickly.

> **Me: Delete or die.**

> **Hunter: Never. You'll have to catch me first.**

> **Me: That's not fair. I don't have any embarrassing photos of you.**

The typing dots appear immediately. Then another photo pops up.

Only...this one is very different.

Hunter, sweaty and shirtless, standing in front of a full-length mirror grinning like the devil himself from inside the Hawkeyes locker room. His skates are still on, his hockey pants hanging low on his hips, and his abs are on full display, like he's the cover model for a fitness magazine. There's a tattoo above his left peck. It's the first time I've seen it.

I nearly throw my phone across the room, but I don't. Because, God...I can't stop staring.

> **Hunter: Here. Something for your screensaver. Now we're even.**

Not even close. That's straight spank bank material, and he knows it. That's why he's grinning in the photo. He knows exactly what a half-naked photo of him does to the female libido.

> **Me: Oh my God, Hunter. That's not what I wanted.**

> **Hunter: I'm headed for the showers. Would you rather I take it from there?**

He's screwing with me.

He has to be. But this?

This is just plain cruel. Teasing a sex-deprived woman with locker room thirst traps?

That should be classified as psychological warfare. And now—mark my words—I'll be dreaming about him in the shower one of these nights.

Fantastic. That'll do wonders for keeping this arrangement complication-free.

I toss my phone onto the bed, groaning. This man is dangerous.

And I've officially lost control of this entire situation.

I push out of bed and head for the kitchen to make a cup of tea to start my day. I need to get back to work. At least there is a small piece of that interview that can be salvaged. Then I need to get to work on new questions to ask him that won't lead to him storming out of the house, but that also gives me something to bring in new listeners.

On autopilot, I swipe open Instagram as I walk down the hall, scrolling straight to my podcast account, trying to move mentally past the picture of Hunter. As I enter the kitchen, I notice that the notifications are still going nuts. The kiss photo. The bid. Hunter's smirk. My shocked face. Bethany's icy glare in the background.

Everyone's still eating it up. I figured after a few days it all would have died down by now. I guess I was wrong.

Subscriber Count: 78,450

That's up by almost nine thousand since yesterday.

My stomach flips again, but this time for a different reason.

It's working.

Whether it was the kiss, the drama, or the fact that Hunter Reed's name is now attached to my podcast—it's working. And if I can lock in a better interview and keep the momentum going, I might actually pull this off.

Fake boyfriend.

Real headlines.

Career on the line.

And then my mind decides to wander without my consent. Movie night, heating pad, being spoiled by a man who's done more for me in a few hours than all my worthless relationships combined.

I shake the thought away. I'm not going there. Especially not with the infamous serial dater of the Hawkeyes hockey team. The only reason he did what he did last night was to get back in my good graces—that's all.

I glance over at the kitchen windowsill, surprised to see Sproutacus already out of his box, watered, and ready for the morning—with a French bulldog sticky note that Hunter must have grabbed out of my office after he set Sproutacus up.

Morning plant mom. Have a great day.

-Your son

I laugh out loud... Of course, he would go to that level.

But now it has me wondering. Did Hunter go to all this trouble to cheer me up...or is this some long-game prank that I'm not seeing?

Prank or no prank, this fake thing with Hunter has to work.

Because if it doesn't...I'm out of time to line someone else up at this point.

I back out of my social media screen, and then I see an email notification from Rebecca.

My stomach dips as I swipe it open.

Subject: Podcast Development Check-In — Deadline Approaching

Peyton,

Just checking in to see how everything is coming along. We only have two months left on our deadline, and the other podcast hosts have submitted their teaser clips.

I know you mentioned that you had the Hunter Reed interview yesterday. We would love to get something on that interview asap.

Daily Sports just surpassed you on subscribers, and Mobile Mayhem just got the hot new Seattle Sentinels footballer to spill about his elopement with that pop princess everyone is talking about.

The media is still gossiping about why Bethany Richards is still hanging around. Your interview with Hunter on his past with her and what happened in New Jersey four years ago could be the thing that pushes you over the top.

I'm not supposed to have favorites...but let's just say, I'm rooting for you.

Rebecca Almasy

Podcast Division Producer

I read the email twice, then once more, hoping it might magically say something different the third time.

It doesn't.

I'm falling behind.

Rebecca rooting for me is great and all, but at the end of the day, she's not making the call on her own. It's the board, which includes her and three other executives. I have to win all of them over, and I have to start by nailing this interview.

I knew the whole point of this insane fake dating arrangement was to secure Hunter's interview and catapult me to the top of the list. But seeing it in writing, knowing the other two podcasts are already ahead of me...it hits differently now.

My mind races with every worst-case scenario possible. If I don't land this deal, if I don't get that interview and hit the one hundred thousand subscriber mark, the network will choose someone else. The rent on this townhouse, the studio equipment, the hours I've dumped into *Bleacher Report*—it'll all be for nothing.

The anxiety is building so fast I can barely breathe.

I pull up another social media app, more out of habit than curiosity. But as soon as I open it, my feed is a minefield.

There we are—Hunter and me, frozen mid-kiss at the charity auction, splashed across every headline.

NHL's Hunter Reed Off the Market?

Who Is Peyton Collins and How Did She Snag Hockey's Hottest Bachelor?

Peyton Collins Scores Big—Is This Relationship the Real Deal?

I scroll, the captions all blurring together.
Some comments are sweet.
Some are skeptical.
And some...cutting.
He's a player. He'll chew her up and spit her out.
Didn't he get spotted last month with that Brazilian model?
Pretty sure Bethany Richards isn't done with him yet—girl better watch her back.
This is fake AF.
She's just another puck bunny with a podcast mic.

My stomach twists, because I can't stop myself from reading them even though I know better.

I swipe the screen off, pushing the phone away like it's radioactive.

This is exactly why I made the rules. Why I told him no sex, no puck bunnies, no blurring the lines.

Because I've seen what happens when you believe in something that isn't real.

The memory hits me before I can shove it down.

My dad, sitting in the bleachers at every single tennis meet, even after my injury, even when I quit.

Telling me I was still the best, even when I wasn't.

He would've told me to trust myself.
To stop reading the comments.
To play the game my way.

I close my eyes and breathe him in, like he's still sitting across from me, coaching me from the sidelines.

But I can't call him now.

I can't call anyone.

Because right now, the person I'm pretending to fall for...is the only one who could actually break me.

CHAPTER TEN

Hunter

Slade Matthews's basement is already loud when I walk in—game controllers clicking, trash talk flying, and Wolf yelling at Luka to stop screen-peeking.

I check my phone one last time before tucking it into my pocket. Peyton and I have been texting on and off all day, mostly her still trying to downplay the fact that she woke up halfway on my side of the bed with drool on her chin, and me doing everything I could to tease her about it. Not to mention that I caught her off guard with that photo of me without my practice jersey on.

The alternative is thinking too hard about how soft she felt nestled against me last night watching the movie. How we ended up talking most of the night instead of watching any of it.

Then waking up to find her straddled over the pillow wall, dead asleep, but peaceful.

I've been expecting a snarky text in response to the last thing I said to her, but she must be deep in editing mode because it's been thirty minutes since my last text asking if Sproutacus is taking well to the new place.

BLEACHER REPORT

My phone dings in my hand, and I'm a little too quick to check.

A flash of disappointment settles when it's not her.

It's my agent who I met with earlier today.

> Dale: I still don't get it. New Jersey had you for the last four years and didn't play you in the NHL. I can't believe they're making a play for you now. Don't worry, I'll keep you apprised of any new developments with Bethany. But maybe you want to consider this. You'd be closer to your mom. Just a thought.

He's right. Being close to my mom is probably the only attractive piece to the possibility of a trade. Still, I'm not even sure if my mom needs me there. She's playing this whole thing off, assuring me that it's all going to be fine. And what if it is all going to be fine? What if I'm making something out of nothing?

"Finally," Slade says, pulling me out of my thoughts, and then handing me a beer. "Thought you were going to bail."

"Not a chance," I say, cracking it open and taking a pull off the hoppy beer. He had no idea how badly I needed it after my agent asked me what the hell was going on and why Bethany Richards called him to discuss a trade deal, giving up two of her best players for me. "Had to meet with my agent, and physical therapy took longer than I thought."

He shoots me a concerned glance as if he wants to pry into the conversation with my agent, but he doesn't. Now isn't the time, and there isn't much to tell. My agent said that when he called Everett, he said that this was the first he'd heard of it, though I suspect Everett is holding his cards close to the vest. He's a billionaire for a reason.

He just nods and then the door rings. "Must be the pizza guy. I'll be right back."

The rest of the guys are sprawled around the room. Aleksi's lounging on the bean bag, Scottie and Olsen are double-teaming Luka in *NHL 24*, and Trey—Trey's texting like his thumbs are trying to break the screen.

"You okay over there, Hart?" I ask him.

He looks up from his screen as if just now realizing I've arrived.

"I would be if Adeline's nanny would just give me a straight answer about whether she's going backpacking through Europe with her boyfriend next month," he says, exhaling sharply as he tucks his phone into his pocket and pushes up from the recliner.

I follow him to the wet bar, where there's a generous spread laid out—sliders, chips, wings, and a dangerously large platter of cookies someone probably made from scratch. And apparently, pizza just got here too.

But it will all get polished off before we leave. Morning skate was grueling earlier today, and these guys can put away some food.

He pops the top off a beer and takes a long pull before I ask, "Still having trouble with the nanny?"

He nods, jaw tight. "Yeah. She knows my hockey schedule, knows I've got no one else for Adeline until the season's over. I knew she was a little young and maybe not the most mature hire, but Adeline bonded with her so fast...I let it slide."

"And now she's trying to take a vacation mid-season without anyone to stay with Adeline for away games," I say, knowing exactly how this screws Trey.

Ever since he left the Army last year to take care of Adeline after both of her parents passed away in a car accident, he's been doing the best that he can for her. Trying to give her as normal of a life as he can as her uncle and guardian. I know Trey enough to know that failure isn't an option, and that anyone messing with the peace he's been trying to establish for Adeline is going to get the brunt of a not-so-nice, ex-special-forces badass.

There are only two things Trey Hartley gives a shit about in this world: winning a Stanley Cup and Adeline.

And Adeline? She's firmly planted in the number one spot.

"You've got time though, right?" I say. "Just call up one of the other nanny services. Tell Maddy to go backpacking across Europe and find herself, but she's going to need a new job when she gets back. Easy fix."

He grabs a chip from the bowl and crunches down like it personally offended him. He chews for a second and then responds. "I wish it were that simple. I've already called every agency from here to Tacoma. No one has a nanny willing to do overnight shifts, multiple days a week."

"Shit," I mutter, then a thought hits. "Wait—why don't you talk to Isla? Her sister owns a nanny company, right? She was at Oakley's that night that I, uh…accidentally called Peyton a puck bunny."

A rare grin tugs at his mouth. "Vivi Newport."

I raise a brow. "Yeah. What—do you know her?"

"No. But Vivi's hard to miss."

Before I can ask what the hell that's supposed to mean, Slade walks back in from the kitchen, carrying a stack of pizza boxes that smell like melted cheese, fresh dough, and heaven.

It takes all of three seconds for every guy in the room to hit pause on the game and make a beeline for the food.

Because if there's one thing this team takes more seriously than hockey—it's pizza.

"How's fake domestic bliss going, Reed?" Wolf asks as he walks up to the basement bar, grinning as he grabs a soda from the cooler. "You start picking out his and hers throw pillows yet?"

Luka chimes as he makes his way from the living room. "He's probably got matching monogrammed robes."

Olsen reaches past me for a plate. "Whatever the hell you do, just don't ask me to be a groomsman at your fake wedding if this gets any crazier. I get itchy when I lie. But I will come to the bachelor party. I wouldn't miss that."

"Jesus Christ, Bozey," Trey says. "The man isn't going to marry the girl. Not even dodging his crazy ex is worth that."

I tilt my head and raise my eyebrows. There's just about nothing I wouldn't do to keep out of Bethany's well-manicured claws.

Slade sees my expression. "Seriously? You'd take it that far."

I laugh it off because otherwise, this team might have me committed to a loony bin for even considering it.

"No...of course not. Marriage isn't on the table, even if it's fake."

The guys all chuckle and dive back into their conversations about Thanksgiving plans, and then our next out-of-town game coming up the morning after, and I let them.

Let them assume this is all lighthearted and funny and easy. Because the truth? None of this is easy.

Bethany's circling. My mom's keeping secrets. And I've somehow moved into a stranger's house just to avoid one woman while pretending to date another.

If that's not the definition of a mess, I don't know what is.

But when I picture Peyton's face this morning—still half-asleep, hair sticking out in all directions, sleep lines on her cheek—I can't help the way something settles in my chest.

This might be fake.

But for the first time in a long time, I don't feel like I'm losing.

"Are you headed back to New Jersey to see your mom for Thanksgiving?" Trey asks over his shoulder as I follow him to the large couch, we find a spot to sit down and eat.

"No, it's not enough time to get back. What are you and Adeline going to do?" I ask.

"Oakley's has the bar open for players who can't make it home for the holidays. It sounds like half the team is going there. Since it's just Adeline and me now, it should help to keep her distracted that this is the second year without them. She's excited to go since it's the only time she can get in as a minor."

I nod. Holidays are hard when you lose someone you care

about. My mind flashes to Peyton and how she mentioned that her dad died young and suddenly back to our kiss last night. "Yeah, I might do that too."

"You're not going to spend Thanksgiving with Peyton's family? I know this is all fake, but you two seemed to be getting along last night at the open skate night."

I hadn't even thought about asking Peyton about Thanksgiving, mostly because it feels like I'm encroaching in on her life enough as it is.

I wish I had time to go home and see my mom. But she'd be busy anyway, and I'd be following her around all day. She volunteers at a soup kitchen every year, then her salon does a Thanksgiving dinner, and then she goes with her singing group to an old folks' home to sing Christmas carols.

If I showed up with this little notice, I'd be her plus one she'd be dragging around town.

Oakley's with half the team is good enough for me. And I've heard that the spread that Oakley's puts on is impressive. Unless of course, Peyton wants me to go with her. She did mention that her nephew is one of my biggest fans. Since I'm coming to his career day, it might be a good time to meet him, but I won't bring it up. If she wants to ask, she will.

I stay another hour or so, watching Luka dominate on Slade's PlayStation, putting everyone to shame.

And then I get a text from Peyton. It's a picture...of the bed... with double the pillows for her new and improved pillow wall. Where did she even find all of those? I snicker, wondering how long this took her to build.

> **Me: I hate to tell you but no amount of pillows will make me less desirable. Your efforts are futile.**

> **Peyton: I ordered barbed wire fencing to go over top but shipping says four to five business days. Hopefully I can resist you in my sleep until then.**

I huff out a laugh, and then I get an idea.

I search for a furniture shop, and since it's only just after dinner time, they're open.

A man answers the phone, and I tell him what I need.

"Hi, I'm looking to order a king-size bed for my girlfriend, and I need it as soon as possible."

I see Trey give me a questioning glance.

Yeah, it's unusual, but nothing about this arrangement is normal and we've been making it work.

"A king-size bed sir? If you'd like to bring her down to the store we can—"

I cut him off quickly. "I'm on a time crunch and I'm not available to come by. Can you just give me your best seller that women usually pick out? It needs to be in stock. And can you deliver it the day after Thanksgiving?"

The salesman clears his throat. It's an odd request to not even care what it looks like, but sure enough, the man wants a sale and agrees.

I list off my credit card number and Peyton's address, and there it is. Problem solved.

Another hour later, I say my goodbyes and head out of Slade's. As soon as I walk out his front door, the sun's starting to set.

I round the front of my truck.

And that's when I see it.

A sleek, black Mercedes idles in the spot next to mine, engine still purring like it's waiting for something—or someone.

As I approach, the tinted window glides down just halfway, slow and deliberate.

The smile that greets me is sharp enough to cut glass.

Bethany.

Her perfume hits me instantly—sweet, cloying vanilla with a bitter undertone. It used to be my favorite scent in the world. Now it turns my stomach. It smells as artificial as the rest of her.

She's wearing oversized designer sunglasses and a smug little expression, like she's already won whatever game she's playing.

"Are you really just going to ignore me, Hunter?" Her voice is sweet poison, smooth as ever. "It won't work forever. You know that. We have too much history."

"Are you stalking me? How long have you been waiting out here for me to come out? You know this is a gated community. How the hell did you get in?"

Has she lost her damn mind? Wait, I already know the answer to that.

"I have an old friend I was visiting a few blocks away, and she mentioned that Slade is close by. Then I saw your truck. I would call it a coincidence, but you and I both know that it's fate."

It's not fate. It's Bethany Richards realizing that I'm finally free from under her husband's thumb and now she wants to set my new life ablaze. But I'm not going down without a fight this time.

"What are you really doing here? And don't keep using the friend excuse. We both know that you don't have any," I say flatly.

Her chin lifts, her perfectly manicured nails tapping against the steering wheel like she's bored already. "Just wanted to know when you're going to kick this Bleacher Reporter girl to the curb. I'm not here for games, and we both know that I'm the last woman you dated seriously."

"That's really what you came here to ask? Peyton and I are serious, and I'm staying in Seattle. You can head home without me whenever you want, Beth. No one is going to miss you here."

Her lips twitch. "Haven't you considered that there is someone else to consider here? Like your mom?"

That hits like a punch to the ribs.

She knows exactly where to aim.

"You mean, take the trade you're trying to convince Everett to sign off on," I snap. "Go back to New Jersey. Back to your team."

She shrugs like it's nothing. "Would that really be so bad? Your mom needs you right now...more than ever. I can tell she's not feeling well."

My stomach knots at the mention of Mom.

"What do you mean, 'she's not feeling well?'" I ask, the sound of it causing hair to stick up at the back of my neck.

What does Bethany know?

"She just doesn't sound as chipper on the phone, and her best friend Bonny has shared some concerns with me."

Bonny—my mother's best friend since beauty school and her salon manager.

"What did she say?" I ask, stepping closer to Bethany's car.

"Just that Carly has seemed more tired recently and wanted to know if I was coming back home soon to check in on her."

I hate that Bonny thought to call Bethany instead of me.

Bethany didn't grow up in the best home. She was taken away from her mom when she was young, and then bounced around between uncles, aunts, and grandparents most of her life... anywhere the courts could think to put her, but then she'd run away. They'd have to place her somewhere else because that family member wouldn't take her back.

So when we started dating, she connected with my mom almost instantly, worming her way into my mother's life. Bethany helped take care of her the last time she was sick, back when I was too far away to do anything about it. Mom still talks about her like Beth is her long-lost daughter. She was disappointed with Bethany when she found out what she did to me. She told me that even though Bethany hurt us both with her actions, that my mother wouldn't stop loving her—and that Bethany has deep wounds that need mending.

And that's the problem. My mom loves her, and they're still connected at the hip it seems.

Bethany leans a little closer to the open window, voice

dropping. "But if you want to play house with your little podcast girl, go ahead. Just don't forget—you'll get bored and sabotage things with her soon enough. That's been your thing ever since you lost me. I'm the one that got away, and we both know it."

I cross my arms over my chest, keeping my distance. "We don't have anything, Beth."

Her smile disappears. "You don't mean that."

I do. I mean every damn word. But she's not the type to care.

She shifts her car into gear and pulls away without another word, leaving nothing behind but the faint smell of vanilla and the sinking weight in my chest.

I stare at the spot where her car used to be, jaw clenched, every worst-case scenario running through my head. What if she knows something about Mom's health that I don't? What if she's using it, dangling it in front of me like a carrot on a stick?

And the worst part?

For a second, I almost consider it.

Almost.

But I already burned my career once for Bethany Richards. And unless my mother needs me to move home, I won't do it again.

The drive across town feels longer than usual. Probably because my brain won't shut off.

Bethany's voice keeps looping in the back of my head like a bad soundtrack. The smug smile. The subtle digs. The way she weaponized my mom without blinking.

I tighten my grip on the steering wheel and force myself to breathe. She's bluffing. She has to be.

Still...I can't shake it.

I turn down Peyton's street, the quiet residential block almost too normal after Bethany's ambush today. Like none of it should exist in the same universe as a tidy row of townhomes, and a podcast host who thinks I'm a menace.

Her townhouse comes into view, and despite myself, something in my chest loosens.

The porch light's on. Her little blue SUV parked neatly in

front.

And I hate how much this place feels like home already. At least the closest thing to feeling like home I've had in a while.

I cut the engine and sit there for a second, drumming my fingers against the steering wheel.

What the hell am I even doing? Moving in with a woman I barely know. Faking a relationship. Letting her lay down ground rules like this is some kind of reality show.

But the thing is...she's the only person in my life right now who doesn't want anything from me. Not my money. Not my name. Not control.

Nothing except a few interviews and a kid's career day.

But when she smiles—when she's not rolling her eyes at me—there's something about her that makes it easy to breathe.

I grab my duffel from morning skate and head up the front steps.

Before I can even knock, the door cracks open like she's been waiting.

Peyton stands there in sweatpants and a tank top, her hair pulled up in a messy bun, like she has no idea she looks better than half the women who paid five figures to bid on me.

Her eyes flick down to my bag. "You're late."

I smirk, shaking off the weight of everything that's been crawling under my skin all day. "Miss me already, Collins?"

She doesn't answer—just rolls her eyes and steps aside to let me in.

But the corner of her mouth twitches.

And damn if that doesn't feel a hell of a lot better than anything Bethany Richards could ever offer.

CHAPTER ELEVEN
Peyton

The second we step inside the stadium, the energy hits me like a wall—bright lights, the sharp clicking of cameras going off, the low murmur of fans and media weaving through the open space. It's the annual Hawkeyes Winter Open House, and apparently, it's a bigger deal than I thought.

Hunter's hand hovers at the small of my back as we make our way through the crowd. He spots Penelope, Kendall, and Isla standing off to the side, discussing something, and steers me toward them.

"Good evening, ladies, have you met—"

"Peyton! You're here," Penelope says with a big smile.

"We've already met," I tell him as Penelope steps forward to squeeze my arm, while Isla bends in for a hug and Kendall gives a sweet wave. "I interviewed Penelope two months ago on my show, and I met Kendall and Isla at the bar...the night you and I met, actually," I tell him with a smug grin.

"The night I was a complete gentleman," he says, reaching back to scratch the back of his neck as if that night embarrasses him a little.

Someone comes up behind us and claps Hunter on the back. Slade Matthews—Penelope's husband. "Don't be too hard on yourself. At least you didn't foil her Olympic figure skating dreams," he says, and then sends Penelope a knowing look.

"True," Penelope agrees. "The best love stories come from the worst first impressions. Just ask any retired player on this team."

Before Hunter can reply, someone calls his name. The Hawkeyes' new social media manager waves him over to a group of reporters gathered near the ice. She's only been with the team a few weeks, filling in for the last social media manager that was let go last week, after attempting to step in after Tessa Powers moved to Aspen with her husband, Lake Powers. From what I've heard around the team, losing Tessa has been a tough adjustment for the Hawkeyes, and they haven't found a media manager who can handle the press or the players as well as Tessa did.

"Go," Penelope tells him, already waving him away. "We'll take good care of her."

He hesitates a second longer, his eyes locking on mine for a moment before finally stepping away with Slade to answer interview questions from the press.

The second he's gone, Penelope leans in. "You doing okay?"

I nod, even though I'm not sure if I should be nervous or not.

"He's different when he's on," she adds knowingly, following my gaze as Hunter slips easily into reporter mode. He smiles, laughs at something one of them says, and answers each question like he's done this a thousand times. Because he has.

"He's...good at this," I murmur.

"He is," Penelope agrees. "But don't let him fool you. That's his game face. Speaking of which, I heard that he botched your first interview."

"How did you hear that?" I ask.

"Trust me. Nothing in this stadium stays a secret. These boys gossip harder than a group of southern housewives whispering at a Sunday church luncheon."

Before I can think too deeply into it, the familiar feeling of Hunter's hand on my back returns. I turn to find him at my side.

"All they wanted to talk about was us," Hunter says quietly, leaning in close to my ear. "Every question, every headline—they're circling."

The heat of his breath against my neck sends shivers down my spine. I'm beginning to realize how much I like it when he stands this close, even though I know that I shouldn't let it affect me this way.

"You ladies won't mind if I borrow her for a second, will you?" he asks.

They all nod and as he's leading me away, I hear Isla's voice. "The broom closet at the end of the hall has a lock on it. Just in case..."

My cheeks redden and Hunter huffs out a chuckle as he leads me down one of the quieter hallways.

"I didn't realize how much of a circus this was going to be," he admits, voice low. "We might have to sell this harder than I thought."

I glance up at him, unsure where this is going. "Okay... What does that mean?"

"It means that while we're in public I might need to kiss you to sell it. I've already had a few comments from reporters asking if you and me are planning any lip-locking tonight. I don't want to catch you off guard if it comes down to that."

My stomach does a stupid little flip. "So, what—you'll give me a heads up?"

"Exactly." His eyes meet mine, something unreadable flickering there. "Consider it rule number five. I'll give you a warning."

I nod, swallowing against the sudden dryness in my throat. "Okay. I accept your addendum to the rules."

Hunter's lips curve into that crooked half-smile that makes it way too easy to forget this is all fake. "Good. Let's get out on the rink before Penelope and Isla start planning our wedding."

Hunter helps me lace up my skates and a crisp chill hits my face the second we step through the tunnel that leads to the ice. The rink is practically glowing under the festival lights strung up around the plexiglass. Families are out skating, varying levels of experience, but everyone's having a good time.

Hunter's hand finds the small of my back again, steady and warm. "Ever skated before?"

"Once or twice. I'm more of a tennis court girl, remember?"

He grins down at me, clearly picturing me falling flat on my face. "Good. You'll make me look like a hero."

Before I can argue, he's tugging me onto the ice, one large hand wrapped firmly around mine.

We skate. Or rather, he glides, and I wobble and do my best not to eat it in front of half of Seattle.

It's...fun. More fun than I thought pretending would be.

Until the mood shifts like a cold front.

Hunter stiffens, slowing us to a stop at the edge of the rink, his grip on my hand tightening.

I follow his gaze and feel my stomach drop.

Bethany Richards. Dressed in an elegant, figure-hugging coat, hair sleek, smile sharp. She's standing in the opening of the players tunnel, closer than I'd like her to be, watching us like she's already plotting her next move.

Hunter mutters something under his breath.

"Rule number five," he says low, his eyes still locked on Bethany. "This is your warning, Peyton."

Before I can respond, his fingers brush my cheek, tipping my face toward his. His touch is warm, grounding—and then his lips are on mine.

This time, it's different.

The first kiss blindsided me, all adrenaline and chaos, like he was trying to prove a point. But now... Now he's deliberate. Slower. Like he's making sure I feel every second of it.

His lips move against mine with a steady, calming kind of confidence. Not rushed. Not frantic. Like he's got nothing but time to remind everyone—Bethany included—that I'm his.

And the worst part?

It feels familiar.

Like I've done this before. Like kissing Hunter Reed is something I know how to do, even when I shouldn't.

A spark flickers low in my stomach, unexpected and sharp, and my toes curl in my skates. I force myself to keep breathing when he finally pulls away.

His hand lingers at the side of my face, thumb brushing my cheek like he can't help himself.

The crowd cheers around us, but it all feels muted.

Because I can still feel him everywhere.

And I forget, for one stupid second, that it's fake.

Bethany doesn't wait long after the kiss.

By the time Hunter pulls away—slowly, like he wants it to linger just a second longer—she's already making her way toward us, her steps slow yet intentional on the ice.

She doesn't have to come out more than a few feet before she's too close for comfort.

"Hunter," she purrs, sliding her sunglasses onto the top of her head even though it's eight o'clock at night and we're indoors. "Didn't realize you were so...domestic now."

Her eyes flick to me, sharp and assessing. I recognize the look—it's the one women like Bethany use when they want to make sure you know exactly where you stand.

Hunter shifts subtly, angling his body toward me like a shield. "Beth, this isn't the time."

"Oh, please. Don't mind me." She waves a hand, voice syrupy sweet. "I just wanted to meet the woman who's apparently tamed Seattle's most notorious bachelor."

Her gaze rakes over me, stopping pointedly on my hand still resting in Hunter's.

Isla and Kendall appear like backup, sliding in on either side of me.

"This must be Bethany," Kendall says breezily, like they're

discussing the weather.

Bethany's smile flickers.

Isla leans in to the group, stage-whispering, "Is it too soon to initiate Peyton into the WAGs group chat?"

Bethany's eyes narrow.

Hunter's fingers tighten around mine.

"We were just about to grab drinks," Isla continues smoothly, linking her arm through mine like we're old friends. "Peyton, you're coming, right?"

"Of course," I say, letting them steer me away, Hunter following behind.

As we walk, Kendall murmurs, "Don't let Bethany rattle you. Women like that feed on it."

Isla grins. "And by the way, you're officially a WAG now. Real hockey boyfriend or not."

The VIP lounge is tucked away on the second level of the stadium, far from the reporters, cameras, and fans still milling around the Open House downstairs. It's quieter here—dimly lit with plush couches, a private bar, and enough space for the WAGs to gather without an audience.

Penelope, Kendall, and Isla don't even hesitate to pull me toward a corner booth like I've been part of their circle for years.

Kendall slides into the booth across from me. "I can't believe you and Hunter are faking it to keep Bethany away from him."

I blink, caught off guard. Then I remember that Penelope said that the players all talk. Hunter must have told someone, and it got around the locker room. I'm not completely comfortable with everyone knowing, and yet, in some ways, I'm happy that I don't have to lie to these girls about it.

"It didn't start out like that. At first, he just wanted me to outbid her in exchange for an interview. Then things got a little crazy, and here we are," I say.

Isla grins knowingly. "It doesn't look fake. That kiss out there? It looked like you've been together for years."

My cheeks flush, but I force a laugh. "Well, you know how

hockey players are. Dramatic."

Penelope raises a brow but doesn't press. Instead, she waves over the bartender. "You're one of us now, Peyton. Whether you like it or not."

Kendall leans in conspiratorially. "Speaking of...we usually get together for one of the away games and watch it together at Penelope's house, just a few of us. Drinks, pizza, probably a lot of trash-talking the refs who can't hear us."

Isla grins. "You're coming."

It's not really a question.

Before I can answer, my phone buzzes in my lap—a text from Hunter.

> **Hunter: You okay?**

I glance up at the women around me, all of them smiling, relaxed, like this is just another Thursday night.

And somehow, for the first time tonight, I actually am.

I text back quickly.

> **Peyton: I'm good.**

Then I look at Penelope and nod. "Yeah. Count me in."

The event is starting to wind down by the time Hunter finds me again, the crowd thinning as people filter toward the exits. He's still got that easy smile on his face—the one he saves for the cameras—but it softens when his eyes land on me.

"Did you have fun with the girls?" he asks, slipping his hand to the small of my back like it's second nature now.

"Yeah, I did. They invited me to Penelope's for your away game."

"That should be a good time. Are you going to go?" he asks, nodding at a teammate as we pass by on our way out to his truck.

"Yeah," I nod, glancing up at him. "They insisted."

Something flickers in his expression—almost like relief. "Good. It will make this all more believable, but also you'll have them to hang out with during the home games and events that you agreed to come to."

His explanation makes sense. So why do I feel like there might be more to him wanting me to befriend the Hawkeyes girls' group?

The cool night air hits us as we step outside, the quiet of the parking lot a sharp contrast to the noise inside.

Hunter unlocks his truck and opens the passenger door for me without a word, waiting until I climb in before shutting it and rounding to the driver's side.

For a second, as he pulls out onto the street, neither of us says anything. The tension that's been simmering all night—the media attention, the kiss, the crowd—settles between us like an invisible thread.

Finally, he glances over, voice softer now. "You handled tonight like a pro, Collins."

I shrug, looking out the window to hide my smile. "It wasn't my first circus."

His laugh is low and warm. "Good. Because it won't be the last."

CHAPTER TWELVE
Peyton

I fiddle with the hem of my sweater, my nerves buzzing like I'm about to walk into a final exam unprepared. It's ridiculous. I've survived press scrums and radio interviews and a million awkward first dates. But nothing quite compares to the stomach-knotting anxiety of driving to my mom's house with Hunter Reed behind the wheel.

He's casual about it, one hand resting on the steering wheel, the other flipping through radio stations like he owns the airwaves. We've been driving for almost twenty minutes, and the silence has been...comfortable, mostly. Until he pauses on a classic rock station, and I immediately reach over and change it to an indie folk channel.

Hunter glances at me sideways, smirking. "Seriously? What is this? Sleepy banjo music?"

I grin and prepare for the war about to rage over the radio. "Excuse me, but I am the passenger princess. That means I control the music."

He huffs a laugh, checking over his shoulder before switching lanes smoothly. "Passenger what?"

"Passenger princess," I repeat, teasing him like he's dense. "My dad used to call me that on long drives to tennis tournaments. I got to pick the music, the temperature, the snack stops—full control. He said it was only fair since I was the one doing all the winning."

His smirk softens, and he shoots me a quick glance before focusing back on the road. "You two were close."

I swallow around the lump that always forms when I talk about him. "Yeah. Some days it's really hard to accept that he's gone. I keep thinking he's going to call any second to ask me what he should get mom for their anniversary, but then my phone never rings."

The smile fades from Hunter's face, his jaw tightening ever so slightly. "He sounds like a good dad."

"He was," I murmur, turning my gaze out the window. "I miss him every day. Especially when something exciting happens and I want to call him...or around the holidays."

Silence settles over us again, heavier this time. I glance at him, trying to shake it off. "Do you ever wish you would have grown up with a dad?"

His thumb taps against the steering wheel three times, then stops. "Sure. But my mom did her best."

The answer is short, clipped. His entire posture shifts—shoulders rigid, jaw clenched. It's clear that's all I'm getting, so I let it go.

I reach for the climate control dial and crank it up a degree, flashing him a playful smile. "So, you're not going to bite my hand off if I turn it to seventy-two?"

That earns me a real smile, the corner of his mouth twitching like he can't help himself. "Nah. You're my passenger princess now." A stupid little flutter takes up residence in my chest at the way he says it—like it's a title he's happy to give me. I shove the feeling down before it can root itself too deep. "Just don't make me sweat through this button-up before I meet your mom for the first time. First impressions are important, and I have no idea what you told her about our first meeting. I might have some damage control to do."

"She's already in love with you. She and Jesse watch every televised game you're on."

Hunter just laughs and shakes his head. "Good to know."

And for the first time since we left my place, the weight pressing on my chest lightens.

The second we step inside my mom's house, it smells like cinnamon, roasted turkey, and the faint trace of the lemon cleaner she always uses when company's coming over. It's warm and chaotic—the way every holiday gathering has been since I was a kid.

Mom's already at the door, wiping her hands on her apron as she grins at us. "There you are! I thought you two got lost."

Before I can respond, Hunter holds out a hand. "Thank you for having me, Mrs. Collins."

My mom blinks at him like she wasn't expecting manners from a six-foot-two, muscled hockey player, then shakes his hand warmly. "None of that Mrs. Collins business. Call me Shari."

I glance over at Hunter, catching the flicker of amusement in his eyes.

A soft whirl cuts through the noise behind us, and I turn just in time to see Jesse rolling toward us, a wide grin on his face.

"Hunter Reed's coming to Thanksgiving? No way! No one told me," Jesse's eyes light up like it's Christmas morning.

Hunter's entire face softens, and he crouches down so he's eye-level with Jesse without hesitation. "You must be Jesse. I've heard a lot about you."

Jesse beams, immediately launching into a ramble about his favorite players and how he's working on his wrist shot. Before I know it, Hunter's asking about Jesse's wheelchair modifications and if he's ever tried adaptive sled hockey. He doesn't even blink at the chair, like it's just another part of Jesse's gear.

By the time we make it to the living room, Jesse's already out of the chair, sitting cross-legged on the floor while Hunter shows him how to properly hold a hockey stick using the old ones my mom keeps tucked in the hall closet from past Christmases.

It hits me then, like a sucker punch to the chest—how easy he makes this look. How quickly he slipped into my family like he's always belonged here.

My mom stands beside me, her hands on her hips as she watches them. "He's good with Jesse," she says softly.

"Yeah," I agree, folding my arms tight across my chest. "He really is."

Too good.

Which is dangerous.

Because I know exactly how temporary this is.

After a bathroom break, I step back into the kitchen, and the sound of laughter hits me.

I pause in the doorway, taking in the scene.

Hunter's at the counter with Jesse propped beside him in his chair, both of them peeling potatoes under my mom's supervision. Mom's laughing so hard she's wiping tears from her eyes, and Jesse's grin is huge, like he's never heard anything funnier in his life.

"I swear to God, Shari," Hunter is saying, "if I had a dollar for every time Aleksi Mäkelin's skincare routine has held up team meetings, I wouldn't need my player salary."

"That man does *not* use night cream," my mom giggles.

"He travels with an entire toiletry bag dedicated to moisturizers," Hunter replies with a straight face. "And another one for serums. It's a problem."

Jesse snorts, nearly dropping a slippery peeled potato.

I lean against the doorframe, watching this ridiculously domestic scene unfold. Hunter's sleeves are rolled up, there's a streak of potato peel on his wrist, the ink of his tattoos just barely visible, and he looks so damn at home that it's almost disorienting.

Mom catches sight of me hovering in the doorway. "Hey! You and Abby can set the table. I've got these two wrapped around my finger already."

Abby breezes past me, nudging my shoulder as she passes. "Come on, lovebird. Let's go."

I roll my eyes but follow her anyway, casting one last glance back at the kitchen.

Hunter says something I can't hear, but whatever it is makes Jesse laugh so hard he nearly tips backward in his chair.

That sound is the best thing I've heard in a long, long time.

Abby tosses a stack of napkins onto the dining table as I follow behind her, grabbing plates from the cabinet. The laughter still drifts from the kitchen, Hunter's voice blending in like he's been part of this family for years instead of hours.

Abby sets a fork down and glances at me. "So...how's it going?"

I raise an eyebrow. "You're going to have to be more specific."

She shrugs, arranging silverware like she's not prying. "You know. Living with a hot hockey player. Sharing a bed. Fake dating him in front of the entire city."

I blow out a breath, setting plates around the table. "It's fine."

"Fine?" She snorts. "That man is currently peeling potatoes in Mom's kitchen and making Jesse laugh so hard he's about to fall out of his chair, and you're telling me it's *fine*?"

I glance back toward the kitchen, where the three of them are still talking, the rhythm easy and natural. Too natural.

Abby bumps her shoulder into mine, dropping her voice. "I'm just saying...if you don't want him, I think Mom might finally be ready for a boyfriend."

I roll my eyes and wad up one of the napkins, lobbing it at her head. "Stop."

She laughs but sobers quickly when she catches my expression. "You know I'm kidding, right?"

"Yeah." I press my lips together, smoothing out another napkin. "It's just...he fits here better than I expected. But he's temporary."

Abby doesn't argue. She doesn't have to.

We both know that's the part that's going to hurt.

Dinner is loud and warm, exactly like it always is at Mom's house. It still doesn't mask the fact that my dad isn't here and that my brother Will is still overseas, but this Thanksgiving is turning out to be better than I anticipated it would be.

Abby is making snarky comments about the sweet potatoes being too sweet, Jesse keeps trying to sneak extra rolls when no one's looking, and Mom is laughing at everything like she hasn't had a reason to smile this big in years.

But when Mom finally taps her fork against her glass and says, "All right, before dessert—what's everyone thankful for?" the whole room quiets.

Jesse starts first, grinning shyly as he says, "I'm thankful for my family. And that Dad gets to come home in a few months."

Abby says she's thankful for Jesse and Mom, and for strong coffee on her night shifts at the hospital.

When it's Hunter's turn, he clears his throat, eyes flicking over to me.

"I'm thankful," he starts, voice deceptively casual, "for my passenger princess. Because apparently, I've been driving around my whole life without knowing the right temperature setting."

There's a beat of silence before the table bursts into laughter.

But me? I freeze.

Because I feel her eyes on me. Mom's. Sharp, knowing.

She doesn't say anything, but when I glance over, she's wearing a small smile that says she heard every word and understood exactly what it meant.

Under the table, Hunter's hand slips onto my thigh, his fingers giving it a playful squeeze like he's in on the joke.

And even though I know it's fake, my heart doesn't seem to get the message.

It has me wondering about our second interview, and whether I'm willing to risk making Hunter upset for the ratings I need.

Oh God...am I falling for my fake boyfriend?

After dinner, we're all full and sleepy, lounging around the living room while Jesse wheels himself in and out, bouncing between conversation and trying to snag extra dessert without anyone noticing.

Hunter's been glued to Jesse's side most of the night—not in a forced way, but like it's the most natural thing in the world. Watching them makes something soft settle low in my chest, and I keep reminding myself this isn't real.

Once I get my network deal and Bethany moves back to New Jersey, taking her trade deal with her, this all ends. Doesn't it?

When we finally say our goodnights, Mom hugs me tight and whispers in my ear, "You've got a good one there."

I don't even bother correcting her. Not tonight.

Hunter crouches down next to Jesse's chair. "Hey, buddy. Next time you want to come to a game, you let me know. I'll have a set of tickets waiting for you at will-call."

Jesse's eyes light up, wide and round. "Like, forever?"

Hunter chuckles, scratching the back of his neck. "Not forever," I jump in quickly, knowing full well how Jesse latches onto things. "Hunter plays in different cities. We don't know how long he'll be—"

Hunter cuts me off gently, his gaze never leaving Jesse's. "As long as I'm playing, and wherever I'm playing, you'll have a home game ticket. Deal?"

Jesse beams like Hunter just handed him the Stanley Cup. "Deal."

I glance over at Abby, and she's giving me that look again. The one that says, *this man is perfect.*

Except he's not.

He wouldn't even be here tonight if we weren't pretending.

"And if your aunt is nice to you," Hunter adds with a wink, "maybe she can tag along too."

I roll my eyes. "Cute."

But my heart thumps anyway.

The drive home is quiet.

Not awkward quiet—just that kind of full, satisfied quiet you get after a long day surrounded by family and too much food.

Outside, the streets are nearly empty, the outskirts of Seattle still asleep in its post-holiday haze. Inside the truck, the heat hums low, the dashboard lights casting a soft glow across Hunter's profile.

He hasn't turned on the radio this time. Maybe he's too full of turkey and pie. Maybe he's lost in thought like I am.

I stare out the window, the cool glass pressed against my temple, replaying the night in my head—Jesse's smile, Mom's laugh, the way Hunter fit so easily into all of it.

It's dangerous, how good he is at this. How natural it felt having him there. How easy it was to forget it was all fake.

His hand moves, resting casually on the center console, fingers tapping against the leather.

I glance over.

He catches me looking and flashes that damn crooked grin like he knows exactly what I've been thinking.

My stomach does a little flip.

"Thanks for coming tonight," I say, breaking the silence.

Hunter keeps his eyes on the road but his voice softens. "I wouldn't have missed it."

That's the problem.

He's too convincing.

And I can't afford to forget why he's here.

By the time we get back to the townhouse, my limbs feel like lead, my stomach still too full from two helpings of pie, and my brain buzzing with everything I don't want to think about—how easy it would be to want more of this.

Hunter carries the leftover container of pie into the kitchen while I shuffle down the hall, already tugging my hair tie loose.

When I come back out, he's leaning against the counter, scrolling through his phone. He looks up when he hears me and gives me a soft, tired smile.

"You good?" he asks.

"Yeah. Just tired."

I cross to the bedroom and disappear into the bathroom to

change, brushing my teeth and washing off my makeup like it's any other night. Like I haven't spent the whole day pretending he's my boyfriend.

When I finally crawl into bed, the pillow wall is back, but it doesn't feel like much of a barrier anymore.

Hunter flips the light off and slides under the covers, turning onto his side to face me.

"I'll be gone tomorrow," he says quietly, voice rough with exhaustion.

My stomach dips. "Your away game?"

He nods. "Yeah. We're flying out after morning skate. Three games. Back late next week."

"Okay," I say, rolling onto my side to mirror him. "Good luck."

He's quiet for a beat. Then, softer, "Thanks, Collins."

When I close my eyes, it's the first time I notice how cold the other side of the pillow wall already feels.

This is fake. He's temporary.

And I absolutely, definitely, should not want him.

The next morning, I wake up relieved to find myself on my own side of the bed. No drool. No sprawling. No photographic evidence of my unconscious crimes against the pillow wall. Progress.

But there's something sitting on my bedside table.

A neon pink sticky note shaped like a French Bulldog.

Of course.

I sit up and peel it off the lamp.

P—

There's a delivery coming to the townhouse at two p.m.

Also, I've hidden your favorite mug. If you follow the clues, you'll find a reward.

Good luck.

Love, your boyfriend.

I roll my eyes so hard I'm surprised they don't pop out of my skull.
He hid my mug?
And signed it "your boyfriend?"
I can practically hear the smirk in his voice as if he were saying it out loud. Dripping with sarcasm. So proud of himself he probably flexed while writing it.
Still...a little something flutters in my stomach. Because he's not even here—he left early this morning for the road trip—but this? This stupid little scavenger hunt?
It means he thought about me before leaving.
His words from the podcast flicker through my head: "I only prank people I like."
I throw off my covers with a groan that's equal parts annoyance and reluctant amusement. "Okay, Reed. Let's see what kind of nonsense you left behind."
My feet are barely on the hardwood before I'm heading straight for the kitchen, toward the drying rack by the sink. That's where my mug lives.
That's where I always leave it.
Of course, it's gone.
But another Frenchie sticky note waits in its place, stuck to the faucet.

Cold mornings and your favorite peppermint tea.

You always start your day right here, but I'm holding your mug hostage.

If you want it back, go check the place where we turned a heating pad and Thai food into our first truce.

I blink.
The couch.
I jog back to the living room, already grinning.
Another note is under the throw blanket, wedged between the cushions with ruthless accuracy and curled at the edges.

You laughed, you snacked, and you definitely tried to hog the blanket.

But your mug's not here.

Try the place where I keep things hot...and mildly spicy.

Bonus points if you find leftover noodles.

Oh my god.
The fridge?
I half-sprint back to the kitchen.
I yank open the fridge door. There's a half-empty container of pad thai shoved in the back—and taped to it?
Another pink note.

Not just leftovers—this is where peace offerings live.

But your mug is still MIA. If you're desperate, check the place you go when things get really steamy... like flat hair and melting mascara steamy.

"Seriously?"
He left a clue in the bathroom?
I tug the bathroom door open and find the note taped to the shampoo bottle like it's been mocking me all morning.

Not here either. I'm not that cruel.

But you're so close. You once said this place held all your secrets.

Better check the drawer where your secrets actually live.

Secrets.
My nightstand drawer?
He better not have touched my vibrator.

I pull open the drawer slowly, half-expecting glitter to explode in my face.

No glitter. Just a folded note on top of my usual stash of Advil and emergency chocolate.

Didn't find what you were looking for? Sorry, sweetheart.

But I left your precious mug somewhere that means something—to you and me—our first fight. Go where the stories live.

The studio.
I break into a jog down the hall.
There it is.

Sitting front and center on my desk like it owns the place. My white ceramic "Microphones & Mayhem" mug, flanked by my soundboard and the leftover scent of Hunter's body wash and aftershave from this morning.

Taped to the mug, a note reads:

Turns out I do listen. Don't get smug.

Your reward's in the fridge.

And yes, it's chocolate. Because I'm not a monster.

I'm laughing now, shaking my head as I head back to the fridge.

Inside, tucked behind the takeout, is a glossy red box of truffles.

Another note, this one slightly bent from the condensation.

Consider this your prize for surviving a Hunter Reed scavenger hunt.

Sproutacus says hi. Make sure to talk to him a little while I'm gone. He gets lonely up on the windowsill all alone.

See you soon.

—Your Charming Plant Baby-Daddy

I hold the box and the note in my hands for a second, something warm blooming under my ribs. Because yeah, this is fake. It's all fake.

But for a minute? It doesn't feel that way.

Not even a little.

At exactly two twenty-five p.m., there's a knock at the door.

I pause mid-bite of truffle, still half-lounging on the couch in my pajama pants and fuzzy socks. The scavenger hunt had completely erased any memory of the delivery note.

When I open the door, two guys in branded polos are waiting on the porch with a clipboard and a moving truck behind them.

"We're here to deliver the bed," one says, friendly but professional. "Mr. Reed asked us to set it up and move the old one to your garage."

"Deliver the...bed?" I blink. "What bed?"

He hands me the clipboard. And there it is.

Hunter Reed. King-size custom pillow top. The price tag makes my jaw drop.

The second guy's already unlocking the truck.

"He bought me a bed?" I whisper to myself.

No.

He bought us a bed.

I blink again, scanning the absurd number. Who spends that much on a mattress?

"Uh, yeah—come in," I say quickly, stepping back. "Let me strip the bedding first."

The guy nods and heads to help unload while I half-jog back to the bedroom, still reeling.

I pull the comforter off in a daze.

He bought me—no, us—a bigger bed.

And not just any bed. A ridiculous, luxury, custom, king-size bed.

Hunter freaking Reed.

What am I supposed to do with that?

CHAPTER THIRTEEN

Hunter

The third-period clock ticks under a minute. The crowd is on their feet, roaring like the game's already won, but we're not there yet. Not until that horn sounds.

Slade snags the puck behind our net and launches it toward Aleksi, who flies up center ice like a man on fire. I push off hard, legs burning as I keep pace, scanning the ice as we transition.

Aleksi dodges a defenseman and slips the puck to Trey, just as a guy from the other team barrels toward him. "Heads!" I shout, but it's too late.

The hit comes hard—shoulder to chest. Aleksi goes down, skates first, sliding out of frame.

I cut hard to the left, eyeing the bastard who leveled him. Before he can peel off, I angle myself just right and slam into him from the side. Not enough to draw a penalty, but enough to make him think twice. His balance wobbles, and he goes down—ice scraping up beneath him as he skids into the boards.

The ref doesn't whistle. It's been the theme of the night.

Good. I like games like these.

Trey still has the puck. He winds up, shifts, fires.

Their goalie reads him perfectly—glove snapping the shot out of the air like it's nothing.

Damn it.

But we're still in the lead. As long as we defend, this game is in the bag, but with time on the clock, nothing's a sure thing.

Before the puck even drops from his glove, their left wing is already moving. I spin on my heels, sprinting backwards as they haul ass up the ice. They're as hungry for this win as we are.

Olsen's ready in the net, crouched low.

Their right wing takes the shot, but Olsen blocks it, only the puck gets pushed out to their center who scrambles to make another shot. He does, but it's not good enough. Olsen pounces on the puck, covering it with his entire body.

Wolf and I are in the thick of it, ramming our way through the opposing team to keep them off our goalie.

Slade gets the puck and starts hauling ass the other direction, a one-second delay before anyone realizes he's got it. But before he gets a chance to take the shot, the final horn blows—and the relief is immediate.

We won three to one. A dirty, scrappy, but solid game.

My shoulder held up—through cheap shots and more bullshit than a rodeo. But these are the games I live for as a defenseman, especially when there's a "W" on the board at the end.

The second we step off the ice, though, that relief fades. Because I know what's coming next.

The media circus.

By the time I hit the locker room, there's already a crowd of reporters gathering outside. Trey claps me on the shoulder as he passes. "Good luck, lover boy."

I roll my eyes, but the joke lands closer to the truth than I'm comfortable admitting.

Things with Peyton have started to feel different lately. But I'm in no place to offer anyone a relationship—especially not her.

Peyton's the kind of woman you marry. Settle down with.

Build a life around.

Watching her with her family over Thanksgiving dinner told me everything I needed to know—because that's what she wants. And I get it. Spending Thanksgiving with them felt easier than it should've. Jesse's a good kid, her mom's an actual saint, and Abby... well, Abby and I are cut from the same cloth. I'd probably get along with her brother too.

And honestly? I don't even know if Peyton would give me a chance, even if I asked for one. I've screwed up more than once since the day we met. And after everything that happened with Bethany—the first person I ever let in—I'm not sure I have it in me to risk that kind of vulnerability again.

I don't know if I ever will.

Still...sitting on the couch with Peyton?

It was the most at peace I've felt in a long damn time. I know what the media wants tonight. Gossip. Headlines. They're not here for the game recap. They want stories about the player and the podcaster riding off into some carefully curated, fake sunset.

But if it keeps Bethany at bay—even a little—and Peyton's podcast keeps climbing like it has since this all started...then yeah, I've got to do my part to keep this thing going.

And yeah, I've been keeping tabs on it—checking her sub numbers once...maybe twice a day. Would I do that for anyone else? Probably not, but her success feels like I'm winning too.

After I've showered and dressed in my suit, the media liaison is already motioning me toward the gauntlet.

It starts the way it always does—questions about the game, about the team's performance, my shoulder.

And then—

"So, Hunter, the big question of the night isn't about your game—it's about your relationship. Can you tell us how things started between you and Peyton Collins?"

I school my expression, force a polite smile. "That's private."

Another reporter jumps in. "But there's a video of you two at the charity auction. And at the Open House. Fans are dying to know how the NHL's most notorious bachelor got tamed."

Tamed.

I bite back a laugh. If only they knew.

"We met through mutual friends," I say smoothly. "One thing led to another."

"And now you're living together?" another reporter presses.

I glance at the cameras, knowing full well that whatever I say will be replayed a hundred times by morning.

"We're figuring it out," I answer simply, keeping my voice even.

The questions keep coming, but all I can think about is how fast this thing has snowballed. And how much harder it's going to be to keep this under control.

Because the more they ask, the more I realize...

Everyone's watching.

And the longer I keep playing this game, the harder it's going to be to remember it's not real.

I'm halfway through unwrapping the tape from my wrist when I spot her.

Bethany.

Leaning casually against the wall outside the locker room exit, like she's got every right to be here. Like she isn't the reason I'm technically a rookie in the NHL since I never finished a full year with New Jersey before they shipped me off to the farm team.

She's dressed in black, understated but expensive. Hair curled perfectly. Lips painted red like a damn stop sign.

The second she sees me, her smile curves upward like she knows a secret.

I should keep walking. I should ignore her completely. But I already know she'll find another way to corner me if I don't get this over with now.

"Beth," I greet flatly, coming to a stop a few feet away.

Her smile deepens, like we're old friends catching up instead of...whatever the hell we are.

"You looked good out there tonight," she says, her voice all sweet edges. "You always did play better when you had something to prove."

"What do you want?"

She tilts her head, eyes sweeping over me like she's taking inventory. "Dinner."

I blink. "You're kidding."

She steps in closer, lowering her voice. "Just dinner, Hunter. We used to have fun, remember? It doesn't have to be complicated."

"I have someone at home waiting for me. And unlike you, I'm not the cheating type," I remind her.

She reaches into her clutch and slips something into my hand. A hotel key card.

"She doesn't have to know," she says, like she's the one doing me a favor. "Skip dinner. Just dessert. You've always needed a release after a game. I remember how worked up you used to get, and Peyton's not here to take care of your needs. But I am."

Then, without waiting for an answer, she brushes past me like she's already won.

Aleksi rounds the corner just as she disappears down the hall. His brow lifts at the sight of me still holding the key card.

"What the hell was that?"

I shake my head, and walk over to the trash can nearby, dropping the key into it. "A reminder of all the reasons I don't trust anyone."

His gaze sharpens. "She's persistent, isn't she?"

"Yeah," I mutter. "Something like that."

Aleksi doesn't say anything, but I can feel his eyes on me the entire way back to the locker room, like he's trying to figure out what kind of mess I've signed up for.

And if I'm being honest...

I'm wondering the same damn thing.

By the time I make it back to the team hotel, the weight of the game, the interviews, and Bethany's lingering shadow feels heavier than it should.

I toss my gear bag onto the hotel room chair and sink onto

the edge of the bed, scrubbing a hand over my face.

My phone buzzes on the nightstand.

Peyton.

> **Peyton: Good game tonight. Your shoulder looked solid out there.**

I can't stop the smirk that tugs at the corner of my mouth. It's such a simple message, but it hits harder than it should.

> **Me: It felt solid. You watch the post-game interviews?**

The typing bubbles appear almost immediately...then disappear.

They pop up again. Then vanish.

I watch, amused, knowing she's probably overthinking every word.

Finally, her message lands.

> **Peyton: I did. Looked like you handled yourself well. Even with all the "relationship" questions.**

I lean back against the pillows, thumb hovering over the keyboard.

> **Me: We're the new IT couple of the Hawkeyes. How do you feel about that?**

There's a pause before her reply.

> **Peyton: I feel like you owe me royalties for how many headlines my name's in today.**

That makes me laugh for the first time all night.

> **Me: You want royalties, Collins? I'll pay up when I get back. Dinner's on me.**

Three dots appear.
Disappear.
Then her reply:

> **Peyton: Fine.**

> **Peyton: By the way...the bed was delivered today.**

> **Me: How do you like it?**

> **Peyton: I love it. It's gorgeous but it takes up half the room, and you shouldn't have spent that much.**

> **Me: You're sharing your bed with me. It's the least I can do. And the pillow walls need more room to grow.**

I tease, staring at the blank space, anticipating where I know her text will come up soon.

But she's stalling...the dots appearing again and then disappearing. Did I say something wrong? Why is she having trouble coming up with a response?

> **Peyton: So the bed is to keep me further away?**

Fuck no. The last thing I want is her further away. If it were up to me, I'd be waking up every night to her sneaking over the pillow wall to be closer to me. Though it's probably best that I don't tell her that.

> **Me: I just thought you'd be more comfortable. And a queen bed is small even when I'm all alone in one.**

> **Peyton: True. Well, thank you. I'm looking forward to testing out the bed tonight.**

> **Me: You're welcome.**

I set my phone on the nightstand, but I don't fall asleep right away.

Because the truth is...I'm not sure which part I'm looking forward to more—the next game or getting home to test out that bed with her.

CHAPTER FOURTEEN

Peyton

The buzzing of my alarm cuts through the quiet, vibrating obnoxiously against my nightstand. I groan, cracking one eye open and glaring at the ceiling like it personally offended me.

Six a.m.

Why in the world did I agree to hot yoga this morning?

I roll over, grabbing my phone, half-ready to text Abby and bail. But my thumb hovers over the keyboard without typing. Because right below my alarm notification is the last message I got last night.

Hunter: Sweet dreams, Passenger Princess.

My stomach flips—annoyingly, frustratingly flips—and I hate how much I've reread that stupid text.

I stare at it for a few seconds longer than I should, then toss the phone onto the bed like it's on fire.

God, I need to get a grip.

Dragging myself out of bed, I shuffle toward the bathroom. Maybe sweating out all the confusing feelings tangled up in my chest is exactly what I need. If nothing else, Abby will drag me mercilessly if I cancel on her again. She's already convinced I'm letting this fake relationship spiral out of control.

By the time I tie my hair up in a messy bun and pull on leggings, I've almost talked myself out of overthinking Hunter Reed and his stupid, sweet, flirty texts from last night.

Almost.

"Bye Sprouty," I call out to Sproutacus as I head for the front door. "Going to yoga, be back in a bit."

Have I actually lost my mind? I'm talking to a plant like Hunter told me to. Some things are just getting weirder around here, but it seems even weirder not to say anything to the little terracotta Frenchie staring at me from the windowsill, tiny green sprouts just now starting to show.

When I step outside, the cool morning air hits me like a slap. The kind of slap that says: *Get your shit together, Peyton.*

By the time I back out of the driveway, my phone buzzes again.

> **Abby:** Don't even think about bailing. I've got tea and sisterly judgment waiting.

I shake my head, letting the smallest smile tug at the corner of my mouth.

Fine. Yoga, sister time, and maybe a reminder that real life exists outside of hockey players, fake dating disasters, and the looming podcast deal that is hanging in the balance.

I can survive one hour without checking my phone to see if Hunter's texted again.

Maybe.

Twenty minutes later, I pull into the studio parking lot. Abby's already posted up on the curb like a judgmental gargoyle with my favorite drink—balancing two iced teas in one hand and her yoga mat slung over her shoulder like a weapon of mass destruction.

"You're late," she calls before I've even shut the car door.

"I'm literally two minutes early," I argue, grabbing one of the teas she holds out.

"Which is five minutes late in my world. Also, you look like hell."

"Gee, thanks."

She falls in step beside me as we walk toward the studio.

"I blame the bed," I mutter. "It's too comfortable. I didn't want to get up."

Abby stops short. "Wait—what bed? You said you were broke."

"Oh, I am. It's not my bed. Hunter bought it. Had it delivered yesterday while he was out of town."

She turns to stare at me like I just told her I eloped with Jason Momoa.

"He bought you a bed?"

I nod.

"A whole bed? Like...with a frame and everything?"

"Yes."

Abby scoffs. "Your king-sized fake boyfriend bought you a plow platform?"

I blink. "A what?"

"You know...a sheet shaker, a boom-boom base, a horizontal hustle zone."

I reach over and gently pluck the iced tea from her hand. "I don't think you need any more of this. You're wired enough."

She throws her arms up. "Meanwhile, your brother hasn't given me more than a crick in my neck and a caffeine addiction."

I snort. "The bed's really nice, too."

She smirks over at me. "Oh, I bet it is. Of course it is. Because men like Hunter Reed only come in two modes—emotionally unavailable or accidentally perfect. And you're telling me this man bought you a bed and still hasn't screwed you in it?"

"Abby!"

"I'm just saying," she says as we push through the studio doors, "this man is one pillow talk away from domestic bliss, and you're still calling this fake?"

I roll my eyes, but the little flutter in my stomach doesn't lie. Because the bed? The text? The scavenger hunt yesterday? None of it feels fake.

Abby's eyes go wide. "Oh, I see that look. You're in trouble."

"I am not," I insist, adjusting my mat under my arm as we walk inside. "It's fake, remember?"

She gives me a knowing look. "You keep saying that, but the way you're blushing right now? Fake isn't the word I'd use."

I don't respond because what am I supposed to say? That every time Hunter texts me, it feels less fake and more like the start of something I can't afford to want?

We check in at the front desk, and as we walk toward the back corner of the studio, Abby lowers her voice.

"Look, I'm not saying you're in love with him—"

"Good. Because I'm definitely not," I interrupt.

She ignores me. "I'm just saying...maybe you should figure out what's real and what's not before you wake up one morning and it's too late."

The instructor dims the lights and the class begins, but her words stick like a pebble in my shoe.

Because the truth is, I'm starting to lose track of what's fake and what's not too.

We take our spots at the back of the class because we don't come enough and we're sure to make asses out of ourselves... plus we're loud, and we get glares from the serious yogis upfront if we get too close.

It's fine. I like our corner in the back anyway.

"Did I tell you about Sproutacus?" I ask.

"Who the hell is Sproutacus?" she asks, her nose scrunched up.

She's not a fan of the name, and I wasn't either. But it's

growing on me. No pun intended.

I pull up my phone and show her a picture of Sprouty on the windowsill. His cute little Chia Pet face. I'm sure he'll look cuter once he's filled in.

"He got you a Chia Pet? Are you joking?"

"He said we're plant parents now."

Abby narrows her eyes at me and then turns back to the picture.

"What does that sticky note say on the faucet? Heating pad and pad thai? What the hell are you two doing over there?"

Oh, yeah, I forgot about that. "He hid my mug that you got me for hitting twenty-five thousand subscribers and set up sticky notes for a scavenger hunt." I smile and then glance back up at her.

"You are as blind as a bat when it comes to what this boy is doing to you," she says as our instructor walks in.

"He's not doing anything," I lie, mirroring Abby as we both kneel on the mats and wait for instructions.

"He's love bombing you. But not with malicious intent to pull the rug out from under you. I don't think he realizes what he's doing either. This kid is crazy about you. He just doesn't know it"—she lets out a dramatic sigh—"typical man."

"You're wrong. He's not looking for anything. And definitely not with me."

"I wish I would've recorded you saying that. Then I could have replayed it five years from now when you're pregnant with triplets, living in your giant custom house with your ridiculously gorgeous hockey husband, surrounded by king-size beds, Chia Pets, and shiny little hockey trophies."

I glare over at her. "You're delusional."

She just grins, utterly unfazed. "You'll thank me later."

I open my mouth to argue—but the yoga instructor calls for us to get settled, saving me from whatever nonsense Abby had locked and loaded next.

When we finish class, I'm drenched in sweat, my body deliciously sore in that satisfying post-yoga way that tricks you into thinking you've just solved all your life's problems by holding warrior pose for two minutes.

I always tell myself I'll start coming more.

Spoiler alert: I never do.

I wipe my forehead with a towel and glance over at her, still breathless.

Those forty-five minutes were the first time in weeks I wasn't sweating over the network deal—I was too busy trying not to die.

"Okay, you were right. I needed that."

She nods, still catching her own breath. "Told you."

As we're rolling up our mats, my phone buzzes in the pocket of my jacket. I pull it out to see a text from Cammy.

> **Cammy: Are you coming to Penelope's tonight? Girls-only game watch party. Drinks and snacks included.**

A second text comes through almost immediately after.

> **Cammy: Pen says you have to come. You're one of us. Which means you're not allowed to miss it.**

I can't deny that I'd like to go, and since all of the girls already know that Hunter and I aren't really together, it's not like I have to lie to everyone. I'm also really curious about where Cammy and JP have been the last few days since both of them were absent for the Open Skate event.

Abby peeks over my shoulder. "What's that?"

I show her the texts, and she grins. "Oh, you're so going."

I chew on my bottom lip, hesitating. "Do you think I should?"

"Peyton," she says, slinging her yoga mat over her shoulder. "This could be great for the podcast. Ask people questions about Hunter. Get the inside track on some things that might help you understand him better. The girls have all the tea and you know it."

She's right. And part of me wants to go—wants to sit in a room full of women who understand what this world is like, even if I'm only faking my way through it.

I text Cammy back.

> Me: Wouldn't miss it. See you tonight.

By the time I pull up to Penelope's house, it's dark out, but the place is already buzzing. Cars line the curb, porch lights glowing on a beautiful home in a gated community where I've heard many of the retired Hawkeyes players live. When I step up to the front door, I can hear the sound of laughter filtering through the windows.

Cammy opens the door before I even knock. "There she is! Seattle's newest WAG."

I roll my eyes but can't help the smile tugging at my lips. "Don't start."

"Oh, it's too late. You've officially been inducted," she teases, stepping aside so I can come in.

The living room is already filling up with familiar faces. Penelope's seated on the massive sectional, a glass of wine in her hand, while Kendall and Isla are huddled over a charcuterie board, laughing about something. I even spot a few of the other players' wives and girlfriends, some of whom I recognize from press photos.

When Penelope sees me, she waves me over. "Peyton! We were wondering if you'd show."

I glance at Cammy. "Like I could've said no."

Penelope grins and reaches for another wine glass. "Good.

Because tonight is basically a rite of passage. No better way to learn how this crazy club works than by watching the game surrounded by the women who survive it."

Cammy nudges me. "Come sit. The game is about to start and everyone's taking bets."

As I settle onto the couch, wine glass in hand, bets between girls start flying about who ends up racking up the most time in the sin bin. Penelope's big-screen TV flickers to life, showing the Hawkeyes warming up on the ice. Hunter's name flashes across the screen as the commentators talk about his defensive game.

And just like that, my stomach flips.

I'm not sure how I ended up here, in a room full of girlfriends and wives who actually belong in this world.

And I definitely don't know how to convince myself that this isn't starting to feel real.

The first period is crazy—the game is stacked, no one scores before the break, and Wolf has already been sent to the penalty box with twice as much time as any other player—not a surprise there.

Penelope hits mute as the commercials come, the girls all getting up for refills and snacks. Then Penelope turns to me.

"So," she starts, voice sly, "how's fake dating Hunter going?"

I can feel all the girls turn to face us from wherever they are in the room.

I clear my throat, playing it casual. "It's going well. Just your run-of-the-mill fake relationship."

Cammy snorts. "Oh, please. The way he looks at you? That man is not pretending."

Kendall leans forward, smirking. "Did you see the way he shut down those interview questions last night? He basically said, *I'm taken*, and dared anyone to argue."

Penelope lifts her wine glass. "It's the first time I've seen him act like that about a woman, honestly."

I shake my head, trying to fight off the flush creeping up my neck. "It's just PR. We both know the deal."

Cammy nudges my knee with hers. "Uh-huh. Keep telling yourself that."

Before I can argue, the commercial break ends, and everyone heads back to the couch. Penelope unmutes the TV and then everyone's eyes are back on the game. The Hawkeyes score, and the room erupts in cheers.

The conversation shifts, but the weight of their knowing looks lingers. Because if I'm honest with myself—really honest—every little thing Hunter's been doing lately doesn't feel like just PR.

And I'm not sure what to do with that.

After the game, we're all lingering in Penelope's kitchen, finishing off dessert and the last of the wine. The energy is lighter now—the Hawkeyes won, and the girls are relaxed, chatting easily like they've known each other forever.

I lean against the counter next to Cammy while she scrolls through her phone, grinning at something.

She catches me looking and nudges me with her elbow. "By the way, JP and I are officially dating."

I blink at her, surprised. "Really?"

She nods, cheeks flushing a little. "Yeah. We've been seeing each other quietly for a while, but we decided to stop hiding it."

"That's amazing, Cam. I'm really happy for you."

"Thanks." She shoots me a look. "And not that I'm meddling, but...you and Hunter. Don't rule it out."

"We're too different. I don't do casual, and he doesn't want a serious relationship. Even if both of us were interested. We don't want the same things."

Cammy gives me a knowing smile. "Sometimes the best things start out that way."

Before I can reply, my phone buzzes in my pocket. I pull it out to find a new text from Hunter.

Hunter: Miss me yet?

My heart does an entirely stupid flip in my chest.

Me: You're ridiculous.

Hunter: You didn't answer the question.

I type back quickly before anyone can notice my smile.

Me: Maybe.

By the time I finally slip away from Penelope's house, it's almost midnight. I slide into the driver's seat of my SUV, the quiet of the night wrapping around me like a blanket after the lively chaos of the watch party.

My phone buzzes again just as I'm pulling out of Penelope's driveway.

Hunter: We're headed for the airport now. My flight won't get in until late. I'll try not to wake you up when I get in.

I roll my eyes but bite back a smile.

Me: Okay, sounds good. I'm about to leave Penelope's house soon. I'll keep the porch light on.

Hunter: You're at Penelope's? How did that go?

I wonder if I should tell him what title they gave me, but if it weirds him out, I suppose I should know now before it goes too far.

> Me: Good. They told me that I'm an official WAG, but I'm sure they're just trying to make me feel included. It was nice to watch with everyone.

> Hunter: I'm glad you have them to hang out with when I'm out on away games.

> Me: Me too. It was fun. Have a safe flight. The new bed is waiting for you.

> Hunter: Good. Because I'm counting down until I'm back in your bed.

The breath leaves my lungs in a whoosh, heat crawling up my neck.

I lock my phone and focus on the road, refusing to let the tiny thrill that his words give me take root.

This isn't real.

It's not.

And no title from the wives and girlfriends of the players can change that.

I pull into my driveway, the street quiet and the houses dark except for a few porch lights left on. I kill the engine, slumping back in my seat for a second longer than I need to.

My phone's still in my hand, thumb hovering.

I scroll back up to that photo—Hunter, shirtless in the locker room, grin pure mischief, hockey pants low on his hips, looking like sin and sweat and a very bad idea. I should delete it. For my sanity. But I don't.

Instead, I shake my head and climb out of the car.

The house is dark when I step inside. I lock the door behind me, hang up my jacket, and tiptoe over to the windowsill. "Night, Sprouty," I whisper, checking on our plant baby like a lunatic. His little green leaves are perky. Thriving. Must be nice.

I head straight for my bathroom, still sore from yoga. My muscles are tight, achy in that post-stretch kind of way that screams for a bath. So, I run one—hot and steaming, with bubbles piled high and my lavender soak dumped in with zero restraint.

By the time I step out, my skin's flushed and soft, and my brain is just gooey enough to feel like maybe everything in my life is just a little less of a disaster.

I wrap myself in a plush towel and pad into the bedroom. The new mattress Hunter bought cradles me as I sit on the edge of the bed, the sheets cool beneath me.

My phone buzzes on the nightstand, and I reach for it, heart fluttering as Hunter's name lights up the screen.

> **Hunter: Our flight is about to take off. Sweet dreams, Collins. Tell your pillow wall I said hi.**

A laugh escapes me, and I quickly type back.

> **Me: Pillow wall says you're on thin ice.**

I glance at the pillow barrier beside me, a makeshift divide that's become more symbolic than functional. In a matter of hours, Hunter will be back on the other side of that bed. I just hope this pillow wall is a little stronger than the last.

His reply comes almost immediately.

> **Hunter: Good thing I play well on frozen surfaces.**

I scroll back up to the photo—the shirtless locker room selfie, his smirk as cocky as ever. I should delete it, erase the temptation, but instead, I find myself staring, heat pooling low in my belly.

The ache is familiar now, a constant companion since Hunter moved in. I haven't used my vibrator in over a week, not since the tension between us started simmering just beneath the surface. Tonight, it's unbearable.

But before I can make up my mind, sleep creeps in like a thief.

And the next time I blink, the world is soft and dim and far away—and I'm still in my towel.

And still, very much, alone.

CHAPTER FIFTEEN
Peyton

Warmth. That's the first thing I register.

Then, the steady thump beneath my ear—a heartbeat.

My lashes flutter open, and confusion strikes. Where am I?

More pressingly, where are my clothes?

The comforter is cool against my bare skin. The towel... Oh no. I went to bed wrapped in it after a hot bath. I must have lost it during the night.

I blink slowly, my gaze traveling upward, pausing at the sight of a smooth, bare chest. Golden skin marked with a familiar tattoo—a memory from a photo he sent last week.

Hunter.

Oh God.

I'm on top of him. Not beside him. Not curled up on the edge of my own mattress like a civilized human. I'm straddling him.

One thigh slung over his. My body pressed half on top of him at his side. My breasts smashed against his rib cage. My hand spread across his tattooed pectoral like I'm staking some kind of claim.

The pillow wall is a managed mess. No longer straight and sturdy how I constructed it before I fell asleep.

And I'm naked. Every inch of me.

What the actual hell?

My brain spins. How did I get here? The last thing I remember is climbing into bed wrapped in my towel after a hot bath and too many late-night thoughts about a certain hockey player's abs and him naked in the Hawkeyes' locker room.

Did I move in my sleep? Did I crawl over the wall and drape myself over him like a human weighted blanket?

I steal a glance down.

He's still in his boxer briefs. His body is loose and warm beneath mine, his chest rising and falling in a steady rhythm. One arm is tucked behind his head, the other draped at his side, nowhere near touching me. He didn't pull me over here. He didn't initiate any of this.

I did.

Mortification washes over me.

Worse—my thighs tighten at the memory of the dream I was having. The one where I was backed up against a locker room wall, no clothes between us, his mouth trailing down my body, his hands pinning mine high above my head.

And now... Now I'm pressed against his thigh. My core is still humming from the ghost of that dream.

Jesus. Did I...grind on him in my sleep?

Did he wake up at any point and feel me? Hear me?

My heart pounds harder. I'm going to die. That's it. Actual death by embarrassment. There will be no funeral. Just a closed casket and hushed whispers, like: *She rode him unconscious and never recovered.*

I try to shift off of him, slowly, carefully. But the second I move, he stirs beneath me, his muscles tightening. His breath catches.

And that's when I realize—I'm not the only one affected.

I freeze.

His chest shifts under mine. A low groan escapes him, like he's been yanked out of the best dream of his life—or, more likely, jolted into the worst reality.

I lift my head just enough to meet his bleary gaze.

He looks at me and grins.

"Good morning," he says, voice gravel-thick and teasing. "You're on top of me. Did you miss me?"

Oh God.

"Um...good morning," I mumble, my voice raspy, my body still firmly pressed to his. If I push away right now, he'll see everything. "Did I..."

"Break over the pillow wall again to cuddle?" He cocks a brow. "Yes."

I bite my lip, bracing myself. "I'm sorry—"

"Don't." His grin turns wicked. "For God's sake, don't apologize. I'm a man, Peyton, and you're fucking gorgeous. You have an open invitation to come lay naked on top of me anytime you want. I'm also your fake boyfriend, which means I'm contractually obligated to let you use me like a body pillow."

I roll my eyes. "Hunter, this isn't a joke. We set boundaries—remember those?"

"From the looks of it, I'm not the one who forgot. Which has me confused," he says, his tone playful. "Because you've been rubbing your tits and your wet pussy all over me for the past four hours since I got home."

My mouth goes dry.

"Four hours? Since you got home?" My stomach drops—and then tightens with heat. "You were awake the entire time?"

"I tried to sleep," he says, "but you didn't make it easy."

Oh God.

"How long were you in bed before I climbed over the pillows?"

"It was less than fifteen minutes before you busted through the pillow wall like the Kool-Aid Man."

I cover my face with one hand, the other still trapped between us. "Did I...say anything in my sleep?"

"No words," he murmurs, his voice dropping an octave, "but the sounds... Damn, Collins. Hottest thing I've ever heard."

I peek out from between my fingers. "What kind of sounds?"

"Like my thigh was giving you the best orgasm of your life."

I bury my face against his chest, and he chuckles.

"I can't believe I did that. Why didn't you wake me up and stop me? I practically forced myself on you," I say, finally glancing up to meet his eyes.

"I don't know. I didn't know what to do, but you seemed content lying on top of me. I didn't want to stop you. And trust me, you couldn't force yourself on me even if you wanted to. I'm twice your size. But from my end, it was all consensual, if that makes you feel any better," he teases.

I glance up and notice that one hand is still tucked behind his head and the other at his arm. "You're not touching me."

"I'm not," he confirms. "I wouldn't—not without permission. You should know that I'd never cross the line you already set between us. Not unless you tell me I can."

I do. That's the worst part. I trust him, and yet can he say the same about me?

If the roles were reversed this situation would look a lot different.

His eyes flicker darker. He sucks in his bottom lip like he's trying to behave. "What were you dreaming about?"

"I don't remember," I lie.

He chuckles, low and knowing. "You're a terrible liar."

"Liar or not, I'm not telling you."

"It was about me." He says it like he already knows, and when I don't answer, his gaze darkens. "Was it me in the dream?"

I look away. He lifts my chin with two fingers.

"Where were we?"

I swallow. "Locker room. I blame that picture you sent."

He licks his lips, his eyes darting to mine. "And what were we doing?"

"You had me naked, pressed against the locker room wall. My

hands pinned over my head."

His breath catches, and he mumbles out something akin to "fuck."

"Warning, Peyton," he says softly, and before I can protest, his mouth is on mine.

The kiss is soft at first—sweet, tentative. Then it deepens. His hand tangles in my hair. My fingers clutch his shoulders. His hips press up, and suddenly I'm not thinking anymore.

I'm feeling. I'm aching, desperately pulling him closer.

Then he moves.

An arm wraps behind me. One smooth shift and he's on top of me, nudging my legs apart with the heavy weight of his thigh. His cock presses between us, thick and hard beneath the thin cotton of his briefs. My breath hitches.

"I can make it better than the dream," he says, lips brushing against my throat. "How bad are you aching for release, Peyton?"

"We have rules," I say, but my objection is too weak for either of us to take seriously.

His mouth pulls back, and his green eyes find mine. Dilated and hungry for this as much as I am.

"You never said I can't make you come with my fingers. Tell me yes and I'll take care of you," he says. "It's painful how bad you need this, isn't it?"

I nod, and then his mouth crashes back against mine, his right hand gently caressing down the side of my body.

His phone buzzes, but we both know that if he stops now and this moment is broken, this won't happen again.

He ignores his phone, dips his hand between my legs, and I cry out when his thumb brushes over my clit.

And then—his phone rings again.

We both freeze.

"Maybe you should see who that is?" I say.

He growls in annoyance at the interruption, forehead dropping to mine. "And stop where this is going? Even if it were Everett Kauffman himself offering to triple my contract salary to take his call right now, it wouldn't be worth giving this up."

I laugh, breathless. The thought that Hunter wants to touch me this bad has me enjoying every moment of this.

"You should check. Just in case."

He sighs, pulling away just enough to reach the phone on the nightstand. His jaw clenches.

"It's my agent. His text says 911."

I blink. I know he's worried about what kind of deal Bethany might be conjuring up with Everett Kauffman. "Take it."

He hesitates. "You'll still be here when I get back?"

No, of course not. We both know this is a bad idea, but I couldn't tell him that or he won't take the call.

I want him. I want his lips all over me and his fingers inside me, and I know that's the last thing this complicated situation needs. Worst of all, my inability to stay on my side of the bed put us in this position.

"I don't know," I lie, though the destructive part of me wants a Hunter Reed-produced orgasm.

His eyes search mine, but I can tell he doesn't completely believe me. "Just give me five minutes. Stay."

I don't say anything, but I can see that he's feeling anxious to not miss his second call.

He climbs off me slowly, his body pulling away like we're still magnetized together. Like it's taking every bit of his effort to pull apart from me.

The moment he steps out of bed, he gazes down at my bare body, the comforter pushed off from when he got up. "Fuck, you're beautiful."

I suck in my lower lip, trying not to squirm at him taking me in.

Then he slides his thumb across the screen to accept the call. And starts for the bedroom door. "Hey, Dale...yeah, I was in the middle of something. What's up, can you make it fast?"

I watch carefully, eyeing how far it is from the bed to my nightstand with my vibrator in it. I need release so bad it almost hurts. Next, I eyeball the distance of the bathroom.

If I can get to my vibrator and then to the bathroom, I might be able to get this done before he even knows I'm gone. It wouldn't take long. I'm already on the edge from the wet dream and rubbing against Hunter for hours, and then him flipping me onto my back and rubbing himself between my thighs, his fingers playing with my clit. I'm on a hairpin trigger at this point.

Quickly, I jump to the other side of the bed and open the drawer.

"She's offering all of those players for me? No, I know it's not a done deal but... Have you talked to Kauffman yet?" I hear him ask his agent.

I'm running out of time, and I have to run past him to get to the bathroom door.

I spin around, my pink vibrator in my hand and head straight for the bathroom, almost home free while he stays distracted.

"Not yet? Okay, but you'll tell me if the Hawkeyes seem like they are entertaining the deal? Right, okay, thanks for calling," he tells him.

He ends the call just as I'm about to pass him and then he spins around, hearing me coming.

"Where do you think you're going with that?" he asks.

Just before I get past him, he scoops an arm around my ribs and hauls me up his body, pulling me to the end of the bed, seating me on his lap, facing the full-length mirror against the wall.

He uses his thighs to nudge mine apart, spreading me open in front of the mirror.

The reflection shows everything—my flushed skin, my parted lips, the way I'm sitting on top of him, completely bare, my thighs spread wide over the thick outline of his boxer-covered cock. My nipples are tight, my breathing shallow, and my pussy lips gleam under the low light like I've already surrendered.

And I have.

God, I have.

Hunter's arms wrap around me from behind, holding me

steady, his chest solid against my back. I can feel every controlled breath he takes, every twitch of restraint beneath me.

"You see that?" he murmurs, voice thick. "That's what I see every time I close my eyes. You—wet, open, wrapped around me, begging for more, but I never thought you'd let me get this close."

His words burn with honesty. There's nowhere to hide. Not from the way I shift on his lap. Not from the slick shine between my thighs. Not from him—not from myself.

His gaze rakes over every inch of me, dark and possessive. "Look at you, Peyton. Dripping for me because you know I'm right here—my attention focused on only you—wanting you. Ready to fuck you with my fingers while you watch me do it."

He leans in, his voice a growl at my ear. "Your body should be worshipped...by me."

My breath catches.

My fingers curl tighter around the vibrator.

"Were you planning to run from me and use this instead?" he asks, prying it gently from my grip.

I swallow hard. "You were busy, and I didn't want to—"

He cuts me off, voice low and razor sharp.

"And you were going to rob me of hearing you come with my fingers buried inside you? When I starred in your dirty little dreams? That doesn't seem fair."

My skin heats. I can't look away from the mirror, from the way he's behind me now—partially clothed, fully in control—while I'm trembling and bare.

"This will make everything between us messy," I whisper. I don't even know what I mean anymore. The vibrator? The situation? Me?

His smirk is slow and dangerous as his fingers trail down my inner thigh. "Oh, baby, your wet pussy is already making everything between us messy, and I want it that way."

He meets my eyes in the mirror. "But the real question is—do you want to do this alone? Or with me?" His fingers hover. Barely there. Teasing.

My breath stutters. My thoughts are static.

I should say no.

I should walk away.

But I don't. Because my body already made the choice.

I turn my head slightly, voice a whisper of confession. "With you."

A smile stretches across his face. "Then the next question. Do you want me to use this?" he asks with the vibrator in his hand. "Or do you want my fingers? The choice is yours. I don't care either way...as long as I'm the one making you come in my lap."

"Your fingers."

Hunter grins, happy with my answer. "Good choice," he says, and then tosses the vibrator back on the bed. "Now lay back, relax...and watch."

I do as he instructs, leaning back fully into him, my head falling back against his shoulder.

One hand glides up my stomach, cupping my breast, while the other traces the curve of my hip. His fingers slip between my thighs—slow, teasing, in complete control. My breath catches when a knuckle grazes my clit, the touch so light it steals the air from my lungs.

"Keep your eyes open, Collins," he murmurs against my ear, his voice molten and low. "Watch what I do to you."

I do. God help me, I do.

The mirror reflects everything—my flushed skin, my pebbling nipples, my parted lips, the way my body arches into his hands like it's not even mine anymore. Like it's his.

His palm spreads across my lower stomach, grounding me, while his fingers start to move with more purpose. Each stroke is patient but filthy, circling and sliding, never giving quite enough but driving me wild all the same.

"Hunter..." My voice is barely a whisper, thick with need.

He presses a kiss to the side of my neck, his lips dragging heat down to my collarbone.

"You feel how close you already are?" he asks, his thumb

flicking gently across the bundle of nerves that's now throbbing. "This is what you wanted, right? You were going to slip away to finish on your own?"

My head drops back onto his shoulder, a whimper escaping me. "Yes."

"Say it. Say why you tried to run."

"Because I want you." The words fall from me in a breathless rush. "I wanted this."

"Damn right, you do," he growls, his hand quickening.

The mirror blurs through my lashes, moisture beading at the corners of my eyes. My hips start to move, rolling against his hand, chasing the edge he's pulling me toward with infuriating control.

"That's it," he whispers, voice low and reverent like he's watching something sacred. "You're so fucking beautiful like this. Open and wild for me."

I grind harder, my body rocking against the hard length of him. He groans, his mouth brushing my ear before pressing a kiss just below it.

"Look at how you melt for me," he murmurs, his voice a warm scrape against my skin. "You're soaking my fingers, Peyton. Dripping all over my lap."

A strangled moan escapes me. My hand reaches up, curling around the back of his neck, nails digging into his skin like I need him to keep me grounded, tethered to this moment.

"Don't stop—Hunter, please—don't stop..."

"Never," he promises, his voice dark silk. "I want to watch you fall apart for me, and you're going to watch it too."

And I do.

With one final stroke, he presses deep, curling his fingers inside me just as his thumb presses hard and fast against my clit. The orgasm rips through me, white-hot and staggering, my body jerking in his lap as my head tips forward, a cry strangled in my throat, his name slipping off my lips.

He cradles me there, breathing just as ragged as mine, as if watching me fall apart stole every ounce of his control.

He holds me, his mouth on my shoulder, whispering things I can't even process.

When I finally collapse back against him, trembling and gasping, I catch sight of myself in the mirror—flushed, wrecked, utterly undone—and his gaze locked on me like he's never seen anything more beautiful.

"That was..." I start, trying to catch my breath.

Hunter leans in, his nose nuzzling behind my ear. "That was...better than a dream, wasn't it?"

I can't even answer. My brain is mush, my limbs liquid.

But deep down, I know the truth.

This is more than just chemistry. More than just need.

And I hope this didn't just ruin everything.

Because once you let someone this close—this intimately close—how do you pretend it didn't happen?

"I can't believe we did that."

His arms tighten slightly. "I can't believe it took us this long."

I laugh, breathless. It's the only sound I can make without crumbling all over again.

But then, just like that, the room shifts.

Reality creeps back in.

He shifts me, until he has me in a cradle hold and carries me to my side of the bed, setting me down, and then pulls the covers over me.

"This doesn't change anything, right?" I ask, voice quiet.

He nods, brushing a damp strand of hair off my cheek, then bends down to kiss the top of my head. "Not a thing," he mutters against my hair.

But we both know that's a lie.

I stare at his still-hard cock, straining against his boxers, drenched from me. "What about you?"

I've never been one to leave a man hanging that I was intimate with. I can only imagine that he's hard enough that it's painful.

"Don't worry about me. That's not what we agreed to. I'm going to use the guest bathroom and take a quick shower before I hit the stadium. I'll take care of it," he says, grabbing his phone off the bed and then turning to walk out of the bedroom. "I'll see you later, right?"

"Yeah," I nod. "I'll see you later."

He walks out, shutting the door behind him.

I sit there, almost in disbelief at what just happened. And then I find myself holding my breath when I hear the hallway bathroom door close and then the shower turn on.

Can't blame a girl for wishing to be a fly on that wall.

CHAPTER SIXTEEN

Hunter

It's been four days since Peyton came apart in my arms.

Four days since I felt her tremble and fall against me, her breathy moans filling my ears and replaying in my head on a loop I can't shut off.

And for four nights in a row, we've managed to miss each other.

I come home late from practice or a game, and she's already in bed, curled on her side like she's guarding the damn pillow wall again.

Or she's holed up in her studio, headphones on, lights dimmed, so laser-focused I don't have the heart to interrupt.

Either way, we haven't talked about it. I haven't touched her since.

And it's driving me insane.

I'm the guy who only does casual—who prefers temporary hook-ups that never last more than a week or two, tops.

I shouldn't still be thinking about how much I want a repeat with Peyton. Maybe it's the fact that I can't get laid by anyone else for another six weeks.

Maybe...but I've had dry spells before. I don't sleep with everyone I take out to dinner or drinks, and though it may come as a shock to the media, and probably even Peyton, I haven't slept with every woman I've been photographed with either.

Two months without sex isn't the kind of hiatus to put me in a mental or physical tailspin. I've had plenty of spans that lasted that long, or longer. So this? Peyton getting under my skin like this after only touching her once...it's something I seem to have no control over.

Still, I know that Peyton deserves more than I'm willing to give her. She wants the white picket fence. The dad who takes his daughter across the county to tennis tournaments, the mom who takes care of the entire family and gives great big hugs to absolute strangers who crash Thanksgiving dinner since they're fake dating her daughter.

She wants the syndication deal and the story about Bethany that I can't bring myself to give her. It's not a part of my life that I want to relive. Unfortunately, that puts us at odds, since it's the story she needs to put her in line with winning the network spot.

I grip the steering wheel a little tighter, the cool leather squeaking beneath my fingers as I turn into Jesse's school's visitor parking lot near the entrance of the red-brick building. Kids run wild on the playground, their laughter a blur through my open window.

It's been two weeks since we agreed to fake-date. Two weeks since I moved into Peyton's townhouse to avoid Bethany. And I thought I'd be able to keep a handle on this whole thing. Keep it fake. Keep it safe.

But my cock has been hard since the moment she collapsed against me, gasping my name. I've gotten off in the shower every morning since—eyes closed, one hand braced against the tile, the other replaying that moment with her in my lap, trembling, whispering my name when she came. Feeling her body squeeze my fingers.

I park, kill the engine, and glance at the school entrance where I'm supposed to meet Peyton. I exhale a slow breath and drag a hand through my hair.

Time to get it together.

The second I spot Peyton popping her head out the front door of the school looking for me and waving me over, a relieved smile on her face—I grin from ear to ear.

I head for her with a little bounce in my step. She opens the door wider for me as I walk up. Her face lights up—that full, open smile I swear could stop traffic.

"You're here," she says. "Thank you for coming."

"I said I would." I grin as I pass through the door. "Morning skate went longer than I expected, but I wasn't going to bail on Jesse's big day."

Shari stands next to her. "Yes, thank you. Jesse hasn't stopped telling people that you're coming to Career Day. He said that his classmates don't believe Hunter Reed is coming to speak today. He's going to be so excited that you're here."

I follow Shari and Peyton as they lead me down the hall. The smell of cleaning supplies and library books fill the air. The nostalgic smell of an elementary school I suppose. Mine smelled exactly the same.

As soon as we round the corner, I see a small crowd of what I assume to be parents, standing outside of the classroom, here to discuss their job with the class.

A few murmurs break out as the parents see us coming. I hear some whispered remarks. "Is that Hunter Reed?" But I stay on target.

I barely get to the door of the classroom before Jesse's eyes lock on mine.

"You're really here." I think I hear him say over someone else speaking to the class.

He's sitting in the second row when he jumps up, grabs his cane, and heads for me. No wheelchair in sight. His first couple of steps seem like an effort but then he's moving well.

Shari pipes up behind me as all three of us watch him head our way. "He said that since you were coming he didn't want his wheelchair today. He wanted to show you how strong he's been getting with his physical therapy."

She finishes her explanation just as Jesse nears the door.

Jesse's practically vibrating. "You're going to talk to my class today! That's so cool! I knew you'd come."

"You bet I am," I say, ruffling his hair. "And you look ready to lead the charge."

Peyton's watching me again, something unreadable flickering in her eyes. Pride. Gratitude. Maybe something more, and for some reason, it's the first time in a while that I really want to be that for someone. At least for today.

And just like that, all that pent-up tension from the last few days? It softens a little. Not gone, but...manageable.

The parent who was just in the classroom steps out and finishes with their Q&A from the class.

His teacher steps out quickly. "Mr. Reed. I'm Mr. Laurence, Jesse's teacher. How great you could join us. Jesse has been talking about you all week."

He's a guy in decent shape, probably a decade older than me with glasses and his school lanyard over his neck.

"I'm glad I could be here. We could always use more kids interested in the sport," I tell him, which is true.

Someone has to fill our skates after we retire. There always has to be someone to take on the sport.

"Great, well the floor is yours when Jesse is ready to introduce you," he says, smiling down at Jesse and then heads back into the classroom.

"Ready to introduce me, champ?" I ask Jesse.

He nods enthusiastically and grabs my hand like we've done this a hundred times. "Come on! Everyone's going to want to meet you."

Peyton trails just behind us with Shari. They move inside, finding a place against the wall to listen but to stay out of the way.

I glance over just to catch her watching me. I'm used to having eyes on me since I play a sport that has millions of fans around the world and televised games. But her attention on me hits differently than it ever has with anyone else. I realize that I want her eyes on me all the time.

She always looks at Jesse like he hung the moon. But the way she looks at me now?

It's different. Soft. Open. Like I won't fuck up. But I might. Not for career day, that's in the bag, but making sure that I don't hurt her when this whole thing is over. That I can't promise, though I wish I could.

The second we step into Jesse's classroom, all hell breaks loose.

"This is Hunter Reed," Jesse announces like he's bringing a celebrity into a press conference. "He's my friend—and he plays for the Hawkeyes!"

The room explodes. Not literally. But close.

Kids cheer. One kid drops a pencil case. Someone gasps so loudly you'd think I just announced I was giving away free puppies.

"Hi, everyone," I say, lifting a hand, trying not to laugh. "Thanks for having me."

I keep it light. I talk about teamwork. About getting benched. About coming back from an injury. About the away games, and camaraderie with the players. About seeing the world and doing what I love. I leave out the drama with Bethany and the staged kiss that made the sports blogs combust.

Instead, I tell them about the time I wore two left skates to practice and fell on my ass. The kids lose it.

Jesse's laugh cuts through it all—loud, unfiltered joy. And damn if it doesn't settle something in my chest.

When I wrap up, the teacher opens the floor for questions. That's when chaos really erupts.

"Do you fight a lot?"

"Are you rich?"

"Do you have a tiger like that one guy on the clock app?"

"Will you sign my forehead?"

I'm signing T-shirts, notebooks, even a baseball cap someone swears belongs to their older brother. The whole time, Jesse stands to the side like he's the one who brought in the rock star. Which I guess, technically, he did.

Then someone—a kid with glasses and big energy—pipes up from the back.

"Is it true you're dating Jesse's aunt?"

The room goes silent. Every kid whips their head to look at Peyton, and even the parents outside in the hallway.

I glance over.

She's standing near the door, one brow lifted, like she's waiting to see how I'll answer. Maybe hoping I'll stick to the script.

But I don't.

I smile, easy and sure. "Yeah," I say. "I am."

The kids scream. Jesse turns to Peyton. "I told you he'd say yes!"

Peyton's cheeks flush pink, but she doesn't look away. She just shakes her head, biting back a smile.

She doesn't look mad. She doesn't look freaked.

She looks...proud.

And suddenly, pretending feels a lot harder than it used to.

The classroom slowly empties of parents as the kids have to head to lunch next. Some thank me on their way out. A few try to snap a selfie. One asks if I do birthday parties.

Peyton slips out of the room before I can catch her, her hand lightly brushing Jesse's shoulder as she goes. "I have to take this call with the network," she tells him, her phone ringing. "I'll see you later though. Okay? Love you."

Jesse nods and then walks over to me, his face still flushed with excitement. "That was so cool. You're like...famous."

I chuckle, crouching down to his level. "Don't let it get out. I like being your secret weapon."

"Can you come over soon? I want to show you how I've been improving on my slap shot that we worked on over Thanksgiving.

I think I'm getting pretty good. I could use some more tips."

"Definitely," I tell him. "But how about I do one better and you come out to the stadium to hit some pucks on the ice. You have to clear it with your mom and your grandma. Do you think you're up for that?" I ask and then glance at Shari to make sure I didn't overstep.

She nods that I'm on the right track.

"That would be so cool," he says.

"Okay, we have to go so you can head to lunch. I'll be here to pick you up. Your mom picked up a late-night shift. I'll get Hunter's number and then we can coordinate next week as long as your physical therapist is okay with it," she says.

He seems disappointed as if he thinks he won't get cleared, but then everyone in his class lines up for lunch and a few of the boys in his class call him over.

Shari gives me a soft smile as we exit the classroom and start down the hallway toward the exit. "You were wonderful in there. Thank you for doing this for him."

"It was my pleasure. He's a good kid," I say. "A great one."

We push through the exit to find Peyton standing by her car, still on the phone.

Shari's eyes twinkle at me when she catches me staring—like she's holding back about six follow-up comments. But she doesn't push. Just pats my arm and then heads for her car. "I'll be in touch," she calls over her shoulder.

And then it's just Peyton.

She ends the call and heads for me.

"You were amazing in there. They loved you. And you made Jesse's life by showing up here today. I am going to be his favorite aunt forever, so thanks for that."

"Think I've got a future in second-grade public speaking?"

She laughs, and it's soft and real, tugging something loose in my chest.

"I have a feeling that you could do anything you wanted to do if you put your mind to it," she says, her voice gentler now.

I stop walking. Just for a second. "Thanks for saying that."

She stops too. "You're welcome. And I mean it. You're a very capable person from what I can tell from the time we've known each other."

I step closer. Not too close. But close enough to see the truth flicker in her eyes.

Temptation builds, wanting to ask her what she sees in me. If there's something I'm missing that could make something like her and me work.

She stares back up at me. So close that I could bend down and kiss her if I thought she'd accept it.

I take a breath, then step back, giving her space.

"I'll see you at home," I say, voice quieter now.

She nods once. "Drive safe."

And just like that, the moment passes. She climbs into the car, and I stand there for a beat longer, watching the taillights until they disappear.

Trouble.

That's what this is.

And I'm already in deep.

CHAPTER SEVENTEEN

Hunter

The studio lights feel hotter this time, but the tension that hung thick in the air during our first interview is gone. As I settle into the chair across from Peyton, I can feel the difference—a sense of ease, a shared understanding that we're both here to do a job.

Peyton flashes me a warm smile as she adjusts her headphones. "Welcome back, Hunter. Thanks for being here again."

"Thanks for having me," I reply, my voice steady. No more defensive walls, no more snapping at her questions. This time, I'm ready.

The questions flow more naturally, her voice steady but warm, like she's not just interviewing me—she's trying to understand me.

She starts off with softballs.

"How do you feel like this season is shaping up?"

"What's the weirdest pre-game tradition you've seen from a teammate in the years you've played?"

I'll give it to her, she did a good job warming me up before she gets into the deeper questions.

"When's the moment you realized hockey wasn't just a sport

for you? That this was something you really wanted to do. That it was the NHL or bust?"

"Honestly, I can't remember when the moment clicked for me. As cliché as it sounds, it feels more like hockey chose me," I tell her, thinking as far back as when my mom started me in a hockey league when I was four. "When I first started in the league as a kid, I was just happy to get out and screw around with some other kids my age. I took to ice skating instantly—turned out I had really good balance, so after a few weeks of practice, the ice wasn't a factor like it was for some kids."

"A little skating protégé..."

I chuckle. "Yeah, something like that. But then, my second year on the team, we got a new coach—Coach Murphy," I tell her. I can still remember the lime green windbreaker he wore to practice every day and the handlebar mustache that I always thought was funny.

"And Coach Murphy turned you into a superstar?" she asks.

"No. In fact, he was just an assistant coach—one of my teammates' dads who volunteered to help out to keep the league open—his coaching technique wasn't anything special, and his understanding of the game was basic, at best."

"So what did he do that was so special to have this kind of impact on you as a five-year-old kid who didn't care all that much for hockey?" she asks.

She shifted in her chair and adjusted her mic in front of her.

"There's this little tradition, I guess you could call it, that happens before practice starts. All the kids on the team would line up on this bench and their dads would lace up their skates," I tell her. "Growing up without a dad, I couldn't help but feel left out. I tried not to let my mom see it. I never wanted her to think she wasn't enough or that I was ungrateful to her, so I'd always ask her to lace me up well before practice so that I wouldn't have to feel that void. And then the first week into the new season, my mom had to use the restroom—or take a call—or something, and I wasn't laced up. Coach Murphy didn't even say a single word when he walked up to me, standing away from the other boys whose dads were lacing them on the bench. He knelt down and laced up my skates for me. It was the first time that I realized not having a dad doesn't make me incomplete. That there was someone else to make me feel included. He must have noticed how much it meant to me because he started lacing up my skates for the entire season."

"And that's what made you want to play hockey for the rest of your life."

"No...not exactly. It made me want to play my heart and soul out on the ice for Coach Murphy. I think I wanted him to notice me...or maybe I wanted him to be proud of me. Whatever it started out as, it turned into me outperforming all my teammates. I was a standout, and a coach from a town over with a better hockey program begged my mom to give him a year with me on his team to see what I was capable of. My mom sacrificed a lot to make sure that I got across town to the other team for several years, and it paid off because I kept excelling. It turned out I was good at hockey, but not because I started out loving the sport."

"It was because of the simple act of kindness that changed your entire trajectory in life," she says. And she's right, though I never thought about it like that before now.

"Yeah, pretty much. It's crazy though. I've never told anyone that story before, until right now."

Peyton smiles over at me, and I smile back.

"Have you seen Coach Murphy since that fateful year of Little League hockey?"

"No," I say, shaking my head, wondering where he is now and if he even knows what he did for me. I bet he doesn't.

"Well, in case he's listening...would you like to say anything to him?" she asks.

Fuck, yeah... There's a lot I'd like to say, but I'll keep it simple.

I lean a little closer toward the desk and stare at the mic in front of me. Suddenly, I'm no longer speaking to her, but hoping that Coach Murphy is a listener of her show, or at least someone who knows him might hear this and tell him what I said.

"I'd just like to say, Coach Murphy...if you're listening...thank you for doing something as seemingly insignificant as tying the skates for a kid you barely knew, on a Wednesday night, in a cold-ass rink in New Jersey. You couldn't have anticipated the impact it left...but you saved my life."

I look up and Peyton's eyes are welling with tears.

She takes a deep inhale and looks away from me, using the sleeve of her oversized sweater to wipe her eyes quickly, like she doesn't want me to see it.

"That was a beautiful story, and my listeners are amazing. I guarantee someone is going to know Coach Murphy, and that message is going to get to him."

There's a softness in her expression that makes me want to keep talking, to show her all the ways that I'm different from who she thinks I am, but there's a mic recording in front of me, and a strong sense of self-preservation holding me back.

It's just her and me in a recording studio. She's recording all of this for her podcast.

"Speaking of people who make an impression on athletes in their earlier years. What kind of advice would you give to young players trying to make it in the NHL?" she asks, her tone genuine.

I pause, considering the question carefully. "Stay dedicated. Don't let setbacks define you. Everyone faces challenges but it's how you push through them that matters." My eyes meet hers, and I hope she can see the sincerity there. "And surround yourself with the right people. That makes all the difference."

Peyton nods, a small smile tugging at the corner of her mouth. "That's great advice. I wish I'd had someone like you to look up to when I was younger."

"Right, you were a young athlete too," I say, though it feels like I'm spinning the hot seat around and putting her in it.

"Yeah," she says, her voice quieter now. "A lot of my listeners already know, but for those of you who don't," she says, addressing the listeners who will hear this after she tweaks and posts it. "I was a competitive tennis player. Had dreams of going pro—

Wimbledon, the whole deal. But then I suffered a career-ending injury and everything changed."

The air shifts, and I feel a pang of understanding. Injury. The crushing weight of shattered dreams. I know that feeling all too well.

"That must have been tough," I murmur, and I can see the flicker of pain in her eyes.

"It was," she admits. "But I found my way back somehow. Podcasting became my new outlet. I get to share stories and connect with athletes. It's not the same, but it's fulfilling."

I nod, a surge of admiration rising in my chest. "I get that. You've got a good thing going here. It's not about the trophies, it's about the passion."

"Exactly," she says, the tension easing from her shoulders. "And I still get to be a part of the sports world, even if it's from a different angle."

"Right. And who knows—maybe you'll be the one to break the next big story." I can't resist a teasing grin. "Or maybe you'll just end up writing about how your roommate is the hottest player in the league."

Peyton rolls her eyes, but I catch the smile she's trying to hide. "Please, the last thing I need is another headline about you and me."

"Why not?" I tease, leaning in. "We'll give them something to talk about."

The tension shifts again, but this time, it feels lighter—almost playful. Peyton shakes her head, a spark of amusement in her eyes.

"Let's focus on you. The listeners want to hear about you."

"I'm an open book. What would you like to know?" I tease, settling back into my chair as we continue the interview.

By the time we wrap up, I feel a sense of satisfaction. She skated around some of the bigger questions she wanted to ask. I have a feeling that in the next interview, she's going to dive deeper. But at least this time I didn't storm out.

Progress.

Half the team's already gathered around our usual table by the time Peyton and I step into Oakley's. The familiar din of laughter, the clinking of pint glasses, and the thrum of classic rock vibrating from the old jukebox settles something in me. Warm lighting glows overhead, and the scent of beer and fried food wraps around us like a worn-in hoodie.

Cammy spots us immediately and makes a beeline, looping her arm through Peyton's. "I'm borrowing her from you," she says with a grin.

The look on my face must give me away, because Cammy smirks and adds, "I'll give her back. Promise."

Reluctantly, I let go of Peyton's hand.

Trey catches sight of me from across the room and raises his beer. "Look who finally decided to show up."

I grin. "Yeah, yeah. Where's the rest of the crew?" I ask, glancing around the bar.

"Easton and Ziegler are at the pool table, Bozeman's in the bathroom, and Dumont's getting a round at the bar," Trey replies. "Mäk's over there trying to convince Kendall to let him cook her some kind of Finnish sautéed reindeer dish or whatever. Let's just hope she doesn't have a soft spot for Rudolph or any of his furry friends."

"Where's Popovich?" I ask, knowing that Luka doesn't usually miss a night out with the team.

"He had a beer and then left with some chick he met at the bar."

I chuckle, not surprised that Luka left with a puck bunny. That's about on-brand for him, and it used to be for me, too, on occasion. Until Peyton showed up at the charity event. The last four weeks have been different.

I scan the room until I spot her again—this time deep in conversation with Cammy and Isla. She looks relaxed, at ease. So different from that first night in this very bar.

Trey nudges me with his elbow. "So...heard anything from your agent? Bethany still trying to trade you like a deck of baseball cards?"

I shake my head. "Not a word. I'm taking that as a good sign. Hopefully, this whole fake relationship thing with Peyton is wearing her down."

I'm mid-conversation when Trey goes quiet. Not silent—just...still. And that's when I feel it too.

A shift in the air.

I turn.

Bethany.

Striding through the front doors like she's walking onto a red carpet—flawless posture, red lips, high-end perfume that hits before she's even within reach.

My stomach knots.

Across the bar, Peyton catches my eye. She's already seen her. Her spine stiffens as she sets her drink down and heads toward me with measured steps, her eyes locked on mine.

Bethany gets to me first. "Hunter. Good—I'm glad you're here. I need to talk to you. Later."

"Anything you want to say, you can say right here. Hart doesn't care," I say, glancing at Trey. "Do you, Hart?"

"Nope," he says, arms crossed over his chest, watching like he's front row at a prize fight.

Bethany lifts her chin. "It's important we discuss this privately—"

She doesn't finish.

Because that's when Peyton arrives.

She steps right into my space without hesitation, the curve of her hip brushing against my leg as she turns slightly toward me. Then, before I can blink, she's sliding onto my lap like it's the most natural thing in the world—like she belongs there.

Her hand drapes over my shoulder, her sweet scent invading every one of my senses.

"What are our plans for bye week?" she asks, her voice low, meant for me but pitched just loud enough for Bethany to hear. "Cammy thinks we should head to Mexico with her and JP. I just bought a tiny bikini that barely covers anything...though I'm sure I wouldn't be wearing it for long." She bites her lip, a wicked shimmer in her eyes.

"Fuck me," I mumble in a groan.

I blow out a breath, my cock already stirring at the image she's painting. I don't care how much sand we end up with in places it shouldn't be—fucking Peyton on a beach just shot to the top of my fantasy list.

"You, me, and no bikini?" I ask, locking eyes with her.

She nods. She knows exactly what she's doing.

This thing we agreed to? It's supposed to end before bye week. Two months—that's all we gave it. If I'd known how easy it is being with her, I would've fought for more time.

Bethany clears her throat sharply. "Hunter."

But I don't take my eyes off Peyton, perched perfectly in my lap.

There's a mischievous glint in her eye as she shifts, angling herself so that Bethany has a perfect view of the back of her jersey—my name and number stretched across her body.

"Warning, Reed," she murmurs under her breath.

Then she leans in and kisses me.

Her hands land on my chest, mouth pressing to mine. It starts slow—just enough to make my heart hammer—but then her fingers slip behind my neck, pulling me closer. Her lips part. My tongue finds hers.

And suddenly, it's not about Bethany. Not about fake dating. It's just Peyton and me.

The kiss deepens—hotter, hungrier than we've ever let it get before outside of that night she crawled over the pillow wall naked, dreaming of me.

When we finally break apart, I'm breathless. So is she.

"I'll tell Cammy we're in for bye week," she says, and slides off my lap, her warm body leaving a trail of fire in its wake. My hands skim down her thighs on instinct, not ready to let her go just yet.

"Oh—Bethany," Peyton adds sweetly. "Didn't see you there. I'll let you two talk."

She gives Trey a nod. "Hi, Hart."

Trey smirks, a rare sound of amusement slipping past his lips. He knows exactly what just happened.

Peyton saunters off, hips swaying with just a touch more intention. I don't know if she's proud of herself, or if she just wants my eyes on her ass.

Either way, she wins. My eyes are always on her ass.

Bethany clears her throat again.

"Do you need someone to take care of that for you?" Bethany asks, her voice dripping fake sweetness. I find her blatantly staring at the outline of my hard cock through my jeans. "The bathroom's right over there. I know someone who'd be *more* than happy to relieve you."

To Hart's credit, he doesn't even blink. Just leans back in his chair like he's watching a show he's already seen a hundred times.

Bethany's tactics aren't surprising.

Pathetic, sure. But not surprising.

This is what usually works for her, and I get why she's been successful up until now. The problem is, I've already been burned bad enough to know that it's all about her ego, and has nothing to do with her wanting me.

I shift lazily in my seat, stretching my arm over the back of the chair like I've got all the time in the world.

"That won't be necessary," I say, letting a slow grin pull at my mouth. "My girlfriend gets worked up after watching me win on the ice. She already has plans to put me to good use tonight. I'll get more *relief* than I know what to do with."

It's a lie. Peyton isn't likely going to let me anywhere close enough to make that happen, but Bethany doesn't need to know that.

Bethany's face turns dark, her perfectly placed expression

cracking through her not getting her way. "Fine. Then can we talk? Privately," she huffs out.

"I have nothing to say to you. You're not going to trade me that easily."

She rolls her eyes. "It's a family matter."

Shit.

A family matter can only mean one thing. My stomach dips at the thought that this has to do with my mom.

I sigh and rise from my stool. "After you."

We step outside into the cold night. The street's quiet, only the distant sound of cars passing on the main drag. The neon glow of Oakley's sign flickers above us.

A few steps out, she spins to face me, heels clicking sharply.

"Are you in love with her?" she demands.

"That's none of your business. And it's not a family matter, either, because we're not family," I snap. "Besides, what the hell do you care about love?"

"I'm not the monster you think I am," she says, her voice suddenly too soft. "You were never around after you got drafted. I was lonely. You had women chasing you everywhere you went, throwing themselves at you. What was I supposed to do—wait around until you cheated?"

"Good to know you had such high expectations of me," I mutter. "So your plan was to cheat first? Secure a billionaire while I was trying to build us a life? Trying to give you everything you never had growing up? Like financial security and a man who didn't hurt you like your mom's ex-boyfriends?"

She shrugs like that's fair logic. "You wouldn't understand."

"Try me."

"Forget it," she says, shaking her head. "That's not why I came."

"Then spit it out, Bethany. You're keeping me from my team... and my girlfriend."

A patron from the tattoo parlor walks by us and then heads into Oakley's. It's a freezing December night, though at least there's a break in the rain.

"Have you talked to your mother recently?"

"Yeah. A couple days ago."

"And what did she say? About the doctors? The tests?"

"She said the doctors aren't concerned. That we're waiting on results."

Bethany's eyes flare. "It's been months, Hunter. You seriously believe they're still waiting?"

I hesitate.

"What are you saying?" I ask.

"I have my sources," she says. "And I know she's not being honest with you. She's not even being honest with me—and she tells me everything."

The chill of her words sinks in.

"What do you want me to do?"

"Come home. Move back to Jersey. Be closer to her. If not for us...then at least for her. One day, you'll see this was always meant to happen. Peyton and Seattle aren't your home. *We* are."

She brushes her hand down my arm.

The door swings open behind me.

Peyton.

She takes one look—Bethany's touch, my clenched jaw—and walks straight over.

I pull my arm away.

"My mother isn't your concern anymore, Bethany. And neither am I."

I reach for Peyton. She takes my hand without hesitation, her cold gaze locked on Bethany.

"You ready to go home?" I ask, tugging her gently to my side.

"Yeah," she says. "I'm ready for our big, comfy bed."

She walks past Bethany without looking back, calm and cool.

"Goodnight, Bethany," I say. "Thanks for your concern. But I can handle it—from Seattle."

At least, that's what I tell myself.

The truth is...I'm not so sure.

And I'd be lying if I said the concern in Bethany's eyes didn't rattle me a little.

She could be faking it. Hell, manipulation is her specialty.

But she's tugging on a thread I've already been ignoring.

And if there's one thing I know about Bethany...she does care about my mom.

Probably more than she cares about anyone else on this planet—

Besides herself, of course.

CHAPTER EIGHTEEN

Peyton

It's been a week since our second interview went semi-viral, and I jumped into Hunter's lap in front of Bethany.

Maybe I was a little jealous, or maybe I was just holding up my end of the deal. It's hard to say.

Now, with five weeks left on our fake dating agreement, and my subs list now at eighty-six thousand, I'm so close I can taste it. The *Daily Sports* podcast is still in the lead at ninety-three thousand subs and the *Mobile Mayhem* podcast had a great interview as well. I'm not home free—not even close.

Stepping into Serendipity's, the familiar warmth of the cozy café instantly puts me at ease. I spot Penelope, Cammy, Kendall, and Isla already gathered at their usual table, mugs in hand and laughter filling the air.

I head for the barista, put in my order, and then head for them.

Penelope catches my eye and waves me over.

I take a seat in between Isla and Kendall as they discuss Trey's nanny situation.

"Couldn't you ask Vivi if she has someone in her office who could help Trey out?" Kendall asks.

Isla nods. "I could, but the thing is, he still technically has a nanny, and Adeline is attached to her from what I understand. Trey hasn't asked for my help yet, and the last thing I want to do is take someone from Adeline. She's honestly the sweetest girl, and she's been through so much."

"Vivi owns a nanny service, right?" I ask, only having heard something like that weeks ago when I first met her.

"She started out as a nanny service, but as her clients have needed more help, she's brought on a lot more. Now her business is a full range of household services: nannies, private chefs, chauffeurs, personal assistants...you name it. Half of her clients are pro athlete families, the other half are CEOs."

"That's impressive. She really has that many professional athlete clients? Do you think she would be interested in being on my podcast?"

"She's not an athlete. And besides the occasional yoga class, she's not all that athletic. Are you sure you want her on your show?"

I don't have to consider it. I think it's a great idea.

Fans of the show are always interested in the inner workings of the day-to-day life of celebrities and athletes, but not many of them want to discuss their private chefs, tutors for their kids...the things that run in the background of their lives because they like to shield their personal lives from the media. But Vivi could give an inside that not many fans get to see without an athlete having to speak into it.

I think my listeners would love to get a better idea of the infrastructure that keeps these high-producing athletes able to focus on their craft instead of concerns like grocery shopping and laundry...that sort of thing.

"I think people would love to hear her point of view on what it's like to support a professional athlete's family."

Penelope turns from her conversation with Cammy. "Speaking of interviewing athletes, how are things going with

Hunter? You two look cozy, sitting in his lap and making out in the middle of the bar."

"You saw that?" I ask, my cheeks warming.

"Are you kidding? Everyone saw it," Kendall barks out with a laugh, as if it were the most shocking thing she had ever seen.

The moment I saw Bethany head for Hunter, I didn't think about much else except to make sure she knew that I'm still in the picture, even if it is fake. I hadn't thought about who else witnessed it, besides Trey.

"You should have seen the look on Bethany's face," Cammy interjects. "Like she ate something sour when she saw you sucking face with the player she's after."

"Something sour?" I joke.

"Like she sucked really hard on a lemon," Isla says back.

All the girls laugh.

My phone buzzes in my pocket, and I pull it out to find a message from Rebecca, the executive producer at the network.

"Excuse me for a second. I need to take this," I tell them and stand from my chair, heading for the front exit of the coffee shop.

Large snowflakes start to drift down, and it has me wondering if we'll get a white Christmas. Though, Christmas is still a couple of weeks away.

"Hi, Rebecca," I answer.

"Peyton. So good to hear your voice. How's it going with the podcast? I'm seeing a lot of movement on the subs list, and that interview from last week hit big views."

"Thanks. I think it went really well, and the viewers seem to love Hunter."

"Who wouldn't? He's very charismatic on audio...and that voice of his... Well, I don't have to tell you. You're dating him." She laughs. "He's never opened up in an interview like that before. That was podcast gold, and I can tell you that you swayed the other execs in your favor just a little more with that interview. Great work."

"Thanks. I think I also have a really good lead on a unique

take on the *behind the scenes* of how these athletes run their day-to-day lives with private chefs and—"

"Does she work for a big name? Like the quarterback for the Seattle Sentinels, or a starter on the Seattle Rainiers baseball team?"

"Technically, yes, those are some of her clients, but she's the CEO. She places personal assistants and chefs with them, but she doesn't handle the day-to-day."

She stalls for a second.

"Yeah, sure, let's revisit that after you win over the other execs and you have the syndication deal firmly in place," she says quickly, putting the idea off.

I get it's not the clickbait she's hoping for, but I think it would be interesting.

"Okay…right," I say, not masking the tone of disappointment in my voice.

"Listen, I know you can do this, Peyton. I've already mentioned that I'm not supposed to have favorites, but I just see how big you're going to be, and I know the network is going to be disappointed if they pass on you. Right now, you're the only female podcaster on the list, and it was a fight to get you here. I don't have to remind you that this is a male-dominated industry, and it took everything I had—late hours, failed relationships because I worked too many hours—to get me here. But your podcast is proving that there is an untapped demographic of sports fans that want a female podcaster's perspective on it."

She's right, she's been cheerleading for me this entire time, and I need to remember that she's trying to push me to the end. With the other two podcasters being male, I know that I'm not the instant favorite for the network. I have to prove that I'm the best podcast for the network harder than ever before. And with such little time left, I need to follow her suggestion here, though I still think Vivi would be an interesting guest. Who knows what kind of stories she could tell of past players, even if she kept the names anonymous. I bet she has juicy stuff.

"So what do you suggest I do next?"

"The other two on the board want to see more between you and Hunter. They want to see how much more you can get him to open up. This will be a good indicator of what you can do with other guests on your show in the future. And we want to see you two discuss the WAG lifestyle a little. Like how you two are navigating this attention on your relationship when he is so private about his serious relationships from the past."

"You're right, he's really private, and our relationship is still new. Discussing how we're handling our relationship in public is probably something I can get him to talk about. I'll see what I can do." I say, though, dreading the idea of it.

"The social media team is going wild with the photos from the last home game with you in his jersey. Let's work on getting you and Hunter out there more as a couple."

I feel my stomach twist with a familiar mix of excitement and trepidation. The network is finally taking notice, but at what cost? I know Hunter won't be thrilled about the increased public scrutiny, even if it's part of our agreement.

Chewing my lip, I consider how I'm going to sell this to him for our next interview...and the last one he agreed to.

"Of course. I can do that."

"Great. I'm really looking forward to hearing what you put together, and also, seeing more public photos of you will get your subscriber list where we need it. You're so close, Peyton."

I tell her I'll keep her posted on the interview, and then we say our goodbyes.

I pocket my phone, dreading the conversation I know I need to have. Somehow, the lines between fake and real have become even more blurred, and I'm not sure how much more I want to push him. Could I stand him storming out on me now if I pushed him past what he's comfortable with?

I head back inside, my coffee sitting there waiting for me, and I spend the next hour listening to the conversation around me. Though I barely hear a word because I can't stop thinking about how I'm going to get Hunter to warm up even more than he has. And what will he think if I ask him if we can be photographed together more often? Will I feel more like Bethany to him—using him to get something else I want?

I suppose that both of us are using the other person at some level. Only now, I'm starting to wonder what that means for us. This is only supposed to last for a couple more weeks.

When I pull into the driveway, the sight of Hunter wearing camo Crocs in the front yard, with a bucket of soapy water at his feet, and a sponge in hand instantly brings a smile to my face as he's washing down his own truck. The image is both ridiculous and strangely endearing—especially since he's wearing nothing but a tiny Speedo, his broad shoulders, muscular frame, and tattoos on full display. I never noticed the one on his calf before now.

Not to mention that it's less than thirty degrees outside and the bulge in his speedo is still impressive, even in this frigid weather.

"What are you doing?" I call out, unable to hide the amusement in my voice.

Hunter turns, a crooked grin spreading across his face. "Car wash, of course. It's Sunday, and I've missed the last three. I was cleaning my truck while I was waiting for you to get home to wash yours." He gestures to my car, which still has some snow on it from when I was parked outside of Serendipity's Coffee Shop. "Figured I'd better make up for it."

I shake my head, a smile tugging at my lips as I approach him. "In this weather? And in a Speedo?"

He shrugs, the movement drawing my gaze to the way his muscles shift beneath his skin. "What can I say? I'm a man of my word."

He turns to show me his ass, and I just about swallow my own tongue when I notice that it's a thong. Dear God, this man has the best ass I've ever seen, even though it's hairier than in my dreams.

I must look like I've frozen solid in the December weather

because I stop blinking.

Hunter grins, wide and wicked. "Stop looking at me like a piece of meat. Unless you plan to eat me later."

"I think you just turned me into a vegetarian."

He chuckles and then lobs a sponge at me. It hits me square in the chest, a slap of icy suds soaking through my coat.

I gasp, stumbling back a step, my mouth hanging open. "Hunter Reed, you did *not* just—"

He cuts me off with a cocky shrug, already reaching for the bucket. "You just wounded me. An eye for an eye."

I narrow my eyes, a spark of mischief catching fire. "You're going to regret that."

Before he can react, I snatch the other sponge from the ground and hurl it at him. It nails him right in the thigh, water exploding in all directions.

"Oh, it's *on*, Collins," he growls, laughter rumbling in his chest.

I turn and run in the opposite direction, squealing as he chases me around his truck.

What follows is pure chaos.

We chase each other around the yard like two overgrown kids, slipping on patches of frozen grass, shouting ridiculous threats. Hunter ducks behind the truck just as I whip a half-full sponge at him, but it bounces off the side mirror and smacks him in the shoulder anyway.

"Nice aim," he calls. "Maybe you should try out for the team."

"Maybe I should replace you," I shout back, scooping a handful of snow for the smallest snowball in history and flinging it in his direction.

He yelps when I make contact with his skin, though it was barely enough to cause any damage.

"Oh, that's low, Collins!" He grabs a second bucket—where the hell did that come from?—and *launches* a wave of sudsy water at me. It soaks my leggings down to my socks.

I squeal, slipping as I try to dodge, arms flailing like a drunk baby deer.

Hunter's laughing so hard he can barely stand.

"Truce, truce!" I gasp, holding my arms up like I'm surrendering.

"No chance. If you think you can replace me, let's see how well you block," he says, kicking off his Crocs, and then charges at me.

He catches me around the waist and lifts me off the ground like I weigh nothing. I squeal again, laughing so hard it hurts as he spins me in a circle. Then he pulls me into the cover of the garage and drops us both onto my old queen mattress still living in here from where the movers put it.

We collapse together in a heap, breathless and soaked, our laughter fading into something heavier.

Hunter's body presses against mine, pinning me gently to the cold mattress. But I don't feel the cold. All I feel is *him*. His hard cock rubbing between my thighs, sending sparks to my clit. Thank God I wore leggings today.

The space between us shrinks until there's barely a breath of air left.

His lips find mine, his hand trailing down along the curve of my jaw, his touch featherlight, sending shivers racing down my spine.

His voice is rough against my lips. "You're so beautiful," he murmurs. "Sometimes it fucking hurts to look straight at you... like you're the goddamn sun."

My heart thumps against my chest so hard it almost hurts.

"How do you do that?" I whisper, dizzy from the heat building between us.

"Do what?"

My hands glide up his chest, feeling the hard lines of him, his skin burning hot even after being bare to the freezing air. "Say all the right things."

"Because I mean them," he mutters. "You're shivering. I need to get you inside."

He leans in, pressing his forehead gently to mine. For a second, we just breathe each other in, the world narrowing down to his hands gripping my waist.

Before I can reply, he scoops me into his arms and strides toward the mudroom door. The house is dim and quiet around us, the cold left behind with the slam of the door.

Inside the laundry room, it all unravels.

A flurry of movement begins as Hunter helps me out of my damp, freezing clothes, hands caressing and exploring—until I'm down to my bra and panties, and he's stripped bare—no thong left in sight. His hands move over me, rough and reverent all at once, and then he lifts me again, setting me down atop the rattling dryer.

The vibrations instantly jolt through me, a shocking, delicious thrum that makes me gasp and arch into him.

His lips trail hot, open-mouthed kisses along the column of my throat.

I tilt my head back, giving him more, my fingers tangling in his hair as a shaky moan slips free.

Hunter's hands find my hips, and with a low growl, he bends me forward, pressing me into the rumbling dryer.

The steady vibration throbs against my clit, pulling a gasp from my lips as heat floods my core.

My eyes flutter closed, my body arching instinctively into the sensation, every nerve ending coming alive under his touch.

His lips curve against my skin. "How good does that feel, Peyton?"

I shudder against him, pressing closer. "It's driving me crazy...I need more."

His hands tighten around my hips, anchoring me as the dryer hum buzzes against my core, each vibration making my pulse race harder.

"How much more?" he asks, his voice a low, rough rasp against my ear.

I slide one hand down between us, cupping the hard length

of him that's settled heavy and hot against my lace panties. His entire body jerks at the contact.

"What if we forget rule number one?" I whisper, kissing the corner of his mouth. "Just for tonight. I want all of you, Hunter. Right now."

"I told you Collins, I'm yours for whatever you want until this deal is over. If you want me, you can have me. All of me."

His fingers slide around my hips, slow and sure, before he lifts me off the dryer and into his arms like I'm something fragile he can't afford to drop.

I melt against him, my heart hammering as he carries me toward the hallway without breaking eye contact.

"Where are we going?" I ask, feigning disappointment. "I liked the dryer."

He smirks, brushing a kiss against my mouth before pulling back just enough to lock me in place with a look that's pure sin.

"Now that I've got a one-night hall pass on our rules..." he says, his hands flexing against my ass, sending a pulse straight to my core, "I'm taking you to the shower, Collins—because you and I are about to make a fucking mess out of this little body you just handed over to me."

His eyes drag over the soaked fabric of my bra clinging to my skin, and a heated flush spreads across my chest. He licks his lips.

My body.

His to touch, to ruin, just for tonight.

I swear my whole body vibrates harder than the damn dryer we just left behind.

But I lift my chin anyway, meeting his dark, hungry gaze with a slow, wicked smile. "Then what are you waiting for, Reed?" I whisper. "Make a mess."

He carries me to the hallway shower and closes the door. In the bathroom, he backs me against the tile wall, his hands slipping beneath the last scraps of my clothing. The water splashes cold when he reaches in to turn the shower on, and he grimaces when the icy spray hits him—but he doesn't stop.

He's too busy stripping off my bra and panties like he's starving for the feel of me.

His mouth crashes back onto mine, stealing the words from my lips. His tongue dips inside, deep and hungry, just as he spins me under the warm spray as the water finally heats.

I gasp against him, my frozen body coming alive under the dual assault of the hot water and his scorching kiss.

My hand slides down, finding him—hard, hot, and ready—and I wrap my fingers around his cock, giving a teasing squeeze.

He groans into my mouth, bucking against my hand.

"Slow down, Peyton," he warns, his voice tight with strain. "Or I'll come all over your hand."

I smirk against his lips, feeling a rush of power that's heady and electric.

"Then take me already," I whisper, my voice raw with need.

The steam rises thick around us, turning the world soft and hazy as Hunter lifts me again, pinning me against the tile, his mouth trailing down my throat, my collarbone, lower still.

The vibrations of the dryer are a ghost of a memory now—nothing compared to the pulse building low in my belly, the throbbing need only he can ease.

His hands roam every inch of my body with slow passes—mapping me, worshiping me, like I'm the only thing that's ever mattered.

"Hunter..." I breathe, nails scraping lightly down his back, my entire body quivering for him.

He groans, hips rocking between my thighs as he holds me up, his hardness sliding between us, pressing low against my belly.

"God, Peyton...you feel so fucking good."

The water rushes over us, the heat from the spray mixing with the furnace of our bodies. Our kisses turn desperate again, needy, like we're both chasing the same inevitable crash.

Hunter curses softly under his breath, tearing his mouth from mine. "Don't move," he growls, voice wrecked. "Condom."

I shiver from the loss of his heat, wrapping my arms around

myself even with the hot water pounding down around me. He jumps out of the shower, searching the bathroom for a condom, the sound of a zipper, and then the sound of a foil being ripped open.

The sight of him—water dripping off his hair, muscles flexing as he rolls the condom down his thick length, the sheer focus in his eyes—nearly undoes me.

Before I can even think, he's crowding back into my space.

He lifts me again, pressing me up against the cold tile, and this time there's no hesitation.

Our mouths crash together, hot and clumsy and hungry.

One strong arm bands around my lower back, holding me up with almost no effort, while the other grips the back of my thigh, hitching my leg higher around his hip.

I wrap myself around him, desperate for more friction, more pressure, more him.

Then I feel him—hot, hard, perfect—nudging at my entrance.

He pulls back just enough to catch my gaze, his forehead resting against mine, breathing ragged.

"Last chance, Peyton," he rasps, his voice breaking around my name. "Tell me to stop if you want me to."

I shake my head wildly, digging my fingers into his wet hair.

"I don't want you to stop," I whisper. "I need you."

That's all he needs.

Hunter thrusts forward in one long, hard stroke, sinking into me inch by inch until he's seated fully inside.

I cry out, the stretch almost too much, almost too good, my head falling back against the tile with a soft thud.

He groans low and brutal, like he's barely holding himself together.

"Fuck...you're so tight."

The first few thrusts are slow, deep, like he's savoring every second, every pulse and squeeze of my body around his. Each push drives me higher, winding me tighter, until I'm panting against his mouth, clawing at his shoulders.

"Hunter—please—"

Whatever control he had snaps.

He braces one hand beside my head, the other gripping my thigh to hold me open for him, and starts moving faster—harder—his hips slamming into mine with desperate, relentless rhythm.

The sound of skin-on-skin echoes under the spray of the water, the wet slap of our bodies colliding filling the steamy, fogged-up shower.

Every time he thrusts, it knocks a ragged moan out of me, my nails dragging down his back as I cling to him.

The pressure builds fast, almost unbearable, my entire body tightening, spiraling, trembling against him.

Hunter's hand slides between us, his thumb circling my clit in fast, devastating little strokes that send shockwaves through my entire system.

"Come for me, Peyton," he demands, his voice breaking against my ear. "I want to feel you fall apart around me."

One more thrust, one more rough swirl of his thumb—and I shatter.

Pleasure detonates through me, white-hot and overwhelming, my entire body locking up around him.

I cry out his name, my thighs clenching around his hips as my climax rips through me, violent and unstoppable.

Hunter follows a second later with a guttural curse, driving into me one last time as he buries himself deep, spilling into the condom as his body shudders against mine.

For a long, breathless moment, we stay tangled together, hearts hammering, the spray of the water washing over us like a blessing.

His forehead drops to my shoulder, his hands still gripping me like he's afraid to let go.

Slowly, Hunter pulls back just enough to press a kiss to my collarbone, then my jaw, then finally my lips—this one slow, tender.

When he finally sets me down on shaky legs, his arms stay

wrapped around me, steadying me, like he knows I'm still trying to remember how to stand.

He leans in, his voice rough but laced with something suspiciously close to wonder. "When does my hall pass expire?" he asks, his breath warm against my ear.

"By sunrise. Tomorrow morning," I tell him, my voice barely more than a whisper.

Hunter grins and reaches out past the shower curtain, grabbing a towel off the rack. He wraps it around me and then slings one low around his hips.

"Really? I get you for the rest of the day and all night?"

I nod, but hearing it said out loud has me nibbling my lip, suddenly second-guessing how wide open I left the invitation.

He claps his hands once, rubbing them together with a gleam in his eye.

"Damn, do I have plans for you."

Before I can ask, he turns and strides out the bathroom door, leaving me blinking after him.

"Where are you going?" I call out, still clutching the towel tight around me.

"To get my phone," he yells back casually. "I'm ordering food and snacks. Neither of us is leaving this house until sunrise, Collins. Thai or pizza?"

I follow the sound of his voice into the hallway, peeking around the corner toward the kitchen.

"Pizza, I guess? But, you're worried about food?"

He pops his head out from behind the fridge, phone already in hand, looking like the hottest, most dangerous distraction ever with just a towel barely hanging on.

"This is going to be a sex marathon, Peyton. We're going to need sustenance. And a chick flick. Find something good on TV while I order."

"We're watching a movie now?" I tease, grinning despite myself.

"You're getting the full Reed experience," he says, grinning back like he knows exactly how much trouble I'm in. "Romancing and all. Hope you're prepared, Collins."

And that's when it hits me.

I'm not prepared.

Not even a little bit.

CHAPTER NINETEEN

Peyton

I stare at the rideshare pulling up to the curb, standing in the doorway of my townhouse with Hunter in front of me—backpack slung over one shoulder, small rolling bag at his side, and a twinge of disappointment pulling tight in my chest.

I know he has to go—some important meeting for a sponsorship deal—but that doesn't make it any easier.

It's only been four days since our so-called hall pass expired, and even though we've stuck to our rules since, it's been...different.

Late-night card games. Ice cream sundaes. That ridiculous night he showed up with bright pink face masks and challenged me to a round of Would You Rather? that revealed more about him than I ever would've expected.

Small things.

Easy things.

Things that are starting to slip under my defenses, making this fake thing between us so much more comfortable than any of the real relationships I've had before.

"Don't let anyone steal my spot on that couch while I'm gone."

Promise?" Hunter says, his eyes sparkling with mischief.

I roll my eyes, trying—and failing—not to smile.

"I make no such promises, Reed. That couch is fair game."

He laughs, stepping closer, tugging me gently toward him by the belt loop of my jeans.

Then he kisses me.

Soft and tender, nothing like the heated, desperate kisses we've shared.

This one is slow. Savoring.

The kind of kiss that makes my heart flutter and my bare toes curl against the cool metal door stoop.

He pulls back just a breath—his eyes locking on mine.

"Shit, sorry," he murmurs, the apology brushing my lips. "I know we said no kissing without warning. You just looked too good standing there."

Heat blooms in my cheeks, my whole body suddenly too aware of how close we are.

"It's okay," I whisper. "I don't mind."

Hunter gives me that smile—the slow, devastating one that curls at the edges like he knows exactly what he's doing—and presses a kiss to my forehead before pulling away.

"I'll call you later, Passenger Princess," he says, tossing the nickname over his shoulder like he's trying it on for size and already knows it fits.

I watch him walk toward the rideshare, my chest tightening a little more with each step he takes.

He pauses with one hand on the door. "Oh—and I left a present in the house for you. Good luck finding it."

I blink. "You left me a present? Where?"

He grins. "Telling you would ruin the fun, wouldn't it?"

And then he's gone—climbing into the backseat, the car pulling away with a quiet hum. I stand there a moment longer, hand still on the doorknob, heart thudding in my chest like it's not quite ready to be alone.

When I close the door, the house settles into a silence that feels bigger than it should. Too still. Too empty. Like maybe the space Hunter's worried about losing...isn't just on the couch.

I pad toward the bedroom, peeling off my sweatshirt, preparing for bed and trying to shake the weird flutter still lingering in my chest.

This is an arrangement, I remind myself. A temporary fix. No matter how easy it's starting to feel—or how much I might wish it wasn't pretend—I can't let myself get caught up in the moments between.

I reach for the nightstand drawer to grab my lotion—and freeze.

My trusty vibrator is missing.

In its place, there's a neon yellow sticky note folded over something. My fingers brush the paper, heart skipping like it already knows I've found clue number one.

Written in his sharp, confident scrawl:

Looking for something, Peyton?

You'll have to work for it this time. Follow the clues—if you dare.

I stare at it, half-smiling, half-scowling.
Damn him. The man really left me a sexy scavenger hunt.
And I'm already hooked.

I stare at the note, a mix of confusion and intrigue swirling inside me. Of course Hunter would pull some kind of prank, even when he's not here.

Tucking the note into my pocket, I start searching the room, looking for any other signs of his mischief. It doesn't take long before I spot a pink sticky note, this one taped to the lamp on my dresser.

Warm and cozy, where I like to rest my head. That's where your next clue will be found instead.

I roll my eyes, a smile tugging at my lips. "Typical Hunter," I mutter, already heading for the bed.

Sure enough, there's another note nestled between the pillows, this one slightly crumpled.

Feeling thirsty, are we?

The kitchen is where you'll find the next piece.

Shaking my head, I make my way downstairs, my phone buzzing with an incoming call from Hunter. I debate ignoring it, but my curiosity gets the better of me.

"Where did you put it?" I ask, cutting right to the chase.

I can practically hear the grin in his voice. "Put what?"

"Don't play dumb with me, Reed. The sticky note in my nightstand? Where's my vibrator?"

He chuckles, the sound low and warm. "Oh, that. Couldn't wait until my flight took off before needing a little help, huh sweetheart? You could have asked me to take care of you before I left."

"You moved my vibrator. You're a monster," I tell him.

"We both know that deep down, you're excited to find my little present."

I roll my eyes, already heading for the kitchen. "You're impossible, you know that?"

"Ah, ah, ah. No spoilers," he teases. "Follow the clues, Peyton. You're smart, I know you can figure it out."

I sigh, scanning the kitchen for any sign of another note. My eyes land on the fridge, where a bright yellow square is stuck to the door.

"Keeps my drinks nice and cold, where I like to store my snacks. Check inside, that's where your next clue will be stashed."

Pulling open the fridge, I spot another note attached to a bottle of water. "Hydration is key, especially when you're...well, you know."

I groan, cheeks flushing at the implication. "Hunter, I swear to God—"

"Shh, you'll scare Sproutacus. He doesn't like it when mom and dad fight."

I glance over at the Chia Pet sitting on the counter. "You're enjoying this way too much, aren't you?"

"Maybe a little," he admits, a teasing tone to his voice. "But come on, Peyton. Where's your sense of adventure?"

I shake my head, but I can't fight the smile that spreads across my face. "All right, fine. Lead on, you ridiculous man."

I follow the trail of clues, each one more cryptic than the last. The living room, the laundry room, even the guest bathroom—every time I think I've got it figured out, Hunter throws me a curveball.

By the time I make it to the last clue, tucked inside one of the kitchen cabinets, I'm equal parts exasperated and amused.

The final destination is where I like to get all hot and steamy.

Open me up and you'll find your prize.

I stare at the note, brow furrowed. Hot and steamy...the oven? No. The bathroom? My eyes widen as realization dawns.

"The shower?" I ask.

He says nothing. "Hunter, is it the shower?" I ask as I practically sprint to his shower in the hallway, but I don't find anything besides less of his things on the counter since he packed them with him.

Seeing the bathroom almost bare of his belongings makes me feel—lonely?

Maybe, but wherever these misplaced feelings are coming from, now isn't the time to unpack them.

"Did you find it?" he asks smugly,

"It's not in there and you know it," I say and then run to my room, and then to my bathroom. But again...it's empty. "It's not in my bathroom either. Where is it?"

"Keep looking. What got you hot and steamy the last time we were together?"

I think for a second. "The dryer!" I practically shout and race out of my bathroom, bedroom, and then down the hall.

I can hear him muffling back laughter.

"I'm going to get you back for this, by the way."

"You'd better mean that Peyton. Don't tease me."

I grumble at his enjoyment as I push through the half-open laundry door. Nothing is sitting on top, so I yank open the door. He must hear me.

"Well, well, look who figured it out," he teases. "Go on, open it."

Sure enough, there's a neatly wrapped box sitting inside the dryer drum, a bright red bow perched on top.

"You put my vibrator inside?" I ask, like it's the most outrageous thing imaginable.

"Yeah...that's where it goes. Inside." His voice drops lower, full of wicked amusement. "I'll be happy to demonstrate on you when I get home, if you need a proper tutorial."

I blow out a loud, exaggerated sigh, pretending he's annoying me—pretending I'm not already grinning like an idiot. My fingers work quickly at the wrapping paper, anticipation buzzing under my skin.

When I finally pull off the lid, my breath catches.

Nestled inside the box is a sleek, glittery turquoise dildo—Hawkeye's green, no less—and it looks suspiciously like a certain part of Hunter's anatomy that I've become intimately familiar with.

"What the—" I sputter, heat flooding my cheeks. "Hunter, did you...?"

He chuckles, low and rich, clearly enjoying himself.

"Yep. Had it custom-made, just for you. An exact replica of your favorite phallus," he says, completely unbothered. "You know...since I can't be there to take care of you myself."

I'm torn between mortification and...something else.

Something hot and needy that coils low in my belly and refuses to be ignored.

"You're unbelievable," I mutter, even as my fingers trace the smooth, glittering silicone.

"Oh, I know," he says. "But admit it, Collins. You love it. I even made it Hawkeye's colors—I thought you'd appreciate the team spirit."

I open my mouth to respond—but he keeps going, tone dropping into a mock-serious deadpan.

"And don't even think about returning it. I don't want my cock ending up in some stranger's hands. Plus...That molding wax got everywhere. I was pulling it out of my ass hairs for a week. And the expedite fee they charged to get it here before I left town? Straight highway robbery."

A choked laugh bursts out of me before I can stop it.

God help me, this ridiculous, infuriating man.

I bite my lip, cheeks burning, as my fingers keep skimming the surface of the gift.

Equal parts thoughtful and depraved—and so very him.

And yeah...it's doing things to me that I really shouldn't be thinking about right now.

Hunter's voice softens, the teasing falling away.

"Hey," he says gently. "You okay?"

I swallow hard. "Yeah, I'm... I'm fine. Just, um, processing, I guess."

He chuckles. "Well, take your time. I'm not going anywhere." His voice drops an octave, smooth and sinful. "At least, not the fun parts. Do you like your present? It's an upgrade from that tiny thing in your drawer, right?"

I glance down at the dildo still in my hands, fighting a smile. Now he's fishing for compliments.

"I'm not sure..." I tease. "Maybe we should do a measuring test to be sure which one's bigger."

He groans, like I just stabbed him in the heart.

"You know how to cut a man straight to the core."

I bite back a laugh. "Oh God, I'm sorry. I'm teasing."

"No, no," he says dryly. "I like it. Love being emasculated before my flight."

I glance down at the dildo still in my hands, fighting a wicked smile.

He's clearly waiting for praise—and maybe something else.

"I'm not sure..." I tease. "Might need to take it for a spin before I give a full review."

There's a sharp inhale on the other end of the line.

"You're killing me," he mutters. "You're seriously going to make me hard in a terminal full of families, old ladies, and neck pillows?"

I laugh quietly, brushing my fingers up the length of the toy again, slower this time.

"That depends," I murmur. "Are you going to talk me through it?"

I can hear him rustling around like he's moving. "First, let me find a quiet corner in this godforsaken packed airport."

There's a beat of silence for a moment as I wait for him to find a spot, my body already heating up at the idea of having phone sex with Hunter while he can't do anything to take care of himself.

Then his voice drops—low, rough, and intimate enough to make my knees weak.

"Get in bed," he says. "Keep the phone on speaker."

I don't even hesitate.

I head for my bedroom, the house suddenly feeling warmer, smaller, tighter around me. I flick off the bedside lamp and crawl under the covers, placing the phone on the pillow beside me. The vibrator—his vibrator—is still in my hand, glittering in the dim light.

"Clothes off?" I ask.

"Mm-hmm. Everything. And lay on my side of the bed. I want to know you're coming all over my side of the sheets."

I slide my tank top over my head, shiver as the cool air kisses my skin, and push my panties down my thighs. The sheets catch against my bare legs as I settle back, heart pounding.

"Tell me what you're doing," he says, voice a soft growl now. "Walk me through it."

"I'm lying on your side of the bed..." I say, a little breathless. "Naked. Thinking about how good you felt inside me last week. Wondering if this thing you made actually lives up to the real thing."

He groans quietly, trying to muffle it back from the other passengers within earshot. "Are you wet?"

I drag my finger through my arousal. Wetter than I even realized. Just the sound of his voice is enough to get me dripping. "Yes."

"Wrap your hand around it. Slide it through those sweet pussy lips. Get it nice and wet for me first."

I wrap my fingers around the toy, the familiar weight making me wish it was him in real life instead.

His voice in my ear is everything—commanding, sinful, and somehow still laced with that teasing affection that always ruins me.

"Slow. Go slow. I want you aching for it."

I do exactly as he says—sliding it between my thighs, letting it brush against me, teasing my entrance. My hips lift without meaning to.

"Now, put me inside—just the tip—teasing that pussy. You don't get the whole thing yet. Not until you beg."

I moan as I press the vibrator inside of me—Hunter's tip spreading me open—the stretch feels so good, but I know from experience how thick the rest of his shaft is.

"Now swirl my tip inside of you and then pull out a little before pushing me back in."

"Hunter..." I mutter as I do as he instructs.

"You want more don't you?" He phrases it as a question, but we both know I need more.

I make a muffled "yes" sound.

"Are you wet enough to take all of me?"

"Mm-hmm..." I tell him.

"Beg, Peyton."

"*Please.*"

"That's what I want to hear. Good girl... Now push me in. All the way. Let me hear you."

A soft moan escapes my lips as I sink it inside, the stretch surprisingly familiar.

"Holy shit," I breathe. "You weren't kidding. This thing's... accurate."

"Now you're just stroking my ego," he rasps, but I can hear the strain in his voice. "How wet are you?"

"Soaked."

"Good. Work that little body until you can't think straight."

His voice guides me, patient but filthy, every word fanning the fire building in my core. I move with his instructions, chasing the high he's painting for me with nothing but his voice.

And when I finally come—I cry out—his name is the only thing on my lips.

After a beat, all I can hear is my shaky breath and the subtle crackle of the airport overhead speaker through the phone.

Hunter makes a rough exhale.

"Goddamn, I'm hard as a rock and have nowhere to go."

"You started it," I whisper, chest rising and falling fast. "Next time, don't leave your cock lying around."

A beat of laughter breaks through the phone line, and then his voice drops into that smile I can feel even across the country.

"That was your retaliation, wasn't it?"

"Maybe."

"You're evil."

"And you love it."

There's another pause, and then I hear a flight being announced over the speaker.

"They're boarding my flight," he says reluctantly. "I'll text you when I get to my hotel. Night, Peyton."

I should say something normal. Something casual.

But instead, I smile wickedly at the glittering turquoise cock in my hand, and say sweetly, "Does phone sex count against rule number one? Because that's the best I've ever had."

There's a rough inhale on the other end of the line. A muttered curse.

"Goddamn it," he growls. "I'm standing in line at my gate, and now I have to adjust myself in public."

Laughter bubbles up in my throat as I imagine him, flustered and hard, trying to casually shield himself from the families and businessmen waiting for boarding.

"Serves you right," I say, grinning.

We say our quick goodbyes and then the call cuts off, and I'm left alone with my racing heart and the obscene gift in my hand.

I stare at it for a long moment, fingers lightly tracing the smooth contours, my mind spinning faster than it should. This was supposed to be pretend. Clean. Professional.

And now? I'm in bed, clutching a dildo modeled after the man I swore I wouldn't fall for.

The thing is...I don't want the imposter.

I want the real thing, but I'm not supposed to.

I walk to my bathroom and clean it, then stow it back in my nightstand for future use with zero interest in finding my old vibrator that he hid. Not when I have "him" to use whenever I want.

A few minutes later, a text comes through.

> **Hunter:** Just had to lie to a gate agent about the "bulge in my pants." Apparently, they don't waive baggage fees for emotional support erections. Hope you're satisfied, Collins.

> **Me:** I'm very satisfied. Your gift made sure of that. Also, next time, maybe don't leave me a replica of your cock if you don't want consequences.

> **Hunter:** Just wait. Retaliation is coming.

> **Me:** Is coming? I'm pretty sure your glittery stunt double already came. I was pretty thorough...in all three speeds and with a backup battery.

> **Hunter:** I'm glad at least one of my cocks gets to slide past rule number one. Lucky fucker.

> **Me:** Let me know when you're rechargeable too, Reed.

> **Hunter:** *searching for human solar panels*

I laugh and then type back, imagining him taking his seat after stowing his belongings in the overhead compartment.

> **Me:** Have a safe flight.

And if this fake relationship keeps heading in this dangerously real direction... I'm going to need more drawer space and a lot more backup batteries.

My phone dings again, and my heart thumps against my chest. I grab it to see Hunter's reply, but it's not Hunter—it's an email from Rebecca.

Peyton,

The second interview was a huge success! But the network wants the New Jersey story. Can you deliver on this?

I blow out a frustrated breath. The network wants the one thing that Hunter won't give me, and by pushing him, it threatens the possibility of things between us turning real.

I want this network deal. I've been working toward this for years, a way to honor my father's memory. But is losing Hunter worth it?

CHAPTER TWENTY

Hunter

Another week has passed since I sent Peyton on her sexy scavenger hunt. We only have three weeks left in our fake relationship.

Now, I'm back on home ice.

We're tied with three minutes left in the third, and the puck's a fucking magnet for disaster.

Missouri's top line is bearing down hard, their winger digging in, and Olsen is crouched in the crease, ready to make the save if I don't clear it first.

I don't hesitate.

I throw my body in front of the shot.

The puck ricochets off my pads, but before I can even wheel around to clear it, I catch a flash of blue and white barreling toward me out of the corner of my eye.

No time to brace.

The hit slams into me, a freight train straight to my side, and I hear the sickening pop before I feel it.

My shoulder wrenches back at a brutal angle, my feet flying up over my head. Fire explodes down my arm, and then I hit the ice, headfirst.

The world tilts, and then everything cuts to black.

When I come to, I'm flat on my back on the ice, the rink lights spinning above me.

Kendall's crouched over me, her face sharp with worry, and one of the medics is already peeling my glove off.

"Hunter, look at me," Kendall says, voice steady but firm. "Can you hear me?"

I grunt, trying to nod, but the motion sends a jolt of pain so sharp through my shoulder that stars dance in my vision.

"Yeah," I rasp out.

"Good," she says. "You dislocated your shoulder. Don't move. And you blacked out when you hit the ice."

Fuck.

"How long was I out?" I ask.

"Seconds, but I'm still checking you for a concussion. You took a hard hit."

My heart kicks into overdrive, and it has nothing to do with the pain.

If Everett hears about this—if he thinks I'm a liability—it's one more excuse to trade me. Or even more reason if anything ripped when it dislocated.

I force my eyes open wider, trying to shake off the dizziness.

I need to get up. I need to show them I'm fine.

I—

My gaze flickers past Kendall, scanning the glass.

And there she is.

Peyton.

Standing, hands pressed against the plexiglass, eyes wide—her face almost ghost white—concern coating her beautiful face.

Not moving. Not blinking.

Just watching me.

And for a split second, the only thing I want to do is be next to her, comfort her, and tell her that I'm going to be okay, though I can't promise that until Kendall looks at my shoulder.

Trey and Wolf skate over, dropping to their knees on either side of me.

"We've got you, Reedman," Wolf mutters under his breath.

They help lift me carefully, supporting most of my weight as I stumble toward the bench, cradling my arm to my chest.

Every step is agony, but worse is the sick, twisting panic in my gut. I can't be sidelined. I can't lose this team.

Not now.

Not after four years fighting to get back to the NHL. This can't be my last game.

The crowd buzzes in my ears, loud and distorted, but I don't look away from Peyton.

She's still there, still watching, her hands curled into fists against her chest now.

In the locker room, Kendall doesn't waste time.

"Sit down," she orders, already snapping on a pair of gloves.

I drop onto the bench, grinding my teeth as she examines my arm.

"This is going to suck," she says almost kindly.

"No shit," I grunt.

Before I can brace myself, she grabs, twists, and with a brutal pop, my shoulder slides back into place.

I grunt out a curse, sweat beading on my forehead, but I don't black out.

Small miracles.

"The good news, I think your shoulder is going to be fine, but I want to see you tomorrow before early morning skate. We'll take X-rays if something seems off tonight. The bad news...you're out for the rest of the game," Kendall says, her tone leaving no room for argument.

"I can play," I snap, already trying to stand. Somehow proving to Kendall that I'm ready to get back out there.

But she's a hard ass as the Hawkeyes doctor, and she doesn't let anyone push her around.

"You can't," Coach Wrenley says from behind her, arms

crossed. "She's the doctor here. If she says you're done, you're done."

I glare at both of them, breathing hard, but deep down, I know they're right.

Still. Doesn't make it any easier to swallow.

Kendall tapes me up quickly and efficiently, hands steady.

"Practice tomorrow," she says quietly. "Come see me first thing. I want to reevaluate it after you've iced it all night."

I nod stiffly.

It's not good for my shoulder, but not career-ending.

I'll take it.

Back on the bench, I watch my team.

I sit on the far end, shoulder throbbing under the ice pack tucked into my jersey.

The guys are gassed, scrambling for any chance to pull ahead. Every shift, every shot, I want to be out there helping. Instead, I sit and watch.

My eyes drift up into the crowd.

Peyton's sitting again, but she's wringing her hands, her eyes locked on me, her eyebrows downturned with concern like she's willing me not to fall apart.

Something in my chest squeezes tight.

Bethany used to hate coming to games unless there was press coverage involved. Whereas Peyton's here for me. Not the team— not the win.

I can see it in the way she's not watching anything but me across the ice—concern in her eyes, her fingers clamped together tight, almost like she's praying for me to be okay.

We lose three to five.

No one's fault. We played hard, and so did they. But the weight of it feels crushing. Another uneasy feeling that Everett could have a reason to trade me. Especially if this injury is worse than Kendall thinks it is.

The buzzer sounds, and I skate out for the handshake line. I've played with or against most of these guys over the years, and respect for their hard-fought win is how it's done.

Breathing through the ache in my shoulder, I let the sting of the loss sink into my bones.

And still—when I glance up one last time...

Peyton's looking at me. Not disappointed. Not angry. Just... there. And that means more than she'll ever know.

The locker room is a graveyard after a loss like that.

Nobody says much.

I just sit there, jersey peeled halfway off with an ice pack strapped to my shoulder, letting the frustration burn through me like acid. I feel like I let down my team tonight, though there was little I could have done after Kendall and Coach Wrenley took me off the roster.

A few guys mumble curses under their breath. And then Aleksi strolls in singing some oldies song, breaking the dark cloud hovering over most of us. Then chirps start flying, guys start laughing. There's still an uncurrent of disappointment, but our team is getting back to its normal locker room rumble of lighthearted shit talking and funny YouTube videos making their way around the players.

I head for the shower, ready to get this night behind me and head home with an ice pack, Peyton's couch sounding pretty damn good about now.

I'm freshly showered and headed for my locker to grab my duffel bag to head home when I hear JP's voice.

"Reedman...you've got a visitor." He's standing at the locker room door, smiling and nodding, and just past him, I'd know that blonde hair and smile anywhere.

Peyton stands there, shifting on her heels, my jersey wrapped around her.

The second our eyes meet, her face softens with something achingly close to relief.

I yank my duffel bag off the bench and head straight for her.

"Hey," she says, voice low. "How's your shoulder?"

"It's been better. Nothing a night with an ice pack won't fix," I tell her, keeping it to myself that it hurts like hell. My neck doesn't feel all that great from crashing down on top of it either, but I'd still like to hold on to some remnant of my pride. I'm a defender on an NHL hockey team—complaining about getting served up on the ice won't do well for my reputation.

"Are you going to tell me I'm a sore loser, and that you're going to avoid me on the night that I...how did you put it again? 'Suck a big L?'" I say.

The first night we met.

When I'd been an absolute dick to her after a loss, and she'd promised she'd avoid me like the plague next time I blew it.

"You remember that, huh?"

"Hard to forget it when the most beautiful woman in the room just called out your bullshit."

"Keep going with that compliment, Reed. You're almost out of the doghouse."

Despite the knot of pain in my shoulder, I huff out a laugh.

"Yeah... sorry about that. Again."

Her eyes soften even more. "You're forgiven. You were drunk, emotionally stunted, and hangry. Triple threat."

A real laugh escapes me this time—gravelly, but real.

"I'm still emotionally stunted, by the way," I say. "And continuously hangry."

"Good to know," she teases, stepping closer. "I'll tread carefully."

There's something easy between us now, something that wasn't there before.

Something that feels dangerously close to real.

She looks down at my gear bag.

"You want me to carry that for you?" she offers, reaching for the strap.

I snort. "It's fine. I've got it on my good side."

But Peyton's stubborn. She yanks at it anyway—and immediately lets out a surprised "oof!" as the weight nearly topples her forward onto her face.

I laugh, stepping in and yanking the bag back up off the ground.

"Jesus, Collins. You're going to dislocate something yourself," I tease, slinging it back over my shoulder.

She glares at me, cheeks flushing, but there's laughter dancing in her eyes too.

"I just watched you have your entire clock rung out on the ice, suffer a dislocation and a low-grade concussion, and you're swinging a thousand-pound bag over your shoulder as if it's nothing," she mutters. "Are you even human?"

"Nope. I'm a hockey player," I shoot back easily.

She bumps her shoulder lightly against my good arm as we walk toward the exit.

The simple, casual touch nearly undoes me.

Outside, the night air is sharp against my flushed skin. Peyton shivers slightly, but doesn't complain.

"What's on for tonight? Are we headed to Oakley's?" she asks.

I shake my head. "Nah. I should skip it. Ice this thing, get some sleep. If I want any shot at practicing tomorrow, I can't be worthless."

Relief flashes across her face so fast I almost miss it.

She's happy that I'm going home to take care of my shoulder.

She unlocks her car, hesitating.

"Do you want me to drive you home?" she asks.

I shake my head. "Nah. I'm good. Can't leave my truck here overnight anyway. I won't have a way to get here in the morning, and Kendall wants to see me early."

She nods, chewing her lip like she wants to say something more but holds it back.

I toss my gear bag into the bed of my truck, grimacing a little as the movement tugs my shoulder.

Peyton's still standing there, hands stuffed into her jacket pockets, watching me.

The temptation to just pull her into my arms and say fuck it—to let whatever this is between us snap free—is harder and harder to ignore.

Instead, I flash her a small, crooked smile.

"I'll see you at home, Collins."

Her face lights up in a way that makes the ache in my shoulder feel like nothing.

"Yeah," she says softly. "See you at home."

The second we step inside the townhouse, Peyton flicks on the entry light and turns to me, hands on her hips like she's ready for a fight.

"You. Go change into something comfortable, then the couch. Now," she orders. "I'll get everything."

I smirk, cocking a brow. "Bossy."

"Necessary," she fires back, already kicking off her shoes and heading for the kitchen.

I chuckle under my breath and head for the bedroom, peeling out of my jeans one-handed and tugging on a pair of sweatpants and a T-shirt.

Every movement tugs at my sore shoulder, but I ignore it. Ice, rest, skate tomorrow—that's the goal.

Barefoot, I make my way back into the living room.

Peyton's moving around the kitchen with quick, focused efficiency—grabbing a pint of ice cream from the freezer, tossing a gel ice pack over her shoulder, refilling my water bottle.

She's everywhere at once—like this is second nature—like taking care of me has always been part of our story. There's a natural ease between us I've never had with anyone else, not this fast.

I lower myself carefully onto the couch, grunting a little as I shift into the cushions.

Peyton plops the ice pack onto my shoulder, wrapped in a hand towel, the cold shocking a grunt out of me.

"Sorry," she says, not sounding sorry at all. "Ice first, pizza second."

She snags her phone, already pulling up the pizza place's app.

"Are you hungry?" she asks, glancing over her shoulder.

I snort. "Always."

"Hawaiian, add bacon and extra pineapple?"

"You know me so well," I say, and it slips out before I can stop it.

She ducks her head but smiles.

God, that smile.

A few minutes later, she pads back over and sets the water bottle on the coffee table.

She grabs the remote, and with a few quick clicks, *10 Things I Hate About You* starts playing.

"You're kidding," I say, teasing.

She shrugs, all innocence. "House rules: Nights in require chick flicks."

"Is that a scientific fact?"

"You're the one who started this new tradition...so you tell me."

I huff out a laugh, sinking deeper into the couch as she drapes a blanket over my legs. It barely covers them—most throw blankets are too short—but I don't care, as long as she climbs in under it with me.

And she's right. I've been doing this for her since I moved in. Now, she's doing it for me.

It's not lost on me that she picked up my habit.

My mom would be doing the same thing right now if she were here.

Shit.

Mom.

She called after the game, but I was too busy getting out of there with Kendall patching me up.

I grab my phone from the cushion beside me and check.

One missed call. One text.

Mom: I saw the hit tonight. Please tell me you're okay. You were sitting on the bench, but they didn't show you enough.

With the time difference, it's too late to call now. But she'll see my text in the morning if I send one.

I hear Peyton on hold with the pizza place. It's been a long time since I've felt this domesticated with someone else.

I exhale slowly, thumb flying over the screen.

> **Me: I'm sore but I'm home now. Peyton's taking good care of me, you don't have to worry. I'll call you tomorrow after the morning skate.**

It's not long before I see her reply. Now I feel bad. I probably woke her up.

> **Mom: About how you're finally going to settle down and give me grandkids?**

I shake my head. Of course, being with Peyton is her only takeaway there.

> **Me: No but nice try. About the doctors. Bethany thinks you're hiding something.**

> **Mom: It's nice to see you and Bethany getting along. She's been through a lot. I know that she hurt you but forgiving her could be good for you both.**

I've heard this before. My mom is making excuses for Bethany's behavior. And I get it, because I used to do the same, but Bethany treated me like a stepping stone to get what she wanted when I was there for her, thinking we were building a life together. I don't owe Bethany anything, and if it were my choice, I'd never see her again.

She fucks up everything she touches, and I'd rather not be in reaching distance.

> **Me: This isn't about Bethany. This is about you.**

> **Mom: Nothing to tell. And bring Peyton home for Christmas.**

I stare at the screen a second longer than necessary, my gut twisting with something sharp.

Nothing to tell.

Bethany might be wrong...or she might not be.

Either way, the thought of bringing Peyton home for Christmas sends a rush of panic through me—sharp and immediate.

But just as fast as it hits, it fades. And in its place, a different thought takes hold.

One that whispers about what it might look like if Peyton and I *don't* end this in three weeks like we agreed to. If, instead, we let it become something more.

I shift to adjust the ice pack, and a jolt of pain flashes through my shoulder.

A hiss escapes me before I can stop it.

Peyton notices immediately.

"Hey," she says, crouching beside me. "Let me."

Before I can argue, she's kneeling on the floor next to the couch, reaching for the ice pack.

"You want me to massage it a little?" she asks, voice tentative.

"Might help loosen everything up."

I hesitate for a second—because the idea of her hands on me, while I'm half-broken and half-hard for her already, feels like playing with fire.

But then I nod. "Yeah. That sounds...good."

"How do you want to do this?" she asks. "Where are you comfortable?"

I shift, thinking.

"Probably better if I lie face down," I mutter. "Take the pressure off."

She nods, and I roll carefully onto my stomach, resting my cheek against the armrest.

A second later, Peyton climbs up onto the couch and straddles the backs of my thighs, settling low on my ass.

The weight of her—warm, solid, real—sinks into me like a brand.

I bite back a groan as her fingers start working into my shoulder, slow and careful.

"You're good at this," I mumble into the cushion.

"Tennis has its own injuries," she says, her hands pressing into the tight knots of muscle. "I've had my fair share. Had to learn fast."

I grunt, half in pain, half in pleasure.

"Right. Of course," I say, my voice rough.

The movie plays quietly in the background—Kat Stratford telling Patrick Verona he's not as badass as he thinks—and Peyton's hands work magic on me.

Slow, confident, devastating.

After a few minutes, she leans down close to my ear.

"How does that feel?" she asks.

"Better, but can you reach here?" I squeeze the inner part of my shoulder and bicep.

"Not from this angle. Can you turn over?"

I turn my head to look at her, my heart beating somewhere up in my throat.

"Yeah," I say hoarsely.

She shifts, and I carefully roll onto my back, grimacing as my shoulder twinges. And just like that—Peyton ends up straddling my hips, her perfect ass sitting on top of my pelvis.

My cock reacts immediately, thickening beneath the thin fabric of my sweatpants.

She notices. There's no way she couldn't in those thin leggings she's wearing.

"You're smooth, Reed," she says, laughing softly.

"You're not moving," I point out, my voice thick.

She just smiles, wicked and beautiful, and leans forward to start massaging the front of my shoulder and down my arm.

Her touch is lighter now, more teasing.

Every brush of her fingers feels deliberate, and it's driving me fucking crazy.

"Thanks for doing all this," I say, voice low.

She glances up, confused. "All what?"

"The movie. The pizza. The ice. The massage." I shift slightly, sliding my hand to the curve of her hip. "I've been on my own a long time. I guess I forgot what it's like...having someone have your back."

A soft look crosses her face—sweet and a little sad.

"I'll always have your back, Hunter," she says quietly. "Even after our time's up."

I grin at the idea of it. "Yeah? Are we bonded for life now?"

"Obviously. Fake exes forever," she says, her smile widening. "And what about Sproutacus? We have to stay civil for the plant-child."

I laugh, the sound breaking something open in my chest, and my body shakes, which makes her laugh too and grip onto my chest for stability.

Without thinking, I reach up, pushing back the strands of hair that have fallen in her face when she leaned forward.

Her smile fades slightly, her eyes darkening—finally, we're on the same page.

"Warning, Peyton," I murmur, giving her one last out.

But she doesn't take it.

Instead, she makes the first move—she bends down, her mouth slamming against mine, and every thought scatters.

The kiss is rough, desperate, teeth and tongues and hands that can't get enough.

Her fingers slide into my hair, pulling just hard enough to make me growl against her mouth. She pulls back at the sound, taking it for something else.

"Your shoulder," she says, concerned.

"Fuck my shoulder. Come here," I say and then pull her back down to my mouth.

I slip my hands under her jersey, finding the bare skin of her stomach first—hot and smooth—and then I push higher, cupping the soft weight of her breasts.

She gasps into my mouth, arching into my touch, and I nearly lose it right then and there.

She tastes like a home I've never known, and everything I didn't know I was starving for.

I nip at her bottom lip, feeling her shudder against me, and then her hands are under my T-shirt, skating across my abs, dragging little sounds from the back of my throat.

My hands pull reluctantly from her perfect breasts and slide over her hips, gently rocking her over my cock to test her interest. She moans into my mouth at the friction.

I want her.

God, I want her.

I want—

The doorbell rings.

Peyton jerks back like she's been electrocuted, panting, eyes wide. We stare at each other for one frozen second, chests heaving, the air crackling between us. Then she bursts into laughter—half hysterical, half mortified.

"The pizza," she gasps.

I groan, dropping my head back against the couch.

"Fucking perfect timing."

"It's probably best. Rule number one...remember?" But even I can see the hesitation in her eyes. She wants this as bad as I do. I could already feel her dampening through her leggings.

She scrambles off me, her hair a mess, her jersey wrinkled and riding up.

I watch her go, dazed and more lost for her than I have any damn right to be.

CHAPTER TWENTY-ONE

Peyton

I blow out a breath and press send on an email to Vivi Newport about being on my show.

It might not be the clickbait content that Rebecca wants but I still think it would be an interesting take. However, Vivi may not be interested in telling stories about old clients if it could hurt her reputation. I still think that listeners would appreciate seeing these players' lives from another angle.

And with the pictures circling of Hunter and me walking out together, some photographer getting a photo of an intimate moment between us as we walked through the exit for the stadium after his injury, a headline of the doting girlfriend... The views on our older interview have pushed the already viral status. People are now even more curious about us.

A text chimes in:

> **Rebecca: Congratulations! That picture of you taking care of Hunter as a true WAG was the push you needed.**

Congratulations?

I click back to my video dashboard, hitting refresh a half dozen times, though one would have sufficed. I have to blink a couple of times when I see the number. One hundred and one thousand.

I scream, and just about leap out of my chair. My first reaction is to call Hunter, which shouldn't surprise me anymore. But I know he is at the stadium probably working out with a couple of teammates, so I don't want to bug him. My mom should be at physical therapy with Jesse, so she won't answer anyway. I look at the time, and though Abby is at work, her lunch break is around now.

My subscribers are only half of the requirement, but I have to share this with someone. And I have to share it now.

I grab my phone and scroll to the recent call log. My phone rings. The second she picks up, I practically scream in her ear.

"Abby? You're not going to believe this."

"What? What's going on?"

"I hit one hundred thousand subscribers!" I tell her, tears rushing to my eyes. I still can't believe that I'm saying the words out loud.

"I knew you were going to do it. I'm so freaking proud of you."

"Thank you. I was going to call mom, but I know she's in physical therapy at the clinic with Jesse and—"

"The clinic? No, they stopped those a couple of weeks ago."

"What? Why? He's been doing so good."

"It's been a little overkill for him now that Hunter's been picking him up after school twice a week and taking him to see the Hawkeyes' physical therapist."

Shock fills me. This is the first time I'm hearing of this.

"What? Hunter's been taking Jesse to physical therapy with him?" I ask.

"I thought you knew... He is your boyfriend with whom you live with, I'm shocked you don't know."

"Well then where are they now? I assumed they were at the clinic."

"Hunter asked your mom to bring Jesse down to the stadium today after school. He said he has an early Christmas present for Jesse, and he wants him to try it out. They should be there."

Then I hear someone paging Nurse Collins to the ER.

"Hey, I have to go. Love you. I'm so proud of you and everything you've accomplished. I'm on Christmas and Christmas Eve for the ER, double time, but after, celebratory yoga class," she teases.

"I can't wait," I say sarcastically.

My mom doesn't answer, her phone is off, but Abby told me where they are.

I head for the stadium, my mind is racing. What early gift did he get Jesse, and why didn't Hunter tell me that he's been taking Jesse to PT with him?

When I arrive at the stadium, I spot Jesse first, his face practically glowing with excitement as he wheels himself around in a brand-new, custom-made wheelchair. Hunter is walking beside him, a proud smile on his face.

"Peyton!" Jesse calls out, waving me over. "Look at my new chair!"

I hurry over, taking in the sleek design and the way it seems to move with Jesse's every motion. "Wow, Jess, this is amazing! Where did you get it?"

"Hunter got it for me!" he exclaims, beaming up at the towering hockey player. "Isn't it the coolest?"

I glance up at Hunter, my heart swelling with a mix of emotions. "You did this?" I ask, my voice barely above a whisper.

He nods, his hand coming up to rub the back of his neck. "I, uh, I had a little help from Luka. One of his friends is a Paralympian who uses these chairs. His buddy has an in with the manufacturer, and they were able to fast-track it for Jesse."

My eyes sting with unshed tears as I take in the thoughtfulness of his gesture. "Hunter, this is... This is incredible. Thank you."

"It's nothing," he says, waving me off. "Jesse's been a champ during his PT sessions, and he earned it. Now, he can come out with me to play."

"Are you ready to go, Jesse?" my mom says, holding out his jacket. "I've got dinner in the crockpot, and we'd better get your homework done before school tomorrow."

Jesse heads for my mom in his new wheelchair, and Hunter walks behind him with a bucket of pucks and his hockey stick in his hand.

"Thanks, Grandma," he says, standing out of his wheelchair. She helps him put on his jacket and then hands him his cane. It just about wrecks me to see him so much stronger than ever before. Though he uses his cane a lot, the stadium is a big place, and he would usually bring his wheelchair for this many steps. He's beaming, the smile on his face as big as I've ever seen it, red from the cold ice.

Jesse turns around and hugs Hunter. "Thank you. I can't believe I get to play with you now. This is the best day of my life."

All of a sudden, my jacket feels like it's choking me, and I'm trying to get air, emotions want to overflow, my tear ducts start to water, but I take a deep breath through my nose to stop them. I panic, searching for the exit. This is all supposed to be fake.

With my subscriber numbers reaching my goal and Hunter doing all of this, it's almost too much. And in less than three weeks, he'll go back to being the hockey player on the ice that I once knew, I'll go back to an empty townhouse, free of boxer briefs in my washing machine, protein shakers in the sink, and more food in the refrigerator than I could ever eat.

In a matter of almost six weeks, I gained so much, and yet I'm about to lose so much more.

I see my mom holding back her own tears. "We owe you so much."

Hunter waves her off. "I'm happy to get another future hockey player out on the ice," he says, smiling at her, but then his eyes find mine.

Our eyes lock, and there is so much unspoken in this moment. So much more that he's done for my family that he was under no obligation in our agreement to do. And he did it without asking for recognition from me or anyone else.

Thank you, I mouth to him, trying to keep my emotions from bubbling over.

He gives the faintest nod, almost as if he doesn't want to take the credit, and it only makes me want to kiss him more.

Jesse turns back to my mom. "Did you get the video so I can send it to dad next time he calls from base? He's not going to believe it when I tell him that I'm training with the Hawkeyes. Just wait until my friends hear about this at school," he tells her, his eyes lighting up like a Christmas tree.

I glance over at Hunter, who's watching the exchange with a knowing smile. "PT sessions?" I echo, my brow furrowing.

Hunter buries his hands in his pockets and shrugs like it's no big deal. "Yeah, I've been bringing him a couple times a week," Hunter explains. "Figured he could use the extra support, and the team's trainers have been great about working with him."

I'm speechless, my gaze darting between my mom, Jesse, and Hunter. This man, who I thought was only here because of some mutually beneficial arrangement, has gone above and beyond to make a real difference in my nephew's life. And without telling me—without looking to gain favor with me or to rack up points to get me in bed.

He's been doing it because he cares about my nephew—no ulterior motive in sight.

My mom smiles. "Have a safe flight to your mother's. I'm sure she can't wait to see you. We'll see you after Christmas?"

His eyes break from mine and glance to my mom. "I will, and I'll let you know what the physical therapy schedule is when I get back," he tells her and then looks down at Jesse. "Make sure that you're doing all the strength training over the holidays. No slacking off. The only person it hurts is you."

"Yes, sir," Jesse says, and then my mom turns and follows

Jesse down the player's tunnel.

Hunter steps closer, his eyes searching mine as if he can sense the emotions I'm trying to hold back.

"You've been picking him up from school and bringing him to PT with you? Why haven't you ever mentioned it to me?"

"I got your mom's number at Thanksgiving in case something came up. My PT said he'd like to help, and he's worked with people with spina bifida right out of college. It just worked out. I didn't think it would be a problem."

"It's not a problem, you just never said anything and..."

"You've got a lot on your plate, and he's only gone with me a few times, I wasn't sure it would help. I didn't want to get your hopes up if it wasn't going to work."

I lick my lips, wanting to explain that this isn't a small thing. It's a big thing. To take my nephew who could really use a male figure in his life, who's putting time and energy into his dreams when my brother isn't here to do it—it's a big deal. And I've never seen Jesse so happy.

"And the wheelchair," I ask, breaking eye contact from him to stare at it sitting on the ice. "That was just a small thing too?"

He swallows hard before he speaks. "I called in a favor."

"An expensive favor..." I add.

"It's just money."

"It's more than that and you know it. You've done something for Jesse that none of us could have done. You've given him hope and knocked down barriers that we couldn't have done. And... And..."

"And what?"

"And... I should go. I have an interview I need to edit." I spin around and head down the player's tunnel.

It suddenly dawns on me that I'm falling for a man who I agreed to be temporary with, and there's nothing I can do to stop it. I'm falling fast—and hard.

"Stop...Peyton. Where are you going?" Hunter's voice rings out behind me, laced with concern.

I don't answer, just keep walking, my arms wrapped protectively around myself. I need to get away, to put some distance between us before I completely lose my grip on this fragile thing we've built.

But Hunter isn't letting me go that easily. He catches up to me as I make it down to the locker room, his hand wrapping around my wrist as he pulls me back around to face him. "Peyton, please stop. Tell me what I did wrong. I don't understand why you're running from me."

"You didn't do anything wrong," I insist, my gaze fixed on a point over his shoulder. But I can't ignore the pull of his touch, the way my body yearns to be closer to his.

I want his hands all over me. I want to feel the safety I feel when he wraps his arms around me and pulls me to his chest. But I can't say that. It's not fair. I'd be asking him for something he's been avoiding with other women for the last four years.

His eyes narrow, and he glances around, taking in our surroundings. We've ended up in the players' locker room, the showers just a few feet away. The memory of my fantasy, of being pinned against the locker room wall, flashes through my mind, and I have to fight to keep my composure.

"Obviously I did something you didn't like, because you're running away, making some lame excuse that you have editing to do," he presses, his frustration evident. "What's going on, Peyton? What did I do?"

"Nothing!" I exclaim, the words bursting out of me, echoing loudly through the locker room.

His brow furrows, and his touch trails down to my wrist before settling at my hand, weaving our fingers together like he's trying to tether me to him—and it's all I want.

His eyes lock on mine, steady and searching.

"Then why are you upset?"

"Because you keep doing everything right," I blurt out, my voice shakier than I wish it was. "And it's been so long since I've had someone take care of things in my life. I'm used to keeping things together for everyone else."

Understanding dawns on his face, and he takes another step forward, closing the small gap between us.

"I know you have. I didn't tell you because I didn't want you to think I had some motive. Jesse has talent, and I know what it feels like when someone steps up for you as a kid. Especially with his dad being overseas," he murmurs, his voice soft and tender.

His words gut me—sharp and quiet and true—and I nod, blinking hard.

None of us can fill the hole my brother left behind when he deployed.

But Hunter... Hunter didn't just try. He showed up.

This—this—is exactly what we were supposed to avoid.

Getting attached. Getting invested.

And I tried. God, I tried.

But somehow, Hunter's already under my skin, lodged into my heart, my every thought, wormed his way into places I didn't even know were vulnerable.

My voice barely makes it out, but it's enough.

"You're more than I gave you credit for when we first met," I murmur, the words thick with everything I'm not ready to say yet.

"That's all I've ever wanted you to see."

His gaze locks on mine, so intense it pins me in place.

Then he grabs my waist with his other hand—just enough pressure to steal my breath—and he's kissing me.

Hard, searing, wrecking. Like he's trying to undo both of us in a single breath.

Every thought flees, every fear dissolves, until there's nothing left but the two of us and the heat blazing between us. Urgent, raw, stealing the breath from my lungs.

He cages me against the wall, the chill of the cinder block doing nothing to compete with the wildfire heat of his chest against mine.

I gasp against his mouth as he presses into me, all hard muscle and male heat, every part of him demanding more.

My mind spins—somewhere between *yes yes yes* and *what the hell are we doing?*—because we're standing in the middle of the Hawkeyes' locker room, and someone could walk in at any second.

The thought has panic flickering at the edges of my mind.

But then Hunter groans low in his throat, grinding against me, his hands frantic at the hem of my sweatshirt, and everything rational inside me collapses.

He's not worried. Not even a little.

He's laser-focused—like nothing else exists except for me.

And God help me, I don't want to exist anywhere but here with him, either.

He tugs the sweatshirt, T-shirt, and sports bra up over my head all at once, tossing it somewhere behind him without looking.

His mouth is at my throat, nipping, sucking, dragging heat across my skin as his body presses even tighter against me, my body responding instantly. Heat pools low in my belly.

"You're driving me crazy, Collins," he rasps, his voice wrecked.

I fumble with the hem of his shirt, desperate to feel his skin, and he rips it off one-handed, baring the thick cut of his shoulders, the muscles shifting under inked skin. Next go our shoes, one by one—leggings and pants next until my cotton panties and his boxer briefs are the only two things left.

The sharp smell of ice, rubber, and sweat fills the air—the scent of hockey and male and everything that's so achingly Hunter.

He kisses me again, slower this time, dragging his teeth over my bottom lip, teasing it into his mouth.

It's a claiming.

A slow, devastating claiming.

And I don't want it to ever end.

His hands slide down my ribs, palming my hips.

"Tell me this is against the rules. One word from you will make me stop," he rasps against my mouth, his forehead resting on mine.

The air between us buzzes, so charged I can barely breathe.

I shake my head, my fingers diving into the waistband of his joggers.

"Don't you dare," I whisper.

He lets out a sound that's half groan, half growl, grabbing my thighs and lifting me against the wall with a roughness that sends my pulse skyrocketing.

I wrap my legs around his waist instinctively, feeling the hard, thick ridge of him grinding against me.

It steals another whimper from my throat.

His hand cups the back of my neck, his thumb stroking the side of my throat as his eyes lock on mine.

"I need you," he breathes, voice cracking on the edge of it. "I need you so fucking bad, Peyton. I did it all for you—Jesse, the PT, the movie nights, Sproutacus...every single moment. Because for once in my life, I want to be the kind of man who deserves you."

Tears sting the backs of my eyes, but they're swallowed by the desperate slide of his hand between us, his fingers sliding the thin layer of my cotton panties to the side. The air hits my bare skin, cold and shocking, but he's already there, touching me, stroking me, coaxing me to open for him.

"Please," I gasp, my hips rolling against his hand.

"Fuck," he mutters, leaning his forehead into my shoulder. "You're already soaking wet. So responsive for me, aren't you?"

My legs are already beginning to shake, my body desperate for the deep, thick penetration that only he can deliver.

He slides his finger back out of my panties and slides his boxer briefs down with one hand. His hard cock bobs under me.

"Condom?" he pants, looking down at the rubber mat floor of the locker room for his pants.

"I'm on birth control," I whisper, the words shaking free. "I want to feel you, Hunter. Nothing between us. I want all of you."

His hand trembles as he guides himself to my entrance.

"Are you sure?"

I nod fiercely, digging my nails into his shoulders. "I'm sure."

And then he thrusts into me in one deep, slow slide, and the world tilts off its axis.

I cry out, the stretch, the pressure, the overwhelming fullness of him stealing my breath, making my toes curl, suspended behind him.

He groans something filthy into my neck—something about how tight I am, how good I feel—how he sees stars every time he enters me, but it blurs around the sound of my own heavy panting.

He pulls out slowly, then drives back in, each motion grinding my back against the locker room wall, each thrust shoving the air from my lungs. But I wouldn't want it any other way. Being taken by Hunter Reed is rough, and careful, and protective...and completely addicting.

"I've wanted you like this since the first time you smarted off to me at the charity event," he grits out, fucking me harder now, his hands braced on the wall by my head. "Since the second you told me I was an asshole."

I gasp out a broken laugh, my body already climbing too fast, too high.

"Maybe...I like assholes," I manage to gasp.

He huffs a low laugh, then buries himself deeper inside me, making me sob.

"Then you're in luck because I'm just your type," he growls against my ear.

I'm going to come undone on a damn locker room wall, and I wouldn't change a single second of it.

I'm close.

So close.

Every nerve ending screams for release as he drives into me harder, rougher, his hands grabbing at my hips, anchoring me to him.

"Is this your fantasy? Taking you against the wall of the locker room?" he asks.

I nod. I can't count how many times I've dreamed about this since he moved in, and it's even better than I imagined.

"Come for me, Peyton," he commands, voice dark and

wrecked.

I shatter at his words, coming hard around him, clenching so tight he curses low and filthy against my skin.

He thrusts once, twice more—and then he's following me over the edge, emptying into me with a deep, guttural moan that makes my whole body tighten again.

Afterwards, as we lie tangled together on the bench, our breathing finally slowing, the weight of what just happened settles over us. Hunter's fingers trace idle patterns on my arm, and I savor the intimacy of the moment.

"Peyton," he murmurs, his voice low and rough. "What are we doing?"

I chew on my bottom lip, my heart pounding. "I... I don't know," I admit. "I feel like I can't decipher between real and fake anymore."

He nods, his hand coming up to cup my cheek. "Me neither," he confesses. "I don't think faking it is supposed to feel like...this." He trails off, his thumb brushing over my skin.

"I'm scared, Hunter," I whisper, my eyes searching his. "I don't want to get hurt again."

"Hey," he soothes, pulling me closer. "I'm not going anywhere. Not unless you want me to."

I let out a shaky breath, snuggling into his embrace. "I don't want you to go," I murmur. "But what does that mean?"

"Maybe we figure it out together."

"Really? I thought you didn't do relationships."

"I didn't. But for you? I'd do anything not to lose you." Hunter presses a tender kiss to my forehead. "Will you come to New Jersey with me for Christmas?"

I can't stop the wide grin stretching across my face.

There's still so much to figure out. Like, is he going to get traded to New Jersey? Am I going to win the syndication deal? Where do we both end up after all of this? But I can't worry about any of that because right now, I'm the happiest I've been since... Since, I can't remember when.

"You want me to meet your mom?"

"She's begging to meet you and...she doesn't ask for much."

"This is just for her, then?" I tease, looping my arms tighter around his neck.

He shakes his head, that cocky grin I can never resist tugging at his mouth.

"Absolutely not. I just had a sudden fantasy of trying to fuck you in my childhood bedroom. Sixteen-year-old me would lose his goddamn mind if he knew I was bringing home a girl like you."

He leans in, brushing his lips over mine. "Hope you're cool with twin beds, Collins."

I laugh, the sound bubbling out of me before I can stop it. "You are so kinky, it's almost impressive."

"Almost?" He smirks. "Eliminate rule number one and you'll see just how twisted I can get."

He drops his forehead to mine, voice low and teasing. "So, you'll come?"

"It's the first time I'll have missed Christmas with my family, but I can't seem to bring myself to turn down the promise of you trying to sneak to second base on your twin bed. You really laid the hype on thick."

"Have I told you that baseball was my second-best sport in high school?"

"I'm shocked, can you tell?"

"I'm taking that as a yes, Passenger Princess," he says.

"Yes, I'll come."

Relief washes over Hunter's face, and he pulls me into a fierce hug, his lips finding mine in a kiss that leaves me breathless.

I melt into his embrace. This is uncharted territory for both of us, but the thought of spending the holidays with Hunter, of being welcomed into his family, fills me with a warmth I haven't felt in a long time.

I have no idea what this means for us, or if it means anything, but I can't turn down this opportunity to see where Hunter comes from—what's shaped him into the person I'm falling for, no matter

how much I've tried to resist it.
New Jersey, here I come.

CHAPTER TWENTY-TWO

Hunter

As Peyton and I pull up to my mom's house, a familiar knot tightens low in my stomach.

It's a small Cape Cod tucked into an older neighborhood in northern Jersey, the kind of street lined with mature maple trees and cracked sidewalks that frost over by late November.

There's a light dusting of fresh snow on the lawn, and Christmas lights are strung along the roof line. Christmas has always been my mother's favorite holiday.

The porch light is already on, casting a warm glow over the narrow stoop, a cheerful green Mr. Grinch-themed wreath hanging on the door.

Inside, I can already imagine the blast of cinnamon-sugar from the oven, the hum of the old baseboard heaters that always ticked at night. Why do I miss that sound?

It's been a year since I've been back, trying to make my next step out of the farm team as my contract was winding down, and it paid off with a large Hawkeyes contract that Everett Kauffman himself pushed for with the old owner Phil Carlton while they were still in negotiations.

The effort worked out for my career, but it's been too long.

Maybe if I'd been around more... Maybe if I was still playing for New Jersey...

My gut twists harder.

Maybe my mother wouldn't be keeping so much from me.

I flex my hands on the steering wheel before forcing myself to let go, reaching for Peyton's hand instead.

If Bethany's right—and my mom's sicker than she's letting on—what the hell am I supposed to do?

Take the trade?

Come back here and forget everything that's happening between Peyton and me?

Would she even want to move across the country for me?

The thought barely flickers through my head before I shove it back down.

Too soon.

Too much.

One step at a time.

Peyton squeezes my hand gently, pulling me out of the spiral.

"You okay?" she asks, her voice low and warm.

I nod, forcing a smile. "Yeah. Just... It's been a while, you know? And I'm worried about her."

Peyton holds my gaze a second longer than necessary, then nods, squeezing once more before letting go.

"I'm right here," she says simply.

We grab our bags and walk up the front steps, the December cold nipping at our skin.

When the door opens, my mom stands there, arms wide, that same bright smile stretched across her face.

Only...she's thinner.

There are dark shadows under her eyes that weren't there the last time I saw her.

But she pulls me into a hug that feels exactly the same—tight, fierce, full of unconditional love.

"Hunter, honey, it's so good to see you," she murmurs into my chest.

Then she turns to Peyton and wraps her up just as tightly.

"And you must be Peyton! It's wonderful to finally meet you, dear. I'm Carly."

Peyton beams, cheeks pink from the cold—or maybe from the Reed family welcome assault.

"It's so nice to meet you too, Ms. Reed."

"Please," Mom laughs, waving her off. "It's Carly. And come on in. You must be freezing."

Inside, the house smells like a bakery, the fake tree my mother keeps up in the attic taking its annual spot in the corner of the living room with all the same ornaments that we've had since I was a kid.

The living room is cozy, cluttered in the way of lived-in homes—crocheted throws over the couch, a cluttered side table full of holiday cards, and everywhere, pieces of my childhood.

My hockey trophies line one wall, gathering a little dust but polished with pride.

A lump rises in my throat as I follow her gaze.

"I'll take the bags upstairs," I say quickly, trying to shake it off.

"You do that," Mom says, steering Peyton toward the kitchen. "I could use some help decorating the cookies for the Christmas Eve retirement home cookie exchange. You up for it, Peyton?"

"I love decorating Christmas cookies," Peyton says with an excited tone that I can hear as I ascend the stairs with our luggage. "My mom and I do it every year."

As I head upstairs, I catch snippets of their conversation—Mom explaining how cream of tartar and a little Crisco are the secret to icing that doesn't run, Peyton's easy laughter in response.

For a second, the tension in my chest eases.

Mom still sounds like Mom.

Maybe Bethany's wrong.

Maybe everything's fine.

But the moment I walk into my old bedroom, my stomach drops again.

Gone are the sun-bleached posters, the scratched-up homework desk, the ancient twin bed.

The room's been repainted a soft sage green.

The bed is now a California king with a fresh comforter set that looks straight off a Pottery Barn website.

The dresser's new too—sleek, modern lines—nothing like the battered furniture I grew up with.

Change is hard, but this... This hits harder.

After all these years, after all the times she said she couldn't bear to touch it— she chose now?

Now she changes everything.

I rub a hand over the back of my neck, unsettled, before setting down the bags and heading back downstairs.

I hear my mother's voice float through the house as I hit the bottom of the stairs. "Peyton, what does your family usually do for Christmas?"

"Nothing crazy or out of the ordinary. We used to drive around on Christmas Eve to see Christmas lights, my mom buys store-bought gingerbread houses that we'd decorate as kids, and before my dad passed away, he'd read us *The Night Before Christmas*."

"Oh...I'm so sorry to hear that, dear."

"Thank you. Are these pictures of Hunter?"

Crossing the living room, I catch sight of Peyton again.

She's standing in front of the refrigerator, grinning as my mom ties an apron around Peyton's waist.

Peyton's head tilts as she studies the pictures of a younger me on the fridge.

I don't even realize I'm holding my breath until she turns and spots me watching her.

A smile.

A giggle shakes her shoulders.

"What's this one?" she asks, pointing to a photo.

"Aww that one..." my mom says. "That's his T-ball team picture. He was three."

"He looks so happy here," Peyton points out.

"He was. The photographer told him to give him the kind of stare down he would give a pitcher if he was at bat, but Hunter's always been a fun-loving kid. He couldn't frown to save his life when he was that little."

"And this one?" she asks, pointing to another photo of me with a trophy in my hand. The first one I ever won with my hockey team. After that, I was hooked.

"He made the traveling hockey team across town when he was six. It was a sacrifice to get him there with having to manage the salon as well, but now seeing how far he's come, it was worth it. Though, sometimes I wish I wouldn't have taken him away from the team he was on."

"Really? He said it was a great opportunity to get better," she says, and I lean in to listen too. She's never mentioned it to me.

"I didn't realize how pivotal Coach Murphy was for Hunter. Having a man step in for him like that. I didn't know that's what changed Hunter's drive."

"You didn't know about Coach Murphy?" she asks.

"Not until your show," she says, tightening the bow around Peyton's waist and then patting her on the shoulder to tell her that she's done with the strings. "As far as I know, you're the first person he ever told."

Peyton spins around to look at her, her mouth gaping a little, her eyebrows pulled together.

My mother smiles and then spins back towards the sink as if she's proud of herself to surprise Peyton.

"You have an effect on my son, Peyton. One that no one else seems to have."

"I don't know about that...he's incredibly strong-willed. It's hard to imagine that anyone affects him unless he allows it," she says, and I bite back a chuckle.

"That's not his natural disposition. He's the kind of kid who's never met a stranger—everyone he meets is his friend—a complete chatterbox. The world did a number on him but give him time. He's softening when it comes to you. I can hear it in his voice ever since he started dating you."

I clear my throat and take the few steps into the kitchen, pretending I didn't hear anything.

"Ma, what's up with my room? You changed everything. You got rid of my old bed?"

"Not the twin?" Peyton gasps dramatically, eyes gleaming with laughter as she smirks at me. "I was promised a twin bed, Reed. I packed emotionally for it."

My mom waves a hand. "Please. You're a grown man bringing your girlfriend home. I wasn't about to let you share a mattress built for a tooth fairy. Besides, I've been meaning to turn it into a proper guest room for a while."

I arch a brow. "You kept it the same for ten years."

"I kept it the same because you kept acting like it was still yours," she shoots back, opening the oven door and sliding in another tray of cookies. "Now that you've brought someone home worth impressing, I figured it was time."

Peyton's cheeks flush, but she doesn't look away. I drop the subject. We're only here until Christmas evening, and the last thing I want to do is discuss the contents of a room that I've stayed in a small handful of times since college.

We eat dinner around the small round table in the breakfast nook, the three of us swapping stories while my mom fills us in on the latest salon gossip. Peyton listens with wide eyes as Mom recounts how Lorraine from the Wednesday morning knitting group got turned in to the HOA for harboring an illegal pot-bellied pig.

"Apparently, she walks it on a leash," Mom adds between bites of meatloaf. "And yes, it uses the toilet. Smartest damn animal on the block."

Peyton's laugh is bright and real, and I can't stop staring at her while she laughs like that in my childhood kitchen. It feels... right. Exactly right.

I want to ask my mother about her health—about what the doctors are saying—and if Bethany's intuition is right, but it will have to wait until tomorrow. It's too heavy for our first night.

After dinner, Peyton rinses while I load the dishwasher, both of us elbowing each other playfully until I catch her stifling a yawn.

"All right, I'm stealing her upstairs," I tell my mother, draping a towel over my shoulder. "Long flight."

"Thanks for the cookies and dinner," Peyton says, giving my mom a genuine smile. "And for letting me raid your icing stash."

"You're welcome anytime, sweetheart," my mom replies warmly. "I'm going to head off to the bath as well. I've been on these legs too long."

When we step into my room, Peyton halts in the doorway, eyes sweeping over the neatly made king-sized bed.

"So this is the upgraded childhood lair," she says. "Color me disappointed. Not a single dinosaur bed sheet."

I lean against the doorframe, arms crossed. "They're in the attic. Want me to pull them out? Really complete the fantasy?"

"Only if you're going to return the old playboys under the bed also," she teases.

When we finally settle into bed, Peyton turns to me, her expression soft. "Thank you for bringing me here. I know this place means a lot to you."

I pull her close, pressing a kiss to her forehead. "You mean a lot to me, too."

She snuggles into my side, her hand sliding over my chest.

And this is it.

I know I don't want to just try... I want to make this work.

CHAPTER TWENTY-THREE

Peyton

The smell of cinnamon and coffee greets me before I even open my eyes. I roll onto my side, blinking in the morning light pouring in through Hunter's childhood bedroom window, the snow from last night dusted on the rooftops of the neighboring houses outside.

The new comforter is soft, the mattress firm, and I can hear the faint clinking of dishes from downstairs.

Hunter stretches beside me, shirtless, sleep-ruffled, and already smirking. "I think my mom's trying to seduce us with breakfast."

I laugh. "I'd fall for it."

We eventually make our way downstairs where Carly is already dressed, dishes set out, and bacon sizzling on the stove. She greets us with a warm smile and a plate of scrambled eggs.

"Eat up, kids," she says. "I've got a busy day ahead. Gifts to drop at the animal shelter and the salon. Then I'm heading over to the old folks' home to set up for the cookie exchange."

"We won't see you all day?" Hunter asks.

"I'll be home after the cookie exchange, unless Bonnie

decides she wants to go caroling with the rest of our choir group," she says, loading a cookie tin.

"Ma, it's Christmas Eve..."

"Yeah, I know...but you're aware that I've packed my schedule to help others during the holidays ever since you left for college. And you only gave me a few weeks' notice that you were coming for Christmas. I already committed. And this family follows through on its commitments. I've already taught you that."

"I think it's great," I pitch in.

Carly turns around from the counter and gives me a smile. "See, a girl with a good head on her shoulders." She sets the tin in a huge box that's filled to the brim. "Now, be a good son and take this box out to my car for me. It's heavy. You two have fun today, and I'm sure I'll see you later tonight."

He takes the box, and I watch her follow him out to the car. He sets the box in the trunk of her minivan and then kisses the top of her head before opening her driver's side door, shutting it once she's inside.

My heart swells at how sweet he is with his mother.

After breakfast, Hunter leans close. "Get dressed into something comfortable. I have a surprise."

A short drive later, we pull up in front of a massive tennis and sports complex. It's the kind of place with tall glass windows, indoor courts, and a sleek sign that says "The Net Spot."

"This place is huge," I say as we walk in.

"Figured we could play a round. Or ten," he says.

We change and hit the court. From the other side of the net, Hunter does some over-the-top stretches—groin lunges, arm flaps, even a twirl.

"Hope my thighs in these shorts don't distract you," he calls. "I know what you want, dirty girl, but I'm more than just a pretty face."

I snort. "Pretty? Bold claim from someone about to get destroyed."

"Confidence is key, baby."

To his credit, Hunter's actually good. His footwork is solid, his serves are wicked. But I've been playing since I was four, and by the third round, he's sweating, swearing, and glaring at me in mock betrayal.

"You hustled me," he gasps, winded.

"I told you I had Wimbledon in my sights before my injury."

"Yeah, but you didn't say you were the devil in a ponytail."

We grab lunch at the on-site café, sitting at a small table tucked in the corner. Hunter orders a spinach fruit smoothie, a burger with extra bacon, and a large order of crinkle fries. I grin at the contrast.

"Balance," he says, mouth full. "Athlete logic."

After lunch, he drives us to an indoor hockey rink.

"Where are we?" I ask as he pulls into a parking spot.

"This is where my high school hockey team used to play." A familiar sparkle lighting up his eyes.

The second we get out and meet up behind the car, he reaches for my hand.

It should feel foreign. But somehow, it feels like I've been holding it forever.

"Get out your phone," he says as we walk toward the entrance.

I blink. "What?"

He shoots me a crooked smile. "Can you walk and talk? I'd bet good money you've already memorized the questions you want to ask me for our third interview."

Of course I have them memorized. But there's more riding on this than just the interview. With everything between us shifting, I don't want to push too hard and risk him shutting down—or worse, walking away. Yet, I also know that my opportunity to snag the syndication deal and make my dad proud, is hanging in the balance too.

He squeezes my hand gently. "Record it. I owe you one more. I want you to have this."

Something in his voice makes me stop questioning. I pull out my phone, hit record, and follow him through the front doors.

BLEACHER REPORT

Hunter leads me through a side door, down a narrow hallway that smells like wet gear and sports tape, and into the heart of the rink. He's relaxed here. There's a bounce in his step I haven't seen since before his injury.

We make our way to the bleachers and sit on the cold aluminum bench overlooking the ice. The hum of the overhead lights fills the space, the rink eerily quiet without players slicing across it.

He leans back on the bench, elbows resting on the seat behind us, his eyes scanning the ice like he's watching ghosts from the past.

"You're smiling," I say. "Take me through what you're thinking."

"This place is where it all really clicked for me. But it didn't come easily. High school hockey was a different animal than what I had been used to playing," he says. "Freshman year was the first time I was on the third line. Couldn't land a hit to save my life. Coach joked that I skated like a baby deer on a trampoline."

I smile behind the camera. "Hard to imagine. You're one of the most physical players in the league."

"That's what happens when you're a big fish in a tiny pond, and then they drop you in the ocean with hungry piranhas all looking to catch the eye of scouts. That hadn't been a factor in middle school. There were still kids playing just for the fun of it, but high school hockey isn't for the faint of heart. I've seen more kids lose chiclets in one single game than I had in the years I'd played the sport up until then."

I grin behind the camera. "Sounds brutal. But you clearly adapted."

"Yeah, well, turns out growing six inches in one summer helps with that too." He grins. "By sophomore year, I was big enough to make an impact."

"Cheating," I tease. "You basically leveled up overnight. Meanwhile, I spent all of high school trying to convince recruiters I wasn't too short to return a serve."

He chuckles, that familiar spark in his eyes. "You? Short? You serve with murder in your heart."

I muffle back laughter thinking back on our earlier game and how much I love that he's not the sore loser I called him back at Oakley's that first time we met. A time that feels so far away, almost as if it didn't happen.

"Did you used to dream about playing in the NHL here?"

He nods. "Every damn day. I'd sneak in during open skates and pretend I was scoring the game-winner in a playoff series. Right there—" He points toward the far side of the rink. "Bottom left corner. Coach used to stay late so I could practice that shot."

Something swells in my chest. This isn't just a location—it's a living memory. And he's letting me inside it.

"Is this where you fell in love with hockey?"

"This is where I fell in love with who I was when I played. Before the contracts. Before the agents. Before it all got complicated."

"You didn't get recruited out of high school," I say, knowing his history.

"My mom was going through chemo then, and I didn't want to go far. I had a couple of junior league scouts reach out, but I stayed close and went to college instead. It meant I could still get her to treatments. Cook dinner once in a while. Her best friend Bonnie was a big help too."

My chest tightens.

"And you don't regret it?"

"Not for a second." His voice is steady. "We had a stacked team—I learned a lot in college. And eventually, Jersey picked me up."

He stares back out onto the ice as a few high school players skate out for practice.

"So, no big drama? No rebellious phase? No high school scandal?"

"Oh, there was drama." He smirks. "One time, I broke into the opposing team's locker room before a game and replaced all their warm-up playlists with Celine Dion's greatest hits."

I choke on a laugh. "You didn't."

"They came out to 'My Heart Will Go On.' It backfired though because they were so fucking pissed that they whipped the ice with us."

"So you regret it?"

"Hell no. It was still funny as shit. My coach didn't like it much, though."

"You can take the prankster off the rink..." I say.

He nods toward the far goal line.

"See that crease?"

I follow his gaze.

"That's where I scored my first high school goal. Triple overtime. My stick flew out of my hands, and I tackled my own teammate in celebration. Sprained his wrist. Coach benched me for the next game."

"You don't know when to quit," I tease.

"I never quit," he replies, and then his voice softens. "I haven't been back here in years. But I wanted you to see it."

I lower the phone slightly, feeling that familiar warmth rise in my chest again.

"Why me?"

He doesn't look away from the ice.

"Because this...was sacred. And you make everything feel like it matters again."

I want to shut off my phone and just be present for this moment between us, when he's sharing all of this with me. Unfortunately, I have an interview to turn in, and a part of me is looking forward to having all of our original agreements behind us so that we can move on.

"When you were signed by New Jersey, how did that feel?"

"Looking back, that was a rollercoaster ride. I've never been so high and then hit a low so quickly in my life."

"When they transferred you to the farm team?" I ask.

"I only got to play half a season on professional ice. I thought I might not ever make it back here."

I nod slowly. "There were rumors. About your attitude. About Bethany."

It's a huge gamble, and he might get up and walk out of this rink, leaving me here to walk back to his mom's house, but I have to at least ask the questions even if he doesn't answer them.

He stiffens just slightly, his jaw ticking. But he doesn't look away.

"I don't like thinking back on those days," he says. "It doesn't do anyone any good. Bethany and I dated in college and into my rookie year. It didn't work out. That's it. Nothing more to say about it. Bethany and I grew apart—Richard made a business call regarding his team that I don't agree with—end of story. Now, I'm playing for one of the best teams in the league, and I feel like I'm right where I need to be."

It's not the juicy detail I was hoping for. The truth is that I know what she did, but Hunter just gave me more on the story than anyone else has ever gotten out of him. This might be enough for the syndication deal.

And more importantly, he's still sitting here. Still talking. And that comment he made about being where he needs to be...it feels like I'm part of that now.

I lower the camera just slightly and ask, "If you weren't playing hockey, what would you be doing right now?"

Without missing a beat, Hunter grins. "That's easy. Personal Speedo car washer."

I blink. "You're joking."

"Dead serious," he says, eyes gleaming with mischief. "I'd shave the ice, blast club music, maybe even throw in a little choreography. Make it a full experience."

I laugh, shaking my head. "You're unbelievable."

"But admit it—you'd come watch."

"I'd come for the soapsuds and stay for the tragic tan lines."

He clutches his chest. "Wounded. But noted. No tan lines."

I shake my head, grinning. "You'd make a fortune in tips."

"Obviously," he says, and then slaps the back of his thigh.

"These glutes are money makers."

We sit in silence for a beat, both of us watching a couple of players practice shots.

Then I ask the question I always save for last.

"If you could go back in time and fix a mistake, what would it be—and what would you do differently?"

Hunter's shoulders go still. He doesn't answer right away. Just watches the far end of the rink, the ghost of a dozen younger versions of himself skating in his silence.

Finally, he speaks.

"If I could go back...I'd redo the first night we met at Oakley's. I was drunk and angry and made assumptions about you that I had no right to make." He glances at me. "You didn't deserve that. I'd take it back in a heartbeat. And then I would have asked for your number so I could call you on a night I wasn't plastered."

My throat tightens. It's not the soundbite I was chasing—but it might be the most honest thing he's ever said on camera.

"Thank you," I whisper. "For letting me see this part of you."

He shrugs, trying to play it off, and then straightens his back. "Don't get used to it, Collins. I have a reputation to maintain."

But the small smile pulling at his mouth says otherwise.

I end the video. I got enough and now I want the rest of him to myself.

"You shared a lot. More than you have in past interviews. Are you sure you're okay with me sharing this?" I ask, tucking my phone into my pocket.

"I figured you could use some solid B-roll for your interview cut if you're trying to win that syndication deal. This is what I agreed to, and now that Bethany has left Seattle, I owe you my end of our arrangement."

"We're a good team," I tease.

He nods and then reaches over and gives my thigh a gentle squeeze, making my whole body react. God, do I love his hands on me. "C'mon. I'll show you the snack bar that has the best nachos in town."

"Oh God...*this* is your move, isn't it? Is this how you convinced all the high school girls to kiss you under the bleachers?"

He looks over his shoulder with that troublemaker grin of his that has me laughing. "The last time I tried it, I ended up spilling the entire tray in my lap, covering my crotch in spicy, hot nacho cheese. But if you want to make out under the bleachers, Collins, I'd happily oblige you. I wouldn't want to be a bad host," he says, leading me out to the concessions that are getting ready for some Christmas Eve ice show.

"Slow down, Romeo. Wow me with these nachos first, then we'll see where the night takes us."

He laughs as I follow behind him, my hand in his.

And it occurs to me how much I wish I could have seen the Hunter before Bethany. What Carly said about him warming up has me wishing we had met earlier, but then I wouldn't get the man he is now, and maybe that would be a shame too.

Maybe we met just in time.

By the time we pull back into the driveway, the last of the sunlight is slipping behind the neighbor's roofline.

"I'm going to start dinner," Hunter says as we step inside, dropping the keys on the entryway table. "You want to hang down here or...?"

"Actually," I say, slipping off my coat, "would you mind if I went upstairs for a bit to edit the interview? I know it's Christmas Eve, but the execs are waiting for all my final deliverables."

Hunter nods without hesitation. "Go ahead. I'll holler when it's ready."

I head up to his room, slipping onto the edge of the oversized bed with my laptop. An hour passes in a blur as I cut together clips, keeping the edit light and natural. I leave in the echo of the rink, the squeak of his shoes against the floor, the way his voice softened when he talked about taking care of Carly when she was sick.

But I take out his final answer—the one about Oakley's bar and the apology. That part is just for me.

Once I'm done, I hover over the publish button, then tap

it without second-guessing. I mute my notifications—no one's watching a sports interview on Christmas Eve anyway, and honestly, I don't want to be tethered to my phone tonight.

Not when I've got this.

Downstairs, the house smells like garlic bread and spaghetti sauce. Hunter's at the stove, sleeves rolled up, wooden spoon in hand. I lean in the doorway for a moment, watching him hum along to the holiday music playing low on the speaker, like this is just any regular night.

Dinner is warm and easy. We linger over second helpings, share stories from childhood Christmases, and laugh over the fact that neither of us can remember all the words to "Frosty the Snowman."

Later, we curl up on the couch with a wool blanket and an old black-and-white holiday movie that Hunter says he and his mom watch together every year.

I love that he's bringing me into his traditions—showing me this side of him.

Hunter answers a call from his mom.

"Carolers," he says with a grin as he puts her on speaker.

"I couldn't say no," Carly says cheerfully. "The ladies from my choir group showed up at the old folks' home and demanded. I'll be back late. Don't wait up."

Hunter laughs. "Stay out as long as you want. We're good here."

We hang up, and I shift closer, feeling his arm slide around my shoulders. He looks down at me, eyes warm, lips barely parted like he's about to say something—or kiss me—

When my phone buzzes on the arm of the couch.

I glance at the screen and frown. "It's Rebecca."

He lifts his eyebrows. "On Christmas Eve?"

I answer, and Rebecca launches in without preamble.

"Peyton, your video is blowing up. Like, network-level viral. One of the senior producers just called me. They're talking about fast-tracking the contract."

"Wait, how is it going viral? No one's watching my podcast on Christmas Eve."

Hunter hears my words and then grabs his phone out of the pocket of his sweats. I watch as he quickly pulls up the video, my eyes widen at the number of views.

"That's where you're wrong. It's had over five hundred thousand views, and you only posted it a couple of hours ago. Besides, the network is my life, and the other execs are the same. We never take a day off. Media doesn't sleep."

"Oh my God," I whisper.

My eyes flash back up to Hunter's, and he's smiling wide.

Rebecca's voice comes back in, and I almost forgot that she's still on the line.

"You'll probably be asked to head into the Seattle office the day after Christmas."

My pulse spikes. "You're serious?"

"Absolutely, the comment section is blowing up. The authenticity, the intimacy—people are eating it up. I'll be in touch but prepare yourself for coming into the network's office the day after Christmas. You'll have contracts to sign."

She hangs up before I can respond, and I stare at the phone like it might vanish.

"Was that real?" I ask, still breathless.

Hunter leans in, his voice low and warm. "That was very real."

He's still holding his phone, screen tilted toward me, showing the growing number of views, the flood of heart emojis and fire icons in the comments. I watch the count tick up again—five hundred twenty thousand now.

My heart leaps.

"Peyton," he says, setting his phone aside and taking mine too. "You did it."

Before I can second-guess myself, I lunge at him, laughing, arms wrapping around his neck.

"We did it," I whisper against his jaw, giddy and a little

stunned.

"Yeah, we did," he says, pulling me closer. "Bethany left Seattle, and you just got your syndication deal. And we did it with time to spare."

He presses his lips to mine and my mouth opens for him, his hot tongue searing against mine, each of us fighting to get closer, to have our hands all over each other, to touch everywhere we can.

Soon, his hands slide down to my waist, gripping tight as he lifts me clean off the couch. I gasp, instinctively wrapping my legs around his hips, anchoring myself to him as he straightens to full height.

"Where are we going?" I ask.

"To celebrate the end of our arrangement and the start of something permanent."

Our lips never leave each other as he carries me up the staircase and down the hall to his bedroom.

And I know that he's right. We're on to something so much better.

CHAPTER TWENTY-FOUR

Peyton

Christmas Morning

It's quiet. Still. The kind of quiet that makes me forget where I am for a second. But then I smell baked bread, cinnamon, and nutmeg wafting up the stairs, and I remember—I'm in Hunter's childhood home.

He's already out of bed, the space beside me still warm, and I can hear faint humming from downstairs. Carly's cheerful voice, totally on-key, humming "Baby, It's Cold Outside," has me tempted to jump in and sing the melody, but my voice sounds more like fingernails against a chalkboard than Hunter's mother. I'm not ready to scare Hunter off with my horrifying singing just yet.

I roll over and stretch, my cheek still pressed into the soft pillowcase. Something about this house, this morning, feels like I made the right decision to come.

I slip out of bed, pull out one of Hunter's old college hockey hoodies from the brand-new dressers under the window, and follow the sounds of clattering pans and laughter down the stairs.

Carly's in the kitchen in a Santa apron with flour dusting her hair, smiling like she's been waiting all morning for Christmas to arrive. Her cheeks are pink and flushed, her voice steady and full of happiness. Whatever Hunter's fears were...maybe Bethany was wrong. Carly seems stronger and in good health. Then again, this is the first time I'm meeting her.

"Good morning, dear. Are you hungry?" I hear Carly say, noticing me coming through the kitchen threshold before Hunter does.

But then his eyes are on me in a split second. Those deep green eyes that I know could find me in a crowded room or a packed stadium. A shiver shoots down my spine and my cheeks warm to a blush that must be evident because his soft smile turns to a smirk.

He knows he's winning me over.

Cocky bastard. I can't help it—I smile back.

"Starving. It smells really good in here. Can I help with anything?" I ask, as Carly fills batter into the waffle maker and Hunter turns to open the fridge, reaching in to grab the orange juice carton.

Carly waves me off with a spatula. "You just enjoy. You're our guest."

"I don't mind," I say, stepping up beside her. "I've been known to dominate the cinnamon roll icing game. Legendary, even."

Carly grins. "Then you've come to the right place. The icing's cooling by the window. You want to be on drizzle duty?"

"Drizzle duty is my calling," I say, already moving to the bowl of thick icing. I pick up the spoon and test the consistency, giving Hunter a look. "Cream cheese frosting?"

"Of course," he says, pouring juice into glasses. "This isn't amateur hour, Collins."

I glance up at him as he closes the fridge and catches me staring. He walks coolly up behind me and bends, his mouth close to my ear. "That hoodie on you is doing it for me, by the way. I might like it even better than my jersey," his voice low and private.

"It's almost unfair that we're not alone. I'd take you on this island if it were just us."

There's a deep need in his voice. One that I can relate to wholeheartedly.

I glance down at myself in his oversized hoodie and fuzzy socks. "Your hoodie looked more comfortable than mine."

"I like it," he says and then glances around the kitchen. "In fact, I think you look good in everything of mine." As if meaning that I look good in his childhood home.

And that right there...that undoes me.

Hunter leans in, brushing a kiss to my temple. "Remind me to send you home with every hoodie I own."

Carly clears her throat, clearly amused. "Save it for the mistletoe, you two. You're making the waffles jealous."

We all laugh, the kind of warm, genuine laughter that settles into your bones. I drizzle icing over the cinnamon rolls, and Carly flips waffles with ease, like she's done this every year of her life. Hunter slides up beside me with two mugs of hot tea, offering me one.

"Peppermint. Drizzle of honey," he says, almost shyly.

"You remembered?" I ask, taking it.

"You make things hard to forget," he says simply.

Something flickers in my chest. I glance around—at the steaming food, the snow falling lightly through the kitchen window, the garland strung over the doorway—and realize I've never had a Christmas morning that feels quite like this in a really long time. Not since my dad passed.

Like for once, it doesn't feel as hard to breathe without my dad here.

Carly sets a bowl of eggs on the table. "Okay, time to eat before the food gets cold. Hunter, don't hover over the bacon tray this year."

"Not my fault the bacon and I have unresolved tension," he says, already grabbing a slice. "Don't worry...it's consensual."

I snort into my tea. "Where do you come up with this stuff?"

Carly shakes her head and then looks over at me. "He's always been like this. And I'm sorry to tell you honey, but I don't see it improving anytime soon," she teases.

"Good," I say, plopping down at the kitchen table next to Hunter. "I like him just as he is."

Carly giggles, and Hunter smiles over at me with a mouthful of bacon and then reaches over to squeeze my thigh in solidarity.

We all sit, plates loaded and conversation flowing easily. Carly tells stories about Hunter's middle school years—his obsession with glitter glue in third grade...which brings new light to his previous gift—and his brief phase as a magician's assistant in fifth.

"Wait, you were in a magic show?" I ask, nearly choking on a bite of waffle.

"He wore a velvet cape," Carly says with a wink. "He was so cute."

"A burgundy velvet cape," Hunter mutters. "With gold trim. I'll never live it down."

"I'm going to need photo evidence," I say, reaching for my phone.

"There are photos," Carly confirms. "I'll send them."

"I'm taking back everyone's presents. No Christmas this year," Hunter grumbles, but his grin betrays him.

We eat until we're stuffed, and then—finally, we carry our mugs into the living room. The tree is large, with only a handful of gifts beneath it—nothing extravagant, not with such short notice. But none of that matters. Because somehow, this all feels perfect. Warm, simple, real.

Hunter flops onto the couch beside me, still in sweatpants and a T-shirt, looking way too good for someone who woke up like that. I tuck my legs beneath me with my hot tea in hand.

"Open that one," Carly says, pointing to a soft, fabric-wrapped package.

I pull the ribbon loose and let out a soft gasp. "Is this... handmade?"

"It's a game-day blanket," Carly beams. "Hawkeyes' colors,

and if you look close—"

"My number's stitched all over it," Hunter finishes, smiling proudly.

I smooth a hand along the edges, touched in a way I didn't expect. "This is incredible. Thank you. I'm definitely bringing it to the next home game."

How she could have made it so quickly with the little notice that Hunter had given her about me coming along this year, I have no idea—but I love it.

Hunter leans close and mutters under his breath, "It's also the exact shade of that sparkly toy in your nightstand."

My eyes widen, and I elbow him sharply. "Do you have a death wish?"

Carly doesn't seem to notice. She's already unwrapping the gift that Hunter picked up under the tree from me and handed to her—a sleek, digital photo frame. As soon as the screen lights up and begins rotating through candid snapshots of Hunter over the last few months, she goes still.

"These are beautiful," she whispers. "Are these from the recent games?"

"I have a folder on my phone where I can keep adding more," I say, trying not to sound too emotional. "I just thought...maybe it would feel like you were there. At the games. Behind the scenes. I'll take them while I'm there and upload them so you feel like you're there with us."

She presses a hand to her chest. "Oh, Peyton..."

Hunter looks away, blinking hard, like it's a lot for him, too.

She gets up off the couch and heads straight for me, wrapping her arms around my neck. "I knew he picked a good one. I'm so relieved he finally found you," she whispers against my hair.

"Okay, my turn," Hunter says next to me, handing his mom an envelope.

She takes it in her hand and looks at it for a second, then glances back at him. "You didn't have to get me anything. You two being here is what I really wanted for Christmas."

"I know but I think you'll like this one," he says, reaching her arm over the back of the couch behind me. "Merry Christmas."

The second she sees the paperwork inside, her eyes widen and her face almost goes white. My stomach drops. What the heck did he give her?

"You paid off the deed to the house?"

I glance at him in shock but he's staring at her, his expression calm. He hadn't said anything about this to me. I had no idea. Not that it was my place to know any of this.

Hunter's taking care of her, the way my father made sure that my mother was taken care of if anything ever happened to him. Emotions flood and my eyes begin to well.

"I meant to do it back when I signed with New Jersey," he says softly. "But...life got in the way. I can now. So I did."

He stands and she throws her arms around him, and I swallow the sudden lump in my throat.

"You didn't have to do this," she muffles against his shoulder.

He's so much taller than her, and the height difference makes me smile.

"I didn't have to...I get to, and that's the best part. You took out a second mortgage to put me through hockey camp, then again to help me through college, and again for your first round of chemo. It's my turn to take care of you. Now you can do anything you want to do."

She nods, "Thank you," she says, sliding the paperwork back into the envelope and wipes a tear from her eye.

Hunter reaches for the gift I got him and opens it.

It's a ridiculously oversized weighted blanket that I had to pay an overweight fee to fly here, but it was worth it.

"For movie nights," I grin. "The one we have now doesn't even cover your legs. You let out all the heat."

"Because you're a blanket hog," he shoots back.

He digs deeper into the box and pauses. "Is this...a stroller?"

"For Sproutacus," I say. "Now that mom and dad are staying together, he deserves to see the world. I thought we could take him on nightly walks around the neighborhood."

Carly laughs so hard she nearly spills her tea.

He leans over and gently pulls my chin towards him to lay a kiss on my lips. "It's fucking perfect. I can't wait to take him on his first stroll with you."

"Did I take it too far? People are going to think we're crazy," I say.

Hunter shakes his head. "It's Seattle. Last week I saw a dog pushing a guy in a stroller. We're not even the craziest people on that block."

Then he gets up and grabs a small box from under the tree.

"This one's special," he says, placing it in my lap. "Promise not to yell?"

"Not making any promises," I murmur, tearing into the wrapping paper.

Inside is a black Speedo. A very tiny one. With...my face on it. Right over the, well...front.

I stare. Then blink. "Is this...?"

"For when I wash your car in February," he says, grinning smugly. "Some rules, I think we should keep."

"You got this custom-made with my face over your cock?"

Carly bursts out laughing, and my cheeks go fire-engine red the second I realize I just said *cock*—out loud—in front of his *mother*.

"Yup," Hunter says, grinning. "Had to explain it to the lady at the embroidery shop. Pretty sure I'm banned now."

"You really shouldn't have..." I start.

He ignores me, tapping the side of the box. "Don't forget the coupons."

I reach in and pull out a homemade coupon book, flipping it open—already bracing myself:

Water Sproutacus in a thong
Vacuum the living room in just Crocs
Drive you to yoga, Speedo only

Each one is more ridiculous than the last—a collection of

favors I can cash in, all involving him half-naked and probably violating a few local ordinances.

"You didn't..." I say, laughing as I shake my head.

"Oh, I did," he says proudly.

He's practically vibrating with excitement. He's clearly been dying to give me this gift, and I can see it written all over his face.

Carly watches us, amused but trying not to ask questions.

"This was...creative. And deeply on-brand for you. Thank you," I say, tucking everything back in the box.

The doorbell rings just as I'm closing it up, still laughing.

Hunter stiffens beside me, and Carly pauses mid-sip of her tea. "Who on earth would be stopping by on Christmas morning?"

"Probably Mrs. Bramble from next door," Carly says, standing. "She usually brings over her spiked Christmas morning eggnog—"

"I'll get it," Hunter says quickly, already rising. "But spiked eggnog...at nine in the morning?"

His tone is light, but something in it makes me look up.

I watch him cross the living room, still relaxed, still casual—until he opens the door.

Then I see it.

His body goes still. His shoulders lock.

The shift in the air is instant.

And then I hear her voice.

"Hunter," she says sweetly. "Aren't you going to invite me in?"

I freeze.

My stomach drops.

Bethany.

From the couch, I can't see her, but I hear everything. The soft clack of expensive heels crossing the threshold. The pointed tone in her voice that doesn't quite match the fake smile I know she's wearing.

Carly gasps softly. "Beth! What are you doing here, honey?"

"I was just in the neighborhood," Bethany says, breezing into the living room like she owns it. "Thought I'd stop by with a few gifts. I didn't have anything better to do today."

Of course not.

She's dressed like she's heading to brunch at the Four Seasons—an expensive dress, long peacoat with a fur collar, clinging to every curve, and high heeled boots too high for snow, and more makeup than anyone should be wearing at this hour on Christmas morning. She places a perfectly arranged bouquet in Carly's hands and sets two gifts on the table like she's Santa with a blowout.

One for Carly.

One for Hunter.

My eyes lock on that second box.

Bethany glances at me for the first time, a barely-there smirk tugging at her red-painted lips. Her gaze lingers—calculating, amused, like I'm the entertainment and she already knows the ending.

I keep my smile polite and sip my tea. Barely.

Hunter doesn't move to take the gift.

"Come on," she says, stepping closer. "Don't be rude. It's Christmas."

Carly shoots him a look—the gentle mom kind that's half warning, half plea.

Reluctantly, he takes it and peels off the wrapping. Inside is a silver picture frame, glossy and delicate. A photo sits behind the glass.

I lean forward instinctively, just as Hunter stiffens.

The picture is of them—Bethany and Hunter—on ice skates at the same rink he took me to yesterday. Both their cheeks flushed, her hands in his. They look...young. Happy.

A tiny tremor slides through me.

It's subtle. Barely a crack. But it's there.

And Bethany sees it.

Because she watches me as I look at the photo—her eyes gleaming with something dark and smug. She doesn't need to say anything. The message is clear.

BLEACHER REPORT

I was here first.

My throat goes tight, but I swallow it down.

Not here. Not in Carly's living room. Not in front of Hunter.

"I didn't realize you still had that. I figured you burned everything before moving into Richard's mansion," he says flatly, holding the frame by its edge like it might burn him.

Bethany shrugs. "Not everything can be replaced. Some things are forever. I thought it was a nice memory. You always did say that was your favorite night."

"That was a long time ago. A lot has changed, including your last name, if you remember."

Carly clears her throat, trying to bring the tension down. "Well, thank you, Beth. That was thoughtful." She opens her own gift—something from Tiffany's, of course—and I let the murmur of motherly gratitude and charm bracelets blur into the background.

Because all I can hear is my own heartbeat pounding in my ears.

I feel Bethany's stare before I even turn.

That smile—blinding, predatory, sharp enough to slice through the cinnamon-sugar warmth of the kitchen—burns between my shoulder blades.

"I'll be right back," I say quickly, grabbing my mug. "Just need the restroom."

"Okay, honey," Carly calls after me. "The rest of us will get started on those cinnamon rolls. They should be ready soon, and they'll go great with Mrs. Bramble's eggnog."

"Unless she's already passed out drunk in her kitchen from drinking her own supply," Hunter jokes.

Bethany laughs too loudly, like it's her job.

I duck into the downstairs bathroom. But I don't need to pee. I need to breathe. Because Bethany showing up just when things were finally starting to feel right? That's classic Bethany.

I grip the edges of the sink and stare at my reflection. Hunter doesn't want her. He's chosen me. We're supposed to start something new after this trip. After Christmas. After Carly. After—

The knock comes just as I'm trying to shake it all off.

I don't even have time to respond before the door creaks open—

And five-foot-nine of perfume and perfectly waved hair sweeps in like she owns the place, forcing me to step back just to keep from being steamrolled.

"Bethany—"

"We need to talk."

"I don't think we do. Hunter doesn't want to be with you. That's not on me. That's on you."

"This isn't about Hunter," she snaps. "It's about Carly."

That stops me.

"What about her?"

"She's sick, Peyton. Really sick. And she's been lying to Hunter."

My breath catches. "What are you talking about?"

Bethany pulls four envelopes from her designer purse and drops them dramatically onto the bathroom counter.

I glance down. They're all addressed to Carly Reed. One's from a cancer research center in Texas, another in Michigan, one from Florida, and the last from somewhere in Washington.

"Clinical trials," I breathe. "You stole these? Isn't that a federal offense to steal mail?"

"Technically I didn't open them," she says, like that makes it better. "She'd have to press charges, and honestly? I don't care. She's lying to everyone, and I had to know the truth."

"So you...suspected?"

"She's been missing salon days. Her best friend Bonnie's been calling me, worried. Carly's tired all the time, dropping weight, and brushing it all off like it's nothing."

The air turns colder. Heavier.

"Oh my god. This is going to destroy Hunter."

Bethany nods, just once. "Yeah. Which is why he has to come home. Carly won't ask him to. She's too proud—too independent. She lives for Hunter, and she'd never ask him to give up his dreams for her. But if he doesn't move home, she won't get the treatment. And you know that."

I blink at her. "So, what—you want me to tell him to take the trade?"

"No," she says, lips curving. "I want you to take yourself out of the equation."

"What?"

"He won't leave you behind. You know that. He'd give up the Hawkeyes. But you? That's trickier. He'll hesitate. He'll weigh you against his mother. And that delay could cost Carly everything. So do the right thing. Let him go."

I stare at her, heart pounding.

Bethany leans in. "End it. Tell him you've changed your mind. That you don't want this anymore. That Seattle's where you belong. And let him belong here. I'll make him happy...eventually he'll see it."

The idea of letting him go eats at me, but the thought of Carly not getting treatment and him losing her? That's something I can't allow to happen.

She tucks the envelopes back in her purse, like it's settled.

"What are you going to do with those?"

"I'm going to confront Carly later. Demand she tell Hunter. But until she does? You're the only one who can save her."

She walks out, leaving the door wide open behind her.

So many ideas swirl in my head. Did Bethany make those up? Are they even real? But there's a part of me that does believe that Bethany cares for Carly, and she seems genuinely concerned.

I have no idea what to do, but I do know that I need to talk to Hunter about all of this. If Carly is sick, he needs to know, and maybe the trade is the right thing to do. But does that mean I have to let him go?

Maybe there's another path forward, but I won't know unless I talk to him.

And maybe, just maybe, Bethany is blowing all of this out of proportion just to get Carly and Hunter to herself.

Hunter

Seeing Bethany at the door earlier almost had me slamming the door in her face. If my mother hadn't heard Beth's voice, I would have.

I try to shake the fact that she's still in my mother's house, putting a damper on my first Christmas with Peyton and my mother together. But with Peyton and I leaving tonight so I can be fresh for practice in two days, I need to stay present, since I'm not sure when I'll be back.

Christmas music plays softly in the background, something old-school and jazzy, and for a moment, everything feels...steady.

I glance down the hallway and hear the bathroom sink shut off.

Peyton will be back in the room in a few seconds.

Everything feels more anchored when she's near.

I push off the counter. "Need help with the plates, Ma?"

She doesn't answer.

The sound of footsteps is near but when I look at the kitchen opening, it's just Bethany, beaming over at me as she comes into the kitchen.

"Ma?" I ask as I turn toward her.

Still nothing.

My brow furrows, and I move closer—just as her hands tremble, the stack of plates tilting in her grip.

Then she sways.

"Ma!"

I barely catch her before the dishes hit the floor. They clatter onto the table as she slumps into me, her body heavy and unresponsive.

"Mom, come on. Stay with me."

Her head lolls. Her eyes flutter.

"Peyton!" I yell, heart hammering, and then I hear her footsteps pounding into the kitchen. "Bethany, call 911!" I bark, already lowering her gently to the floor, cradling her against me like I can hold her here—like I can will her to stay.

Because if Bethany's been right this whole time, then this isn't just a faint spell.

This is something we can't ignore anymore.

CHAPTER TWENTY-FIVE

Peyton

The hospital hallway is full of the sounds of machines beeping and nurses walking around. It's been almost eight hours since we showed up at the hospital this morning.

Everything smells like disinfectant and overused hand sanitizer. The overhead lights buzz faintly, and somewhere behind the next set of double doors, someone coughs. I sit in the plastic chair outside Carly's room, a paper cup of water cradled in my hands.

Hunter steps out from her room, keeping the door open so that he can see her, his expression unreadable. His shoulders are tense, eyes rimmed red but dry. He walks over and sinks into the chair beside me, elbows on his knees.

"She's resting now," he says softly. "The fluids are helping. They're keeping her for observation overnight."

I nod, swallowing hard. "Did they say what caused it?"

Hope blooms that Bethany was wrong in the bathroom and that it was just stress related.

He runs a hand down his face. "Combination of things. Low

iron, dehydration, and overexertion. The cookie drop-offs, the old folks home event, caroling last night... She just overdid it. Her body couldn't keep up."

I let out a breath. "But she's going to be okay?"

Hunter hesitates.

"The cancer's back."

His voice barely makes it out—raw and splintered. The weight of those words seems to drain what's left of the fight in him.

I blink, not sure I heard right, but this is what Bethany warned me about. "What?"

He nods once, a jerky motion. "She didn't want me to know. Said it would distract me. But the tests...they confirmed it."

The paper cup crumples slightly in my hands. "God."

"Yeah, God," he exhales. "I don't know what to do, Peyton. I can't leave her like this. And if I don't force her into treatment, I'm not sure she'll go."

I reach out and pull him into me. His arms wrap around my shoulder as we comfort each other. "Then you make her go," I mumble against his chest. "You're her son. She listens to you."

He pulls back, his gaze searching mine. "And the team? Practice starts back the day after tomorrow. If I don't show up..."

"Call Coach Haynes. Explain the situation. Ask for a few days."

"He might bench me for a game since I'm not there to practice with the team, but you're right. I should call."

I can see him considering it.

"You should stay," I say, quietly. "She needs you. I can stay too, if you want me to."

"Of course I want you here," he says. "But there's nothing you can do. And you've got your meeting with the network. You should go home on the flight tonight like we planned. Do what you've worked so hard for. I won't let you give up the syndication deal. I'll cancel my flight until I know what's going on."

The idea of leaving him here alone stings. But I know he's right. There's nothing I can do except be here for him. But there's still a sting that he's telling me to go, as if the syndication deal means as much to me as he does, but I won't take it personally that he's sending me home. He's trying to do the best for everyone in this situation.

I nod, not wanting him to worry about my concerns or feelings at this point. He needs to focus all of his energy on Carly.

The sound of Carly stirring in bed has both of us glancing toward her room. She fell asleep after all the tests they ran this morning, wiping her out. "Hunter?" Her soft voice reaches out to us.

"Go take care of her," I say gently. "I'll go grab coffee."

He presses a quick kiss to my temple and heads back into the room.

I glance across the hallway and spot Bethany deep in conversation with Bonnie, her voice low, her expression serious. The moment stretches, and for once, Bethany doesn't look smug. She just looks...resolute.

Our eyes meet.

There's something quiet in her gaze this time. Less challenge, more calculation. I turn away, heart pounding, and make my way to the elevators.

The ride down feels like it takes hours.

I stare at the metal doors, the hospital lights flickering faintly overhead, the scent of antiseptic thick in the air. All I can think about is the way Hunter's face collapsed when he said the word *cancer*. The way he leaned into me like I was the only thing keeping him upright.

I've never seen him look so wrecked.

And I've never wanted so badly to fix something I can't.

By the time I reach the main floor, my decision is made. I need to find a way to be here. With him. For however long he needs. Even if it means reshuffling everything else.

Because I'm not just worried about him. I'm *in love* with him.

Somewhere along the way—from fake interviews and made-up contracts to secret glances and unspoken promises—I fell.

Hard. And I want to be the one standing beside him through this. Not watching from three thousand miles away while Bethany fills the gaps I leave behind.

I pause outside the cafeteria, pulling out my phone with trembling fingers.

Outside, the sky is a flat, winter gray. It's Christmas. Everything beyond these hospital walls feels like it's paused—frozen in place. But inside me, everything is moving too fast. I don't want to make a choice between love and career. Not yet. Maybe I don't have to, but either way, Hunter is worth everything.

I scroll to Rebecca's contact and hit call.

She answers on the first ring. "Peyton! What a pleasant surprise."

I was expecting to leave a voicemail today, but it's just as well that I get my answer now so that Hunter and I can make plans moving forward.

"You're working? It's Christmas."

"Holidays are when I get the most done, and the news doesn't care what day it is," she replies. "I don't have anyone at home waiting on me, and the office is quiet. No distractions from the assistants around here." I hear her adjust in her chair. "What can I do for you?"

I take a deep breath. "It's about the network deal. Can I do the show from New Jersey? If I relocate."

A pause. "You mean...move?"

"Yes. I need to know if that's even on the table."

Another pause. "So, the trade rumors are true."

I don't answer.

"Peyton, the network will need you in Seattle. At least a year. Maybe two. After that, I'm sure the network would be open to you moving."

That's not the answer I was hoping for.

My throat tightens. "Rebecca, it's Hunter's mom. She's really sick. And Hunter says she already told him that she won't move to Seattle."

She lets out a *tsk* sound, debating my dilemma. "You're in a tough spot, Peyton, I get it. I can't tell you what to do, but the execs want to move fast. Do you want a couple of days to think about this? See if there is another option? Because if you turn this down, I'll be required to call the other podcaster on the list right now in order to get things moving. I won't be able to go back after we end this call."

I nod to myself. I figured that if I turned this down they'd have to move to the next viable option. "Then I have to say no. I need to be here with him."

She's quiet for a beat. "I can't say that I understand. I chose my career over having a family and I don't regret that, but you have to make your own call. You're sure Hunter is worth this?"

"Yes." I don't have to question it for a second. I know the answer immediately.

She exhales. "If you're sure, then I respect it. I was really looking forward to having another woman podcaster on the network. It's a sausage fest around here," she jokes. "I won't lie and say that I'm not disappointed, but I think big things are still on the horizon for you, and I hope that Hunter knows what he has in you as a partner."

"Thank you. For everything."

We hang up just as I step up to the counter.

"One coffee and a green tea, please."

I pay, then drift over to the pickup counter, scrolling through new messages from Abby and my mom—Christmas morning snapshots from back home. One shows Jesse holding up a giant chocolate Santa, another has my brother on a video call, grinning from a grainy laptop screen in his base quarters, wishing them a Merry Christmas from across the world.

A lump rises in my throat.

I'm about to respond when movement catches my eye near the elevators.

Bethany.

I immediately drop my gaze, hoping she's just headed to the

coffee line too. But instead, she veers sharply toward me—heels clicking with familiar precision—cutting me off before I can pretend to be busy.

"He's not going to make the choice, Peyton," she says, her voice low and cold. "You know that. He'll try to juggle it all. And someone will get hurt. Probably Carly."

"Bethany, don't—he doesn't have to stay in Seattle. I'm working it out."

Bethany lifts her brows. "If you don't break it off, I'll kill the deal."

My jaw clenches. "Then is it me who's hurting Carly? Or you?"

She doesn't answer. Doesn't blink. Just stares at me like she's already won.

"You want what's best for him?" she adds softly. "Give him a clean break."

And then she walks away. Just like that. No fight. No hesitation.

The barista calls my name.

"Order for Peyton!"

I grab the drinks with shaking hands. The cardboard tray creaks slightly in my grip, and the heat from the coffee sears my palm—but it's nothing compared to the burn in my chest.

Everything hurts.

Back upstairs, I round the corner and freeze.

Hunter and Bethany are sitting on either side of Carly's bed, each holding one of her hands.

They look like a team.

A fractured one, maybe. But still a team.

I stand there for a moment, just breathing, trying to calm the storm building behind my ribs. As much as I hate Bethany, she's not wrong about one thing—Hunter is loyal. Too loyal. And he's going to need help getting Carly into treatment. Help from someone relentless. And unfortunately, that might be Bethany.

Hunter notices me and gets up, crossing the hall to meet me.

I paste on a smile so fake I'm shocked it doesn't crack.

"I called Coach Haynes," he says, as I hand him the coffee. "He's giving me the time I need."

"That's great," I say, keeping my voice from wobbling. "I knew they'd understand."

His brow furrows as if he can tell something up. "Yeah. They were good about it."

He takes a sip, but he's watching me too closely now. "Everything okay?"

"Yeah," I lie. "Everything's fine."

But it's not. Because Carly needs him more than I ever will. And Hunter won't walk away unless I force him to.

"Thanks for the coffee," he murmurs.

I glance back toward Carly's room. Bethany is watching us now, careful and still...unsure if I'm going to do what she wants.

I take a breath I don't want to take.

I almost don't say it.

I want to tell him I turned down the deal. That I'm staying. That we'll figure it out.

But then I think of Carly. Of Bethany. Of the letters in that purse. Of the New Jersey deal that Bethany will squash.

So I make myself lie.

"Hey, listen...now that everything's out in the open, maybe you should rethink that trade deal with New Jersey."

Hunter stops mid-sip, brow rising. "You're serious? That would put me three thousand miles away."

"I know." I keep my voice steady. "But with Carly being sick... and not willing to move..."

He stares at me. "What does that mean for us?"

I look down, searching for the words. When I meet his eyes again, I hate myself for what I'm about to say.

"We both got what we started this whole thing for, didn't we? You wanted to shake Bethany. I got the syndication deal."

His jaw ticks. "We both got what we wanted," he repeats, but his tone has gone cold. Guarded.

"I just mean...we came into this without expectations, and now—"

"And now you got what you wanted. The network meeting's tomorrow."

"Hunter, that's not what I—"

"No," he cuts in, stepping back. "I get it. We had an agreement. One I have to take full responsibility for since it was my stupid idea. And I'm the one who went and fell in love with you while it was all supposed to end."

"Hunter—wait."

"It's fine, Peyton. I'm used to being used to further someone else's goals. This time we used each other, right? Call it a draw."

"That's not what this is," I whisper. "It's just...you should be in New Jersey. And my life is in Seattle. It's just...bad timing."

I want to tell him everything. That Bethany threatened to pull the deal if I don't break it off, but then he'll burn his bridge with Bethany and that won't help Carly. They need to do this together or Carly won't budge.

"You don't have to worry about me, Peyton." His voice is brittle. "I'll be fine."

"Do you want me to send you your stuff from the townhouse so you have things here?"

"Already kicking me out?" he says, and I have no idea how to respond. I just know that seeing his things in my house is going to keep this cut from healing. But I didn't mean to hurt him with the idea of moving his things out.

"I don't care what you do with them," he says finally.

He takes another slow sip of his coffee and then glances at me before turning back to check in on his mother. "You should head back to the house. If you want to make your flight, you'll need time to pack. Safe travels."

Then he walks away without another word, back into Carly's room.

Bethany doesn't look smug when our eyes meet. She just looks tired.

I don't have the strength to glare. Or argue.

My heart splinters in my chest, a hundred sharp pieces pressing against my ribs. But I know—deep down—I did the right thing.

Even if it's the most painful thing I've ever done.

I turn down the hallway, blinking fast to keep the tears from forming. When I glance down, the tea is dripping down the cardboard cup, my hand squeezing it too tight. I didn't even realize it until now.

I toss it into the trash and keep walking.

I hope my father would be proud of me...because right now, that's the only thing keeping me upright.

CHAPTER TWENTY-SIX

Hunter

The sun's beginning to set as I steer the rental car onto I-280, a road I could drive in my sleep. It's late by the time the hospital discharges my mother, the sky is a dull steel gray, heavy with low clouds that look like they could split open any minute. The kind of winter evening that settles in your chest and refuses to let go.

It's been two days since Peyton left New Jersey.

Beside me, my mom sits bundled in a thick scarf one of her salon clients crocheted for her as a Christmas gift. Her cheeks are pale, her eyes a little sunken, but she's awake, alert, better than she was when she collapsed in the kitchen. I grip the wheel tighter, my knuckles whitening.

She collapsed in my arms on Christmas morning, and the memory is still seared in my mind. Bethany was the one who made the call to 911, and Peyton was the one who kept me grounded while the paramedics wheeled my mother out of the house.

Now Peyton's gone. And I'm still trying to figure out if I let her leave or if she just walked away without giving me a say.

"You're quiet," Carly says softly, her voice still raspy from the hospital air.

I nod. "Just thinking."

What I don't say is that Peyton's voice keeps echoing in my head.

Maybe this is the right move for you.

She said it like it was a kindness. Like she wasn't cutting herself out of the equation entirely. She didn't ask me to stay. She didn't ask if I wanted her to.

And yeah, maybe I'm pissed. Not just at her. At myself too. Because I didn't fight her on it. But what could I do? We agreed to temporary.

My phone buzzes in the center console. I glance down and see my agent's name.

"Mind if I take this?" I ask my mom.

"Go ahead," she says.

I hit the button on the steering wheel to answer.

"Hunter, hey," he says. "Got a second?"

"Driving Ma home from the hospital, but shoot."

"I won't take up a lot of your time, but you're not going to believe who called me just now."

I glance over at my mother—both our curiosities piqued. "Who?"

"The head lawyer for the New Jersey hockey team, and get this...Mrs. Richards."

"Bethany Richards?" I ask.

"Nope. The real original Mrs. Richards—Kevin's mother. Turns out that the New Jersey team is part of a family trust that Kevin's father set up years ago—Kevin doesn't own it. In fact, he owns very little, as it turns out."

"You're kidding," I say, though I'm now not sure what this means for the trade offer that Bethany made to me if Kevin doesn't own it.

"Mrs. Richards was furious and divulged more information than she might have done otherwise. I told her that I was surprised to hear from her since I was under the impression that Bethany and Everett Kauffman were working this trade deal."

"And what did she say?"

"She said a lot. Mostly about how she didn't know about Kevin giving Bethany half the rights to the team in their prenup. She only found out since Kevin asked for more money from the trust to hire an investigator to prove that Bethany has been unfaithful, which would void her prenup. She gets nothing if she cheated on Kevin, and from what his mother says, they have surveillance of Bethany sleeping with every player on the team...inside the stadium."

I glance over to my mother, as if to say, "This is the woman you keep telling me to forgive."

My mother says nothing, but I can see her mind running a mile a minute. This is the kind of stress I didn't want her under right now.

"So what does this mean for my trade deal?"

"It means that not only was Bethany never entitled to make that deal since the family trust owned the team and not Kevin, but that Bethany isn't getting anything in the divorce at all."

I blink. "She's not getting anything?"

"Not besides the jewelry and clothes he bought her—nope. Her car was purchased through the trust as well."

I say nothing. The road blurs a little.

"Why would she call and tell you all of this?"

"Because Mrs. Richards wants you back on the team. She is willing to make an even better deal with Everett to get you. And from my conversation with Mr. Kauffman this morning, he's only willing to make the deal if you want to go because of your mother's health. It's all up to you. What do you want to do?"

I grip the wheel tighter and then glance over at my mother who doesn't look happy. "I don't know. Maybe."

"Well, give me a call...soon. We need to work this deal asap if this is something you want to do."

"I will. Thanks for calling."

The call ends, and it's quiet in the car for a moment.

"One of your clients is a realtor in the area, isn't she? You think she has listings available nearby?"

She shoots me a glare. "Are you seriously thinking about moving back?"

I shrug. "You need help. You need someone checking in on you. I can't do that from Seattle."

Her voice sharpens. "Hunter, no."

"What?"

"Don't make life decisions out of guilt. And don't use me as an excuse."

I say nothing.

She turns fully toward me. "Is this about Peyton?"

I don't answer.

"Hunter."

"She left, Ma. Said I should be here. That this was the best move for me. That we got what we wanted from the arrangement, and we should be done."

My mother lets out a disbelieving scoff. "That girl is in love with you."

"She didn't act like it."

"Bullshit. I don't believe that for a minute. Before you make a huge decision like this, you need to go home and talk to her first."

"There's nothing to talk about. It was fake for her the entire time. It's fine—I'll move on. And being here to make sure you go through treatment is more important."

I can't even look at her.

"Don't take that damn trade," she says firmly.

"Why not? It would fix everything."

"No, it wouldn't. It would just be easier. You were happy in Seattle. Don't throw that away because you're scared."

I want to argue. I want to tell her it's more complicated than that. But maybe it isn't.

We ride the rest of the way in silence.

When we get home, I settle her on the couch with a heating pad and a movie. She dozes off within minutes, and I finally let myself breathe.

And that's when my phone rings again.

Aleksi.

"What's up, Mäk?"

"You tell me. I just ran into Peyton. She was dropping your stuff off at your apartment. Cammy had the spare key."

My stomach drops. I told her to do whatever she wanted with my things, but I didn't think she'd find a way not to see me again. Subconsciously, maybe I thought I'd have an excuse to see her one last time before I moved back to New Jersey.

"She left it all inside. Boxed up."

I sit down hard on the armrest of the chair across from the couch.

"I thought you two were dating now."

"It didn't work out."

She really meant it.

She's really gone.

CHAPTER TWENTY-SEVEN

Peyton

I roll out my yoga mat at the back of the studio, grateful for the dim lighting and the soft instrumental music playing overhead. Abby plops down beside me, adjusting her ponytail and flashing me a smile that's way too cheerful for someone about to endure hot yoga on a Sunday morning.

"You okay?" she asks, stretching her arms overhead.

"I'm fine," I lie, trying not to groan as I reach for my toes.

She arches her brow. "Liar."

I sigh. "I packed up Hunter's stuff yesterday. Dropped it off at his place."

Even saying his name out loud hurts.

Abby stills. "You what?"

"Cammy got Trey's spare key to Hunter's apartment in The Commons," I say quickly. "I just...needed to do it."

She opens her mouth to speak, but the instructor claps her hands at the front of the class and starts guiding us through our first poses.

"This conversation isn't over. You still haven't told me what happened in New Jersey," she angrily whispers.

We fall into the rhythm—sun salutations, deep breaths, downward dog. But my balance is off, and my head's not in it.

My phone buzzes on the corner of my mat during child's pose. I sneak a glance—the WAGs group chat.

> **Cammy:** Girl, you better be at the game Tuesday. It's New Year's Eve, and the Owner's box is calling. We finally worked Everett into letting us use it since he hasn't been using it for weeks.

> **Penelope:** Still part of the WAG fam even if you're not dating number seventy-two anymore.

> **Isla:** The owner's box is packed with snacks and booze. Plenty of time for you to spill the beans about why Hunter is the worst. We're here to listen. And New Year's Eve in the Hawkeyes stadium is always interesting.

> **Kendall:** I'll be in the stinky locker room waiting for one of our players to get concussed. I always miss the fun. Please live stream.

My throat tightens. Abby catches the look on my face. "What now?" she whispers.

"They all know," I whisper back. "Cammy told them."

Her eyebrows furrow. "Everyone knows but me?"

"No one knows what happened, just that it's better that we ended our fake dating arrangement. This is better for everyone, I promise."

"I don't believe you," she mutters, but then we get shushed by the woman stretching in front of us. Abby sticks out her tongue at her as soon as she turns back around. And I choke back a giggle.

By the time class ends, my muscles are loose, but my chest is tight. Abby hands me a bottle of water and leads me to the bench outside.

"Talk to me," she says. "What really happened?"

I stare at the condensation on my bottle. "I called Rebecca. I turned down the syndication deal."

"What? Peyton, are you out of your mind?"

Possibly.

But no... I know why I did it. I'm heartbroken, but I don't regret giving up the syndication deal for him. Oddly enough, I'd do it again, because somehow, winning it didn't feel as good without him by my side.

It just wouldn't have felt the same.

"I asked if I could do it from New Jersey. She said maybe in a year or two, but not now. I knew Hunter wouldn't leave his mom. I didn't want him to feel like he had to choose between us."

"So you turned down the syndication deal... Why the hell are you still here then? You're free to be in Jersey... Nothing's stopping you."

I take a deep breath, preparing to tell Abby—the woman who I wouldn't put past jumping on an aircraft right now to beat the living shit out of Bethany in my honor—about the moment the last shoe drops.

"Bethany found me downstairs at the hospital. Told me the trade deal was basically done, but that she was going to pull it and not give it to Hunter unless I walked away. She said Carly needs him. And she's right. Getting traded to New Jersey so he can help his mother is the right call for him, and if I stayed, I would have cost him that."

Abby exhales hard. "And what about what you need? What about Hunter? Did you tell him what Bethany threatened to do if you didn't comply?"

"No I didn't, because I love him," I whisper, the sting of hearing him say it in the hallway of the hospital and not being able to say it back felt like I had bottled it in so tight to let the words slip out. He wouldn't have let me leave if I had said it back... I just know it. "I can't ask him to give up everything for me. He would have kicked her out of the hospital, I know he would have, but the truth is he needs Bethany to help him force Carly into treatment."

Abby shakes her head. "You didn't tell him the truth and let him decide. You gave up everything for him—don't rob him of the chance to do the same for you. And by the way, Carly isn't a child, she's a grown woman who can make her own damn decisions without dumb and dumber, okay? Give her some credit."

I close my eyes, heart pounding. "Maybe I'm just scared that he wouldn't have picked me. Or that if he did pick me, he would have resented me for the rest of our lives if something happened to Carly."

"I know," she says, squeezing my hand. "But love's supposed to be worth the risk. Your brother and I don't have the most ideal situation, but we love each other, and we make it work...even long distance. Even with a son that needs a lot of our attention. Life isn't perfect."

I nod—she's right.

"What are you going to do now? Can you get the syndication deal back?"

"No, she called the next podcaster in line after we got off the phone. I'm just going to do what I've been doing for years. Keep my podcast going and move on. Another opportunity will present itself when the time comes."

"You still have us," she says and reaches out to hug me.

"I know. Thank you."

I tuck my water bottle into my bag as we walk out to our cars, the familiar ache of what I gave up flaring sharper.

CHAPTER TWENTY-EIGHT

Hunter

Yesterday I brought Mom back from the hospital and told her to sit her ass on the couch. She told me to go shovel the driveway and stop hovering. Classic Carly Reed logic.

I bundle into my thickest jacket, step outside, and grab the snow shovel from the porch. The driveway is a mess, piled with soft powder and slush from yesterday's flurries. I make it halfway down the walk when I hear the front door creak open.

"Ma, are you expecting anyone?" I call over my shoulder.

"That's Bonnie," she yells back, the smell of fresh-baked bread wafting from the house. "She's dropping off the lease paperwork."

I pause, shovel mid-air. "The what?"

She appears in the doorway, apron dusted with flour, holding a dish towel. "The lease agreement. She and her daughter are going to take the house while I'm in Seattle. It'll help cover treatment costs, and she's going to manage the salon while I'm gone."

I blink at her. "Wait—you're moving to Seattle?"

She lifts a brow like it should be obvious. "Why did you think I redecorated your room? It's for Bonnie's daughter."

305

"You were planning this the entire time?"

"If you think I'm going to let you come back here and join the franchise that banished you to the farm team and then nearly tanked your career, you're crazy. I've been talking with my doctor for the last couple of weeks—since before Christmas—about it. There weren't any openings, but a new trial test came up the day before Christmas Eve. I didn't know how to tell you since I haven't been completely honest about the testing."

"So, your plan was to blindside me and move to Seattle without giving me advance notice?" I ask, a smile spreading across my face, because this is right up Carly Reed's playbook.

I open the door just as Bonnie steps up onto the porch, cheeks pink from the cold.

"Hey, Carly," Bonnie greets warmly. "I brought the copies. But don't worry about signing anything today. I just wanted to check on you."

"Don't be silly. Now's as good a time as any. I feel healthy as ever. Let me get a pen," Mom says, disappearing back inside like she didn't just casually flip my world upside down.

I stand frozen as Bonnie steps in, brushing snow from her coat.

Mom returns a minute later, pen in hand, ready to sign away her house and her role as boss of the local salon like it's just another Sunday.

"I can't believe you've been planning this," I finally say.

She feigns interest in my confusion as she signs the first page. "Once I heard how serious things were with Peyton, I started looking at treatment facilities near Seattle."

"So you wanted me to go back?"

She nods. "Seattle's your life now. I just needed to catch up."

I stand in the driveway, reeling.

A while later, after Bonnie leaves and the bread is cooling on the counter, I step onto the porch and pull out my phone.

I have a flight tomorrow. I need to be back for our home games at least, but with the news of my mom moving to Seattle,

I know that I need to let Tom know that I won't be taking New Jersey's deal.

There's one other thing I need to do.

> **Me: Hey, can I still pick Jesse up tomorrow for PT like usual?**

> **Abby: You're going to be back in Seattle tomorrow?**

> **Me: Yeah. Flying out tonight.**

> **Abby: Sure. He'd love that.**

The next morning, I show up at Abby's house. Jesse greets me first, his cane in hand, and I'm happy to see that he's using his wheelchair less and less.

Abby steps outside too, her arms crossed.

"Got a minute?" she asks.

I nod, stepping closer to the front stoop of their house. The look on her face saying that this is serious. I hope that what happened between Peyton and I won't change her allowing me to work with Jesse.

"Go jump in the truck, Jesse. I'll be there in a minute."

He nods and heads off.

"So when does the trade happen?"

"What trade?"

"The one with New Jersey. And are you planning to tell Jesse about it today? I just want to make sure you let him down easily. He's going to be really disappointed in losing you."

"I told them no," I say, shaking my head. "I'm staying here. My mom is moving here for treatment. Is that what Peyton told you was happening?"

"She told me that your mother didn't want to move, and that

New Jersey offered you a spot, so this was the best option for you," she says in a huff. "You're telling me that you're not taking the trade and moving to New Jersey."

"No. I'm not. I'm staying here. It's where I'm the happiest, and I have more than just a team I want to be here for...including Jesse."

"Oh God...just wait until Peyton realizes that she gave up the syndication deal and you're not moving."

"Wait...what the fuck? She gave up the syndication deal? That can't be right. She had a meeting the day after Christmas with the network."

"Peyton left some things out," Abby says, taking a step closer. "She's going to kill me for telling you, but I think you should know."

My spine straightens. "What should I know?"

"She gave up the syndication deal. Called Rebecca from the hospital cafeteria. Told her she wouldn't take the offer if it meant leaving you."

Air rushes out of my lungs.

"Bethany cornered her," Abby continues. "Told her she'd pull the trade offer unless Peyton walked. So she did. Because she didn't want you to have to choose between your mom and her."

I stare at the sidewalk, jaw clenched.

"She loves you, Hunter. That part I definitely shouldn't be telling you, but I know you love her too. That's why she did it."

It hits me like a damn freight train.

All this time, I thought she didn't choose me. But the truth is, she chose me so hard she walked away.

There's a long pause between us as I relive that moment of Peyton telling me that she was leaving and that I should stay. And then how smug Bethany acted after Peyton left, but I didn't read into it...until now. And that entire time, Bethany already knew that her divorce wasn't going down the way she wanted. She knew when she told Peyton to walk away that she didn't have the authority to offer me a trade deal.

"Did you hear what I said?"

I nod, knowing that I have to get Peyton back. "How do you feel about grand gestures?" I ask Abby.

She smirks. "Big fan."

"Good," I say, unlocking my phone. "I'm going to need your help."

CHAPTER TWENTY-NINE

Peyton

New Year's Eve

I should be at the stadium, surrounded by snacks and champagne-flavored gummy bears in the owner's box. At least, that's what Cammy texted me about an hour ago.

> Cammy: Are you coming out tonight? New Year's Eve games are the best. There's always something in the air, and we're all going out after.

> Me: Thanks, but I'm going to lay low. Maybe edit some, watch a movie, and then head to bed early.

The part I don't tell her—"*...and try not to think about the man I gave up, the syndication deal I turned down, or the way the* *silence in my townhouse echoes now that he's gone."*

I settle into the couch, curled up in my sweats, when a knock sounds at the door.

I didn't call for a food delivery and as far as I know, no one should be coming over today.

I rise, peeking through the window—and freeze.

Jesse.

Standing on the porch with his cane, bundled in a jacket two sizes too big and a smug little smirk on his face. Abby's parked at the curb, idling like she knows this is a quick drop.

I pull open the door. "Jesse? What—"

He hands me a thick envelope, then shrugs like it's no big deal. "He asked me to give this to you. And we're kind of best friends now, so don't screw this up for me," he says with a wink.

"Who are you best friends with?" I ask...though I already have a feeling I know who he's talking about.

"Hunter Reed."

I shake my head and ruffle his hair. "You're unbelievable."

He grins, already turning. I watch him walk carefully down the porch steps and back to Abby's car. His steps are steadier. More confident.

My chest squeezes because I'm holding something in my hands from Hunter, and that my nephew is doing so well because of Hunter's encouragement. Whatever this is...it's from the man I think about most of the day.

Maybe it's a goodbye.

Maybe it's a final rent check.

Or maybe—God help me—it's a custody agreement for Sproutacus. That would be just the sort of thing Hunter would do to make me laugh.

I tear into the envelope.

Inside, a season ticket to his section—and a French bulldog sticky note. Did he steal them from my house, or did he purchase his own? Considering I just tucked mine into my desk days ago to keep from seeing them and thinking of him, I'm pretty sure he didn't break into my house for sticky notes.

Hunter's handwriting curls across the paper:

Don't worry...it's not another glitter cock. Come to my game tonight. One last time. Please.

I suck in a breath.
Is this his last game?
A final farewell before New Jersey becomes home again?
I haven't seen any trade announcements, but if I'm honest...I haven't checked. Any breaking news with the Hawkeyes, I've intentionally ignored. I just don't think the reality of seeing the news release of Hunter getting traded to New Jersey is something I can handle.

I exhale slowly, trying to calm my heartbeat, but it's no use. I want to see him. Even if it breaks me.

Five minutes later, I'm in my closet, pulling on jeans. I reach for the spot where I always kept his jersey that he made me wear as part of our arrangement. I got used to being wrapped up in his number. And then I sink into the memory of why it's not where it should be—I gave it back with the rest of his things.

Disappointment prickles.
I grab my black puffy jacket instead and head for the door.
That's when I see it.
A gift.
A gift box, perched on the hood of my car.
Another sticky note taped on top with his handwriting on it. I glance around quickly, almost hoping to find him crouching in the brushes nearby...but nothing.

Some things don't fit right from the start...

I unwrap it, a breath catches in my throat.
Inside is his jersey. And another note:

...and some things fit perfectly from the very beginning. This jersey is yours. It's never looked better on anyone. No matter where I'm playing, I hope you'll wear it.

Tears sting my eyes.

God, he knows what he's doing.

I peel off my coat, tug the jersey over my head, and climb into my car.

When I enter the stadium, I head for our old seats—my steps quick, heart pounding.

As I approach, I look up overhead to spot familiar faces behind the glass high up in the owner's box.

Isla notices me first, then Cammy, then all the girls.

They cheer, banging on the glass like we just won the Stanley Cup.

I smile, cheeks burning.

But just as I reach my seat, I stop—someone's sitting there.

"Excuse me, I think this is my—"

The woman turns.

"Carly?"

She beams. "There you are! I've been waiting an hour."

She immediately jumps up and hugs me. It takes me a second to connect with what's happening, and then I stretch my arms around her too.

Finally, we both pull back from our hug.

"What are you doing here? Should you even be traveling? I thought you were starting treatment."

She pats the seat beside her. "Next month. I'm getting settled first. The moving van just got here."

I blink. "Settled? Where?"

"In the guest house behind the house that Hunter just bought. It's in that nice subdivision where all the retired players live," she tells me as if this news doesn't have more questions that are bubbling up. I have no idea where to even start now. "And I believe that Hunter told me Coach Haynes lives three doors down."

I sit, stunned. "Hunter...bought a house in Seattle? I don't understand...why?"

"Because he didn't take the trade. He's staying," I hear a voice, and someone flips around in front of me in their seat.

Jesse.

Now I feel like I'm in a tailspin. *What is going on?*

"What are you doing here?" I ask.

"We were invited," a deep male voice echoes next to him. A voice I've known since childhood.

My brother, with Abby sitting to the right of him, my mom on the left.

"Oh my God! You're home!" I say, as he stands from the seat in front of me and we hug. "I'm so confused as to why all of you are here."

"We're here for you and Hunter sweetheart," Carly says.

"And the moving van you just mentioned? I thought you already told Hunter that you wouldn't move."

"I was waiting for my doctor to find me an opening in Seattle. I didn't want Hunter to be let down if nothing opened up in time. But the rest of it... Well, that's the fun part...and you'll have to wait and see. Hunter wants to tell you all about it."

The lights dim.

The jumbotron flares to life.

A close-up shot appears.

Of a sticky note.

Shaped like a bulldog.

Come down to the ice. One last surprise.

And that's when I see him.

Hunter Reed—skating out onto the ice in the darkness and spotlights of the stadium...with something in his hands.

The announcer's voice booms. "Can we get Peyton Collins to center ice, please? Peyton Collins? We promise this won't take long."

My body moves before my brain catches up.

The usher waves me forward, and I climb over the railing to the players tunnel, with help from a couple of players, to get down.

Hunter's there.

Skates on, helmet off, jersey half-untucked.

And in his arms... A French bulldog puppy.

I gasp.

He grins, crossing the ice until he's right in front of me.

I reach out to scratch behind the ear of the little puppy.

"What is going on, Hunter? The notes, the announcer, your mom and my family being here...this puppy?"

"I didn't take the trade, Peyton. Bethany and her ex are out. My mom got into a trial here, and this is where my life is."

"Hunter..."

He steps closer. "I fell for you the second you rolled your eyes at me at the charity event while you were ordering your drink. I should've seen it then. I should have known what was standing right in front of me. But I was too drunk at Oakley's, and I was too stupid, and my vision was too clouded after everything Bethany put me through to see that you were about to flip my life upside down—for the better," he says, leaning in closer, and I welcome it. I miss him so close. "I should have asked you on a real date. I shouldn't have needed a charity auction or a fake dating pact. But I don't regret it, because it brought me here."

"And the puppy?"

He hands the sleeping pup off to me, and I cradle it in my arms.

"You said your life was too chaotic for a puppy. I figured we could try chaos together."

Tears spill freely now.

"I don't care where we live, Peyton. In your townhouse, in the house I bought for us, in New Jersey, in Seattle. None of it matters to me. I just want to be with you."

I laugh through the tears. "Did you bring me out here in front of all these fans to give me a puppy?" I ask with a smirk.

He smiles. "No. I brought you out here to ask you once more… to bet on me. One last time."

"Okay," I whisper. "I'll bet on you. Again and always."

He kisses me.

The crowd erupts. I get a glimpse up in the owner's box where the girls are jumping up and down, and then down to where Jesse, my brother, Abby, Mom, and Carly are all applauding and hugging.

Our family just got bigger, and there's nothing more I want.

It hits me that this is exactly what my father always wanted for me. He wanted me to find my voice, and most importantly, to find love and passion in life again. To find my place in this world. And I know that with Hunter and our family by my side, that's exactly what I have.

Trade contracts and network deals aren't what make you happy. It's the people in your life that make every day worth living, and that's what I have here.

And there's one more final truth. That nothing between Hunter and I was ever fake. Not for a moment.

"What's his name?" I ask, scratching the pup's chin.

"Sproutacus the Second. But we can call him Sprout. What do you think of him?" he asks, reaching over to scratch his chin.

I grin. "I'm just glad he's not another glitter dildo."

He steps closer and rests his forehead against mine, his arms wrapping around Sprout and me. "As long as I'm around, you won't be needing any more silicone cocks. I promise, Passenger Princess."

And then I kiss him again, puck drops forgotten, the roar of the fans long forgotten.

The girls were right—New Year's Eve at the stadium is crazy.

But I wouldn't want this life any other way.

EPILOGUE

Hunter

"Sold!"

I say, slamming the gavel against the podium, and the crowd erupts in laughter and applause. Luka shoots a mock glare at the woman in the back of the ballroom who just won him for a dog-walking date. He gives a dramatic bow, and the table full of Hawkeyes players howls like lunatics.

This is my first year MCing the Hawkeyes' annual Date with a Player charity auction, and I've been doing it while trying not to draw attention to the ring box in my pocket.

My hands have never sweated this much.

I grip the edge of the podium and force myself to breathe.

One more paddle raise. One more cheesy joke. Then I get to change my entire life.

"All right, folks," I say into the mic, my voice steady even if my pulse isn't. "Before we wrap up the live auctions and head to the ice for the goalie shootouts—I have one more thing to say."

The ballroom quiets.

I scan the crowd until I find her.

Peyton.

Wearing a different dress that she pulled from Abby's closet for this event, but it looks just as good as the blue gown she wore to this same event one year ago, when I asked her to bet on me.

The second-best decision I've ever made in my entire life. And today, I'll make the first best decision.

"Last year," I begin, voice tightening slightly, "I was just another player on the Hawkeyes who was willing to stand up here with the rest of the guys and bring in funds for an amazing cause. JP and Cammy talked me into signing up for one of the Date a Player spots, and I was happy to do my part. They needed a warm body with a decent smile... They weren't picky," I say, glancing around as most everyone gives a lighthearted chuckle, and then my eyes land back on her again. "I was expecting a date with a stranger, candle-lit dinner, maybe drinks, and definitely small talk. But what I got instead is something I wasn't prepared to find."

I see Peyton adjust her stance. From standing freely, leaned up against the open bar, stirring her drink, to standing straighter, her eyes glued to me.

I swallow and keep going.

"What I didn't expect was to fall in love with the woman who bid on me." I pause. "What I didn't expect was her changing my life."

Now, it's dead silent.

Peyton's eyes widen, lips parting slightly.

I step down from the stage, and I pass by Penelope and Slade's table, hearing Penelope whisper, not all that quietly, "Oh my God, he's going to propose!"

But Peyton's not close enough to hear her, and it wouldn't matter anyway. The moment I step down those steps, her eyes look like a deer in headlights. She already knows.

"Peyton Collins," I say, crossing the floor toward her, my heart pounding in my chest like I'm back on the ice in overtime. "You mocked me that night. You rolled your eyes so hard I thought they might get stuck. But you still raised your hand. You still gave me a shot."

I reach her standing next to the bar, her hand frozen in place.

"You bet on me when I needed it the most. You showed me what family looks like outside of my own. And even when I thought that our story was over, you proved to me how far you're willing to go, and what you're willing to give up for me. And I want to spend the rest of my life returning that kind of love and devotion."

I pull out the ring box from the pocket it my slacks. The moment the box is visible, I hear the WAGs table collective sigh and Peyton's gasp, as she quickly discards her blueberry lemon drop drink on the bar top.

"Hunter..." she whispers, shocked with a ghost of a smile on her lips. Her eyes flick to me and then back to the unopened box.

"Marry me. For real this time. No sticky notes. No fake dating. Just us, and Ma...and our dogs—both real and of the plant variety."

Her hands are shaking when she reaches for me. "Yes," she whispers, the tears in her eyes turning her smile into something I'll never forget. "Of course I'll marry you."

She jumps into my arms before I can even get the ring on. I slide my arms around her to catch her, laughing into her neck. She finally pulls back, and the moment I slide the ring on her finger, the room explodes.

Players pound their tables. Penelope throws confetti she found scattered on the table. Cammy and Kendall are jumping out of their chairs, shrieking and taking photo after photo with their phones. My mother is clapping, wiping a tear from her eye as she stands next to Coach Murphy who reached out to me months ago and came out to a few of our games. The rest of the players are applauding and catcalling.

I pull Peyton in and kiss her hard, and for a second, the world just...disappears.

Then I turn to the crowd, with Peyton tucked under my arm.

"Thank you all for coming this evening and being a part of this incredible organization. I know that your donations will be put to good use helping families pay for unexpected expenses during treatment. Something that is near and dear to my heart."

Cammy walks over and takes the mic to announce that JP and Olsen will be conducting the second annual goalie shoot off and where guests can purchase tickets to take a shot.

And that's when I spot her.

A woman weaving her way through the crowd. Designer dress. Red lipstick. And a cell phone in her hand.

Peyton sees her a split second before I do.

"Rebecca?"

The media exec offers her a warm smile. "Congratulations, you two. That was a beautiful proposal, Hunter. You clean up well."

I smirk. "Told you I had good timing."

Peyton blinks. "What are you doing here?"

"Hunter called," she says, glancing at me with something close to fondness. "Right after last New Year's, trying to get your spot back with the network when he found out that you had given it up."

Peyton looks up at me, her eyebrows pulled together, almost in disbelief. "You did?"

I just shrug. My call hadn't made a difference then—since the network had already signed a different podcast, so I never bothered to mention it.

"He said I was making the biggest mistake of my career letting you go."

Peyton looks at me, stunned. "I can't believe you did that."

"I might've made a few phone calls when Abby told me that you gave up everything for me. I was hoping to get it back for you." I admit, pulling her in closer.

Rebecca nods. "At the time, there wasn't much I could do. But a few weeks ago, I landed a huge investor. Someone who believes in a women-led sports media network. And I want you, Peyton, to be the first face of it."

Peyton's jaw drops. "You're serious?"

"Dead serious. The contract is already drawn up. Bigger than the last offer, full creative control, and you can live wherever you want."

Rebecca lifts a brow. "New Jersey. Seattle. Timbuktu. Doesn't matter. I just want you on the team."

Peyton stares at her, stunned silent.

Then slowly, her eyes drift back to me.

"I won't be leaving Seattle any time soon," she says, voice thick with emotion. "This is home."

I kiss the top of her head.

Rebecca smiles. "You'll be receiving the contract by tomorrow morning for you to look over. Of course, I hope you agree to this offer, but I know that you've been getting deals since my old network signed the other podcaster—and I know I'm not the only contract on the table."

"Nothing felt like the right fit. And having full control of my voice is what I think my father wanted most."

"That's what I'm offering, but take your time and think it over. I hope you pick me... I think we can do some great things together."

Peyton nods. "Thank you for coming. I'll look over the contract tomorrow."

Rebecca glances at me and then back to Peyton. "Oh, trust me. I wouldn't have missed this. After all, with all the pressure I put on you, I like to think I had a little to do with this," she smiles and then heads back toward the exit.

And I suppose she's right.

It turns out that Rebecca, the Hawkeyes, New Jersey, Ma, and even Bethany, all played their roles perfectly. How else could the woman who hated me have come to fake date me long enough for us both to see we have a whole life together ahead of us?

And marrying her? That's going to be the easiest win of my life.

BONUS CHAPTER

Peyton

Six Years Later

The smell of buttery popcorn and over-priced stadium nachos hits me the second we push through the main entrance of the Hawkeyes stadium. It smells like home. Or at least our home away from home.

A few nights from tonight, our twin girls and I will be back here, sitting in "daddy's seats," watching Hunter and the Hawkeyes play a home game.

"Are we late?" Ellie asks, our three-year-old, wide-eyed and bouncing in my arms.

"Nope," I say, shifting her on my hip and glancing over at Hunter, who's carrying her twin sister, Sadie, and already scanning for the nearest concession stand. "But your dad might make us late if he doesn't stop getting distracted by snacks."

"Guilty." Hunter grins, kissing Sadie's cheek as she reaches for the bright lights blinking along the cotton candy cart.

God, that smile. It still hits me like it did the first time he used it on me—only now, it comes with extra lines around his eyes and a whole lot more love behind it. Six years with this man, and it still feels like it will never be enough.

We snake our way through the concourse, stopping at every stand that offers something sugar-coated or dripping in cheese. It's loud, chaotic, sticky-floored mayhem—and I love every second of it.

It's not as busy tonight as it is during a home game for the Hawkeyes, but this is the championship for Jesse's wheelchair hockey league, and the community support that has shown up is bigger than I could have ever imagined.

"Remember when we used to come here and pretend we weren't into each other?" I tease as he grabs a tray of fries, two sodas, a bag of cotton candy—at Ellie's persistence—and a bucket of popcorn the size of Sadie's head.

He winks. "I was never pretending."

I roll my eyes, but my heart does that annoying squeeze thing it still hasn't stopped doing since the day he jumped off the stage and kissed me in front of a packed charity event like he had nothing left to lose.

We find our seats just behind the glass. Almost the exact spot where I watched Hunter for the first time–the PR favor from Penelope after the podcast we did together. Now these seats are basically part of our family's DNA. Abby and Noah are already waiting, waving us over.

My brother retired from the military two years ago. He now runs a high-security detail for a large government building. The pay is good, and the insurance is even better. More importantly, having him home feels like the missing piece our family needed to be complete.

As we get closer, I notice my mom sitting with them too. Carly wanted to be here, but she flew back to New Jersey to make final arrangements to sell the house for good, and to sign over the salon to Bonny and her daughter to run.

After a long fight, Carly is now in full remission, and she wants to spend the rest of her time being a full-time grandma to our girls. We love her living in the guest house behind our home and I can't imagine not having her help as my podcast has continued to grow, hitting almost a million subscribers, and Hunter's hectic hockey schedule.

"Auntie Abby!" the girls shout in unison, wiggling out of our arms like greased-up otters. Abby catches them mid-leap, expertly wrangling them onto her lap while peppering them with kisses.

Before Hunter and I are even settled, Ellie is in Abby's lap and Sadie is sitting with my mom.

Noah leans back in his seat, his signature smirk already in place. "Look who finally showed up. I was starting to think Hunter got lost in the hot dog line."

Hunter sets the food down with dramatic flair. "I rarely get to be on this side of the plexi...let a man enjoy himself. Besides, I have to fuel up before tomorrow's drills."

Our attention quickly shifts as Jesse's team wheels onto the ice, the crowd erupting into cheers as his name is announced.

The girls go ballistic, running down to the plexiglass and pounding their little hands against it. "Go, Jesse!" they both yell.

I glance over at Hunter, who's already watching the ice like it holds every good thing that's ever happened to him.

He reaches for my hand and squeezes, like he can sense my nerves. "He's got this."

I squeeze back. "He's got us," I murmur, the truth of it wrapping warm around my ribs.

From that first reluctant moment he let me into his life—into Carly's—he's been building this. A family that roots for each other. That shows up. That makes room.

The game flies by in a blur of fast breaks, shots on goal, and Jesse playing like he was born to do this. Hunter and Noah are yelling like they're on the bench, Abby's filming the girls waving their handmade signs, my mom is lifting the girls to give them a better view above the boards, and I just sit there, soaking it all in.

By the time the buzzer sounds, and Jesse's team secures the

win, my cheeks hurt from smiling and my voice is almost gone from yelling.

Jesse wheels over to the glass, bumping his fist against the plexi for the girls to match him, and they do. Each getting a fist bump of their own like they do with Dad every home game.

"Did you see that last assist I made? That was sick, right?" he shouts through the pane.

"Your fan club saw every second," I yell back, gesturing to our two sugar-drunk daughters jumping up and down like groupies.

Hunter laughs, pushing up from his seat to meet Jesse at the railing near the player tunnel. "You crushed it, kid."

Jesse beams, letting Hunter reach down and slap his helmet like a proud big brother who can't quite believe how far this kid has come.

"Peyton," Jesse calls, still breathless from the game, "when do I get to be on the podcast?"

I arch a brow. "The second you stop saying 'sick' every five words," I say as Noah steps up next to me.

"So never?" Noah teases.

We all laugh.

Hunter leans his forearms against the railing. "She's not wrong."

We linger long after the arena starts to clear, our crew the kind that doesn't rush through the good stuff. Eventually, we head out into the frosty night, the girls sleepy but still buzzing from cotton candy and a big win. Hunter carries one, Noah the other.

In the car, they pass out instantly—tiny snores, sticky fingers, and full hearts.

"You know none of this would've been possible without everything you did for Jesse," I say quietly.

Hunter glances over, then reaches for my thigh, his thumb rubbing slow circles. "What *we* did for Jesse. Family's a team sport."

Yeah...he's right.

I glance behind us—our girls snuggled in their car seats, Noah and Abby's car following close behind, my mom tucked into the back seat with them. Jesse's off celebrating with his team. My inbox is overflowing with emails from my producer, confirming an exciting slate of podcast guests for the next month. Hunter's game schedule is still taped to the fridge in the beautiful house we've turned into a home.

This chaotic, noisy, love-filled life we built from one fake dating stunt and a whole lot of unexpected love? It may not have been the plan—but maybe it was always meant to be the ending.

A family. A team. A life we fought for.

And maybe, in the end, this is what my father wanted for me all along—not a perfect career, not a perfect plan—but to get off the bleachers and back in the game of life.

And I'm so damn glad I did.

Because we're not done yet.

Not even close.

ABOUT THE AUTHOR

Author of "spice on ice" romance novels.

As an avid reader myself, and a Westcoast girl, I love two things: swoon-worthy pro athlete book boyfriends, and writing stories about them living in the beautiful Northwest where I'm blessed to call home.

I do my best work late at night after I've tucked in my three littles, and my hard-working husband.

Learn more at: kennaking.com

Available Fall 2025

STORIES WITH IMPACT

WWW.PAGEANDVINE.COM

ALSO BY KENNA KING

The Rookie Hawkeyes Series
Match Penalty
Bleacher Report
Bottle Rocket (Autumn 2025)
Player Misconduct (Autumn 2025)
Playbook Breakaway (Spring 2026)

The Hawkeyes Hockey Series
Cocky Score
Filthy Score
Brutal Score
Rough Score
Dirty Score
Lucky Score
Tough Score
Wrong Score